'Does it live up to the hype? Yes.'
DAILY EXPRESS

'It's well-paced, exciting and – in places –
frightening and bloody.'
PHILIP ARDAGH, THE GUARDIAN

'There is a genuine Potteresque momentum to the story . . .'
THE OBSERVER

'It's a good adventure yarn, about a 14-year-old boy who
discovers an underworld ruled by a violent regime.'
THE TIMES

'A well-imagined and absorbing read.'
THE BOOKSELLER

'. . . violent, gruesome and engrossing.'
FINANCIAL TIMES

'. . . [I] found the world of digging and archaeology just as
compelling as Harry's world of wizarding.'
THE SUNDAY TELEGRAPH

'Wonderfully imagined subterranean fantasy that draws you
completely into its world.'
PUBLISHING NEWS

'This is a must read for anyone!'
FIRST NEWS

A MESSAGE FROM CHICKEN HOUSE

The authors first published this book themselves, putting all their effort, hope and cash into a wonderful piece of imagination. Then word of this great book spread to me – but it had sold out! Finally, I tracked one down, and we dug deeper into their dark and mysterious world to bring you a new, extended adventure. And TUNNELS was born!

I've always loved the idea of a mysterious underground world, so close you can dig down into it . . . but I never imagined it would be this strange!

BARRY CUNNINGHAM
Publisher
Chicken House

TUNNELS

RODERICK GORDON and BRIAN WILLIAMS

Chicken House

2 PALMER STREET, FROME, SOMERSET BA11 1DS

Text © Roderick Gordon and Brian Williams 2007
Cover illustration © Dan Mumford 2020
Inside illustrations © Brian Williams

First published in Great Britain in 2007
This edition published 2020
Chicken House
2 Palmer Street
Frome, Somerset BA11 1DS
United Kingdom
www.chickenhousebooks.com

Cover design by Steve Wells
Cover illustration by Dan Mumford
Designed and typeset by Dorchester Typesetting Group Ltd
Printed and bound in Great Britain by CPI Group (UK) Ltd, Croydon CR0 4YY

The paper used in this Chicken House book is made
from wood grown in sustainable forests.

1 3 5 7 9 10 8 6 4 2

British Library Cataloguing in Publication data available.

PB ISBN 978-1-912626-72-4
eISBN 978-1-908435-22-4

PART ONE

Breaking Ground

CHAPTER ONE

*S*CHLAAK! The pickaxe hit the wall of earth and, sparking on an unseen shard of flint, sank deep into the clay, coming to a sudden halt with a dull thud.

'This could be it, Will!'

Dr Burrows crawled forwards in the cramped tunnel. Sweating and breathing heavily in the confined space, he began feverishly clawing at the dirt, his breath clouding in the damp air. Under the combined glare of their helmet lamps each greedy handful revealed more of the old wooden planking beneath, exposing its tar-coated grain and splintery surface.

'Pass me the crowbar.'

Will rummaged in a satchel, found the stubby blue crowbar and handed it to his father, whose gaze was fixed on the area of wood before him. Forcing the flat edge of the tool between two of the planks, Dr Burrows grunted as he put all his weight behind it to gain some purchase. He then began levering from side to side. The planks creaked and moaned against their rusted fixings until, finally, they bellied out, breaking free with a resounding crack. Will recoiled slightly as a clammy breeze bled from the ominous gap Dr Burrows had created.

Urgently they pulled two more of the planks out of place, leaving a shoulder-width hole, and paused for a moment in silence. Father and son turned and looked at each other, sharing a brief conspiratorial smile. Their faces, illuminated in each other's light beams, were smeared with a war paint of dirt.

They turned back to the hole and stared in wonder at the dust motes floating like tiny diamonds, forming and reforming unknown constellations against the night-black opening.

Dr Burrows warily leaned into the hole, Will squeezing in beside him to peer over his shoulder. As their helmet lamps cut into the abyss a curved, tiled wall came into sharp focus. Their beams, penetrating deeper, swept over old posters whose edges were peeling away from the wall and waving slowly, like tendrils of seaweed caught in the drift of powerful currents at the bottom of the ocean. Will raised his head a little, scanning even further along until he caught the edge of an enamelled sign. Dr Burrows followed his son's gaze until the beams of their lamps joined together to clearly show the name.

'*Highfield & Crossly North*! This is it, Will, this is it! We found it!' Dr Burrows' excited voice echoed about the dank confines of the disused train station. They felt a slight breeze on their faces as something blew along the platform and down on to the rails, as if sent into an animated panic by this rude intrusion, after so many years, into its sealed and forgotten catacomb.

Will kicked wildly at the timbers at the base of the opening, throwing up a spray of splinters and hunks of rotting wood, until suddenly the ground below him slid away and spilled into the cavern. He scrambled through the opening, grabbing his spade as he went. His father was immediately behind him as they crunched a few paces on the solid surface of the platform, their footsteps echoing and their helmet lamps cutting swathes into the surrounding gloom.

Cobwebs hung in skeins from the roof, and Dr Burrows blew as one draped itself across his face. As he looked around, his light caught his son, a strange sight with a shock of white hair sticking out like bleached straw from under his battle-scarred miner's helmet, his pale-blue eyes flashing with enthusiasm as he blinked into the dark. It was difficult to describe Will's clothes, other than to say that they appeared to be of the same red-brown hue and texture as the clay he had been working in. Such was the pasting, it covered him right up to his neck, making him appear like an artist's sculpture which had been miraculously infused with life.

As for Dr Burrows himself, he was a wiry man of average height – one wouldn't have described him as tall or, for that matter, short, just somewhere in the middle. He had a round face with piercing brown eyes that appeared all the more intense due to his gold-rimmed pebble glasses.

'Look up there, Will, look at that!' he said, as his light picked out a sign above the gap through which they had just emerged. WAY OUT, it read in large black letters. They turned on their hand-held torches, and the beams combined with those of their weaker helmet lamps, ricocheting through the darkness to reveal the full length of the platform. Roots hung from the roof, and the walls were caked with efflores-cence and streaked with chalky limescale where fissures had seeped moisture. They could hear the sound of running water somewhere in the distance.

'How's this for a find?' Dr Burrows said with a self-congratulatory air. 'Just think, nobody has set foot down here since the new Highfield line was built in 1895.' They had emerged on to one end of the platform, and Dr Burrows now shone his torch into the opening of the train tunnel to their side. It was blocked by a mound of rubble and earth. 'It'll be just the same down the other end – they would've sealed both tunnels,' he said.

As they picked their way along the platform, gazing at the walls, it was just possible to make out blocks of crazily cracked cream tiles with dark-green edging. Gas lamps sprouted every three metres or so, a number with glass shades still on them.

'Dad, Dad, over here!' Will called. 'Have you seen these posters? You can still read them. I think they're adverts for land or something? And here's a good one . . . *Wilkinson's Circus . . . to be held on the Common . . . 10th day of February 1895.* There's a picture,' he said breathlessly as his father joined him. The poster had been spared any water damage, and they could make out the crude colours of the red big top, with a blue man in a top hat standing in front of it. 'And look at this,' Will said. '*Too Fat? Doctor Gordon's Elegant Pills!*' The heavy line drawing depicted a portly man with a beard, holding up a small container.

They walked further along, stepping around a mountain of rubble that spilled on to the platform from an archway. 'That would've led through to the other platform,' Dr Burrows told his son.

They paused to look at an ornate cast-iron bench. 'This'll go nicely in the garden. All it needs is a rub down and a few coats of gloss,' Dr Burrows was muttering as Will's torch beam alighted on a dark wooden door hidden in the shadows.

'Dad, wasn't there an office or something on your plan?' Will asked, staring at the door.

'An office?' Dr Burrows replied, fumbling through his pockets until he found the piece of paper he was searching for. 'Let me have a look.'

Will didn't wait for an answer, pushing at the door, which was stuck fast. Quickly losing interest in his plan, Dr Burrows went to the aid of his son and together they tried to shoulder the door open. It was badly warped in the frame, but on the third attempt it suddenly gave and they tumbled into the room, a downpour of silt covering their heads and shoulders. Coughing, and rubbing dust from their eyes, they pushed their way through a shroud of cobwebs.

'Wow!' Will exclaimed quietly. There, in the middle of the small office, they could make out a desk and chair, furred with dust. Will moved cautiously behind the chair and, with his gloved hand, brushed away the layer of cobwebs on the wall to reveal a large, faded map of the railway system.

'Could've been the stationmaster's office,' Dr Burrows said as he swept dust off the top of the desk with his arm to reveal a blotter, upon which rested a grimy teacup and saucer. Next to them a small object, discoloured with age, leaked green on to the surface of the desk. 'How fascinating! A railway telegraph, exquisitely made – brass, I would say.'

Two of the walls were lined with shelves stacked with decaying cardboard boxes. Will selected a box at random and carried it over to the desk quickly, as it threatened to fall apart in his hands. He lifted off the misshapen lid and looked in wonder at the bundles of old tickets. He picked one of them out, but the perished rubber band crumbled, sending a confetti of tickets spewing over the desktop.

'They're blanks – they won't have been printed up,' Dr Burrows said.

'You're right,' Will confirmed, never ceasing to be amazed at his father's knowledge, as he studied one of the tickets. But Dr Burrows wasn't listening. He was kneeling down and tugging at a heavy object on a lower shelf, wrapped in a rotten cloth that dissolved at his touch. 'And here,' Dr Burrows announced as Will turned to look at the machine, which resembled an old typewriter with a large pull handle on its side, 'is an example of an early ticket-printing machine. Bit corroded, but we can probably get the worst off.'

'What, for the museum?'

'No, for *my* collection,' Dr Burrows replied. He hesitated, and his face took on a serious expression. 'Look, Will, we're not going to breathe a word about this, any of this, to anyone. Understand?'

'Huh?' Will spun around, a slight frown creasing his brow. It wasn't as if either of them went around broadcasting the fact that they embarked on these elaborate underground workings in their spare time – not that anyone would be seriously interested anyway. Their common passion for the buried and the as yet undiscovered was something they didn't share with anyone else, something that brought father and son together . . . a bond between them.

They stood in the office, their miner's lamps lingering on each other's faces. As his son hadn't made any sort of response, Dr Burrows fixed him with a stare, and went on.

'I don't have to remind you what happened last year with the Roman villa, do I? That bigwig professor turned up, hijacked the dig and grabbed all the glory. *I* discovered that site, and what did I get? A tiny acknowledgement buried in his pathetic effort of a paper.'

'Yeah, I remember,' Will said, recalling his father's frustration

14

and outbursts of fury at the time.

'Want that to happen again?'

'No, of course not.'

'Well, I'm not going to be a footnote on this one. I'd rather *nobody* knew about it. They're not going to nick this from me, not this time. Agreed?'

Will nodded in assent, sending his light bouncing up and down the wall.

Dr Burrows glanced at his watch. 'We really ought to be getting back, you know.'

'All right,' Will replied grudgingly.

His father caught his tone. 'There's no real hurry, is there? We can take our time to explore the rest tomorrow night.'

'No, I suppose,' Will said half-heartedly, moving towards the door.

Dr Burrows patted his son affectionately on his hard hat as they were leaving the office. 'Sterling work, Will, I must say. All those months of digging really paid off, didn't they?'

They retraced their steps to the opening and, after a last look at the platform, clambered back into the tunnel. Six metres or so in, the tunnel blossomed out so they could walk side by side. If Dr Burrows stooped slightly, it was just high enough for him to stand.

'We need to double up on the braces and props,' Dr Burrows announced, examining the expanse of timbers above their heads. 'Instead of one every metre, as we discussed, they're about one in two.'

'Sure. No problem, Dad,' Will assured him, rather unconvincingly.

'And we need to shift this lot out,' Dr Burrows continued, nudging a mound of clay on the tunnel floor with his boot.

'Don't want to get too constricted down here, do we?'

'Nope,' Will replied vaguely, not really intending to do anything about it at all. The sheer thrill of discovery resulted all too often in him flouting the safety guidelines his father tried to lay down. His passion was to dig, and the last thing on his mind was to waste time on 'housekeeping', as Dr Burrows called it And, in any case, his father rarely volunteered to help with any of the digging itself, only making an appearance when one of his 'hunches' paid off.

Dr Burrows whistled abstractedly through his teeth as he slowed to inspect a tower of neatly stacked buckets and a heap of planking. As they continued on their way the tunnel climbed, and he stopped several more times to test the wooden props on either side. He smacked them with the palm of his hand, his obscure whistling rising to an impossible squeak as he did so.

The passage eventually levelled out and widened into a larger chamber, where there was a trestle table and a pair of sorry-looking armchairs. They dumped some of their equipment on the table, then climbed the last stretch of tunnel to the entrance.

Just as the town clock finished striking seven, a length of corrugated-iron sheeting lifted a couple of centimetres in a corner of the Temperance Square car park. It was early autumn, and the sun was just tipping over the horizon as father and son, satisfied the coast was clear, pushed the sheeting back to reveal the large timber-framed hole in the ground. They poked their heads a little way out, double-checking that there was nobody else in the car park, then clambered from the hole. Once the sheeting was back in place over the entrance, Will kicked dirt over it to disguise it.

A breeze rattled the hoardings around the car park and a newspaper rolled along the ground like tumbleweed, scattering its pages as it gained momentum. As the dying sun silhouetted the surrounding warehouses and reflected off the burgundy-tiled façade of a nearby Peabody Estate tenement block, the two Burrows ambling out of the car park looked every inch a pair of prospectors leaving their claim in the foothills to return to town.

CHAPTER TWO

On the other side of Highfield, Terry Watkins, 'Tipper Tel' to his mates at work, was dressed in pyjama bottoms and cleaning his teeth in front of the bathroom mirror. He was tired and hoping for a good night's sleep, but his mind was still somersaulting because of what he'd seen that afternoon.

It had been an awfully long and arduous day. He and his demolition team were pulling down the ancient white lead works to make way for a new office block for some government department or other. He'd wanted more than anything to go home, but he had promised his guv'nor that he would take out a few courses of brickwork in the basement to try to make an assessment of how extensive its foundations were. The last thing his company could afford was an overrun on the contract, which was always the risk with these old buildings.

As the portable floodlight glared behind him, he had swung his sledgehammer, cracking open the handmade bricks which revealed their bright-red innards like eviscerated animals. He swung again, fragments spinning off on to the soot-covered floor of the basement, and swore under his breath because the whole place was just too damned well built.

After further blows, he waited until the cloud of brick dust settled. To his surprise he found the area of wall he'd been attacking was only one brick thick. There was a sheet of old pig iron where the second and third layers should have been. He belted it a couple of times, and it resounded with a substantial clang on each blow. It wasn't going to give up easily. He breathed heavily as he pulverized the bricks around the edges of the metal surface to discover, to his sheer amazement, that it had hinges, and even a handle of some type recessed into its surface.

It was a *door*.

He paused, panting for a moment while he tried to work out why anyone would want access to what should rightfully be part of the foundations.

Then he made the biggest mistake of his life.

He used his screwdriver to lever the handle out, a wrought-iron ring which turned with surprisingly little effort. The door swung inwards with some help from one of his work boots and clanged flat against the wall on the other side, the noise echoing for what seemed like for ever. He took out his torch and shone it into the pitch blackness of the room. He could see it was at least six metres across and was, in fact, circular.

He went through the doorway, stepping on to the stone surface just inside it. But on the second step, the stone floor disappeared and his foot encountered nothing but air. *There was a drop!* He teetered on the very edge, his arms wind-milling frantically until he managed to regain his balance and pull himself back from the brink. He fell back against the door jamb and clung on to it, taking deep breaths to steady his nerves and cursing himself for his rashness.

'Come on, this won't do,' he said aloud, forcing himself to get going again. He turned and slowly edged forwards, his torch revealing that he was indeed standing on a ledge, with an ominous darkness beyond it. He leaned over, trying to make out what lay below – it appeared to be bottomless. He had walked into a huge brick well. And, as he looked up, he couldn't see to the top of the well – the brick walls curved dramatically up into the shadows, past the limits of his little pocket torch. A strong breeze seemed to be coming from above, chilling the sweat on the back of his neck.

Playing the beam around, he noticed that steps, maybe half a metre wide, led down around the edge of the wall, starting just below the stone ledge. He stamped on the first step to test it and, since it felt sound, began to descend the stairway cautiously, so as not to slip on the fine layer of dust, straw and twigs that littered it. Hugging the diameter of the well, he climbed down, deeper and deeper, until the floodlit door was just a tiny dot way above him.

Eventually the steps ended and he found himself on a flagstone floor. Using his torch to look around, he could see many pipes of a dull gunmetal colour lacing up the walls, like a drunken church organ. He traced the route of one of these as it meandered upwards and saw that it opened into a funnel, as if it were a vent of some kind. But what caught his attention more than anything else was a door with a small glass porthole. Light was unmistakably shining through it, and he could only think that he had somehow blundered into the Underground, particularly as he could hear the low humming sound of machinery and feel a constant downdraught of air.

He slowly approached the window, a circle of thick glass mottled and scored with time, and peered through. He couldn't believe his eyes. Through its undulating surface, there was a scene resembling a scratchy old black-and-white film. There appeared to be a street and a row of buildings. And, bathed in the light of glowing spheres of slow-moving fire, people were milling around. Fearsome-looking people. Anaemic phantoms dressed in old-fashioned clothes.

He wasn't a particularly religious man, attending church only for weddings and the odd funeral, but he wondered for a moment if he had stumbled upon an annexe of hell, or at least some sort of purgatorial theme park. He recoiled from the window and crossed himself, mumbling woefully inaccurate Hail Marys, and scuttled back up the stairs in a blind panic, barricading the door lest any of the demons escape.

He ran through the deserted building site and padlocked the main gates behind him. As he drove home in a daze, he wondered what he would tell the guv'nor the next morning. Although he had seen it with his own eyes, he couldn't help but replay the vision over and over in his mind. By the time he had reached home, he really didn't know what to believe.

He couldn't resist bringing it up with his family; he had to talk to somebody about it. His wife Aggy and their two teenage sons assumed he'd been drinking and so he got short shrift from them over supper. Between peals of cruel laughter they held up imaginary bottles and pretended to glug from them, until he fell silent. But he just couldn't drop the subject, and eventually Aggy told him to put a sock in it and stop babbling about infernal white-haired monsters and glowing balls of fire as she was trying to watch 'Stenders on the telly.

So here he was in the bathroom, scrubbing away at his

molars and wondering if hell really did exist, when he heard the start of a scream – his wife's scream, the one usually reserved for mice or errant spiders in the bath. But it was cut short before she could follow through into the usual full-bodied wail.

His instinctive alarm bells rang, his nerves jittering like short circuits as he spun round, only to have the lights go out and the world turn upside down, as he was whisked off his feet and suspended by his ankles. His arms and legs were pinned to his sides by something so much stronger than him that he could find absolutely no way to fight back. Then thick material was wound around him, binding his whole body, until he became a human roll of carpet, and he was rotated to the horizontal and carried off, just as if he was one.

Shouting was out of the question, as his mouth was obstructed, and it was only with the greatest effort that he managed to breathe. At one point, he thought he heard one of his son's voices, but it was so brief and muffled that he couldn't be sure. He had never been so terrified for his family, and himself, in his whole life. Or so thoroughly helpless.

CHAPTER THREE

The Highfield Museum was a glory hole – a repository for redundant belongings that had been spared the town dump. The building itself was the former town hall, which had been converted simply by the haphazard arrangement of glass cases, themselves as old as the objects they housed.

In a grim turn-of-the-century dentist's chair Dr Burrows settled down to his sandwiches, using, as he habitually did, a display case of early twentieth-century toothbrushes as a makeshift table. He flicked open his copy of *The Times* and gnawed on a limp salami and mayonnaise sandwich, seemingly oblivious to the dirt-encrusted dental implements below, which local people had bequeathed to the museum as an alternative to throwing them away.

In the cabinets around the main hall where Dr Burrows now sat, there were many similar arrangements of spared-from-the-dustmen articles. The 'Granny's Kitchen' corner featured an extensive assortment of tawdry egg whisks, apple corers and tea strainers. A pair of rusty Victorian mangles stood proudly by a long since defunct 1950s *Old Faithful Electric* washing machine that now shed rust flakes as voraciously as it once had consumed the soap variety.

The 'Clock Wall' was just as fascinating for its mediocrity. True, there was one item that caught the eye – a Victorian picture clock with a scene painted on a glass panel of a farmer with a horse pulling a plough – but unfortunately the glass had been broken and a vital chunk was missing where the horse's head would have been. Around it was a carefully arranged display of 1940s and 1950s wind-up and electric wall clocks in dull plastic pastel hues – none of these were working, as Dr Burrows hadn't quite got around to fixing them yet.

Highfield, one of the smaller London boroughs, had a rich past, starting as it had in Roman times as a small settlement, and, in more recent history, swelling under the full impact of the Industrial Revolution. However, not much of this rich past had found its way into the little museum, and the borough had become what it was now: a desert of bedsits, two-up-two-downs, and nondescript shops that couldn't afford more central locations.

Dr Burrows, the curator of the museum, was also its sole attendant, except on Saturdays, when a rota of old-age pensioners manned the fort. And always at his side was his brown leather briefcase, which contained a number of periodicals, half-read textbooks and historical novels. For reading was how Dr Burrows occupied his days, punctuated by the odd nap and very occasional clandestine pipe-smoking in 'The Stacks', a large storage room chock-full of boxed postcards and abandoned family portraits that would never be put out on display due to the lack of space.

Tucked in amongst the dusty exhibits and old mahogany showcases, he would put his feet up and read voraciously all day with Radio 4 playing in the background on a 'tranny' that had been left to the museum by a well-meaning local. Other than the occasional school party desperate for a local outing in wet weather, very few visitors at all came to the museum and, having seen it once, they were unlikely ever to return.

Dr Burrows, like so many others, was doing a job which had originally been a stopgap. It wasn't as if he didn't have an impressive academic record: a degree in history had been followed up with yet another, in archaeology, and then, for good measure, topped off with a doctorate. But with a young child at home and few positions on offer in any of the London universities, he had happened to spot the museum job in the *Highfield Bugle,* and sent in his details, thinking he had better get *something*, and quickly.

He'd been offered the curatorship, accepting it with the notion that he would seek out a more fulfilling job in the near future. And, as with so many other people, the security of a regular pay cheque had meant that twelve years had passed in a flash and with them any thoughts of looking for something better.

So, here he was, with a doctorate in Greek antiquities, his dark tweed jacket replete with professorial patches on the elbows, watching the dust settle on the rather tired and ordinary exhibits, only too painfully aware that the dust was also settling on himself.

Finishing off his sandwich, Dr Burrows crumpled the greaseproof wrapper into a ball and playfully launched it at a 1960s orange plastic wastepaper basket on display in the 'Kitchen' section. It missed, bouncing off the rim and coming to rest on the parquet floor. He let out a small sigh of disappointment and reached into his briefcase, rummaging around until he retrieved a bar of chocolate. It was a treat he tried to save until mid-afternoon, to give the day some shape. But he felt particularly forlorn today and willingly gave in to his sweet tooth, ripping the paper off in an instant and taking a large bite out of the bar.

Just then, the bell on the entrance door rattled and Oscar Embers tapped in on his twin walking sticks. The eighty-year-old former stage actor had formed a passion for the museum, and signed up for the occasional Saturday afternoon vigil after donating some of his autographed 'Spotlight' portraits to the archives.

Dr Burrows, seeing the old man bearing down on him, tried to finish his crammed mouthful of chocolate, but found that he had rather overstepped his capacity. Chewing manically, he realized that the pensioner, still very much in possession of his wits, was closing in far too quickly. Dr Burrows thought of fleeing to his office but knew it was too late now. He sat still, his cheeks puffed out like a hamster's as he attempted a smile.

'Good afternoon to you, Roger,' Oscar said cheerfully while fumbling in his coat pocket. 'Now, where did that thing go?'

Dr Burrows managed a tight-lipped 'Hmmm,' as he nodded enthusiastically. As Oscar began to wrestle with his coat pocket, Dr Burrows managed to get a couple of crafty chews in, but then the old man looked up, still grappling with his coat as if it was fighting back. Oscar stopped trawling his pockets for a second, and peered myopically around the glass cases and walls. 'Can't see any of that lace I brought you the other week. Are you going to put it on display? I know it was a little threadbare in places, but good stuff all the same, you know.' As Dr Burrows did not answer, he added, 'So it's *not* out then?'

Dr Burrows tried to indicate the storeroom with a flick of

his head. Never having known the curator to be so silent for so long, Oscar gave him a quizzical look, but then his eyes lit up as he found his quarry. He took it slowly from his pocket and held it, cupped in his hand, in front of Dr Burrows.

'I was given this by old Mrs Tantrumi – you know, the Italian lady who lives just off the end of the High Street. It was found in her cellar when the gas board were doing some repairs. Stuck in the dirt, it was. One of them kicked it with his foot. I think we should include it in the collection.'

Dr Burrows, cheeks puffed, braced himself for yet another not-quite-antique egg timer or battered tin of used pen nibs. He was taken off guard when, with a magician's flourish, Oscar held up a small, gently glowing globe, slightly larger than a golf ball, encased in a metal cage which was a dull gold in colour.

'It's a fine example of a . . . a light . . . thing of some . . .' Oscar tailed off. 'Well, as a matter of fact, I don't know *what* to make of it!'

Dr Burrows took the item, and was so fascinated that he quite forgot Oscar was watching him intently as he chewed his mouthful of chocolate.

'Teeth giving you gyp, my boy?' Oscar asked. 'I used to grind them like that too, when they got bad. Just awful – know exactly how you feel. All I can say is that I'm glad I took the plunge and had them all out in one go. It isn't so uncomfortable, you know, once you get used to one of these.' He started to reach into his mouth.

'Oh no, my teeth are fine,' Dr Burrows managed to say, quickly trying to head off the prospect of seeing the old man's dentures. He swallowed the last of the chocolate in his mouth with a large gulp. 'Just a bit dry today,' he explained, rubbing his throat. 'Need some water.'

'Ohhh, better keep an eye on that, y'know. Might be a sign that you've got that diabetes malarkey. When I was a lad, Roger,' Oscar's eyes seemed to glaze over as he remembered, 'some doctors used to test for diabetes by tasting your . . .' he lowered his voice to a whisper and looked down in the direction of the floor, '*waters*, if you know what I mean, to see if there was too much sugar in them.'

'Yes, yes, I know,' Dr Burrows replied automatically, far too intrigued by the gently glowing globe to pay any attention to Oscar's medical curiosities. 'Very strange. I would venture to say, offhand, that this dates from possibly the nineteenth century, looking at the metalwork . . . and the glass I would say is early, definitely hand-blown . . . but I have no idea what's inside. Maybe it's just a luminous chemical of some type – have you had it out in the light for long this morning, Mr Embers?'

'No, kept it safe in my coat since Mrs Tantrumi gave it to me yesterday. Just after breakfast, it was. I was on my constitutional – it helps with the old bowel mov—'

'I wonder if it could be radioactive,' Dr Burrows interrupted sharply. 'I've read that some of the Victorian rock and mineral collections in other museums have been tested for radioactivity. Some pretty fierce specimens were uncovered in a batch up in Scotland – powerful uranium crystals that they had to shut away in a lead-lined casket. Too hazardous to keep out on display.'

'Oh, I hope it's not dangerous,' Oscar said, taking a hasty step back. 'Been walking around with it next to my new hip – just imagine if it's melted the—'

'No, I don't expect it's that potent – it probably hasn't done you any real harm, not in twenty-four hours.' Dr Burrows gazed into the sphere. 'How very peculiar, you can see liquid moving inside . . . looks like it's swirling . . . like a storm . . .' He lapsed into silence, then shook his head in disbelief. 'No, must be the heat from my hand that's making it behave like that . . . you know . . . thermoreactive.'

'Well, I'm delighted you think it's interesting. I'll let Mrs Tantrumi know you want to hang on to it,' Oscar said, taking another step back.

'Definitely,' Dr Burrows replied. 'I'd better do some research before I put it out, just to make sure it's safe. But in the meantime I should drop Mrs Tantrumi a line to thank her, on behalf of the museum.' He hunted in his jacket pocket for a pen, but couldn't find one. 'Hold on a tick, Mr Embers, while I fetch something to write with.'

He walked out of the main hall and into the corridor, managing to stumble over an ancient length of timber, dug out of the marshes the previous year by some overzealous locals who swore blindly that it was a prehistoric canoe. Dr Burrows opened the door with 'Curator' painted on the frosted glass. The office was dark, as the only window was blocked by crates stacked high in front of it. As he groped for the light on his desk, he happened to uncurl his hand a little from around the sphere. What he saw completely astounded him.

The light it was giving off appeared to have turned from the soft glow he'd witnessed in the main hall to a much more intense light-green fluorescence. As he watched it, he could have sworn that the light was growing even brighter, and the liquid inside moving even more vigorously.

'Remarkable! What substance becomes more radiant the *darker* the surroundings?' he muttered to himself. 'No, I must be mistaken, it can't be! It must be that the luminosity is just more noticeable in here.'

But it *had* grown brighter; he didn't even need his desk light to locate his pen, as the globe was giving off a sublime green light, almost as bright as daylight. As he left his office and returned with his donations ledger to the main hall, he held the globe aloft in front of him. Sure enough, the moment he emerged back into the light, it dimmed again.

Oscar was about to say something, but Dr Burrows rushed straight past him, through the museum door, and out on to the street. He heard Oscar shouting, 'I say! I say!' as the museum door slammed shut behind him, but Dr Burrows was so intent on the sphere that he completely ignored him. As he held it up in the daylight, he saw that the glow was all but extinguished and that the liquid in the glass sphere had darkened to a dull greyish colour. And the longer he remained outside, exposing the sphere to natural light, the darker the fluid inside became, until it was almost black, and looked like oil.

Still dangling the globe in front of him, he returned inside, watching as the liquid began to whip itself up into a miniature storm and shimmer eerily again. Oscar was waiting for him, with concern on his face.

'Fascinating . . . fascinating,' Dr Burrows said.

'I say, thought you were having an attack of the vapours, old chap. I wondered if maybe you needed some air, rushing out like that? Not feeling faint, are you?'

'No, I'm fine, really I am, Mr Embers. Just wanted to test something. Now, Mrs Tantrumi's address, if you'd be so kind?'

'So glad you're pleased with it,' Oscar said. 'Now, while we're about it, I'll let you have my dentist's number, so you can get those teeth seen to, pronto.'

CHAPTER FOUR

Will was leaning on the handlebars of his bicycle at the entrance to a stretch of wasteland encircled by trees and wild bushes. He glanced at his watch yet again and decided he would give Chester another five minutes to turn up, but no more. He was wasting precious time.

The land was one of those forgotten lots you find on the outskirts of any town. This one hadn't yet been covered by housing, probably due to its proximity to the municipal waste station and the mountains of rubbish that rose and fell with depressing regularity. Known locally as 'the Forty Pits', owing to the numerous craters that pitted its surface, some almost reaching three metres in depth, it was the arena for frequent battles between two opposing teenage gangs, the Clan and the Click, whose members were drawn from Highfield's rougher housing estates.

It was also the favoured spot for kids on their track bikes and, increasingly, stolen mopeds, the latter being run into the ground and then torched, their carbon-black skeletons littering the far edges of the Pits, where weeds threaded up through their wheels and around their rusting engine blocks. Less

frequently, it was also the scene for sinister adolescent amuse-
ments such as bird- or frog-hunting; all too often, the
creatures were slowly tortured to death and their sorry little
carcasses impaled on sticks in sadistic youthful glee.

As Chester turned the corner towards the Pits a bright
metallic glint caught his eye. It was the polished face of Will's
shovel, which he wore slung across his back, like a samurai
navvy.

He smiled and picked up his pace, clutching his rather
ordinary, dull garden spade to his chest and waving enthusiastically to the lone figure in the distance, who was
unmistakable with his startlingly pale complexion, and his
baseball cap and sunglasses. Indeed, Will's whole appearance
was rather odd; he was wearing his 'digging kit' which consisted of an oversized cardigan with leather elbow pads, and a
pair of dirt-encrusted old cords, of indeterminate colour
owing to the fine patina of dried mud that covered them. The
only things Will kept really clean were his beloved shovel and
the exposed metal toecaps of his work boots.

'What happened to you then?' Will asked, as Chester
finally reached him. Will couldn't understand how *anything*
could have held his friend up, how *anything* could possibly be
more important than this.

This was a milestone in Will's life, the first time he'd ever
allowed somebody from school – or anywhere else, for that
matter – to see one of his projects. He wasn't sure yet whether
he'd done the right thing; he still didn't know Chester that
well.

'Sorry, got a puncture,' Chester puffed apologetically. 'Had
to drop the bike back home and run over here – bit hot in this
weather.'

Will glanced up uneasily at the sun, and frowned. It was no friend to him: his lack of pigmentation meant that even its meagre power on an overcast day could burn his skin. His albinism gave him the almost pure-white hair that stuck out from under his hat, and his pale-blue eyes, which were now darting impatiently towards the interior of the Pits.

'Right then, let's get straight to it. Lost too much time already,' Will said curtly. He pushed off on his bicycle with barely a glance at Chester, who began to run after him. 'Come on, this way,' he urged, as the other boy failed to match his speed.

'Hey, I thought we were already there!' Chester called after him, still trying to catch his breath.

Chester Rawls – almost as wide as he was tall and strong as an ox, known as Cuboid or Chester Drawers at school – was the same age as Will, but evidently had either benefited from better nutrition, or had inherited his weightlifter's physique. One of the less offensive pieces of graffiti in the school lavatories proclaimed that his father was a wardrobe and his mother a bow-fronted desk.

Although the growing friendship between Will and Chester seemed unlikely, the very thing that had helped to bring them together had also been the same thing that singled them out at school: their skin. For Chester, it was severe bouts of eczema, which resulted in flaky and itchy patches of raw skin. This was due, he was told unhelpfully, to either an unidentifiable allergy or nervous tension. Whatever the cause, he had endured the teasing and jibes from his fellow pupils, the worst ones being ''orrible scaly creature' and 'snake arse', until he could take no more and had fought back, using his physical advantage to quash the taunters with great effect.

Likewise Will's milky pallor separated him from the norm, and for a while he had borne the brunt of chants of 'Chalky' and 'Frosty the Snowman'. More impetuous than Chester, he had lost his temper one winter's evening when his tormentors had ambushed him on the way to a dig. Unfortunately for them, Will had used his spade to great effect, and a bloody and one-sided battle had ensued in which teeth were lost and a nose was badly broken.

Understandably, both Will and Chester were left alone for a while after that, and treated with the sort of grudging respect given to mad dogs. However, both boys remained distrustful of their classmates, believing that if they let their guards down, the persecution would more than likely start all over again. So, other than Chester's inclusion in a number of school teams because of his physical prowess, both remained outsiders: loners at the edge of the playground. Secure in their shared isolation, they talked to no one and no one talked to them.

It had been many years before they'd even spoken to each other, although there'd long been a sneaking admiration between the two for the way they'd both stood their ground against the school bullies. Without really realizing it they gravitated towards each other, spending more and more of their time together during school hours. Will had been alone and friendless for so long, he had to admit it that it felt good to have a companion, but he knew that if the friendship was going to go anywhere he'd sooner or later have to reveal to Chester his grand passion – his excavations. And now that time had come.

Will rode between the alternating grassy mounds, craters and heaps of rubbish left by fly-tippers, careering to a halt as he reached the far side. He dismounted and hid his bicycle in a small dugout beneath the shell of an abandoned car, its make unrecognizable as a result of the rust and salvaging it had endured.

'Here we are,' he announced, as Chester caught up.

'Is this where we're going to dig?' Chester panted, looking around at the ground by their feet.

'Nope. Back up a bit,' Will said. Chester took a couple of paces away from Will, regarding him with bemusement.

'Are we going to start a new one?'

Will didn't answer, but instead knelt down and appeared to be feeling for something in a thicket of grass. He found what he was looking for – a knotted length of rope – and stood up, took up the slack, then pulled hard. To Chester's surprise, a line cracked open in the earth and a thick panel of marine ply rose up, soil tumbling from it to reveal the dark entrance beneath.

'Why do you need to hide it?' he asked Will.

'Can't have those scumbags messing around with my excavation, can I?' Will said possessively.

'We're not going in there, are we?' Chester said, stepping closer to peer into the void.

But Will had already begun to lower himself into the opening, which, after a drop of a metre or two, continued to sink deeper, at an angle.

'I've got a spare one of these for you,' Will said from inside the opening as he donned a yellow hard hat and switched on the miner's light mounted on its front. It shone up at Chester, who was hovering indecisively above him.

'Well, are you coming or not?' Will said testily. 'Take it from me, it's completely safe.'

'Are you sure about this?'

'Of course,' Will said, making a show of slapping a support to his side and smiling confidently to give his friend some encouragement. He continued to smile fixedly as, in the shadows behind him and out of Chester's sight, a small shower of soil fell against his back. 'Safe as houses. Honest.'

'Well . . .'

Once inside, Chester was almost too surprised to speak. A tunnel, a couple of metres wide and the same in height, ran at a slight incline into the darkness, the sides shored up with old timber props at frequent intervals. It looked, Chester thought, exactly like the mines in those old cowboy films they showed on the telly on Sunday afternoons.

'This is cool! You didn't do all this by yourself, Will, you can't have!'

Will grinned smugly. 'Certainly did. I've been at it since last year – and you haven't seen the half of it yet. Step this way.'

He replaced the ply, sealing the tunnel mouth. Chester watched with mixed emotions as the last chink of blue sky disappeared. They set off along the passage, past stores of planks and shoring timbers stacked untidily against the sides.

'Wow!' Chester said under his breath.

Quite unexpectedly, the passage widened out into an area the size of a reasonably large room, two tunnels branching off each end of it. In the middle were a small mountain of buckets, a trestle table and two old armchairs. The timber planking of the roof was supported by rows of Stillson props, adjustable iron columns scabbed with rust.

'Home again, home again,' Will said.

'This is just . . . wild,' Chester said in disbelief, then

frowned. 'But is it really all right for us to be down here?'

'Course it is. My dad showed me how to batten and prop – this isn't my first time, you know . . .' Will hesitated, catching himself just in time before he said anything about the train station he'd unearthed with his father. Chester regarded him suspiciously as he coughed loudly to mask the lull in the conversation. Will had been sworn to secrecy by his father and he couldn't break that confidence, not even to Chester. He sniffed loudly, then went on. 'And it's perfectly sound. It's better not to tunnel under buildings – that takes stronger tunnel props and a lot more planning. Also, it's not a good idea where there's water or underground streams – they can cause the whole thing to slip in.'

'There isn't any water around here, is there?' Chester asked quickly.

'Just this.' Will reached into a cardboard box on the table and handed his friend a plastic bottle of water. 'Let's just chill out for a while.'

They both sat in the old armchairs, sipping from the bottles, while Chester looked up at the roof and craned his neck to peer at the two branch tunnels.

'It's so peaceful, isn't it?' Will sighed.

'Yes,' Chester replied. 'Very . . . er . . . quiet.'

'It's more than that, it's so warm and *calm* down here. And the smell . . . sort of comforting, isn't it? Dad says it's where we all came from, a long time ago – cavemen and all that – and of course it's where we all end up eventually – underground, I mean. So it feels sort of natural to us, home from home.'

'Suppose so,' Chester agreed dubiously.

'You know, I used to think that when you bought a house,

you owned everything under it as well.'

'What do you mean?'

'Well, your house is built on a plot of land, right?' Will said, thumping his boot on the floor of the cavern for effect. 'And anything below that plot, going right down to the Earth's core, is yours as well. Of course, as you get nearer to the centre of the planet, the "segment", if you want to call it that, gets smaller and smaller until you hit the very middle.'

Chester nodded slowly, at a loss to know what to say.

'So I've always imagined digging down – down into your slice of world and all those thousands of miles that are going to waste, instead of just sitting in a building perched on the very crust of the Earth,' Will said dreamily.

'I see,' Chester said, catching on to the idea. 'So if you were to dig down, you could have like a skyscraper, but facing the wrong way. Like an ingrown hair or something.' He involuntarily scratched the eczema on his forearm.

'Yes, that's exactly right. Hadn't thought of it like that, good way of putting it. But Dad says you *don't* actually own all the ground under you – the Government has the right to build Tube lines and things if they want to.'

'Oh,' Chester said, wondering why they had been talking about it in the first place, if that was the case.

Will jumped up. 'Right, grab yourself a pick, four buckets and a wheelbarrow, and follow me down here.' He pointed to one of the dark tunnels. 'There's a bit of a rock problem.'

Meanwhile, back up at ground level, Dr Burrows strode purposefully along as he made his way home. He always enjoyed the chance to think while he walked the couple of kilometres, and it meant he could save on the bus fare.

He stopped outside the newsagent's, abruptly halting in mid-pace, teetered slightly, rotated ninety degrees, and entered.

'Dr Burrows! I was beginning to think we'd never see you again,' the man behind the counter said as he looked up from a newspaper spread open before him. 'Thought you might've gone off on a round-the-world cruise or something.'

'Ah, no, alas,' Dr Burrows replied, trying to keep his eyes off the Snickers, Mars bars and Walnut Whips that were displayed enticingly in front of him.

'We've kept your backlog safe,' the shopkeeper said as he bent below the counter and produced a stack of magazines. 'Here they are. *Excavation Today*, *The Archaeological Journal* and *Curators' Month*. All present and correct, I hope?'

'Tickety-boo,' Dr Burrows said, hunting for his wallet. 'Wouldn't want you to let them go to anyone else!'

The shopkeeper raised his eyebrows. 'Believe me, there isn't exactly an excessive demand for these titles round here,' he said as he took a twenty-pound note from Dr Burrows. 'Looks like you've been working on something,' the shopkeeper said, spotting Dr Burrows' grimy fingernails. 'Been down a coal mine?'

'No,' Dr Burrows replied, comtemplating the dirt encrusted underneath his nails. 'I've actually been doing a spot of DIY in my cellar. Good thing I don't bite them, isn't it?'

Dr Burrows left the shop with his new reading matter, trying to tuck it securely into the side pocket of his briefcase as he pushed the door open. Still grappling with the magazines, he backed blindly out on to the pavement, straight into somebody moving at great speed. Gasping as he rebounded off the short but very heavy-set man he'd blundered into, Dr Burrows dropped his briefcase and magazines. The man, who had felt as solid as a locomotive, seemed totally unaffected and merely continued on his way. Dr Burrows, stuttering and flustered, tried to call after him to apologize, but the man strode on purposefully, readjusting his sunglasses and turning his head slightly to give Dr Burrows an unfriendly sneer.

Dr Burrows was flabbergasted. It was a *man-in-a-hat*. Of late, he had begun to notice, amongst the general population of Highfield, a type of person that seemed – well, *different*, but without sticking out too much. Being a habitual people-watcher, and having analysed the situation as he always did, he assumed that these people had to be related to each other in some way. What surprised him most was that when he raised the subject nobody else in the Highfield area seemed to have registered the rather peculiarly slope-faced men, wearing flat caps, black coats and very thick dark glasses, at all.

As Dr Burrows had barged into the man, slightly dislodging his jet-black glasses, he'd had a chance to see a 'specimen' at close hand for the very first time. Apart from his oddly sloping face and wispy hair, he had very light-blue, almost white eyes against a pasty, translucent skin. But there was something else: a peculiar smell hung about the man, a *mustiness*. It reminded Dr Burrows of the old suitcases of mildewed clothes that were occasionally dumped on the museum steps by anonymous benefactors.

He watched the man stride purposefully down the High Street and into the distance, until he was only just in view. Then a passer-by crossed the road, interrupting Dr Burrows' line of sight. In that instant, the *man-in-a-hat* was gone. Dr Burrows squinted through his spectacles as he continued to look for him, but although the pavements were not that busy, he couldn't locate him again, try as he might.

It occurred to Dr Burrows that he should have made the effort to follow the *man-in-a-hat* to see where he was going. But, mild-mannered as he was, Dr Burrows disliked any form of confrontation and quickly reasoned with himself that this was not a good idea, given the man's hostile manner. So any thought of detective work was quickly abandoned. Besides, he could find out on another day where the man, and perhaps the whole family of hatted lookalikes, lived. When he was feeling a little more intrepid.

Underground, Will and Chester took turns at the rock face, which Will had identified as a type of sandstone. He was glad that he'd recruited Chester to help with the excavation, as he really seemed to have a knack for the work. He watched with quiet admiration as Chester swung the pickaxe with immense force and, once a fissure opened up in the face, seemed to know exactly when to pry out the loose material, which Will quickly shovelled into buckets.

'Need a break?' he suggested, seeing that Chester was beginning to tire. 'Come and have a breather.' Will meant this literally, because with the entrance to the dig covered up, it all too soon became very airless and stuffy where they were, six metres or so from the main chamber.

'If I take this tunnel much further,' he said to Chester as they both pushed loaded wheelbarrows before them, 'I'll have to sink a vertical shaft for ventilation. It's just that it's such a drag putting one of those in, when I could be making more headway down here.'

They reached the main chamber and sat in the armchairs, drinking the water appreciatively.

'So what do we do with all this?' Chester said, indicating the filled buckets in the wheelbarrows.

'Lug it to the surface and tip it in the gully at the side.'

'Is it all right to do that?'

'Well, if anyone asks I just say I'm digging a trench for a war game,' Will replied. Taking a swig from his bottle, he swallowed noisily. 'What do they care anyway? To them we're just a bunch of dumb kids with buckets and spades,' he added dismissively.

'They *would* care if they saw this – this isn't what ordinary kids do,' Chester said, his eyes flicking around the chamber. 'Why *do* you do it, Will?'

'Have a look at these.'

Will gently lifted a plastic crate from the side of his chair and on to his lap. He then proceeded to take out a series of objects, leaning across to place them one by one on the table-top. Amongst them were Codswallop bottles – Victorian soft-drink bottles with strangely shaped necks that contained a glass marble – and a whole host of medicine bottles of different sizes and colours, all with a beautiful frosty bloom from their time in the ground.

'And these,' Will said reverentially, as he produced an entire range of Victorian pâté jars of differing sizes with decorative lids, and names in swirly old writing that Chester had never seen before. Indeed, Chester seemed to be genuinely interested, picking up each jar in turn and asking Will questions about how old they were and where exactly he'd dug them up. Encouraged, Will continued until every single find from his recent excavations was laid out on the table. Then he sat back, carefully watching his new-found friend's reaction.

'What's this lot?' Chester asked, probing a small pile of

heavily rusted metal with his finger.

'Rosehead nails. Probably eighteenth century. If you look carefully, you can see that each one is different, as they were handmade by—'

But in his excitement Chester had already moved down the table to where something else had caught his eye.

'This is so cool,' he said, holding up and turning a small perfume bottle so that the light played through its wonderful cobalt-blue and mauve tones. 'Incredible that someone just chucked it out.'

'Yeah, isn't it,' Will agreed. 'You can have it if you want.'

'No!' Chester said, astonished by the offer.

'Yeah, go on, I've got another one just like it at home.'

'Hey, that's great . . . thanks,' Chester said, still admiring the bottle with such rapture that he didn't see Will break into the widest grin imaginable. Will practically lived for the moments he could show his father his latest crop of finds, but this was more than he could have ever hoped for – someone his own age who seemed to be genuinely interested in the fruits of his labours. He surveyed the cluttered tabletop and felt a swell of pride. He often pictured himself reaching back into the past and plucking out these little pieces of discarded history. To Will the past was so much nicer a place than the grim reality of the present. He sighed as he began to replace the items in the crate.

'I haven't found any fossils down here yet . . . anything *really* old . . . but you never know your luck,' he said, glancing wistfully in the direction of the branch tunnels. 'That's the thrill of it all.'

CHAPTER FIVE

Dr Burrows whistled, swinging his case in time with his brisk pace. He rounded the corner at 6.30 p.m. precisely as he always did, and his house came into view. It was one of many crammed into Broadlands Avenue – regimented brick boxes with just enough room for a family of four. The only saving grace was that this side of the road backed on to the common, so at least the house had views of a big open space, even if one was forced to see them from rooms barely large enough to swing a mouse, let alone a cat.

As he let himself in and stood in the hall, sorting the old books and magazines from his briefcase, his son was not far behind. At breakneck speed Will careered into Broadlands Avenue on his bicycle, his spade glinting under the first red glow of the newly lit street lights. He skilfully slalomed between the white lines in the middle of the road and banked wildly as he shot through the open gate, his brakes reaching a squealing crescendo as he pulled up under the carport. He dismounted, locked up his bicycle and entered the house.

Will was the sort of boy who needed space. As a result, he was rarely to be found in the house except at meal times and to sleep, treating it much like a hotel as many kids his age did. The only problem with his constant yearning to be outside was that, as he couldn't be exposed to sunlight for any length of time, he was effectively forced to go underground at any opportunity he could find. Not that he minded that, of course.

'Hi, Dad,' he said to his father, who was now poised awkwardly just inside the sitting room, still holding his open briefcase in one hand as he watched something on television.

Dr Burrows was unarguably the biggest influence in his son's life. A casual comment or snippet of information from his father could inspire Will to embark on the wildest and most extreme 'investigations', usually involving ludicrous amounts of digging. Dr Burrows always managed to be 'in at the kill' on any of his son's digs if he suspected that there was going to be something of true archaeological value unearthed, but most of the time he preferred to bury his nose in the books he kept down in the cellar, *his* cellar. Here he could escape family life, losing himself in dreams of echoing Greek temples and magnificent Roman colosseums.

'Oh, yes, hello, Will,' he answered absent-mindedly after a long pause, still absorbed in the television. Will looked past his father to where his mother was sitting, equally mesmerized by the programme.

'Hi, Mum,' Will said and then left, not waiting for a response.

Mrs Burrows' eyes were glued to an unexpected and rather fraught turn of events in the casualty ward.

'Hello,' she eventually replied, although Will had already left the room.

Will's parents had first met at university when Mrs

Burrows had been a bubbly media student, dead set on a career in television.

Unfortunately, these days television filled her life for a completely different reason. She watched it with an almost fanatical devotion, juggling schedules with a pair of video recorders when her favourite programmes, of which there were so very many, clashed.

If one has a mental snapshot of a person, an image that is first recalled when one thinks of them, then Mrs Burrows' would be of her lying sideways in her favourite armchair, a row of remotes neatly lined up on the arm and her feet resting on a footstool topped with television pages ripped from the newspapers. There she sat, day after day, week after week, surrounded by a haphazard slag heap of video tapes, frozen in the flickering light of the small screen, occasionally twitching a leg just to let people know she was still alive. The sitting room, her domain, was furnished with furniture that had seen better days: an assortment of odd wooden chairs painted shades of purple and turquoise, a couple of mismatched armchairs with faded, dark-blue loose covers and a sofa with threadbare arms, all of which she and Dr Burrows had inherited over the years.

As he did every night, Will had beaten a path to the kitchen or, more specifically, the fridge. He was opening the door as he spoke, but didn't so much as glance at the other person in the room as he acknowledged her presence.

'Hi, sis,' he said. 'What are we having? I'm starved.'

'Ah, the mud creature returns,' Rebecca said to him. 'I had the funniest feeling you'd show up about now.' She rammed the fridge door shut to stop her brother from nosing inside, and, before he had a chance to complain, thrust an empty packet into his hands. 'Sweet and sour chicken, with rice and some vegetable stuff. It was on a two-for-one at the supermarket.'

Will looked at the picture on the packet, and, without comment, passed it back to her.

'So how's the latest dig going?' she asked, just as the microwave gave a *ting*.

'Not great – we've hit a layer of sandstone.'

'We?' Rebecca shot him a quizzical glance as she took a dish out of the microwave. 'I'm sure you just said *we*, Will. You don't mean Dad's working on it with you, do you? Not during museum hours?'

'No, Chester from school is giving me a hand.'

Rebecca had just placed a second dish in the microwave, and very nearly trapped her fingers in the door as she was closing it. 'You mean you actually asked somebody to help you? Well, *that's* a first. Thought you didn't trust anybody with your "projects"?'

'No, I don't usually, but Chester's cool,' Will replied, a bit taken aback at his sister's interest. 'He's been a real help.'

'Can't say I know much about him, except that he's called—'

'I know what they call him,' Will cut her off sharply.

At twelve, Rebecca was two years younger than Will, and couldn't have been more different from him; she was slim and dainty for her age, in contrast to her brother's rather stocky physique. And with her dark hair and sallow complexion, she wasn't bothered by the sun, even at the height of summer, while Will's skin would begin to redden and burn in a matter of minutes.

The two of them being so completely dissimilar, not just in appearance but also in temperament, their home life had something of the feel of an uneasy truce, and each showed only a passing interest in the other's pursuits.

There weren't the family outings that you would ordinarily expect, either, because Dr and Mrs Burrows also had completely divergent tastes. Will would go off with his father on expeditions – a habitual destination was the south coast, Lyme Regis being a firm favourite, where they would go fossil-hunting, scouring the coastline for recent landfalls.

Rebecca, on the other hand, would arrange her own holidays, regularly taking herself off on outings – where, or to do what, Will did not know or care. And on the rare occasions Mrs Burrows ventured out of the house she would just trudge around the shops in the West End or catch the latest films.

Tonight, as was the case most nights, the Burrows were sitting with their meals on their laps watching an oft-repeated 1970s comedy that Dr Burrows seemed to be enjoying. No one spoke during the meal except Mrs Burrows, who at one point mumbled, 'Good . . . this is good,' which may have been in praise of the microwaved food, or possibly the finale of the dated sitcom, but nobody made the effort to enquire.

Having rushed his food, Will left the room without a word, placing his tray by the kitchen sink before he went bounding up the stairs, a canvas sack of recently discovered items clutched in his hands. Dr Burrows was the next out, walking into the kitchen where he deposited his tray on the table. Although she hadn't finished her food yet, Rebecca followed closely behind him.

'Dad, a couple of bills need paying. The cheques are there on the table.'

'Have we got enough in the account?' he asked as he dashed his signature off on the bottom of the cheques, not even bothering to read the amounts.

'I told you last week, I got a better deal on the house insurance. Saved us a few pennies on the premium.'

'Right . . . very good. Thanks,' Dr Burrows said, picking up his tray and turning purposefully towards the dishwasher.

'Just leave it on the side,' Rebecca said a little too quickly, stepping protectively in front of the dishwasher. Only last week she'd caught him attempting to programme her beloved microwave by furiously jabbing at the buttons in random sequences, as if he was trying to crack some secret code. Ever since then she had been making sure she turned all the major appliances off at the wall.

As Dr Burrows left the room, Rebecca shoved the cheques in envelopes and then sat down to prepare a shopping list for the next day. At the tender age of twelve, she was the engine, the powerhouse behind the Burrows' home. She took it upon herself not just to do the shopping, but also to organize the meals, supervise the cleaning lady and do just about everything else that, in any ordinary household, the parents would have taken responsibility for.

To say Rebecca was meticulous would have been a gross understatement. A schedule on the kitchen notice board listed all the provisions she required for at least a fortnight in advance. She kept carefully labelled wallet files of the family's bills and financial situation in one of the kitchen cupboards. And the only times when this smooth operation of the household began to falter were on the occasions that Rebecca was absent. Then the three of them, Dr and Mrs Burrows and Will, would subsist on the food Rebecca had left for them in the freezer, helping themselves when they felt like it, with all the delicacy of a pack of marauding wolves. After these absences, Rebecca would simply return home and put the house back in order again without protest, as if she accepted that her lot in life was to tidy up after the other members of her family.

Back in the sitting room, Mrs Burrows flicked a remote to commence her nightly marathon of soaps and chat shows while Rebecca cleared up in the kitchen. By nine o'clock, she had completed her chores and, sitting at the half of the kitchen table that wasn't taken up by the numerous empty coffee jars Dr Burrows kept promising he'd do something with, had finished off her homework. Deciding it was time for bed, she picked up a pile of clean towels and went upstairs with them under her arm. Passing the bathroom, she caught her step as she happened to glance in. Will was kneeling on the floor admiring his new finds and washing the soil off them using Dr Burrows' toothbrush.

'Look at these!' he said proudly as he held up a small pouch made of rotten leather, which dripped dirty water everywhere. He proceeded to very gently prise open the fragile flap and lift out a series of clay pipes. 'You usually only find the odd piece . . . bits the farm labourers dropped. But just look at these. Not one of them is broken. Perfect as the day they were made . . . think of it . . . all those years ago . . . the eighteenth century.'

'Lovely,' Rebecca said, without the vaguest suggestion of any interest. Flicking back her hair contemptuously, she continued across the landing to the airing cupboard, into which she put the towels, and then into her room, closing the door firmly behind her.

Will sighed and resumed the inspection of his finds for several minutes, then gathered them up in the mud-stained bathroom mat and carefully conveyed them to his bedroom. Here he thoughtfully arranged the pipes and the still sopping leather pouch next to his many other treasures on the shelves that completely covered one wall of the room – his museum, as he called it.

Will's bedroom was at the back of the house, and it must have been about two o'clock in the morning when he was woken by a sound. It came from the garden.

'A wheelbarrow?' he said, immediately identifying it as his eyes flicked open. 'A loaded wheelbarrow?' He scrambled out of bed and went to the window. There, in the light of the half-moon, he could make out a shadowy form pushing a barrow down the path. He screwed his eyes up, trying to see more.

'Dad!' he said to himself as he recognized his father's features and saw the glint of moonlight from his familiar specs. Mystified, Will watched as his father reached the end of the garden and passed through the gap in the hedgerow, and then out on to the common. Here, Will lost sight of him behind some trees.

'What *is* he up to?' Will muttered to himself. Dr Burrows had always kept strange hours because of his frequent catnaps in the museum, but this level of activity was unusually lively for him.

Will recalled how, earlier that year, he had helped his father to excavate and lower the floor of the cellar by nearly a metre, and then lay a new concrete floor to increase the headroom down there. Then, a month or so later, Dr Burrows had had the bright idea of digging an exit from the cellar up to the garden and putting in a new door as, for some reason or other, he'd decided that he needed another means of entry to his sanctuary at the bottom of the house. As far as Will knew, the job had finished there, but his father could be unpredictable. Will felt a pang of resentment – what was his father doing that meant he had to be so secretive, and why hadn't he asked Will to help him?

Still groggy with sleep and distracted by thoughts of his own underground projects, Will put it from his mind for the time being and returned to bed.

CHAPTER SIX

The next day after school Will and Chester resumed their work at the excavation. Will was returning from dumping the spoils, his wheelbarrow stacked high with empty buckets as he trundled to the end of the tunnel where Chester was hacking away at the stone layer.

'How's it going?' Will asked him.

'It's not getting any easier, that's for sure,' Chester replied, wiping the sweat from his forehead with a dirty sleeve and smearing dirt across his face in the process.

'Hang on, let me have a look. You take a break.'

'Right.'

Will shone his helmet lamp over the rock surface, the subtle browns and yellows of the strata gouged randomly by the tip of the pickaxe, and sighed loudly. 'I think we'd better stop and think about this for a bit. No point banging our heads on a sandstone wall! Let's have a drink.'

'Yeah, good idea,' Chester said gratefully.

They went into the main chamber where Will handed Chester a bottle of water.

'Glad you wanted to do some more of this. It's pretty

addictive, isn't it?' he said to Chester who was staring into the middle distance.

Chester looked at him. 'Well, yes and no, really. I said I'd help you get through the rock, but after that I'm not so sure. My arms really hurt last night.'

'Oh, you'll get used to it and, besides, you're a natural.'

'You think so? Really?' Chester beamed.

'No doubt about it. You could be nearly as good as me one day!'

Chester punched him playfully on the arm and they laughed, but their laughter petered out as Will's expression turned serious.

'What is it?' Chester asked.

'We're going to have to rethink this. The sandstone vein might just be too thick for us to get through.' Will knitted his fingers together and rested his hands on top of his head, an affectation he had picked up from his father. 'What do you feel about . . . about going under it?'

'Under it? Won't that take us too deep?'

'Nah, I've gone deeper before.'

'When?'

'A couple of my tunnels went much further down than this,' Will said evasively. 'You see, if we dig under it, we can use the sandstone, as it's a solid layer, for the roof of the new tunnel. Probably won't even need to use any props.'

'No props?' Chester asked.

'It'll be perfectly safe.'

'What if it isn't? What if it collapses with us underneath?' Chester looked distinctly unhappy.

'You worry too much. Come on, let's get on with it!' Will had already made up his mind and was starting off down the tunnel when Chester called after him.

'Hey, why are we breaking our backs on this . . . I mean, is there anything on any of the plans? What's the point?'

Will was quite taken aback by the question, and it was several seconds before he replied. 'No, there's nothing marked on the Ordnance Surveys or Dad's archive maps,' he admitted. He took a deep breath and turned to Chester. 'The *digging* is the point.'

'So you think there's something buried there?' Chester asked quickly. 'Like the stuff in those old rubbish dumps you were talking about?'

Will shook his head. 'No. Of course the finds are great, but *this* is far more important.' He swept his hand extravagantly in front of him.

'What is?'

'All this!' Will ran his eyes over the sides of the tunnel and then the roof above them. 'Don't you feel it? With every spadeful, it's like we're travelling back in time.' He paused, smiling to himself. 'Where no one has gone for centuries . . . or maybe *never* gone before.'

'So you've got no idea what's there?' Chester asked.

'Absolutely none, but I'm not about to let a bit of sandstone beat me,' Will replied resolutely.

Chester was still flummoxed. 'It's just . . . I was thinking, if we aren't heading for anything in particular, why don't we just work on the other tunnel?'

Will shook his head again, but offered no further explanation.

'But it would be so much easier,' Chester said, a tone of exasperation creeping into his voice as if he knew he wasn't going to get a sensible answer out of Will. 'Why not?'

'A hunch,' Will said abruptly, and was off down the tunnel before Chester could utter another word. He shrugged and reached for his pickaxe.

'He's mad. And *I* must be bloody mad too. What on earth am I doing here?' he mumbled to himself. 'Could be at home, right now . . . on the PlayStation . . . and warm and dry.' He looked down at his mud-sodden clothes. 'Bloody mad!' he repeated several times.

Dr Burrows' day had been the same as usual. He was reclining luxuriously in the dentist's chair with a newspaper folded in his lap, on the brink of slipping into his post-teatime nap, when the door of the museum burst open. Joe Carruthers, former Major of the Queen's Own, strode purposefully in and scanned the room until he located Dr Burrows, whose head was lolling drowsily in the dentist's chair.

'Look sharp, Burrows!' he bellowed, almost taking pleasure in Dr Burrows' reaction as his head jerked up. Joe Carruthers, a veteran of the Second World War, had never lost his military bearing or his brusqueness. Dr Burrows had given him the rather unkind nickname 'Pineapple Joe' because of his strikingly red and bulbous nose – possibly the result of a war injury or, as Dr Burrows sometimes speculated, more likely due to his consumption of excessive amounts of gin. He was surprisingly sprightly for a man in his seventies, and tended to bark loudly. He was the last person Dr Burrows wanted to see right now.

'Saddle up, Burrows, need you to come and recce something for me, if you can spare a mo? Course you can, see you're not busy here, are you?'

'Ah, no, sorry, Mr Carruthers, I can't leave the museum

unattended. I'm on duty, after all,' Dr Burrows said sluggishly, reluctantly abandoning the last vestiges of sleep.

Joe Carruthers continued to bellow at him from across the museum hall. 'Come on, man, this is a *special* duty, y'know. Want your opinion. My daughter and her new hubby bought a house just off the High Street. Been having work done on the kitchen and they found something . . . something funny.'

'Funny in what way?' Dr Burrows asked, still irked by the intrusion.

'Funny hole in the floor.'

'Isn't that something for the builders to deal with?'

'Not that sort of thing, old man. Not that sort of thing at all.'

'Why?' Dr Burrows asked, his curiosity roused.

'Better if you come and have a gander for yourself, old chap. I mean, you know all about the history hereabouts. Thought of you immediately. Best man for the job, I told my Penny. This chappie really knows his stuff, I said to her.'

Dr Burrows rather relished the idea that he was regarded as the local historical expert, so he got to his feet and self-importantly put on his jacket. Having locked up the museum, he fell into step beside Pineapple Joe's forced march along the High Street, and they soon turned into Jekyll Street. Pineapple Joe spoke only once as they turned another corner, into Martineau Square.

'Those damn dogs – people shouldn't let them run wild like that,' he grumbled as he squinted at some papers blowing across the road in the distance. 'Should be kept on a lead.' Then they arrived at the house.

Number 23 was a terraced house, no different from all the

others that lined the four sides of the square, built of brick with typical early Georgian features. Although each property was rather narrow with just a thin sliver of garden at the rear, Dr Burrows had admired them on the occasions he'd happened to be in the area, and welcomed the chance to have a look inside one.

Pineapple Joe hammered on the original four-panelled Georgian door with enough force to cave it in, Dr Burrows wincing with each blow. A young woman answered the door, her face lighting up at the sight of her father.

'Hello, Dad. You got him to come, then.' She turned to Dr Burrows with a self-conscious smile. 'Do come down to the kitchen. Bit of a mess, but I'll put the kettle on,' she said, closing the door behind them.

Dr Burrows followed Pineapple Joe as he stomped over the dust sheets in the unlit corridor, where the wallpaper had been half stripped from the walls.

Once in the kitchen, Pineapple Joe's daughter turned to Dr Burrows. 'Sorry, how rude, I didn't introduce myself. My name's Penny *Hanson* – I think we've met before.' She emphasized her new surname proudly. For an awkward moment, Dr Burrows looked so totally mystified by this suggestion that she flushed with embarrassment and quickly mumbled something about making the tea, while Dr Burrows, indifferent to her discomfort, began to inspect the room. It had been gutted and the plaster stripped back to the bare brick, and there was a newly installed sink with half-finished cupboard units along one side.

'We thought it was a good idea to take out the chimney breast, to give us the space for a breakfast bar over there,' Penny said, pointing at the wall opposite the one with the new units. 'The architect said we just needed a brace in the ceiling.' She indicated a gaping hole where Dr Burrows could see that a new metal joist had been bedded in. 'But when the builders were knocking out the old brickwork, the back wall collapsed and they found this. I've rung our architect, but he hasn't called me back yet.'

To the rear of the fireplace a heap of soot-stained bricks indicated where the hearth wall had been. With this wall removed, a sizeable space had been revealed behind it, like a priest's hole.

'That's unusual. A second chimney flue?' he said to himself, almost immediately uttering a series of 'No's' as he shook his head. He moved closer and looked down. In the floor was a vent about one metre by half a metre in size.

Stepping between the loose bricks, he crouched down at the edge of the opening, peering into it.

'Ah . . . have you got a torch handy?' he asked. Penny fetched one. Dr Burrows took it from her and shone it down into the opening. 'Brick lining, early eighteenth century, I would venture. Seems to have been built at the same time as the house,' he muttered to himself as Pineapple Joe and his daughter watched him intently. 'But what the blazes is it for?' he added. The strangest thing was that as he leaned over and peered down into it, he couldn't see where it ended. 'Have you tested how deep it is?' he asked Penny, straightening up.

'What with?' she replied simply.

'Can I have this?' Dr Burrows picked up a jagged half-brick from the pile of rubble by the collapsed hearth. She nodded, and he turned back to the hole and stood poised to drop it in.

'Now listen,' he said to them as he released it over the vent. They heard it knocking against the sides as it fell, the sounds growing quieter until only faint echoes reached Dr Burrows, who was now kneeling over the opening.

'Is it—?' Penny began.

'Shhh!' Dr Burrows hissed impolitely, giving her a start as he held his hand up. After a moment he raised his head and frowned at Pineapple Joe and Penny. 'Didn't hear it land,' he observed, 'but it seemed to bounce off the sides for ages. How . . . how can it be *that* deep?' Then, seemingly oblivious to the grime, he lay down on the floor and stuck his head and shoulders into the hole as far as he could, probing the darkness below him with the torch in his outstretched arm. He suddenly froze and started to sniff loudly.

'Can't be!'

'What's that, Burrows?' Pineapple Joe asked. 'Anything to report?'

'I might be mistaken, but I could swear there's a bit of an updraught,' Dr Burrows said, pulling his head out of the gap. 'Why that should be, I just don't know – unless the whole terrace was built with some form of ventilation system between each house. But I can't for the life of me imagine why it would have been. The most curious thing is that the duct . . .' he rolled over on to his back and shone his torch upwards, above the hole, '. . . appears to carry on up, just behind the normal chimney. I presume it also vents as part of the chimney stack, on the roof?'

What Dr Burrows did not tell them – did not dare tell them, because it would have appeared too outlandish – is that he had smelled that peculiar mustiness again: the same smell he had noticed on his collision with the *man-in-a-hat* the day before in the High Street.

*

Back in the tunnel, Will and Chester were finally making progress. They were digging out the soil below the sandstone when Will's pickaxe hit something solid.

'Damn! Don't tell me the rock carries on down here too!' he yelled, exasperated. Chester immediately dropped his barrow and came running in from the main chamber.

'What's the matter, Will?' he asked, surprised at the outburst.

'Shit! Shit! Shit!' Will said, violently hacking at the obstacle with his pickaxe.

'What? What is it?' Chester shouted. He was shocked. He had never seen Will lose his cool in this way before; he was like a boy possessed.

Will increased his attack with the pickaxe, working at fever pitch as he struck wildly at the rock face. Chester was forced to take a step back to avoid his swings and the torrents of soil and stone he was throwing out behind him.

Suddenly Will stopped and fell silent for a moment. Then, slinging aside his pickaxe, he sank to his knees to scrape frantically at something in front of him.

'Well, look at that!'

'Look at what?'

'See for yourself,' Will said breathlessly.

Chester crawled in and saw what had excited his friend so much. Where Will had cleared the soil away there were several courses of a brick wall visible under the sandstone layer, and he'd already loosened some of the first bricks.

'But what if it's a sewer or railway tunnel, or something else like that? Are you sure we should be doing this?' Chester said anxiously. 'It might be something to do with the water supply. I don't like this!'

'Calm down, Chester, there's nothing on the maps around here. We're on the edge of the old town, right?'

'Right,' Chester said hesitantly, unsure what his friend was getting at.

'Well, there won't have been anything built in the last hundred to a hundred and fifty years – so it's unlikely to be a train tunnel, even a forgotten one, way out here. I went through all the old maps with Dad. I suppose it might be a sewer, but if you look at the curvature of the brick as it meets the sandstone, then we're probably near the top of it. It could just be the cellar wall of an old house – or maybe some foundations, but I wonder how it came to be built *under* the sandstone? Very odd.'

Chester took a couple of steps backwards and said nothing, so Will resumed his efforts for a few minutes and then stopped, aware that his friend was still hovering nervously behind him. Will turned and let out a resigned sigh.

'Look, Chester, if it makes you happy, we'll stop for today and I'll check with my dad tonight. See what he thinks.'

'Yeah, I'd rather you did, Will. You know . . . in case.'

Dr Burrows said goodbye to Pineapple Joe and his daughter, promising to find out what he could about the house and its architecture from the local archives. He glanced at his watch and grimaced. He knew it wasn't right to leave the museum closed for so long, but he wanted to look at something before he went back.

He walked around the square several times, examining the terraced houses on all four sides. The whole square had been built at the same time, and each house was identical. But what interested him was the idea that they might all have the mysterious ducts running through them. He crossed the road and went through the gate into the middle of the square, which had at its centre a paved area surrounded by some borders of neglected rose bushes. Here he had a better view of the roofs, and he pointed with his finger as he tried to count exactly how many chimney pots there were on each one.

'Just doesn't add up,' he frowned. 'Very peculiar indeed.'

He turned, left the square and, making his way back to the museum, arrived just in time to close up for the day.

CHAPTER SEVEN

In the dead of night, Rebecca watched from an upstairs window as a shadowy figure loitered on the pavement in front of the Burrows' house. The figure, its features obscured by a hoodie and a baseball cap, glanced furtively both ways along the street, behaving more like a fox than a human. Satisfied that it wasn't being observed, it descended on the bin bags and, seizing hold of the bulkiest ripped a hole in it and quickly began to rummage through the contents with both hands.

'Do you really think I'm that stupid?' Rebecca whispered, her breath clouding the glass of her bedroom window. She wasn't in the slightest bit concerned. Following warnings about identity theft in the Highfield area, she had been fastidiously destroying any official letters, credit card or bank statements – in fact anything containing the family's personal details.

In his haste to find something, the man was tossing out rubbish from the sack. Empty tins, food packaging and a series of bottles were being strewn across the front lawn. He snatched out a handful of papers and held them close to his face, rotating them in his fist as he scrutinized them under the dim street light.

'Go on,' she challenged the scavenger. 'Do your worst!'

Wiping the grease and old coffee grounds off one piece of paper with his hand, he twisted around so he could see it more clearly under the street light.

Rebecca watched as he feverishly read the letter, then smiled as he realized it was worthless. He tensed his arm in a gesture of disgust and threw it down.

Rebecca had had enough. She'd been leaning on the windowsill but now stood up, throwing back the curtains.

The man caught the movement and flicked his eyes up. He saw her and froze, then, twisting around to check both ends of the street again, he slouched off, glancing back at Rebecca as if defying her to call the police.

Rebecca clenched her small fists in fury, knowing she would be the one who'd have to clear up the mess in the morning. Yet another tedious chore to add to the list!

She closed the curtains, pulled back from the window and went out of her bedroom on to the landing. She stood, listening; there were several staccato snores. Rebecca turned on her slippered feet to face the door of the main bedroom, at once recognizing the familiar sound. Mrs Burrows was asleep. In the lull that followed she listened even harder, until she was able to discern Dr Burrows' long nasal breaths, then cocked her head towards Will's bedroom, listening again until she caught the rhythm of his faster, shallower breathing.

'Yes,' she whispered with an exultant toss of her head. Everyone was in a deep slumber. She felt instantly at ease. This was *her* time now, when she had the house to herself and could do what *she* wanted. A time of calm before they awoke and the chaos resumed again. She drew back her shoulders, and stepped noiselessly to the doorway of Will's room to look in.

Nothing moved. Like a shadow flitting across the room, she whisked over to the side of his bed. She stood there, gazing down at him. He was asleep on his back, his arms splayed untidily above his head. Under the faint moonlight filtering between the half-closed curtains she studied his face. She stepped closer until she was leaning over him.

'Well, look at him, not a care in the world,' she thought, and leaned even further over the bed. As she did so, she noticed a faint smudge under his nose.

Her eyes scanned the unconscious boy until they settled on his hands. 'Mud!' They were covered in it. He hadn't bothered to wash before getting into bed and, even more revolting, must have been picking his nose in his sleep.

'Dirty dog,' she hissed quietly. It was enough to disturb him, and he stretched his arms and flexed his fingers. Blissfully unaware of her presence, he made a low, contented noise deep in his throat, wriggling his body a little as he settled again.

'You're a total waste of space,' she whispered finally, then turned to where he'd thrown his filthy clothes on the floor. She gathered them up in her arms and left his room, going over to the wickerwork laundry basket that stood in a corner of the landing. Feeling inside all the pockets as she bundled the clothes into the basket, she came across a scrap of paper in his jeans, which she unfolded but could not read in the diminished light. Probably just rubbish, she thought, tucking it away in her dressing gown. As she withdrew her hand from her pocket, she caught a fingernail on the quilted material. She bit thoughtfully at the rough edge and strolled towards the main bedroom. Once inside, she made sure she stepped only on the precise areas where the floorboards under the old and worn shag pile carpet wouldn't creak and betray her presence.

Just as she had watched Will, she now watched Mrs and Dr Burrows, as if she was trying to divine their thoughts. After several minutes though, Rebecca had seen enough, and picked up Mrs Burrows' empty mug from the bedside table, giving it an exploratory sniff. Horlicks again, with a hint of brandy. With mug in hand Rebecca tiptoed out of the room and went downstairs into the kitchen, navigating her way easily through the darkness. Placing the mug in the sink, she turned and left the kitchen to return to the hallway. Here she stopped again, her head inclined slightly to one side, her eyes closed, listening.

'So calm . . . and peaceful,' she thought. 'It should always be this way.' Like someone in a trance, she remained standing there, unmoving, until finally she drew in a deep breath through her nose, held it for a few seconds, then released it through her mouth.

There was a muffled cough from upstairs. Rebecca glared resentfully in the direction of the staircase. Her moment had been broken, her thoughts disrupted.

'I'm so tired of all this,' she said bitterly.

She padded over to the front door, unlatched the safety chain, and then made her way into the sitting room. The curtains were fully open, giving her a clear view of the back garden, which was dappled in shifting patches of silvery moonlight. Her eyes never once left the scene as she lowered herself into Mrs Burrows' armchair, settling back as she continued to watch the garden and the hedge that divided it from the common. And there she remained, relishing the solitude of the night and enshrouded in the chocolatey darkness, until the early hours. Watching.

CHAPTER EIGHT

The next day, Dr Burrows was in the museum, sorting out the button cabinet under the window. He was leaning over the showcase, adding some newly acquired verdigrised brass army buttons from assorted regiments to the erratic lines of plastic, mother-of-pearl and enamel buttons in the display. He was becoming rather impatient because the loops on the backs of the buttons meant that they just wouldn't lie flat on the baize-covered backing board, however hard he pressed down on them. He exhaled loudly with sheer frustration and, hearing a car horn in the road outside, happened to glance up.

Out of the corner of his eye, he caught sight of a man walking on the opposite side of the road. He wore a flat cap, a long coat and, although the day was distinctly overcast with only intermittent glimpses of the sun, a pair of dark glasses. It might easily have been the man he had bumped into outside the newsagent's, but he couldn't be sure, as they all looked so similar.

What was it that was so compelling about these people? Dr Burrows felt in his bones that there was something special about them, something decidedly incongruous. It was as if they had stepped straight out of another time, perhaps from the Georgian era, given the style of their clothing. For him, this was on a par with finding a piece of living history, like those reports he'd read of Asian fishermen netting coelacanths, or maybe something even more tantalizing than that . . . the discovery of the 'missing link' in the evolution of man. These were the things that occupied his dreams and distracted him from his humdrum and uneventful life.

Never a man to rein in his obsessions, Dr Burrows was well and truly hooked. There had to be a rational explanation to the hatted-man phenomenon, and he was determined to find out what it was.

'Right,' he decided on the spot, 'now's as good a time as any.'

He put down the box of buttons and hurried through the museum to the main door, locking it behind him. As he stepped outside on to the street, he located the man up ahead, and, keeping a respectable distance, he followed him down the High Street.

Dr Burrows kept pace with the man as he left the High Street, turned into Disraeli Street and then crossed the road to take the first right into Gladstone Street just past the old convent. He was about twenty metres behind him when the man drew to a sudden halt and turned to look directly at him.

Dr Burrows felt a tremor of fear as he saw the sky reflecting off the man's glasses and, sure the game was up, immediately spun around to face the opposite direction. At a loss to know what else to do, he squatted down and pretended to tie an imaginary shoelace on his slip-on shoe. Without getting up he peered furtively over his shoulder, but the man had completely vanished.

His eyes frantically scanning the street, Dr Burrows began to walk briskly, then broke into a run as he approached the spot where he had last sighted his quarry. Coming to it, he discovered that there was a narrow entrance between two small almshouses. He was slightly surprised that in all the times he'd been this way before he'd never once noticed it. It had an arched opening and ran like a narrow tunnel until it passed beyond the back of the houses, and then continued for a short distance as an uncovered alleyway. Dr Burrows peered in, but the lack of daylight in the passage made it difficult to see very much. Beyond the stretch of darkness, he could make out something at the far end. It was a wall, cutting off the alleyway altogether. A dead end.

Checking the street one last time, he shook his head in disbelief. He couldn't see anywhere else the man might have gone, vanishing as abruptly as he had, so he took a deep breath and started down the passage. He picked his way cautiously, wary that the man might be lying in wait in an unseen doorway. As his eyes adjusted to the shadows, he could see that there were soggy cardboard boxes and milk bottles, mostly broken, scattered across the cobblestones.

He was relieved when he emerged back into the light again and paused to survey the scene. The alleyway was formed by garden walls to the left and right, and was blocked at its far end by the wall of a three-storey factory. The old building had no windows below its uppermost storey and couldn't possibly have provided the man with any means of escape.

So where the blazes did he go? thought Dr Burrows as he turned and looked back up the alleyway, to the street, where a car flashed by. To his right, the garden wall had a metre-high trellis running along it, which would have made it almost impossible for the man to climb over. The other wall had no such encumbrance, so Dr Burrows went up to it and peered over. It was a garden of sorts, neglected and barren, with a few withered shrubs and a stretch of muddy ground where the lawn should have been. This was peppered with faded plastic dishes containing dark-green water.

Dr Burrows gazed helplessly into the private wasteland and was about to forget the whole thing when he had a sudden change of heart. He slung his briefcase over the wall and rather awkwardly clambered after it. The drop was greater than he'd expected and he landed badly, in a sitting position in the mud. He tried to get up, but his shoes lost their purchase and he sat back down again, his outstretched hand managing to flip over one of the dishes, splattering its contents up his arm and neck. He swore silently, brushed off as much of it as he could and then rose to his feet again, stumbling and flailing like a drunken man until he regained his balance.

'Damn, damn and damn!' he said through clenched teeth as he heard a door open behind him.

'Hello? Who's there? What's going on?' came an apprehensive voice.

Dr Burrows wheeled around to face an old lady who was standing not two metres away, with three cats around her feet observing him with feline indifference. The old lady's sight was apparently not good judging by the way she was moving her head from side to side. She had wispy white hair and wore a floral housecoat. Dr Burrows guessed she was at least in her eighties.

'Er . . . Roger Burrows, pleased to meet you,' Dr Burrows said, not able to think of anything to explain why or how he had come to be there. The expression on the old lady's face was suddenly transformed.

'Oh, Dr Burrows, how very kind of you to drop by. What a nice surprise.'

Dr Burrows was himself surprised, and not a little confused. 'Yes, er . . . well . . . I happened to be passing this way.'

'So very courteous of you. Something you don't see much of these days. It's very nice of you to call.'

'Er . . . not at all,' he replied hesitantly. 'My pleasure entirely.'

'Gets a bit lonely with just my pussycats for company. Would you care for some tea? The kettle's on the boil.'

Dr Burrows was floundering – he'd anticipated having to make a quick getaway over the wall when he first saw her. This reception of such hospitality and warmth was the last thing he'd expected. Lost for words, he simply nodded and stepped forward, his shoe catching the rim of another plastic dish, which flipped its contents up his leg. He stooped to remove a slimy gob of algae from his sock.

'Oh, do be careful, Dr Burrows,' the old lady said. 'I put those out for the birds.' She turned, her entourage of cats darting before her into the kitchen. 'Milk and sugar?'

'Please,' Dr Burrows said, standing outside the kitchen door as she bustled around, getting a teapot down from a shelf.

'I'm sorry to turn up unannounced like this,' Dr Burrows said, in an attempt to fill the silence. 'This is all so very kind of you.'

'No, it's you who is very kind. I should be thanking you.'

'Really?' he stuttered, still frantically trying to work out exactly who the old lady was.

'Yes, for your very nice letter. Can't see as well as I used to, but Mr Embers read it to me.'

Suddenly it all fell into place and Dr Burrows sighed with relief, the fog of confusion blown away by the cool breeze of realization.

'The glowing sphere! It is certainly an intriguing object, Mrs Tantrumi.'

'Oh, good, dear.'

'Mr Embers probably told you I need to get it checked.'

'Yes,' she said. 'Don't want everyone to become radio-controlled, do we?'

'No,' agreed Dr Burrows, trying not to smile, 'wouldn't do at all. Mrs Tantrumi, the reason I dropped in . . .'

She held her head on one side, waiting expectantly for him to continue while she stirred the tea.

'. . . well, I was rather hoping you could show me where you found it,' he finished.

'Oh, no, dear, wasn't me – it was the gas men. Shortbread or custard cream?' she said, holding out a battered biscuit tin.

'Er , . . shortbread, please. You were saying the gas men found it?'

'They did. Just inside the basement.'

'Down there?' Dr Burrows asked, looking at an open door at the bottom of a short flight of steps. 'Mind if I take a look?' he said, pocketing the shortbread as he began to negotiate the mossy brick steps.

Once inside the doorway he could see that the basement was divided into two rooms. The first was empty, save for some dishes of extremely dark and desiccated cat food, and loose rubble strewn across the floor. He crunched through to the second room, which lay beneath the front of the house. It was much the same as the first, except that the light was poorer in here and there were several items of furniture. As his eyes roamed through the room he saw an upright piano in one corner, which looked as if it was falling apart from the damp, and, tucked in a shadowy recess, an old wardrobe with a broken mirror. He opened one of its doors and was immediately still.

He sniffed several times, recognizing the same musty odour he had smelled on the man in the street and more recently in the duct at Penny Hanson's house. As his eyes became used to the darkness he could see that inside the wardrobe were several overcoats – black, as far as he could tell – and an assortment of flat caps and other headwear stacked in a compartment to one side.

Remarkably the interior of the wardrobe didn't feel gritty to the touch, unlike everything else in the vicinity, which was coated with a fine layer of dust. In addition, when he rocked it away from the wall to check if there was anything behind it, the wardrobe itself appeared to be in surprisingly good shape. Finding nothing there, he turned his attention once again to its interior. Beneath the hat compartment, he found a small drawer which he slid open. Inside were five or six pairs of glasses. Taking one of these and pulling an overcoat from its hanger, he made his way back out into the garden.

'Mrs Tantrumi,' he called from the bottom of the steps. She waddled to the kitchen door. 'Did you know there's quite a few things in a wardrobe down here?'

'Are there?'

'Yes, some coats and sunglasses. Do they belong to you?'

'No, hardly ever go down there myself. The ground's too uneven. Would you bring them closer so I can see?'

He went to the kitchen door, and she reached out and ran

her fingers over the material of the overcoat as if she was stroking the head of an unfamiliar cat. Heavy and waxy to the touch, the coat felt strange to her. The cut was old-fashioned, with a shoulder cape of heavier material.

'I can't say I've ever seen this before. My husband, God rest his soul, may have left it down there,' she said dismissively, and returned to the kitchen.

Dr Burrows examined the dark glasses. They consisted of two pieces of thick and absolutely flat, almost opaque glass, similar to welders' goggles, with curious spring mechanisms on the arms either side – evidently to keep them snug against the wearer's head. He was puzzled. Why would the strange people keep their belongings in a forgotten wardrobe in an empty basement?

'Does anyone else come here, Mrs Tantrumi?' Dr Burrows said to her as she started to pour the tea with a very shaky hand, the spout rattling against the rim of the cup so violently that he thought she was going to knock it clean off the saucer.

There was a lull in the rattling as she looked confused. 'I really don't know what you mean,' she said, as if Dr Burrows was suggesting she had been doing something improper.

'It's just that I've seen some rather odd characters around this part of town – always wearing big coats and sunglasses, like these . . .' Dr Burrows tailed off, as the old lady was looking so anxious.

'Oh, I hope they aren't those criminal types one hears about. I don't feel safe here any more – my friend Oscar is very kind though. He visits me most afternoons. You see, I don't have anyone close by, any family. My son went to America, you know. He's a good boy. The firm he works for moved him and his wife—'

'So you haven't seen any people in coats like these – men with white hair?'

'No, dear, can't say I know what you're talking about.' She looked enquiringly at him, then resumed pouring the tea. 'Do come in and sit down.'

'I'll just put these back,' Dr Burrows said, returning to the basement. Before he left, he couldn't resist a quick inspection of the piano, lifting the lid and pressing a few keys that gave either dull clunks or completely out-of-tune twangs. He tried to pull it away from the wall, but it creaked and threatened to fall apart, so he stopped. Then he walked around both basement rooms and stamped on the ground, hoping to find a trap door. He did the same in the small garden, stamping around the lawn whilst trying to avoid the plastic dishes, all the time watched curiously by Mrs Tantrumi's cats.

On the other side of town, Chester and Will were back in the Forty Pits tunnel.

'So what did your dad say? What does he think we've found?' Chester asked as Will used a mallet and coal chisel to loosen the mortar between the bricks in the unidentified structure.

'We looked at the maps again and there's nothing on them.' He was lying, as Dr Burrows had not emerged from the cellar before Will had gone to bed, and had left the house before Will was up in the morning.

'No water mains, sewers or anything on this plot,' Will went on, trying to reassure Chester. 'The brickwork is pretty solid, you know – this thing was built to last.' Will had already removed two layers of bricks, but hadn't yet broken through. 'Look, if I'm wrong about this and anything gushes out, just make sure you get yourself to the far side of the main chamber. The flow should carry you up to the entrance,' Will said, redoubling his efforts on the brickwork.

'What?' Chester asked quickly. 'A flow . . . carry me up? I don't like the sound of that one bit. I'm off.' He turned to go, paused as if undecided, then made up his mind and began walking towards the main chamber, grumbling to himself all the way.

Will simply shrugged. There was no way he was going to stop, not with the possibility that he could bring to light some fantastic mystery, something so important that it would bowl his father over, and that he'd discovered by himself. And no one was going to stop him, not even Chester. He immediately proceeded to chisel around another brick, chipping away at the wedge of mortar at its edge.

Without warning, part of the mortar exploded with a high pneumatic hiss, and a chunk of it shot straight past Will's gloved hands like a stone bullet and struck the tunnel wall behind him. He dropped his tools and flopped back on to the ground in astonishment. Shaking his head, he pulled himself together and set about the task of removing the brick, which he accomplished in seconds.

'Hey, Chester!' Will called.

'Yeah, what?' Chester shouted gruffly from the main chamber. 'What is it?'

'There's no water!' Will shouted back, his voice echoing oddly. 'Come and see.'

Chester reluctantly retraced his steps. He found that Will had indeed penetrated the wall, and was holding his face up to the small breach he'd made and sniffing at the air.

'It's definitely not a sewage pipe, but it *was* under pressure,' Will said.

'Could it be a gas pipe?'

'Nope, doesn't smell like it and anyway they've never been made of brick. Judging by the echo, it's quite a large space.' His eyes flashed with anticipation. 'I just knew we were on to something. Fetch me a candle and the iron rod from the main chamber, will you?'

When Chester returned Will lit the candle a good distance back from the hole and then carried it slowly before him, nearer and nearer to the opening, watching the flame intently with every step he took.

'What does that do?' Chester asked as he looked on in fascination.

'If there are any gases you'll notice a difference in the way it burns,' Will answered matter-of-factly. 'They did this when they cracked open the pyramids.' There was no change in the flickering flame as he brought it closer, then held it directly in front of the opening. 'Looks like we're all clear,' he said as he blew the flame out and reached for the iron rod Chester had leaned against the tunnel wall. He lined the three-metre pole up carefully with the hole and then rammed it through, pushing it all the way in until only a short length protruded from between the bricks.

'It hasn't hit anything – it's pretty big,' Will said excitedly, grunting with exertion as he checked the depth by letting the end of the pole swing down. 'But I think I can feel what might be the floor. Right, let's widen this a bit more.'

They worked together and within moments had removed enough bricks for Will to slither through head first. He landed with a muffled groan.

'Will, are you all right?' Chester called.

'Yes. Just a bit of a drop,' he replied. 'Come in feet first and

I'll guide you down.'

Chester made it through after a tremendous struggle, his shoulders being broader than Will's. Once he was in, they both began to look around.

It was an octagonal chamber, with each of its eight walls arching up to a central point about six metres above their heads. At its apex was what appeared to be a carved stone rose. They shone their torches in hushed reverence, taking in the Gothic beading set into the perfectly laid brickwork. The floor was also constructed from bricks laid end on end.

'Awesome!' Chester whispered. 'Who'd have ever expected to find anything like this?'

'It's like the crypt of a church, isn't it? Will said. 'But the strangest thing is . . .'

'Yes?' Chester shone his torch at Will.

'It's absolutely bone dry. And the air's sort of sharp, too. I'm not sure—'

'Have you seen this, Will?' Chester interrupted, flicking his torch around the floor and then over the wall nearest to him. 'There's something written on the bricks. All of them!'

Will immediately swivelled around to study the wall closest to him, reading the elaborate Gothic script carved into the face of every brick. 'You're right. They're names: James Hobart, Andrew Kellogg, William Butts, John Cooper . . .'

'Simon Jennings, Daniel Lethbridge, Silas Samuels, Abe Winterbotham, Caryll Pickering . . . there must be thousands in here,' Chester said.

Will pulled his mallet from his belt and began to knock on the walls, taking soundings to see if there was any sign of a hollow or adjoining passage. He had methodically tapped away at two of the eight walls, when for no apparent reason he suddenly stopped. He clapped a hand to his forehead and swallowed hard.

'Do you feel that?' he asked Chester.

'Yeah, my ears popped,' Chester agreed, sticking a gloved finger roughly into one of his ears. 'Just like when you take off in a plane.'

They were both silent, as if waiting for something to happen. Then they felt a tremor, an inaudible tone, somewhat akin to a low note played on an organ – a throbbing was building, seemingly within their skulls.

'I think we should get out.' Chester looked at his friend blankly, swallowing now not because of his ears, but because of the waves of nausea welling up inside him.

For once Will did not disagree. He gulped a quick 'Yes', blinking as spots appeared before his eyes.

They both clambered back through the gap in double-quick time, then made their way to the armchairs in the main cavern and slumped down in them. Although they had said nothing of it to each other at the time, the inexplicable sensations had ceased almost immediately they were outside the chamber.

'What *was* that in there?' Chester asked, opening his mouth wide to flex his jaw, and pressing the palms of his hands against his ears.

'I don't know,' Will replied. 'I'll get my dad to come and see it – he might have an explanation. Must be a pressure build-up or something.'

'Do you really think it's a crypt, from where a church once stood . . . what with all those names?'

'Maybe,' Will replied, deep in thought. 'But somebody – craftsmen, stonemasons – built it very carefully, not even leaving any off-cuts or rubbish behind as they went, and then just as carefully sealed it up. Why on earth would they go to all that trouble?'

'I didn't think of that. You're right.'

'And there was no way in or out. I couldn't find any sign of connecting passages – not a single one. A self-contained chamber with names, like some sort of memorial or something?' Will pondered, completely foxed. 'What *are* we on to here?'

CHAPTER NINE

Having learned that Rebecca could be very unforgiving, and that it was really not worth incurring her wrath – not just before mealtimes, at any rate – Will shook himself down and stamped the worst of the mud from his boots before bursting in through the front door. Slinging his rucksack to the floor, the tools inside clattering against each other, he froze in astonishment.

A very odd scene greeted him. The door to the sitting room was closed and Rebecca was crouched down beside it, her ear pressed to the keyhole. She frowned the moment she saw him.

'What—?' Will's question was cut short as Rebecca rose swiftly, shushing him with a forefinger to her lips. She seized her bemused brother by the arm and pulled him forcibly into the kitchen.

'What's going on?' Will demanded in an indignant whisper.

This was all very odd indeed. Rebecca, the original Little Miss Perfect, was in the very act of eavesdropping on their parents, something he would never have expected from her.

But there was something even more remarkable than this: the sitting-room door itself. It was *closed*. Will turned his head to look at it again, not quite believing his eyes.

'That door has been wedged open for as long as I can remember,' he said. 'You know how she hates—'

'They're arguing!' Rebecca said momentously.

'They're *what*? About what?'

'I'm not sure. The first thing I heard was Mum shouting at him to shut the door, and I was just trying to hear more when you barged in.'

'You must have heard *something*.'

Rebecca didn't answer him immediately.

'Come on,' Will pressed her. 'What did you hear?'

'Well,' she started slowly, 'she was screaming that he was a *bloody failure* . . . and that he should stop wasting his time on *complete rubbish*.'

'What else?'

'Couldn't hear the rest, but they were both very angry. They were sort of growling at each other. It must be really important – she's missing *Neighbours*!'

Will opened the fridge and idly inspected a yogurt before putting it back. 'So what could it be about then? I don't remember them ever doing this before.'

Just then the sitting-room door was flung open, making both Will and Rebecca jump, and Dr Burrows stormed out, his face bright red and his eyes thunderous as he made a bee-line for the cellar door opposite. Fumbling with his key and muttering incomprehensibly under his breath, he unlocked it and then banged it shut after him.

Will and Rebecca were still peering around the corner of the kitchen door when they heard Mrs Burrows shouting.

'YOU'RE GOOD FOR NOTHING, YOU BLOODY FOSSIL! YOU CAN STAY DOWN THERE AND ROT FOR ALL I CARE, YOU STUPID OLD RELIC!' she shrieked at the top of her lungs, as she slammed the sitting-room door with an almighty crash.

'That can't be good for the paintwork,' Will said distantly.

Rebecca was so intent on what was happening, she didn't appear to have heard Will.

'God, this is so bloody annoying. I really need to talk to him about what we found today,' he grumbled.

This time she did hear him. 'You can forget that! My advice is just stay out of the way until things blow over.' She stuck out her chin with great self-importance. 'If they ever do. Anyway the food's ready. Just help yourself. In fact, you can help yourself to the lot . . . I don't think anyone else is going to feel like any.'

Without a further word, Rebecca spun around and left the room. Will moved his eyes from the empty doorway to the oven, and gave a small shrug.

He wolfed down two and a half of the oven-ready meals and then made his way upstairs in the now uncannily quiet house. There weren't even the usual strains of the television coming from the sitting room below as, propped up in his bed, he meticulously polished his spade with a cloth until it gleamed and sent reflections rippling across the ceiling above him. Then he leaned over to lay it gently on the floor, switched off the light on his bedside table, and slid under his duvet.

CHAPTER TEN

Will woke with a lazy yawn looking blearily around the room until he noticed the light creeping in at the edges of the curtains. He sat up sharply as it dawned on him that something was not quite right. There was a surprising lack of the usual morning hubbub in the house. He glanced at his clock. He'd overslept. The events of last night had completely thrown him and he had forgotten to set the alarm.

He found some relatively clean items of his school uniform in the bottom of his wardrobe and, quickly throwing them on, went across to the bathroom to brush his teeth.

Emerging from the bathroom he saw that the door to Rebecca's room was ajar and paused outside to listen for a moment. He'd learned not to blunder straight in; this was her inner sanctum, and she had berated him for entering unannounced several times before. As there were no signs of life, he decided to take a look. It was as spotless as ever – her bed immaculately made and her home clothes laid out in readiness for her return from school – everything clean and shipshape and in its place. He spotted her little black alarm clock on her bedside table. 'Why didn't she get me up?' he thought to himself.

He then saw that his parents' door was ajar, and couldn't resist putting his head round the corner. The bed hadn't been slept in. This was not right at all.

Where were they? Will reflected on the previous evening's argument between his parents, the gravity of which now began to sink in. Contrary to the impression he usually gave, Will did have a sensitive side. It wasn't that he didn't care, he just found it difficult to show his emotions, preferring to hide his feelings behind a show of flippant bravado where his family were concerned, or a mask of total indifference where other people were involved. It was a defence mechanism he'd developed over the years to cope with taunts about his appearance. *Never show your feelings, never react to their mindless jibes, never give them the satisfaction.*

Although he'd never stopped to give it much thought, Will was aware that his home life was pretty strange, to say the least. All four members of the family were so different, as if they'd been thoughtlessly thrown together by circumstances beyond their control, like four complete strangers who happen to share the same carriage on a train. Somehow it had hung together; each knew their place, and the end result, if not entirely happy, had seemed to have found its own peculiar equilibrium. But now the whole thing was in danger of coming crashing down. At least that was how it felt to Will that morning.

As he stood in the middle of the landing, he listened to the disquieting silence again, glancing from bedroom door to bedroom door. *This was serious.*

'It *would* have to happen now . . . just when I've found something so amazing,' he muttered to himself. He longed to speak to Dr Burrows, to tell him about the Pits tunnel and the strange chamber that he and Chester had stumbled upon. It was as if it all meant nothing without his approval, his 'Well done, Will,' and his fatherly smile of pride in his achievement.

As he tiptoed downstairs, he had the oddest feeling of being an intruder in his own home. He glanced at the sitting-room door. It was still closed. Mum must have slept in there, he thought as he went into the kitchen. On the table was a single bowl; from the few remaining Rice Krispies clinging to it, he could tell that his sister had already had her breakfast and left for school. The fact that she hadn't cleared up after herself, and the absence of his father's cornflakes bowl and teacup on the table or in the sink, caused vague alarm bells to ring in his head. This frozen snapshot of everyday activity had become the clue to a mystery, like the little pieces of evidence at a crime scene which, if read in the right way, would give him the answer to what exactly was going on.

But it was no good. He could find no answers here, and he realized he had to be on his way.

'This is like a bad dream,' he grumbled to himself as he hastily poured his Weetos into a bowl. 'Total cave-in,' he added, glumly crunching on the cereal.

CHAPTER ELEVEN

Chester lolled in one of the two broken-down armchairs in the main chamber of the Forty Pits tunnel. He formed yet another little marble of clay between his fingertips, adding it to the growing pile on the table next to him. He then began to aim them half-heartedly, one after another, at the neck of an empty Volvic bottle that he had balanced on the rim of a nearby wheelbarrow.

Will was long overdue, and as Chester threw the little projectiles he wondered what could have possibly got in the way of his friend's arrival. This alone wasn't of great concern, but he was anxious to tell Will what he'd discovered when he had first entered the excavation site.

When Will finally appeared, he was walking at a snail's pace down the incline of the entrance tunnel, his shovel resting on his shoulder and his head hung low.

'Hi, Will,' Chester said brightly, as he lobbed a whole handful of the clay balls at the defiant bottle. All of them predictably failed to hit the mark. There was a moment of disappointment before Chester turned to Will for a response. But Will merely grunted, and, when he did look up, Chester was disturbed by the marked lack of sparkle in his friend's eyes. Chester had noticed something wasn't right over the past couple of days at school – Will seemed to be avoiding him, and when Chester had caught up with him his friend had been withdrawn and uncommunicative.

An uneasy silence grew between them in the chamber until Chester, unable to stand it any longer, blurted out, 'There's a block—'

'My dad's gone,' Will cut across him.

'What?'

'He locked himself in the cellar, but now we think he's gone.'

Suddenly it became clear to Chester why his friend's behaviour had been odder than usual. He opened his mouth and then shut it again. He had absolutely no idea what to say.

As if exhausted, Will slumped down in the closest armchair.

'When did this happen?' Chester asked awkwardly.

'Couple of days ago – he had some sort of row with Mum.'

'What does she think?'

'Hah, nothing! She hasn't said a word to us since he went,' Will answered.

Chester glanced at the tunnel branching off the chamber and then at Will, who was contemplatively rubbing a smear of dried mud from the shaft of his spade. Chester took a deep breath and spoke hesitantly. 'I'm sorry, but . . . there's something else you should know.'

'What's that?' Will said quietly.

'The tunnel's blocked.'

'What?' Will said. In a flash, he became animated again. He sprang out of the armchair and dashed into the mouth of the tunnel. Sure enough, the entrance to the peculiar brick room was impassable – in fact, only half of the six-metre passage still remained.

'I don't believe it.' Will stared helplessly at the tightly packed barrier of soil and stone which reached right up to the roof of the tunnel, closing it off completely. He tested the props and stays immediately in front of it, tugging at them with both hands and kicking their bases with the steel toecap of his work boot. 'Nothing wrong with those,' he said, squatting down to test several areas of the spoil from the pile with his palms. He cupped his hand, scooped up some of the earth and examined it as Chester watched, admiring the way his friend was investigating the scene.

'Weird.'

'What is?' Chester asked.

Will held the earth up to his nose and sniffed it deeply. Then, taking a pinch of the soil, he discarded the rest of it. He continued to rub it slowly between his fingertips for several seconds and then turned to Chester with a frown.

'What's up, Will?'

'The props further into the tunnel were completely sound – I gave them a once-over before we left last time. And there hasn't been any rain recently, has there?'

'No, I don't think so,' Chester replied.

'No, and this earth doesn't feel nearly damp enough to cause the roof to slip in – there's no more moisture than you'd expect. But the weirdest thing is all this.' He reached down, plucked out a chunk of stone from the pile and tossed it over to Chester, who caught and examined it with a bewildered expression.

'I'm sorry, I don't understand. What's important about this?'

'It's *limestone*. This infill has bits of limestone in it. Feel the surface of the rock. It's chalky – totally the wrong texture for sandstone. That's *particulate*.'

'Particulate?' Chester asked.

'Yes, much more grainy. Hang on, let me check to make sure I'm right,' Will said as he produced his penknife and, folding the largest blade out, used it to pick at the clean face of another piece of the rock, talking all the while. 'You see, they're both sedimentary rocks, and they look pretty much the same. Sometimes it's quite hard to tell the difference. The tests you can use are to drop acid on it – it makes limestone fizz – or look at it with a magnifying glass to see the coarser quartz grains you only get in sandstones, but this is the best method by far.'

'Here we go,' Will announced as he took a minute flake of the stone he'd prised from the sample and, to Chester's amazement, slipped it off the blade and into his mouth. Then he began to nibble it between his front teeth.

'What *are* you doing, Will?'

'Mmmm,' Will replied thoughtfully, still grinding it. 'Yes, I'm pretty sure this is limestone . . . you see, it breaks down into a smooth paste . . . if it was sandstone, it'd be crunchier, and even squeak a little as I bit it.'

Chester winced as he heard the sounds coming from his friend's mouth. 'Are you serious? Doesn't that knacker your teeth?'

'Hasn't yet,' Will grinned. He reached into his mouth to reposition the flake and chewed on it for a little longer. 'Definitely limestone,' he finally decreed, spitting out what was left of the flake of rock. 'Want a go?'

'No, I'm fine, really,' Chester replied without a moment's

hesitation. 'Thanks anyway.'

Will waved his hand in the direction of the roof over the cave-in. 'I don't believe there'd be a deposit – an isolated pocket of limestone – anywhere near here. I know the geology of this area pretty well.'

'So what are you getting at?' Chester asked, with a frown. 'Someone came down here, and blocked up the tunnel with all this stuff?'

'Yes . . . no . . . oh, I don't know,' Will said, kicking the edge of the huge heap in frustration. 'All I do know is that there's something very funny about all this.'

'It might've been one of the gangs? Could be the Clan?' Chester suggested, adding, 'Or maybe even the Click?'

'No, that's not likely,' Will said, turning to survey the tunnel behind him. 'There'd be other signs that they'd been here. And why would they've just blocked up this tunnel? You know what they're like - they would've wrecked the whole excavation. No, it doesn't make sense,' he said, bemused.

'No,' Chester echoed.

'But whoever it was, they really didn't want us to go back in there, did they?' Will said.

Rebecca was in the kitchen doing her homework when Will returned home. He was just slotting his spade into the umbrella stand and hanging his yellow hard hat on the end of it when she called to him from around the corner.

'You're back early.'

'Yeah, we had some trouble in one of the tunnels and I couldn't be bothered to do any digging,' he said as he slumped down rather dejectedly in the chair on the opposite side of the table.

'No digging?' Rebecca said with mock concern. 'Things must be worse than I thought!'

'We had a roof fall in.'

'Oh, right . . .' she said remotely.

'I can't figure out what happened. It couldn't be seepage, and the really odd thing was that the infill . . .' He tailed off as Rebecca rose from the table and busied herself at the kitchen sink, clearly not listening to a word he was saying. This didn't bother Will unduly; he was used to being ignored. He wearily rested his head in his hands for a moment, but then raised it with a start as something occurred to him.

'You don't think he's in trouble down there, do you?' he said.

'Who?' Rebecca asked as she rinsed out a saucepan.

'Dad. Because it's been so quiet, we've all assumed he's gone somewhere, but he could still be in the cellar. If he hasn't eaten for two whole days, he might have collapsed.' Will rose from his chair. 'I'm going to take a look,' he said decisively to Rebecca's back.

'Can't do that. No way,' she said, spinning around to face him. 'You know he doesn't let us go down there without him.'

'I'm going to fetch the spare key.' With that, Will hurried out of the room leaving Rebecca standing by the sink, clenching and unclenching her fists in her yellow Marigolds.

He reappeared seconds later. 'Well, are you coming or not?'

Rebecca made no move to follow him, turning her head to look out through the kitchen window as if mulling something over.

'Come on!' A flash of anger suffused Will's face.

'Fine . . . whatever,' she agreed as she seemed to come to again, snapping off her gloves and placing them very precisely on the drainer at the side of the sink.

They went to the cellar door and unlocked it very quietly, so their mother wouldn't hear. They needn't have worried, as the sound of a barrage of gunfire was coming thick and fast from inside the sitting room.

Will turned on the light and they descended the varnished oak stairs that he had helped his father fix into place. As they stood on the grey-painted concrete floor, they both looked around in silence. There was no sign of Dr Burrows. The room was crammed with his belongings, but nothing was that different from the last time Will had seen it. His father's extensive library covered two walls, and on another were shelves housing his 'personal' finds, including a railwayman's lamp, the ticket machine from the disused railway station and a careful arrangement of primitive little clay heads with clumsy features. Against the fourth wall stood a workbench, on which his computer sat, with a half-finished Curly Wurly in front of it.

As Will surveyed the scene the only thing that seemed out of place was a wheelbarrow filled with earth and small rocks by the door to the garden.

'I wonder what that's doing in here?' he said.

Rebecca shrugged.

'It's funny . . . I saw him taking a load out to the common,' Will went on.

'When was that?' Rebecca asked, frowning thoughtfully.

'It was a couple of weeks ago . . . in the middle of the night. I suppose he could have brought this in for analysis or something.' He reached into the wheelbarrow, took some of the loose soil into his palm and examined it closely, rolling it around with his index finger. Then he held it up to his nose and breathed in deeply. 'High clay content,' he pronounced, and sunk both hands deep into the soil, lifting out two large fistfuls which he squeezed and then released, sprinkling them slowly back into the barrow. He turned to Rebecca with a quizzical expression.

'What?' she said impatiently.

'I was just wondering where this lot could have come from,' he said. 'It's . . .'

'What *are* you going on about? He's obviously not here, and none of this is going to help us find him,' Rebecca said with such unnecessary vehemence that Will was left speechless. 'Come on, let's go back upstairs,' she urged him. Not waiting for Will to respond, she stomped up the wooden steps, leaving him alone in the cellar.

'Women!' Will muttered, echoing a sentiment his father often imparted to him. 'Never know where you are with them!' Rebecca in particular had always been a total mystery to Will – he couldn't decide whether she said the things she did on a whim, or if there was really something much deeper and more complex going on in that well-groomed head of hers, something that he couldn't even begin to understand.

Whatever it was, it was no use worrying about that now, not when there were other, more important things to consider. He blew dismissively and rubbed his hands together to get the soil off, then stood motionless in the centre of the room until his inquisitiveness got the better of him. He went over to the bench, flicking casually through the papers on top of it. There were photocopied articles about Highfield, pictures of old houses in faded sepia tones and tatty sections of maps. One of these caught his eye – comments had been scribbled on it in pencil. He recognized his father's spidery handwriting.

Martineau Square – the key? Ventilation for what? Will read, frowning as he traced the network of lines drawn in pencil through the houses on each side of the square. 'What was he up to?' he asked himself out loud.

Peering under the bench, he found his father's briefcase and emptied out its contents, mostly magazines and newspapers, on to the floor. In a side pocket of the briefcase, he found some loose change in a small brown paper bag and a clutch of empty chocolate wrappers. Then, crouching down, he began to check through the archive boxes stored under the bench, sliding each one out and flicking through its contents.

His search was cut short by his sister's insistence that he should come and eat his supper before it got too cold. But before returning upstairs, he made a short detour over to the garden door to check the coats hanging there. His father's hard hat and overalls had gone.

Back up in the hallway, he passed a cacophony of applause and laughter from behind the closed sitting-room door as he went into the kitchen.

The two of them ate in silence until Will looked up at Rebecca. She had a fork in one hand and a pencil in the other as she did her maths homework.

'Rebecca, have you seen Dad's hard hat or his overalls?' he asked.

'No, he always keeps them in the cellar. Why?'

'Well, they're not there,' Will said.

'Maybe he left them at a dig somewhere.'

'Another dig? No – he would've told me about it. Besides, when would he have had the chance to go off and do that? He was always here or at the museum – he never went anywhere else, did he? Not without telling me . . .' Will tailed off as

Rebecca watched him intently.

'I know that look. You've thought of something, haven't you?' she said suspiciously.

'No, it's nothing,' he replied. 'Really.'

CHAPTER TWELVE

The next day, Will awoke early and, wanting to forget about his father's disappearance, donned his work clothes and ran energetically downstairs, thinking he would grab a quick breakfast and maybe hook up with Chester to excavate the blocked tunnel at the Forty Pits site. Rebecca was already in the kitchen; by the way she collared him the moment he turned the corner, it was obvious she had been waiting for him.

'It's up to us to do something about Dad, you know,' she said, as Will looked at her with a slightly startled expression. 'Mum's not going to do anything – she's lost it.'

Will just wanted to get out of the house; he was desperately trying to pretend to himself that everything was normal. Since the night of the argument between his parents, he and Rebecca had been getting themselves to school as usual. The only break from the norm was that they had been taking their meals in the kitchen without their mother. She had been stealing out to help herself to whatever was on offer in the fridge and had been eating it, predictably enough, in front of the television. It was clear what she'd been up to, because pies and chunks of cheese had gone missing, along with whole loaves of bread and tubs of margarine.

They had seen her on a couple of occasions in the hallway, as she shambled to the lavatory in her nightie and her slippers with the backs trodden down. But the only acknowledgement Will or Rebecca received on these chance encounters was a vague nod.

'I've decided something. I'm going to call the police,' Rebecca said, standing in front of the dishwasher.

'Do you really think we should? Maybe we ought to wait a bit?' he said. He knew the situation didn't look good, but surely this was going a bit far, and he wasn't quite ready to take that step yet. 'Anyway, where do you think he could have gone?' he asked.

'Your guess is as good as mine,' Rebecca answered sharply.

'I went by the museum yesterday and it was still all shut up.' It hadn't been open for days now – not that anyone had rung to complain.

'Maybe he just decided he'd had enough of . . . of everything,' Rebecca suggested.

'But why?'

'People go missing all the time. Who knows *why*?' Rebecca shrugged her slim shoulders. 'But we're going to have to take the matter in hand now,' she said resolutely. 'And we have to tell Mum what we're going to do.'

'All right,' Will agreed reluctantly. He glanced at his spade with longing as they entered the hallway. He just wanted to get away from the house and back to something he understood.

Rebecca knocked on the sitting room door and they both shuffled in. Mrs Burrows didn't seem to notice them; her gaze didn't waver from the television for an instant. They both stood there, unsure what to do next, until Rebecca went up to Mrs Burrows' chair, took the remote from where it rested on the arm and turned the television off.

Mrs Burrows' eyes remained exactly where they had been on the now blank screen. Will could see the three of them reflected in it, three small unmoving figures trapped within the bounds of the darkened rectangle. He drew in a deep breath, telling himself *he* was the one who should take charge of the situation, not his sister as she usually did.

'Mum,' Will said nervously. 'Mum, we can't find Dad anywhere and . . . it's been four days now.'

'We think we should call the police . . .' Rebecca said, quickly adding, '. . . unless you know where he is?'

Mrs Burrows' eyes dropped from the screen to the video recorders below it, but they could both see that she wasn't focusing on anything, and that her expression was terribly sad. She suddenly seemed so very helpless; Will just wanted to ask her what was wrong, what had happened, but couldn't bring himself to.

'Yes,' Mrs Burrows replied softly. 'If you want to.' And that was it. She fell silent, her eyes still downcast, and they both filed out of the room.

For the first time, the full implications of his father's disappearance came home to Will. What was going to happen to them without him around? They were in serious trouble. All of them. His mother most of all.

Rebecca rang the local police station and two officers arrived several hours later, a man and a woman, both in uniform. Will let them in.

'Rebecca Burrows?' the policeman asked, looking past Will

into the house as he removed his hat, then took out a small notebook from his breast pocket and flipped it open. Just then, the radio on his lapel issued a burp of unintelligible speech and he slid the switch on its side to silence it. 'Sorry 'bout that,' he said.

The female PC spoke to Rebecca. 'You made the call?'

Rebecca nodded in response, and the female PC gave her a comforting smile. 'You mentioned your mother was home. Can we talk to her, please?'

'She's in here,' Rebecca said, leading the way to the sitting room and knocking lightly on the door. 'Mum,' she called softly, opening the door for the two PCs and then standing to one side to let them through. Will started to follow them in, but the policeman turned to him.

'Tell you what, son, I could murder a cup of coffee.'

As the policeman shut the door behind him, Will turned to Rebecca with an expectant look.

'Oh, all right, I'll make it,' she said irritably and headed for the kettle.

Waiting in the kitchen, they could hear the low drone of adult conversation coming from behind the door, until – several cups of coffee and what felt like an eternity later – the policeman emerged alone. He walked in and placed his cup and saucer on the table next to them.

'I'm just going to have a quick dekko over the place,' he said. 'For clues,' he added with a wink, and had left the kitchen and gone upstairs before either of them could react. They sat there, peering up at the ceiling as they listened to his muffled footsteps moving from room to room on the floor above.

'What does he think he's going to find?' Will said. They

heard him come downstairs again and walk around the ground floor, and then he appeared back in the kitchen doorway. He fixed Will with an enquiring look.

'There's a basement, isn't there, son?'

Will took the policeman down into the cellar and stood at the bottom of the oak steps while the man cast his eye over the room. He seemed to be particularly interested in Dr Burrows' exhibits.

'Unusual things your dad has. I suppose you've got receipts for all these?' he said, picking up one of the dusty clay heads. Noticing Will's startled expression, he continued, 'Only joking. I understand he works in the local museum, doesn't he?'

Will nodded.

'I went there once . . . on a school trip, I think.' He spotted the earth in the wheelbarrow. 'So what's all that?'

'I don't know. Could be from a dig that Dad's been doing. We usually do them together.'

'Dig?' he asked, and Will nodded in reply.

'I think I'd like to take a look outside now,' the policeman announced, his eyes narrowing as he studied Will intently, and his demeanour taking on a sternness that Will hadn't seen before.

In the garden, Will watched as he systematically searched the borders. Then he turned his attention to the lawn, crouching down every so often to examine the bald patches where one of their neighbour's cats was accustomed to relieving itself, killing off the grass. He spent a little time peering at the common over the hedgerow at the end of the garden before coming back into the house. Will followed him in, and as soon as they entered he put his hand on his shoulder.

'Tell me, son, no one's been doing any digging out there

recently, have they?' he asked in a low voice, as if there was some dark secret that Will was dying to share with him.

Will merely shook his head, and they moved into the hall, where the policeman's eyes alighted on his gleaming spade in the umbrella stand. Noticing this, Will tried to manoeuvre himself in front of it and block his view.

'Are you *sure* you – or any members of your family – haven't been digging in the garden?' the policeman asked again, staring at Will suspiciously.

'No, not me, not for years,' Will replied. 'I dug a few pits on the common when I was younger, but Dad put a stop to that – said someone might fall in.'

'On the common, eh? Big holes, were they?'

'Quite big. Didn't find anything much there, though.'

The policeman looked at Will strangely and wrote something in his notebook. 'Like what?' he asked, frowning with incomprehension.

'Oh, just some bottles and old junk.'

At that point, the policewoman came out of the sitting room and joined her colleague by the front door.

'All right?' the policeman said to her, tucking his notebook back into his breast pocket. He gave a last penetrating look at Will.

'I got everything down,' the policewoman replied, and then turned to Will and his sister. 'Look, I'm sure there's nothing to worry about, but as a matter of course we'll make some enquiries about your father. If you hear anything or need to talk to us, about anything at all, you can contact us on this number.' She handed Rebecca a printed card. 'In many of these cases, the person just comes back – they just needed to get away, have some time to think things over.' She gave them a reassuring smile and then added, 'Or calm down.'

'Calm down about what?' Rebecca ventured. 'Why would our father need to calm down?'

The policeman and woman both looked a little surprised, glancing at each other and then back at Rebecca.

'Well, after the disagreement with your mother,' the police-woman said. Will was waiting for her to say more, to explain exactly what the argument had been about, but she turned to the other officer. 'Right, we'd better be off.'

'Ridiculous!' Rebecca said in an exasperated tone, after she had shut the door behind them. '*They* obviously haven't got the faintest idea where he's gone, or what to do about it. Idiots!'

CHAPTER THIRTEEN

'W ill? Is that you?' Chester said, shielding his eyes from the sun as his friend emerged from the kitchen door into the rather cramped back garden behind the Rawls' house. He had been whiling away the time that Sunday morning by swatting bluebottles and wasps with an old badminton racket, easy targets as they grew lazy in the noonday heat. He cut a comical figure in flip-flops and a beanie hat, his oversized frame accentuated by baggy shorts, and his shoulders reddened by the sun.

Will stood with his hands in the back pockets of his jeans, looking a little preoccupied. 'I need a hand with something,' he said, checking behind him that Chester's parents weren't in earshot.

'Sure, what with?' Chester replied, flicking the mutilated remains of a large fly off the frayed strings of his racket.

'I want to take a quick look around the museum tonight,' Will replied. 'At my dad's things.'

He had Chester's undivided attention now.

'To see if there are any clues . . . in his office,' Will went on.

'What, you mean break in?' Chester said quietly. 'I'm not—'

Will cut him short. 'I've got the keys.' Taking his hand from his pocket, he held them up for Chester to see. 'I just want to have a quick look, and I need somebody to watch my back.'

Will had been completely prepared to go it alone but, when he stopped to think about it, it seemed natural to enlist the help of his friend. He was the only person he could turn to now his father had gone. He and Chester had worked very effectively together in the Forty Pits tunnel, like a real team – and, besides that, Chester seemed genuinely concerned about his father's whereabouts.

Lowering his racket to his side, Chester thought for a moment as he gazed at the house and then back at Will again. 'All right,' he agreed, 'but we'd better not get caught.'

Will grinned. It felt good to have a real friend, someone he could trust, other than his father, for the first time in his life.

After it had grown dark the boys stole up the museum steps. Will unlocked the door and they slipped quickly in. The interior was just visible in the zigzag shadows thrown by inter-lacing bands of weak moonlight and the yellow neon from the street lamps outside.

'Follow me,' Will whispered to Chester and, crouching low, they crossed through the main hall towards the corridor, dodging between the glass cabinets and grimacing as their trainers squeaked on the parquet flooring.

'Watch the—'

'Ouch!' Chester cried, as he tripped over the marsh timber lying on the floor just inside the corridor, and went sprawling. 'What the hell's that doing there?' he said angrily as he rubbed his shin.

'Come on,' Will whispered urgently.

Near the end of the corridor, they found Dr Burrows' office.

'We can use the torches in here, but keep your beam down low.'

'What are we looking for?' Chester whispered.

'Don't know yet. Let's check his desk first,' Will said in a hushed voice.

As Chester held his torch for him Will sifted through the piles of papers and documents. It wasn't an easy task; Dr Burrows was clearly as disorganized at work as he was at home, and there was a mass of paperwork spread across the desk in arbitrary piles. The computer screen was all but obscured by a proliferation of curling yellow Post-it notes stuck around it. As they searched, Will focused his efforts on anything that was written on loose-leaf pages in his father's barely legible scrawl.

Finishing the last of the piles of papers, they found nothing of note, so they each took one side of the desk and set about searching the drawers.

'Wow, look at this.' Chester produced what appeared to be a stuffed dog's paw fixed to an ebony stick from amongst a load of empty tobacco tins. Will simply looked at him and frowned briefly before resuming his search.

'Here's something!' Chester said excitedly as he was investigating the middle drawer. Will didn't bother to look up from the papers in his hand, thinking it was another obscure object.

'No, look, it's got a label with writing on it.' He handed it to Will. It was a little book with covers of purple and brown marbling and a sticker on the front that read *Ex Libris* in ornate and swirling copperplate lettering, with a picture of an owl wearing massive round glasses.

'*Journal*,' Will read. 'That's definitely my dad's writing.' He opened the cover. 'Bingo! It looks like a diary of some sort.' He fanned through the pages. 'He's written something on quite a few of these.' Pushing it into his bag, he asked, 'Are there any others?'

They hurriedly searched the remainder of the drawers and, finding nothing else, decided it was time to leave. Will locked up and the boys made their way towards the Forty Pits, as it was close by and they knew they wouldn't be interrupted there. As they slunk through the streets, ducking behind cars when anyone appeared, they felt alive with the thrill of the forbidden mission at the museum and couldn't wait to look at the journal they'd unearthed. Reaching the Pits they descended into the main chamber, where they arranged the inspection lights and made themselves comfortable in the armchairs. Will began to pore over the pages.

'The first entry is not long after we discovered the lost train station,' he said, looking up at Chester.

'What train station?'

But Will was too engrossed in the journal to explain. He recited slowly in broken sentences as he struggled to decipher his father's writing. '*I have recently become aware of a small and . . . in . . . incongruous grouping of interlopers coming and going amongst the general populace of Highfield. A group of people who have a physical appearance that sets them apart. Where they come from or what their purpose is I have yet to ascertain but, from my limited observation of them, I believe that all is not what it seems. Given their apparent numbers (5+?) . . . remarkably similar features . . . I suspect they may cohabit or at the very least . . .*' He tailed off as he scanned the rest of the page. 'I can't quite make out the rest,' he said, looking up at Chester. 'Here's something,' he said, flicking the page over. 'This is clearer.'

'*Today a rather intriguing and baffling artefact came into my possession by way of a Mr Embers. It may well be linked to these people, although I have yet to . . . substantiate this. The object is a small globe held in a cage of some type of metal, which, as at the time of writing, I have not been able to identify. The globe emits light of varying intensity depending on the degree of background illumination. What confounds me is that the relationship is directly inverse – the darker the surroundings, the brighter the light it emits. It defies any laws of physics or chemistry with which I am familiar.*'

Will held up the page so that Chester could examine the rough sketch his father had made.

'Have you actually seen it?' Chester enquired. 'This light thing?'

'No, he's kept all this to himself,' Will replied thoughtfully. Turning the page, he began to read again. '*Today I had the opportunity to . . . scrutinize, albeit for a brief moment, one of the pallid men at close quarters.*'

'Pallid? As in pale?' Chester said.

'Suppose so,' Will answered, and then read out his father's description of the mysterious man. He went on to the episode with Pineapple Joe and the inexplicable duct in the house, and his father's thoughts and observations on Martineau Square. There followed a large number of pages debating the likely structure within the terraced houses that lined the square; Will leafed through these until he came to a photocopied extract from a book, stapled into the journal.

'It says *Highfield's History* at the top of the page and it seems to be about someone called Sir Gabriel Martineau,' Will said.

'Born in 1673 he was the son and heir of a successful cloth dyer in Highfield. In 1699, he inherited the business, Martineau, Long & Co., from his father and expanded it considerably, adding a further two factories to the original premises in Heath Street. He was known to be a keen inventor, and was widely recognized for his expertise in the fields of chemistry, physics and engineering. Indeed, although Hooke (1635–1703) is generally credited with being the architect behind what is essentially the modern air pump, there are a number of historians who believe that he built his first prototype using Martineau's drawings.

'In 1710, during a period of widespread unemployment, Martineau, a deeply religious man who was renowned for his philanthropic and paternal attitude towards his workforce, began to employ a substantial number of labourers to build dwellings for his factory workers, and personally designed and oversaw the construction of Martineau Square, which still stands today, and Grayston Villas, which was destroyed in the Blitz. Martineau soon became the largest employer in the Highfield district and it was rumoured that Martineau's Men (as they became known) were engaged in digging a substantial underground network of tunnels, although no evidence of these remains today.

'In 1718 Martineau's wife contracted tuberculosis and died, aged thirty-two. Thereafter Martineau sought solace by joining an obscure religious sect, and was rarely seen in public for the remaining years of his life. His home, Martineau House, which formerly stood on the edge of Highfield old town, was destroyed by a fire in 1733, in which Martineau and his two daughters are believed to have perished.'

Underneath, Dr Burrows had written:

'*Why is there no trace of these tunnels now? What were they for? I haven't been able to find any mention of them in the town hall records or the borough archives, or anywhere. Why, why, why?*'

Then, scrawled with such gusto the paper was rucked and even torn in places, were large, crude capitals in blue biro:

FACT OR FICTION?

Will frowned and turned to Chester. 'This is incredible. Have you ever heard of this Martineau?'

Chester shook his head.

'Very weird,' Will said, slowly rereading the photocopied extract. 'Dad never mentioned any of this, not once. Why would he have kept something like this from me?'

Will chewed his lip, his expression transforming from exasperation to one of deep preoccupation. Then he suddenly jerked his head up, as if he had been elbowed in the ribs.

'What is it?' Chester said.

'Dad was on to something that he didn't want anyone to nick from him. Not again. That's it!' Will cried, remembering the time when the professor from London University had pulled rank on his father and taken the Roman villa dig away from him.

Chester was about to ask what Will was talking about when, in a flurry, Will began flipping forward through the journal.

'More stuff about these *pallid* men,' Will said, continuing on until he came to a part of the notebook where there were only the ragged stubs of missing pages. 'These have been torn out!'

He thumbed through a few more pages to the final entry. Chester saw him hesitate.

'See the date,' Will said.

'Where?' Chester leaned in.

'It's from last Wednesday . . . the day he had the row with Mum,' Will said in a quiet voice, then took a deep breath and read aloud:

'*Tonight's the night. I have found a way in. If this is what I think it is, my hypothesis, wild as it may seem, will be proved correct. This could be it! My chance, my last chance to make my mark. My moment! I have to follow my instincts. I have to go down there. I have to go through.*'

'I don't understand—' Chester began.

Will held up his hand to silence his friend, and continued:

'*It could be dangerous, but it's something I have to do. I have to show them – if my theory is right, they'll see! They'll have to. I am not just a bloody curator.*'

And then Will read the final sentence, which was underscored several times.

'*I will be remembered!*'

'Wow!' Will exclaimed, sitting back in the damp armchair. 'This is incredible.'

'Yes,' Chester agreed rather half-heartedly. He was beginning to think that Will's father had perhaps not been completely sane. It sounded to him suspiciously like the ramblings of someone who was losing it, big time.

'So what was he on to? What was this *theory* he was talking about?' Will said, flipping back to the ripped-out pages. 'I'll bet this is where it was. He didn't want anyone to steal his ideas.' Will was buzzing now.

'Yes, but where do you think he's actually gone?' Chester asked. 'What does he mean by *go through*, Will?'

This took the wind out of Will's sails. He looked blankly at Chester.

'Well,' he began slowly, 'two things have been bugging me. First is, I saw him working on something at home very early one morning – 'bout a fortnight before he disappeared. I reckon he was digging on the common . . . but that doesn't stack up.'

'Why?'

'Well, when I saw him, I'm sure he was pushing a barrowload of spoil *to* the common, not *away* from it. Second thing is, I can't find his overalls or hard hat anywhere.'

CHAPTER FOURTEEN

'Oi, Snowflake, I hear your old man's done a runner,' a voice shouted at Will as soon as he entered the classroom. There was an immediate hush in the room as everyone turned to look at Will, who, gritting his teeth, sat down at his desk and started to take his books out of his bag.

Speed, a vicious, skinny kid with greasy black hair, was the self-appointed leader of a gang of similarly unpleasant characters called 'the Greys'. They were frequently to be found clumped together like a swarm of blackfly behind the bike sheds, where they would sneak off for cigarettes when the duty teacher's back was turned. Their name had come from the dirty clouds of smoke wafting around their heads as they huddled together, coughing and trying to finish their cigarettes before they were caught in the act.

They all dressed in uniforms in a similar state of disarray with unfeasibly large tie knots, threadbare sweaters, and crumpled shirts half tucked into baggy trousers. They had the appearance of a band of malnourished orphans that had been pulled out of the canal and then left to dry in the wind. And they were mouthy and obnoxious to anyone in the school unfortunate enough to cross their paths.

One of their more disagreeable turns was to surround an unsuspecting pupil and, like a pack of hyenas, frogmarch him to the centre of the playground, where they would taunt and tease him until he broke down. Will had had the misfortune to witness one of these events, a terrified Year Seven who, encircled by Speed and his gang, had been forced to sing 'Baa Baa Black Sheep' at the top of his voice, over and over again. As the petrified boy stumbled over the words until he was mouthing them soundlessly, Speed prodded him mercilessly in the ribs to make him sing up. A crowd of onlookers sniggered self-consciously and nudged each other with barely concealed relief that they'd been spared the same fate. Will had never forgotten the boy choking over the words as he sobbed with fear. Now it was Will who was the focus of Speed's unwanted attention.

'Can't blame him, can you? Probably got hacked off with you!' Speed sneered, his voice dripping with derision.

Hunched doggedly over his desk Will did his best to pretend he was searching for a page in his textbook.

'Hacked off with his *freak* of a son!' Speed shouted, in that horribly guttural yet slightly squeaky way that only someone whose voice is in the process of breaking can do.

The fury welled up inside Will. His pulse raced and his face felt hot; he hated that it would be betraying his anger. As he remained with his eyes fixed steadfastly on the absolutely meaningless page before him, he experienced, just for a fraction of a second, a moment of incredible self-doubt and guilt. Maybe Speed was right. Maybe it was his fault . . . maybe he was partly to blame for his father's departure.

He dismissed the thought almost immediately, telling

himself that it couldn't have been because of him. Whatever the reason was, his father wouldn't have just walked out. It must have been something serious . . . something deadly serious.

'And *bloody* pissed off with your *mental* mum!' Speed bawled on even more loudly. At this, Will heard gasps and the odd giggle around him in the otherwise completely silent classroom. So it was already general knowledge about his mother.

Will gripped his textbook with such force that the cover was beginning to buckle. He still didn't look up, but shook his head slowly. This was only going one way . . . he didn't want to fight, but the little creep was pushing it too far. It was a matter of pride now.

'Oi, Mr Whippy, I'm talking to you! Are you or are you not fatherless? Are you or are you not a b—'

That did it! Will suddenly stood up, sending his chair shooting back. It scraped across the wooden floor and then toppled over. He locked eyes with Speed, who also rose from his desk, his face contorted with spiteful relish as he realized he'd hit the bull's-eye with his jibes. Simultaneously, three of the Greys sitting behind Speed leaped excitedly out of their chairs with predatory glee.

'Has the Milky Bar Kid had enough?' Speed sneered, moving with a swagger between the desks towards Will, his sniggering entourage in tow.

Reaching Will, Speed stood close to him, his fists clenched by his sides. Although Will wanted to take a step back he knew he had to stand his ground.

Speed pushed his face even closer, so that it was inches away from Will's, then arched his back like a second-rate boxer. 'Well, . . . have . . . you?' he said, emphasizing each word with a finger jab at Will's chest.

'Leave him alone. We've all had enough of *you*.' Chester's imposing bulk suddenly moved into view as he positioned himself behind Will.

Speed glanced uneasily at him, then back at Will.

Aware the whole class was watching him, and that he was expected to make the next move, Speed could only think of hissing dismissively through his teeth. It was a lame attempt to save his pride, and everyone knew it. Two of Speed's entourage deserted him, slinking back to their desks and leaving only the smallest Grey in attendance. Although he was a small, wiry boy who looked as though he should still be in short trousers, he was jigging from one foot to the other, clearly up for a fight.

'Well, what are you going to do now with just a midget as backup?' Chester smiled coldly at Speed.

Fortunately, at that very moment, the teacher entered and, realizing what was afoot, cleared his throat loudly to let them know he was in the room. It did nothing to deflate the stand-off between Will, Chester and Speed, and he had to march over and order them in no uncertain terms to sit down.

Will and Chester took their places, leaving Speed still standing with his henchman lingering just behind him. The teacher glowered at them and, after a few seconds, they skulked back to their desks. Will leaned back in his chair and smiled at Chester. Chester was a true friend.

Returning from school later that day Will stole into the house, taking pains not to alert his sister that he was home. Before he opened the cellar door, he paused in the hallway to listen. He heard the strains of 'You Are My Sunshine'; Rebecca was singing to herself as she did the housework upstairs. He quickly descended into the cellar and unbolted the door to the garden where Chester was waiting.

'Are you sure it's all right for me to be here?' he asked. 'Feels sort of . . . well . . . wrong.'

'Don't be daft, course it is,' Will insisted. 'Now, let's see what we can find in here.'

They searched through everything stored on the shelves, and then the archive boxes that Will had made a start on the time before. Their efforts were fruitless.

'Well, that was a complete waste of time,' Will said despondently.

'So where d'you think the earth came from?' Chester asked, going over to the wheelbarrow to examine it more closely.

'Haven't figured that out yet. I suppose we could have a shufty around the common. See if he was up to something there.'

'Big area,' Chester said, unconvinced. 'Anyway, why would he bring it down here?'

'Don't know,' Will replied as he ran his eyes over the book-shelves for one last time. He frowned as he noticed something at the side of one of the units.

'Hang on a minute, that's odd,' he said as Chester ambled over.

'What is?'

'Well, there's a plug in a socket down here, but I can't see where the cable goes.' He switched the socket on and they both looked around; it didn't appear to have had any effect.

'What's it for, then?' Chester said.

'It's definitely not an outside light.'

'Why's that?' Chester asked.

'Because we haven't got any,' Will replied as he went to the other end of the shelves, peering into the dark corner between the two units, then stepping back and regarding the shelves thoughtfully. 'Funny. It doesn't seem to come out again on this side.'

Taking the stepladder from beside the garden door, he set it up in front of the bookshelves and climbed up to inspect the top of the unit.

'No sign of it here either,' he said. 'This just doesn't make sense.' He was about to climb down when he stopped and ran his hand over the top of the shelves.

'Anything?' Chester asked.

'Load of brick dust,' Will replied. He hopped down from the ladder and immediately tried to pull the end of the shelf unit away from the wall.

'There's definitely a bit of give. Come on, give me a hand,' he said.

'Maybe it's just badly fixed on,' Chester suggested.

'Badly fixed on?' Will said indignantly. '*I* helped put these up.'

They both pulled together with all their strength and, although a thin sliver opened up at the rear of the unit, the shelves appeared to be firmly secured at the top.

'Let me check something,' Will said as he mounted the stepladder again. 'There seems to be a loose nail lodged in this bracket.' He yanked it out and let it fall on to the concrete floor by Chester's feet. 'We used screws to fix this to the wall, not nails,' he said, looking down at Chester with a bewildered expression.

Will leaped down from the ladder and they both pulled on

the unit again. This time, shuddering and creaking, it swung out from the wall to reveal that it was hinged on one side.

'So that's what the cable's for!' Will exclaimed, as both of them stared at the rough-hewn opening in the bottom half of the wall. The bricks had been removed to form a hole approximately a metre square. Inside, a passage was visible, illuminated by a motley array of old neon strip lights burning along its length.

'Wow!' Chester gasped, his face a picture of surprise. 'A secret passage!'

Will smiled at Chester. 'Right, let's check this out.' Before Chester had time to say anything, Will ducked into the passage and was crawling along it at a fair lick. 'There's a bend here,' came his muffled voice.

As Chester watched, Will started to go around the corner and then, very slowly, came back into view again. He sat back and turned his head to Chester, his face disconsolate in the glow of the lights. 'What is it?' Chester asked.

'The tunnel's blocked. It's caved in,' Will said.

Will slowly crawled back out of the passage, then clambered through the hole in the wall and into the cellar again. He straightened up and sloughed off his school blazer, dropping it where he stood. It was only then that he noticed his friend's grim expression.

'What is it?'

'The cave-in . . . you don't think your dad's under it, do you?' Chester said almost in a whisper, barely able to contain a shudder as he pictured the horrific possibility. 'He might have been . . . crushed,' he added ominously.

Will looked worriedly away from his friend and thought for a moment. 'Well, there's only one way to find out.'

'Shouldn't we tell someone?' Chester stammered, taken aback by his friend's seeming detachment. But Will wasn't listening. His eyes had narrowed with the look of preoccupation that meant his mind was churning away, formulating a plan of action.

'You know, the infill is exactly the same as in the Pits tunnel – it's all wrong. There are chips of limestone again,' he said, loosening his tie and pulling it over his head before discarding it next to the crumpled blazer on the floor. 'This is too much of a coincidence.' He returned to the mouth of the passage and leaned in. 'And did you notice the props?' he said, running his hand over one that was just within reach. 'This was no accident. This lot has been hacked at and pulled in on purpose.'

Chester joined his friend at the opening and examined the props, which had deep notches sliced into them. They were cut almost right through in places, as if someone had been swinging an axe at them.

'God, you're right,' he said.

Will rolled his sleeves up. 'Better make a start then. No time like the present.' He ducked into the passage, dragging behind him a bucket that he'd found just inside the opening.

Chester looked down at his school uniform. He opened his mouth to say something, but then thought better of it, removed his blazer and hung it neatly on the back of a chair.

CHAPTER FIFTEEN

'Go!' said Will in an urgent whisper, as he crouched low within the shadows of the hedgerow bordering the common at the bottom of the garden.

Chester growled with the effort as he heaved the over-laden wheelbarrow into motion and then weaved precariously between the trees and shrubs. Reaching open ground, he veered off to the right towards the gullies they were using to dump the spoil. From the mounds of fresh earth and small cairns of rock already deposited there, it was evident to Will that his father had been using these gullies for the very same purpose.

Will kept a watchful eye open for any passers-by whilst Chester swiftly emptied the barrow at the top of the gully. He deftly spun it around for the return journey, while Will remained behind to push in any large pieces of rock or clumps of soil and clay.

Once that was done, Will caught up with Chester. As they were retracing the well-trodden route back to the garden the wheel on the old barrow began to squeal piercingly, as if protesting at the countless trips it had been forced to make.

The noise cut through the peaceful calm of the balmy summer evening.

Both boys froze abruptly in their tracks, looking around to check whether it had attracted any attention from the nearby houses.

Trying to catch his breath, Chester bent forward with his hands resting on his knees as Will stooped to examine the offending wheel.

'We'll have to oil that bloody thing again.'

'Duh, do you think so?' Chester puffed sarcastically.

'I think you'd better carry it back,' Will replied coldly as he straightened up.

'Do I have to?' Chester groaned.

'Come on, I'll give you a hand,' Will said as he grabbed hold of the front of the barrow.

They lugged it the remaining distance, grunting and cursing under their breath, but maintaining a strict silence as they crossed the back garden. They trod lightly as they negotiated the small ramp down to the rear entrance into the cellar.

'My turn at the face, I suppose,' Will groaned as they both flopped with exhaustion on to the concrete floor. Chester didn't answer.

'You all right?' Will asked him.

Chester nodded groggily, then squinted at his watch. 'I think I should be getting home.'

'S'pose so,' Will said, as Chester slowly pulled himself to his feet and began to gather his things. Will didn't say so, but he was very relieved that Chester had decided to call it a day. They were both dog-tired after the intensive digging and tipping, to the point that he could see Chester was a little unsteady on his feet from fatigue.

'Same time tomorrow, then,' Will said quietly, flexing his fingers and then stretching one shoulder in an effort to reduce the stiffness.

'Yeh,' Chester croaked in reply, without even looking at Will as he shuffled out of the cellar by the garden door.

They went through this same ritual every evening after school. Will would very carefully open the garden door, without making a sound, to let Chester in. They would get changed and immediately begin working for two or three hours at a stretch. The excavation was particularly slow and torturous, not only because of the limited space in the tunnel and the fact that they couldn't let anyone above hear them, but because they could tip the excavated material on to the common only under cover of nightfall. At the end of every evening after Chester had gone, Will made sure that the shelf unit was pushed back into place and secured, and the floor was swept.

This time he had an additional task; as he saturated the axle of the noisy wheel with oil, he wondered how much further it was to the end of the tunnel and, not for the first time, whether there would be anything there. He was concerned that they were running out of supplies; without his father's help with materials, he had been forced to salvage as much timber as he could from the Forty Pits, so that as the tunnel beneath the house progressed, the other one became more and more precarious.

Later, as he sat hunched over the kitchen table, eating yet another supper that had gone stone cold, Rebecca appeared in the doorway as if from nowhere. It made Will start, and he swallowed noisily.

'Just look at the state of you! Your uniform is filthy – do

you expect me to wash everything *again*?' she said, folding her arms aggressively.

'No, not really,' he replied, avoiding her eyes.

'Will, what exactly are you up to?' she demanded.

'I don't know what you mean,' he said, ramming in another mouthful.

'You've been sneaking off somewhere after school, haven't you?'

Will shrugged, pretending to examine a dry slice of curling beef on the tip of his fork.

'I know you're up to something, all right, because I've seen that big ox sneaking around in the garden.'

'Who?'

'Oh, come on, you and Chester have been tunnelling somewhere, haven't you?'

'You're right,' Will admitted. He finished his mouthful and, taking a breath, tried to lie as convincingly as he could. 'Over by the town dump,' he said.

'I knew it!' Rebecca announced triumphantly. 'How can you even *think* of digging another of your useless holes at a time like this?'

'I miss Dad too, you know,' he said as he took a bite out of a cold roast potato, 'but it's not going to help any of us if we just mope around the house, feeling sorry for ourselves . . . like Mum.'

Rebecca stared at him distrustfully, her eyes shining with anger, then turned on her heels and walked out of the room.

Will finished the congealed meal, staring into space as he slowly chewed each mouthful, and ruminating on the events of the past month.

Afterwards, up in his bedroom, he took out a geological

map of Highfield, marking the spots where he thought the house stood and the direction he calculated his father's tunnel in the cellar was taking, and, while he was at it, Martineau Square and Mrs Tantrumi's house. Will looked long and hard at the map, as if it was a puzzle he could solve, before he finally put it aside and climbed into bed. Within minutes he'd slipped into an uneasy and fitful slumber, in which he dreamed of the sinister people his father had described in his journal.

In the dream he was dressed in his school uniform, but it was covered in mud, and tattered and torn at the elbows and knees. He'd lost his socks and shoes, and was walking barefoot down a long, deserted terraced street, which felt familiar although he couldn't quite place where he knew it from. As he glanced up at the low sky, which was yellowy-grey and formless, he fidgeted anxiously with the ragged material of his sleeves. He didn't know if he was late for school or for supper, but he was certain he was meant to be somewhere, or doing something – something vitally important.

He kept to the centre of the street, wary of the houses on both sides. They stood ominous and dark; no light shone from behind their dusty windows, nor did any smoke rise from their precariously tall and twisted black chimney stacks.

He was feeling so very lost and alone when, far off in the distance, he spotted someone crossing the street. He knew instantly that it was his father and his heart leaped with joy. He began to wave, but then stopped as he sensed that the buildings were watching him. There was a brooding malevolence to them, as if they harboured an evil force, like a tightly coiled spring, holding its breath and lying in wait for him.

Will's fear grew to an unbearable pitch and he broke into a

trot towards his father. He tried to call to him, but his voice was thin and ineffectual, as though the air itself was swallowing his words the instant they left his lips.

He was running at full pelt now, and with every stride the street was becoming narrower so that the houses on either side were closing in on him. He could now clearly see that there were shadowy figures lurking threateningly in their dark doorways, and that they were beginning to spill out on to the street as he passed them.

Terrified out of his wits, he was tripping and sliding on the slick cobblestones as the figures amassed behind him in such numbers that they were indiscernible from each other, sweeping into a single blanket of darkness. Their fingers extended like wisps of animated black smoke, clutching at him as he desperately tried to elude them. But the shadowy figures had hold of him; they were tugging him back with their inky tendrils until he was forced to a complete standstill. Catching a last brief glimpse of his father in the distance, Will screamed a silent scream. The jet-black blanket folded over him; he was all at once weightless and falling into a pit. He hit the bottom with such an impact that it knocked the air from his lungs and, gasping for breath, he rolled on to his back and saw for the first time the stern and disapproving faces of his pursuers as they peered down at him.

He opened his mouth, but before he knew what was happening, it was filled with earth – he could taste it as it smothered his tongue, and stones dashed and scratched against his teeth. He was being buried alive – he couldn't breathe.

Gagging and retching, Will awoke, his mouth dry and his body dripping with cold sweat as he sat up. In a panic he fumbled for his bedside light. With a click, its comforting yellow glow bathed the room in reassuring normality as he glanced at his alarm clock. It was still the middle of the night. He fell back on to his pillow, staring at the ceiling and breathing heavily, his body still trembling. The memory of the soil clogging his throat was as fresh and vivid in his mind as if it had really happened. And as he lay there, catching his breath, he was plagued by a renewed and even more acute sense of loss for his father. However hard he tried, he just couldn't shake off the overwhelming hollowness, and in the end he gave up any pretence of sleep, watching as the cold light of dawn began to lick around the edges of the curtains, and finally stole into the room.

CHAPTER SIXTEEN

The weeks passed, until finally a police inspector called to speak to Mrs Burrows about her husband's disappearance. He wore a dark-blue raincoat over a light-grey suit and was well spoken, if a little brusque, as he introduced himself to Will and Rebecca and asked to see their mother. They showed him to the sitting room where she sat waiting.

As they followed the policeman they gasped, thinking that somehow they must have entered the wrong room. The television, that eternal flame that burned in the corner, was silent and dark and – just as remarkable – the room was incredibly neat and tidy. During the time when Mrs Burrows had led her hermit-like existence and neither Will nor Rebecca had set foot inside, both of them had assumed it had degenerated into an unholy mess, and pictured it littered with half-consumed food, empty packets, and dirty plates and cups. But they couldn't have been more wrong. It now looked spotless – but what was more astounding was their mother herself. Instead of her drab couch-potato garb of dressing gown and slippers she had changed into one of her best summer dresses, done her hair and even put on some make-up.

Will stared at her with sheer disbelief, wondering what on earth could have brought about this abrupt transformation. He could only think that she was imagining she was playing a part in one of the murder mystery series she so adored, but this didn't make the scene before him any more explicable.

'Mum, this is . . . this is . . .' he spluttered.

'Detective Chief Inspector Beatty,' his sister helped him out.

'Please do come in,' Mrs Burrows said, rising from her armchair and smiling pleasantly.

'Thank you, Mrs Burrows . . . I know this is a difficult time.'

'No, not at all,' Mrs Burrows beamed. 'Rebecca, would you please put the kettle on and make us all a nice cup of tea?'

'That's very kind, thank you, ma'am,' DCI Beatty said, hovering awkwardly in the centre of the room.

'Please,' Mrs Burrows motioned towards the sofa. 'Please, make yourself comfortable.'

'Will, you can give me a hand,' Rebecca said, grabbing her brother by the arm as she tried to shepherd him towards the door. He didn't move, still rooted to the spot by the sight of his mother who, it seemed, was once more the woman she hadn't been for years.

'Er . . . yeah . . . oh yes . . .' he managed.

'Do you take sugar?' Rebecca asked the DCI, still tugging at Will's arm.

'No, white and no sugar, thank you,' he replied.

'Right, milk, no sugar – and, Mum, just the two sweeteners?'

Her mother smiled and nodded at her, and then at Will, as if she was amused by his bewilderment. 'And maybe some custard creams, Will?'

Will snapped out of his trance, turned and accompanied Rebecca into the kitchen, where he stood in wide-mouthed disbelief, shaking his head.

While Will and Rebecca were out of the room, the DCI spoke to Mrs Burrows in a low, serious voice. He said that they had been doing everything they could to locate Dr Burrows, but since there was no news at all of his whereabouts they had decided to step up the investigation. This would entail circulating the photograph of Dr Burrows more widely and conducting a 'detailed interview', as the DCI put it, with her down at the station. They also wanted to speak to anyone else who had had contact with Dr Burrows just prior to his disappearance.

'I'd like to ask you a few questions now, if that's all right. Let's start with your husband's job,' the DCI said, looking at the door and wondering when his tea was going to arrive. 'Did he mention anyone in particular at the museum?'

'No,' Mrs Burrows replied.

'I mean, is there someone there he might have confided in?'

'About where he's gone?' Mrs Burrows completed the sentence for him, and then laughed coldly. 'You won't have any joy on that line of investigation, I'm afraid. That's a dead end.'

The DCI sat up in his chair, a little baffled by Mrs Burrows' response.

She continued, 'He runs the place single-handed; there aren't any other staff. You might consider interviewing the old codgers that hung out with him, but don't be surprised if their memories aren't what they used to be.'

'No?' the DCI said, a small smile showing at the edges of his mouth as he wrote in his notebook.

'No, most of them are in their eighties. And why, may I ask, do you want to interview me and my children? I have already told the uniformed police everything I know. Shouldn't you be putting out an APB?'

'An APB?' The DCI grinned broadly. 'We don't use that term over here. We put emergencies out on the radio—'

'And my husband isn't an emergency, I suppose?'

At that moment, Will and Rebecca appeared with the tea, and the room went quiet as Rebecca put the tray on the coffee table and handed the mugs around. Will, clutching a plate of biscuits, had also entered the room and, as the DCI didn't seem to object to either him or Rebecca remaining there, they both sat down. The silence grew uneasily. Mrs Burrows was glaring at the policeman, who was looking into his tea.

'I think we may be getting ahead of ourselves here, Mrs Burrows. Can we just focus on your husband again?' he said.

'I think you will find that we are all *very* focused on him. It's you I'm worried about,' Mrs Burrows said tersely.

'Mrs Burrows, you have to realize that some people don't . . .' the DCI began, 'don't *want* to be found. They want to slip off because, maybe, life and its pressures have become too much for them to handle.'

'Too much to handle?' Mrs Burrows echoed furiously.

'Yes, we have to take that possibility into consideration.'

'My husband couldn't take pressure? What pressure, exactly? The problem was that he never *had* any bloody pressure at all, or drive, for that matter.'

'Mrs B—' The DCI tried to get a word in, glancing helplessly at Will and Rebecca, who were both looking back and forth from him to their mother, as if they were spectators watching a rally in a particularly savage tennis match.

'Don't think I don't know that most murders are committed by family members,' their mother proclaimed.

'Mrs Burr—'

'That's why you want to question us at the station, isn't it? To find out whether we *dunnit.*'

'Mrs Burrows,' the DCI began again quietly, 'nobody's suggesting that a murder has been committed here. Do you think we might start again, and see if we can get off on the right foot this time?' he proposed, valiantly trying to regain control of the situation.

'Sorry. I know you're only doing your job,' Mrs Burrows said in a calmer voice, and then sipped her tea.

The DCI nodded, grateful that she had stopped her tirade, and took a deep breath as he glanced down at his notebook. 'I know it's a difficult thing to think about,' he said, 'but did your husband have any enemies? Maybe from business dealings?'

At this, much to Will's surprise, Mrs Burrows put her head back and laughed out loud. The DCI muttered something about taking that as a 'no' as he scribbled in his little black notebook. He seemed to have recovered some of his composure.

'I have to ask these questions,' the DCI said, looking straight at Mrs Burrows. 'Did you ever know him to drink excessively or take drugs?'

Again Mrs Burrows unleashed a loud hoot of laughter. 'Him?' she said. 'You've got to be joking!'

'Righto. So what did he get up to in his spare time?' the DCI asked in a flat voice, trying his very best to get the questions over and done with as quickly as he could. 'Did he have any hobbies?'

Rebecca immediately shot a glance at Will.

'He used to do excavations . . . archaeological digs,' Mrs Burrows answered.

'Oh, yes.' The DCI turned to Will. 'I understand you helped him out, didn't you, son?' Will nodded. 'And where did you do all this digging?'

Will cleared his throat and looked at his mother, and then at the DCI who was waiting, pen held expectantly in hand, for an answer.

'Well, all over, really,' Will said. 'Round the edge of town, on rubbish tips and places like that.'

'Oh, I thought they were proper affairs,' the DCI said.

'They *were* proper digs,' Will said firmly. 'We found the site of a Roman villa once, but mostly it was eighteenth- and nineteenth-century stuff we were after.'

'Just how extensive . . . I mean, how *deep* were the holes you dug?'

'Oh, just pits, really,' Will said evasively, willing him not to pursue this line of questioning.

'And were you engaged in any such activities around the time of his disappearance?'

'No, we weren't,' Will said, very aware of Rebecca's eyes burning into him.

'You're sure he wasn't working on anything, maybe without your knowledge?'

'No, I don't think so.'

'Right,' the DCI said, putting away his notebook. 'That's enough for now.'

*

The next day Chester and Will didn't hang around for long outside school. They spotted Speed and one of his faithful followers, Bloggsy, loitering a little distance beyond the gates. Speed was eyeing them as he lounged against the railings with his hands in his pockets, whilst Bloggsy, a nasty little specimen with frizzy ginger hair that gave his head the appearance of a burst cushion, was taking great delight in throwing small stones, which he fished out of the pockets of his parka, at any girls who happened to pass within range. This would elicit squeals and indignant curses which made Bloggsy cackle with a demonic relish.

'I think he's looking for a return match,' Will said, glancing over at Speed, who glared straight back at him until Chester caught his eye. At this point, Speed contemptuously turned his back on them, muttering something under his breath to Bloggsy, who simply sneered in their direction and gave a harsh, derisive laugh.

'Couple of jerks,' Chester growled, as he and Will set off, deciding to take the short cut home.

Leaving their school behind them, a sprawling modern yellow-brick and glass job, they sauntered across the road and entered the adjoining housing estate. Built in the 1970s, the estate was known locally as Roach City, for obvious reasons, and the infested blocks that made up the estate were in a constant state of disrepair, with many of the flats empty or burned out. This in itself didn't cause the boys any hesitation, but the trouble with the route was it took them right through the home turf of the Click, who made Speed and his gang look like Girl Guides.

As they walked side by side through the estate, the weak rays of the sun glinting off broken glass on the tarmac and in the gutters, Will slackened his pace almost imperceptibly, but enough that Chester noticed.

'What's up?'

'I don't know,' said Will said, glancing up and down the road and peering apprehensively into a side street as they passed by.

'Come on, tell me,' Chester asked, looking quickly around. 'I really don't fancy getting jumped in here.'

'It's just a feeling, it's nothing,' Will insisted.

'Speed's got you all paranoid, hasn't he?' Chester replied with a smile, but nevertheless he sped up, forcing Will to do likewise.

As they left the estate behind them, they resumed a more casual pace. Very soon they reached the start of the High Street, which was marked by the museum. As Will did every evening, he glanced at it in the vain hope that the lights would be burning, the doors open and his father back in attendance. Will just wanted everything to be normal again – whatever that was – but once again the museum was closed, its windows dark and unfriendly. The council had evidently taken the decision that for now it was cheaper to simply shut it rather than look for a temporary stand-in for Dr Burrows.

Will looked up at the sky; heavy clouds were beginning to pull across and blank out the sun.

'Should go well tonight,' he said, his mood lifting. 'It's getting dark earlier, so we won't have to wait to start tipping.'

Chester had begun to talk about how much faster the proceedings would be if they could do away with the need for all this cloak-and-dagger subterfuge, when Will mumbled something under his breath.

'Didn't catch that, Will.'

'I said: don't look now, but I think there's somebody following us.'

'You what?' Chester replied and, not being able to stop himself, immediately turned to look behind.

'Chester, you prat!' Will snapped.

Sure enough, twenty metres or so behind them was a short, stocky man in a trilby, black glasses and a dark, tent-like overcoat that reached almost to his ankles. His head was facing in their direction, although it was difficult to tell if he was actually looking at them.

'Shit!' Chester whispered. 'I think you're right. He's just like the ones your dad wrote about in his journal.'

Despite Will's previous instruction to Chester not to look at the man, he now couldn't stop himself from peering back for another glimpse.

'A "man-in-a-hat"?' Will said with a mixture of wonder and apprehension.

'But he's not after *us*, is he?' Chester asked. 'Why should he be?'

'Let's slow down a bit and see what he does,' Will suggested.

As they reduced their speed, the mysterious man did likewise. 'Right,' Will said, 'how about if we cross the road?'

Again the man mirrored their actions, and when they increased their pace again, he quickened his, to maintain the distance between them.

'He's definitely following us,' Chester said, the panic audible in his voice for the first time. 'Why, though? What does he want? I don't like this – I think we should take the next right and leg it.'

'I don't know,' Will said, deep in thought. 'I reckon we should confront him.'

'You've got to be *joking*! Your dad has disappeared off the face of the Earth not long after seeing these people and, for all we know, this man could've been responsible. He might be part of the gang or something. I say we get out of here and call the police. Or get help from someone.'

They were silent for a moment as they looked around.

'No, I've got a better idea. What if we turn the tables on him? Trap him,' Will said. 'If we split up, he can only follow one of us, and when he does the other can come up behind him and . . .'

'And what?'

'Like a pincer movement – sneak up from behind and nobble him.' Will was getting well into his stride now as the plan of action firmed up in his mind.

'He could be dangerous, totally *hat stand* for all we know. And what are we going to nobble him *with*? Our school bags?'

'Come on, there's two of us and only one of him,' Will said as the shops in the High Street came into view ahead. 'I'll distract him while you rugby-tackle him – you can do that, can't you?'

'Oh, great, thanks,' Chester said, shaking his head. 'He's bloody huge – he'll make mincemeat of me!'

Will looked into Chester's eyes and smiled mischievously.

'All right, all right.' Chester sighed. 'The things I do,' he said as he looked quickly back and then made to cross the road.

'Whoa! Scrub that,' Will said. 'I think they've got the jump on us!'

'They?' Chester gasped as he rejoined his friend. 'What do you mean, *they*?' he asked, following Will's gaze to a point further up the street.

There in front of them, some twenty paces ahead, was another of the men. He was almost identical to the first one, except that he sported a flat cap pulled down low over his forehead so that his dark glasses were only just visible under its peak. He also wore a long voluminous coat, which was flapping gently in the wind as he stood in the middle of the pavement.

There was now no question in Will's mind that these two men were after them.

As he and Chester drew level with the first of the shops in the High Street, they both stopped and peered around. On the opposite pavement two old ladies were chatting to each other as they bundled along with their wicker trolleys creaking on their wheels. One was dragging behind her a recalcitrant Scottish terrier decked out in a tartan dog coat. Apart from that, there were only a few people, in the distance.

Their minds were racing with thoughts of shouting for help, or flagging down a car if one happened to pass by, when the man in front started towards them. As the two men closed in, they both realized they were rapidly running out of options.

'This is too weird, we're well and truly snookered . . . who the hell *are* these guys?' Chester said, his words running into one another as he stared back over his shoulder at the man in the trilby. As the man advanced towards them, the heavy thud of his boots on the pavement sounded like a pile-driver. 'Any bright ideas?' Chester asked desperately.

'Right, listen, we hoof it across the road straight towards the one in the flat cap, feint right, then cut left and duck into Clarke's. Got that?' Will said breathlessly as the flat-capped man in front of them loomed closer and closer. Chester hadn't got the remotest idea what he was proposing, but in the circumstances he was ready to agree to anything.

Clarke Bros. was the main grocery shop in the High Street. Run by two brothers known locally as 'Junior' and 'Middling', the shop had a brightly striped awning and immaculately arranged stalls of fruit and vegetables either side of its entrance. Now that the light was beginning to dwindle, the glare spilling out from the shop windows beckoned to them invitingly, like a beacon. The man in the flat cap was caught in its glow, his wide muscular form almost blocking the entire width of the pavement.

'Now!' Will shouted, and they charged into the road. The two men swept in to intercept the boys, who were haring down the tarmac at full tilt, their school bags bouncing wildly on their backs. The men were moving much faster than either Will or Chester had anticipated, and the plan quickly went to hell, turning into a chaotic game of tag as the two boys dodged and weaved between the lumbering men, who tried to snatch at them with huge outstretched hands.

Will squawked as one of the men caught hold of him by the scruff of his neck. Then, more by accident than by design, Chester hurtled straight into the man. The impact knocked off the man's dark glasses to reveal bright pupils, shining devilishly like two black pearls under the brim of his hat. As he turned in surprise, Will took the opportunity to push away from him, with both hands against the man's chest. The collar of Will's blazer ripped off with a rending tear as he did so.

The man, momentarily distracted by the impact with Chester, growled and whipped around to Will again. Slinging the detached collar away, he lunged in a renewed effort to grab him.

In a blind panic, Chester, his head down and his shoulders bunched up, and Will, half falling and half whirling like an uncoordinated dervish, somehow made it to the door of Clarke's as the man wearing the trilby lurched forward, took a last swipe at them and missed.

Will and Chester's momentum carried them straight through the door, squashed together between the jambs, as the bell above the door rang like a demented morris dancer. They ended up in an unruly heap on the floor of the shop, and Chester, coming to his senses, immediately twisted around and slammed the door shut, holding it closed with both feet.

'Boys, boys, boys!' said Mr Clarke Junior, teetering perilously on a stepladder as he arranged a display of corn dollies on a shelf. 'What's all the pandemonium? A sudden desperate yearning for my exotic fruits?'

'Er, not exactly,' Will said, trying to catch his breath as he picked himself up from the floor and made an attempt to act naturally, despite the fact that Chester was now standing somewhat awkwardly with his shoulder braced against the door behind him.

At this point, Mr Clarke Middling rose from behind the counter like a human periscope.

'What was that terrible racket?' he asked, clutching papers and receipts in both hands.

'Nothing for you to worry about, dear,' Mr Clarke Junior smiled at him. 'Don't let us distract you from your paperwork. It's just a couple of tearaways in search of some rather special fruit, I'll wager.'

'Well, I hope they don't want kumquats, we are all out of kumquats at the moment,' Mr Clarke Middling said in a dour voice, as he slowly retracted below the counter again.

'Then kumquat may,' laughed Mr Clarke Junior in a singsong voice, at which Mr Clarke Middling groaned from behind the counter.

'Don't you mind Middling; he always gets in such a tizzy when he's doing the books. Paper, paper everywhere, and not a drop to ink,' Mr Clarke Junior declaimed, adopting a theatrical pose in front of an imagined audience.

The Clarke brothers were a local institution. They had inherited the business from their father, as he had from his father before him. For all anybody knew, there had probably been a Clarke in business when the Romans invaded, selling turnips or whatever vegetables were in vogue at the time. Mr Clarke Junior was in his forties, a flamboyant character with a penchant for hideously garish blazers, which he had made by a local tailor. Dazzling lemon-yellow, puce-pink and powder-blue stripes danced between the tables of sensibly red tomatoes and the downright sober greens of the cabbages. With his infectious high spirits and seemingly endless repertoire of quips and puns he was a great favourite amongst the ladies of the borough, both young and old, yet oddly enough he had remained a confirmed bachelor.

On the other hand, Mr Clarke Middling, the elder brother, couldn't have been more different. A staunch traditionalist, he frowned upon his brother's exuberance, both in appearance and in manner, insisting on the time-honoured dress code: the old shop coat his forefathers had sported. He was painfully clean and neat; his clothes could have been ironed whilst he was wearing them, such was the crispness of his mushroom-brown shop coat, white shirt and black tie. His shoes were so beautifully polished, and his hair, cut in the short back and sides of a new conscript, was oiled flat with such a glistening sheen that from behind one would have had a hard time telling which way up he was.

The two brothers, within the shady green interior of the shop, were not unlike a caterpillar and a butterfly trapped in a pod. And with their constant bickering, the flippant joker and his straight-laced brother resembled a variety act in constant rehearsal for a performance that would never take place.

'Expecting a rush on my lovely gooseberries, is it?' Mr Clarke Junior said in a mock Welsh accent and smiled cheekily at Chester who, still propped against the door, made no effort at a response, as if struck dumb by the whole situation. 'Ah, the strong, silent type,' Mr Clarke Junior lisped as he danced down the stepladder and whirled in a flourish to come face to face with Will.

'It's young Master Burrows, is it not?' he said, his expression suddenly becoming serious. 'I am so sorry to hear about your dear father. You've been in our thoughts and in our prayers,' he said, placing his right hand softly on his heart. 'How is your mother bearing up? And that delightful sister of yours . . .'

'Fine, fine, both fine,' Will said distractedly.

'She's a regular here, you know, a valued customer.'

'Yes,' Will blurted, a little too quickly, as he tried to pay attention to Mr Clark Junior at the same time as keeping an eye on the door against which Chester remained buttressed, as if his life depended on it.

'A highly valued customer,' the invisible Mr Clarke Middling echoed from behind his counter, accompanied by the rustle of papers.

Mr Clarke Junior nodded and smiled. 'Indeedy, indeedy. Now you just park your lovely selves there while I get a little something for you to take home to your mother and sister.' Before Will could utter a word, he had spun gracefully on his heels and practically tap-danced into the stockroom at the rear of the shop. Will took the opportunity to go over to the window to check the whereabouts of their two pursuers, and recoiled with surprise.

'They're still there!' he said.

The two men were standing on the pavement, one directly in front of each window, staring in over the display tables of fruit and vegetables. It had now turned quite dark outside, and their faces glowed like ghostly white balloons under the illumination from the shop's interior. They were both still wearing their impenetrable glasses, and Will could make out their bizarre hats and the waxy shine of their angular coats with the unusual shoulder mantles. Their craggy, slanting faces and their clenched mouths looked uncompromising and brutal.

Chester spoke in a strained, low voice. 'Get them to call the police.' He gestured with his head at the counter, where they could hear Mr Clarke Middling grumbling as he thumped so forcefully on a stapler that it sounded like he was using a jackhammer.

Just then, Mr Clarke Junior fluttered back into the shop carrying a basket piled high with an impressive array of fruits, a large pink bow tied to the handle. He offered it to Will with both hands outstretched as if he was about to break into an aria.

'For your mother and sister and, of course, you, old chap. A little something from me and the old codger over there, as a token of our sympathy for your predicament.'

'Better a codger than an upstart,' came the muffled voice of

Mr Clark Middling.

Pointing at the windows, Will opened his mouth to explain about the mysterious men.

'All clear,' Chester said loudly.

'What's that, dear boy?' Mr Clarke Junior asked, looking past Will at Chester, who was now standing in front of one of the windows and peering up and down the street.

'What's all clear?' Mr Clarke Middling sprang up like a deranged jack-in-the-box.

'Papers!' Mr Clarke Junior ordered in the voice of an angry schoolmistress, but his brother remained above the counter.

'Er . . . just some kids,' Will lied. 'We were being chased.'

'Boys will be boys,' Mr Clarke Junior giggled. 'Now please do remember me to your dear sister, Miss Rebecca. You know, she really has such a good eye for quality produce. A gifted young lady.'

'I will.' Will nodded and forced a smile. 'And thanks for this, Mr Clarke.'

'Oh, think nothing of it,' he said.

'We do hope that your father returns home soon,' Mr Clarke Middling said dolefully. 'You shouldn't worry; these things happen from time to time.'

'Well . . . it's like that Gregson boy . . . terrible thing, that,' Mr Clarke Junior said with a knowing look and a sigh. 'And then there was the Watkins family last year.' Will and Chester watched him as he seemed to focus on a point somewhere between the ranks of the courgettes and the cucumbers. 'Such nice people, too. No one's seen hide nor hair of them since they—'

'It's not the same thing, not the same at all,' Mr Clarke Middling interrupted his brother sharply, then coughed

145

uneasily. 'I don't think this is the time or place to bring that up, Junior. A little unsympathetic, do you not think, given the situation?'

But 'Junior' wasn't listening; he was in full flow now and not to be stopped. Crossing his arms and with his head tilted to one side, he took on the aura of one of the old dears he habitually gossiped with. 'Like the flippin' *Marie Celeste* it was, when the police got there. Empty beds, the boys' uniforms all laid out for school the next day, but they were nowhere to be found, none of them. Mrs W had half a kilo of our green beans that day, if I recall, and a couple of watermelons. Anyway, no sign of any of them anywhere.'

'What . . . the watermelons?' Mr Clarke Middling asked in a deadpan voice.

'No, the *family*, you silly sausage,' Mr Clarke Junior said, rolling his eyes.

In the silence that ensued, Will looked from Mr Clarke Junior to Mr Clarke Middling, who was staring daggers at his wistful sibling. He was beginning to feel as Alice must have done when she'd stepped through the looking glass.

'Ho hum, better get on,' proclaimed Mr Clarke Junior, with a last lingering look of sympathy at Will, and he pranced delicately back up his stepladder, singing: 'Beetroot to me, *mon petit chou . . .*'

Mr Clarke Middling had sunk out of sight once again and the sound of rattling papers resumed, accompanied by the whirr of an old-fashioned adding machine. Will and Chester cautiously opened the shop door halfway and peeked nervously into the street.

'Anything?' Chester asked.

Will moved out on to the pavement in front of the shop.

'Nothing,' he replied. 'No sign of them.'

'We should've got the police, you know.'

'And told them what?' Will said. 'That we were chased by two weirdos in sunglasses and silly hats, and then they just disappeared?'

'Yes, exactly that,' Chester said, irritated. 'Who knows what they were after?' He suddenly looked up as a thought reoccurred to him. 'What if they *were* the gang that took your dad?'

'Forget it – we don't know that.'

'But the police . . .' Chester said.

'Do you really want to go through all that rubbish when we've got work to do?' Will interrupted him sharply, scanning the High Street up and down and feeling more at ease now that more people were about. At least they would be able to call for help if the two men turned up again. 'The police would probably think we're just a couple of kids horsing around. It's not as if we've got any witnesses.'

'Maybe,' Chester agreed grudgingly, as they started towards the Burrows' house. 'There's no shortage of fruitcakes around here,' he said, looking back at the Clarkes' shop, 'that's for sure.'

'It's safe now, anyway. They've gone, and if they do come back, we'll be ready,' Will said confidently.

Strangely enough, the incident had not deterred him in the slightest. As he thought about it, quite the opposite was true; it confirmed to him that his father *had* been on to something, and now he was on the right track. Although he didn't mention any of this to Chester, his resolve to continue with the tunnel and his investigations hardened even further.

Will had begun to pick at the grapes in the garish basket,

and the pink ribbon, now undone, flapped in the breeze behind him. Chester appeared to have got over his misgivings and was looking expectantly at the basket, his hand poised to help himself.

'So do you want to bottle out? Or are you still going to help me?' Will quizzed him in a teasing voice, moving the basket tantalizingly out of his reach.

'Oh, all right then, hand me a 'nana,' his friend replied with a smile.

CHAPTER SEVENTEEN

'All this evidence points to a deliberate dismantling,' Will said, squatting next to Chester on a pile of rubble in the cramped confines of the workface.

They had now reclaimed about ten metres of the tunnel, which had begun to dip down in a sharp incline, and found they were running critically short of timber. Will had hoped they would be able to salvage some of the original props and planking from the tunnel itself. What confounded them both was that very little of it was still there, and that much of the timber they did find was damaged beyond use. They had already stripped out every last piece they could from the other tunnel over at the Forty Pits, as well as removing the Stillson props, without bringing the whole excavation crashing down.

Will patted the workface, looking at it with a frown. 'I just don't get it,' he said.

'So what do you really think happened? That your dad pulled it in behind him?' Chester asked, as he too looked at the plug of earth and solidly compacted rock that they had yet to remove.

'Backfilled it? No, that's impossible. And even if somehow

he had, where are the struts? We'd have found more of them. No, none of this makes any sense,' Will said. Leaning forward, he picked up a handful of gravel. 'Most of this is virgin infill. It's all been lugged here from somewhere else – precisely the same thing that happened at the Pits.'

'But why go to all the trouble of filling it in when you could simply collapse the whole thing?' Chester asked, still mystified.

'Because then you'd have trenches opening up under people's houses or across their gardens,' Will replied despairingly.

'Oh, yes,' Chester agreed.

They were both exhausted. The last section had been particularly hard going, made up mostly of sizeable chunks of rock, some of which even Chester found it difficult to manhandle into the wheelbarrow by himself.

'I just hope we haven't got far to go,' Chester sighed. 'It's really beginning to get to me.'

'Tell me about it.' Will rested his head in his hands, staring vacantly at the tunnel wall opposite. 'You do realize, don't you, there might be nothing at all at the end of this? *A dead end?*'

Chester looked at him, but was too tired to say anything. So they sat there in silence, deep in their own thoughts, and after a while Will spoke. 'What was Dad thinking of, doing all this and not telling us what he was up to? *Me*, especially,' he said, with a look of sheer exasperation. 'Why would he do that?'

'He must have had a good reason,' Chester offered.

'But all the secrecy; keeping a secret journal. I don't understand it. We were never a family that kept things . . . *important* things . . . from each other like that. So why wouldn't he have told me what he was up to?'

'Well, you had the Pits tunnel,' Chester interjected.

'Dad knew about that. But you're right. I never bothered to tell Mum, because she's just not interested. I mean, we weren't exactly a . . .' Will hesitated, searching for the right word, '. . . *perfect* family, but we all got on and everyone sort of knew what everyone else was up to. Now everything's so messed up.'

Chester rubbed some soil out of his ear. He looked at Will thoughtfully. 'My mum thinks people shouldn't keep secrets from each other. She says they always have a knack of coming out and causing nothing but trouble. She says a secret's just the same as a lie. That's what she tells my dad anyway.'

'And now I'm doing exactly that to Mum and Rebecca,' Will said, bowing his head.

After Chester had gone and Will finally emerged from the cellar, he made straight for the kitchen, as he always did. Rebecca was sitting at the kitchen table opening the post. Will noticed straight away that his father's hoard of empty coffee jars that had cluttered up the table for months had vanished.

'What've you done with them?' he demanded, looking around the room. 'With Dad's jars?'

Rebecca studiously ignored him as she scrutinized the post-mark on an envelope.

'You threw them out, didn't you?' he said. 'How *could* you do that?'

She glanced up at him briefly, as if he was a rather tiresome gnat that she couldn't quite be bothered to swat, and then continued with the post.

'I'm starving. Anything to eat?' he said, deciding it wasn't wise to ruffle her feathers by pursuing the matter, not so close to a mealtime. As he passed her on the way to the fridge, he stopped to examine something lying on the side. 'What's this?'

It was a package neatly wrapped in brown paper.

'It's addressed to Dad. I think we should open it,' he said without a moment's hesitation, snatching up a dirty butter knife left on a plate by the sink. Cutting into the brown paper, he excitedly tore open the cardboard box inside, then ripped away a cocoon of bubble wrap to reveal the luminous sphere, glowing from its time in the darkness.

He held it up before him, his eyes sparkling both with excitement and the waning light emanating from the sphere. It was the object he'd read about in his father's journal.

Rebecca had stopped reading the telephone bill and had risen to her feet. She was looking at the sphere intently.

'There's a letter in here as well,' Will said, reaching into the cardboard box.

'Here, let me see it,' Rebecca said, her hand snaking towards the box. Will took a step back, holding the sphere in one hand while he shook open the letter with the other. Rebecca withdrew her hand and sat back down, watching her brother's face carefully as he leaned on the counter by the sink and began to read the letter aloud. It was from University College's Physics Department.

'Dear Roger,

It was wonderful to hear from you again after all these years – it brought back warm memories of our time together at university. It was also good to catch up on your news – Steph and I would love to visit when convenient.

As regards the item, I apologize for taking so long to respond, but I wanted to be sure I had collated the results from all concerned. The upshot is that we are well and truly stumped.

As you specified, we did not breach or penetrate the glass casing of the sphere, so all our tests were non-invasive in nature.

On the matter of the radioactivity, no harmful emissions registered when it was tested – so at least I can put your mind at rest on that one.

A metallurgist carried out an MS on a microscopic shaving from the base of the metal cage, and he agreed with your view that it's Georgian. He thinks the cage is made out of pinchbeck, which is an alloy of copper and zinc invented by Christopher Pinchbeck (1670–1732). It was used as a substitute for gold and only produced for a short while. Apparently, the formula for this alloy was lost when the inventor's son, Edward, died. He also told me that genuine examples of this material are scarce and it's hard to find anyone who can give an unequivocal identification. Unfortunately I haven't yet been able to get the cage assessed by a historical expert to confirm its likely age – maybe next time?

What is particularly interesting is that an X-ray revealed a small, free-floating particle in the centre of the sphere itself that does not alter its position even after rigorous agitation – this is puzzling, to say the least. Moreover, from a physical inspection, we agree with you that the sphere appears to be filled with two distinct liquid factions of differing densities. The turbulence you noted in these factions does not correspond to temperature variations, internal or external, but is unquestionably photoreactive – it only seems to be affected by a lack of light!

Here's the rub: the boys over in the Chemistry Department have never seen anything like it before. I had a fight on my hands to get it back from them – they were dying to crack the thing open in controlled conditions and run a full analysis. They tried spectroscopy when the sphere was at its brightest (at maximum excitation its emissions are in the visible spectrum – in layman's terms, not far off daylight, with a level of UV within acceptable safety levels), and the 'liquids' appeared to be predominantly helium- and silver-based. We can't make any more progress on this until you allow us to open it.

One hypothesis is that the solid particle at the centre may be acting as a catalyst for a reaction that is triggered by the absence of light. We can't think how, at this juncture, or come up with any comparable reactions that would occur over such a long period of time, assuming the sphere really does date from the Georgian era. Remember, helium was not discovered until 1895 – this is at odds with our estimate for the date of the metal casing.

In short, what we have here is a real conundrum. We would all very much welcome a visit from you for a multi-faculty meeting so we can schedule a programme for further analysis of the item. It may even be useful for some of our team to drop into Highfield for a quick investigation into the background.

I look forward to hearing from you.

With kindest regards,

Tom
Professor Thomas Dee'

Will put the letter on the table and met Rebecca's stare. He examined the sphere for a moment, then went over to the light switch and, shutting the door to the kitchen, flicked off the lights. They both watched as the sphere grew in brightness from a dim greenish luminescence to something that indeed approached daylight, all in a matter of seconds.

'Wow,' he said in wonder. 'And they're right, it doesn't even feel hot.'

'You knew about this, didn't you? I can read you as easily as a comic book,' Rebecca said, staring fixedly at Will's face, which was lit by the strange glow.

Will didn't respond as he turned the lights on, leaving the door shut. They watched as the sphere dulled again. 'You know you said no one was doing anything about finding Dad?' he said eventually.

'So?'

'Chester and I came across something of his and we've been . . . um, making our own enquiries.'

'I knew it,' she said loudly. 'What have you found out?'

'Shh,' Will hissed, glancing at the closed door. 'Keep it down. I'm *certainly* not to bother Mum with any of this. Last thing I want to do is get her hopes up. Agreed?'

'Agreed,' Rebecca said.

'We found a book Dad was keeping notes in – a sort of journal,' Will said slowly.

'Yes, and . . .?'

As they sat at the kitchen table, Will recounted what he had read in the journal, and also their encounter with the strange pallid men outside the Clarkes' shop. He stopped short of telling her about the tunnel under the house as, to him, that was just a *little* secret.

CHAPTER EIGHTEEN

It was a week later when Will and Chester finally made the breakthrough. Dehydrated from the heat at the workface, and with muscles that were cramped and fatigued by the relentless cycle of digging and tipping, they were on the verge of winding up for the day when Will's pickaxe struck a large block of stone and it tipped backwards. A pitch-black opening yawned before them.

Their eyes locked on to the hole, which exhaled a damp and musty breeze into their tired and dirty faces. Chester's instincts screamed at him to back away, as if he was about to be sucked into the opening. Neither of them said a word; there were no great cheers or exultations as they gazed into the impenetrable darkness, with the dead calm of the earth all around them. It was Chester who broke the spell.

'I suppose I'd better be off for my tea then.'

Will turned and looked at him with incredulity, then spotted the flicker of a smirk on Chester's face. Filled with an immense sense of relief and accomplishment, Will couldn't help but erupt into a peal of hysterical laughter. He picked up a clod of earth and hurled it at his grinning friend, who ducked, a low chuckle coming from beneath his yellow hard hat.

'You . . . you . . .' Will said, searching for an appropriate word.

'Yeah, what?' Chester beamed. 'Come on, then, let's have a look-see,' he said, leaning into the gap next to Will.

Will shone his torch through the opening. 'It's a cavern . . . can't make out much in there . . . must be quite big. I think I can see some stalactites and stalagmites.' Then he stopped. 'Listen!'

'What is it?' whispered Chester.

'Water, I think. I can hear water dripping.' He turned to Chester.

'You're joking,' Chester said, his face clouding with concern.

'No, I'm not. Could be a Neolithic stream . . .'

'Here, let me see,' said Chester, taking the torch from Will.

Tantalizing as it was, they decided against any further excavation there and then. They would resume the following day when they were fresh and better prepared. Chester went home; he was tired, but quietly elated that their work had borne fruit. It was true that they were both badly in need of sleep and Will was even considering taking a bath as he swung the shelves back into position. He did the usual sweep-up and made his way lethargically upstairs to his room.

As he passed Rebecca's door, she called out to him. Will grimaced and held as still as a statue.

'Will, I *know* you're out there.'

Will sighed and pushed open her door. Rebecca was lying on her bed, where she'd been reading a book.

'What's up?' asked Will, glancing around her room. He

never ceased to be amazed at how infuriatingly clean and tidy she kept it.

'Mum said she needs to discuss something with us.'

'When?'

'As soon as you came in, she said.'

'God, what now?'

Mrs Burrows was in her usual position as they entered. Slumped to one side in her armchair like a deflated mannequin she raised her head dozily as Rebecca coughed to get her attention.

'Ah, good,' she said, pushing herself into a more normal sitting position and, in the process, knocking a couple of remote controls on to the floor. 'Oh, bum!' she exclaimed.

Will and Rebecca sat down on the sofa while Mrs Burrows rummaged feverishly through the mound of video tapes at the base of her chair. Eventually coming up with both remotes, her hair hanging forward in straggles and her face flushed from the effort, she positioned them very precisely on the arm of her chair again. Then she cleared her throat and began.

'I think it's time we faced the possibility that your father isn't coming back, which means we have to make some rather crucial decisions.' She paused and glanced at the television. A model in a spangled evening dress was revealing a large letter 'V' on the *Catchphrase* wall, which had several other letters already on show. Mrs Burrows muttered 'The Invisible Man,' under her breath as she turned back to Will and Rebecca. 'Your father's salary was stopped a few weeks ago and, as Rebecca tells me, we are already running on empty.'

Will turned to Rebecca, who simply nodded in agreement, and their mother continued. 'All the savings have gone and what with the mortgage and all the other outgoings, we're going to have to cut our cloth . . .'

'Cut our cloth?' asked Rebecca.

''Fraid so,' their mother said distantly. 'There won't be anything coming in for a while, so we're going to have to downscale – sell whatever we can – including the house.'

'What?' Rebecca said.

'And *you'll* have to see to it. I'm not going to be around for a while. I've been advised to spend a little time in a . . . well . . . sort of hospital; somewhere I can rest and get myself back on form.'

At this, Will raised his eyebrows, wondering just what 'form' his mother could be referring to. She had been set in her current form for as long as he could remember.

His mother went on. 'So while I'm gone you two will have to go and stay with your Auntie Jean. She's agreed to look after you.'

Will and Rebecca glanced at each other. An avalanche of images fell through Will's mind: the tower block where Auntie Jean lived, with the public spaces crammed with rubbish bags and disposable nappies, and the graffitied lifts reeking of urine. The streets filled with burnt-out cars and the endlessly screaming scooters of the gangs and small-time drug dealers, and the sorry groups of drunks that sat on the benches, squabbling ineffectually amongst themselves as they downed their purple cans of 'Trampagne'.

'No way!' he suddenly blurted out as if waking from a nightmare, making Rebecca jump and his mother sit bolt upright, once again knocking the remotes off the arm of her chair.

'Damn!' she said, craning her neck to see where they had fallen.

'I'm not going to live there. I couldn't bear it, not for a second. What about school, what about my friends?' Will said.

'What friends?' Mrs Burrows replied spitefully.

'You can't really expect us to go there, Mum. It's awful, it smells, the place is a pigsty,' Rebecca piped up.

'*And* Auntie Jean smells,' Will added.

'Well, there's nothing I can do about that. I have to get some rest; the doctor said I'm very stressed, so there's no debate. We've got to sell the house and you're just going to have to stay with Jean until—'

'Until what? You get a job or something?' Will put in sharply.

Mrs Burrows glared at him. 'This is not good for me. The doctor said I should avoid confrontations. This conversation is over,' she snapped suddenly, and turned on her side again.

Out in the hall, Will sat on the bottom step of the stairs, numbed, while Rebecca stood with her arms folded, leaning against the wall.

'Well, that's an end to it all,' she said. 'At least I've got next week away—'

'No, no, no . . . not now!' Will bellowed at her, holding his hand up. 'Not with all this going on!'

'No, maybe you're right,' she said, shaking her head. Then they both lapsed into silence.

After a moment, Will stood up decisively. 'But I know what I have to do.'

'What?'

'Take a bath.'

'You need one,' Rebecca said, watching him climb wearily up the stairs.

CHAPTER NINETEEN

'M atches.'
    'Check.'
  'Candles.'
  'Check.'
  'Swiss army knife.'
  'Check.'
  'Spare torch.'
  'Check.'
  'Balls of string.'
  'Check.'
  'Chalk and rope.'
  'Yep.'
  'Compass.'
  'Er . . . yep.'
  'Extra batteries for the helmet lights.'
  'Check.'
  'Camera and notebook.'
  'Check, check.'
  'Pencils.'
  'Check.'

'Water and sandwiches.'

'Ch— planning a long stay, are we?' Chester asked as he looked at the absurdly large packet wrapped in silver foil. They were carrying out a last-minute equipment check down in the Burrows' cellar, using a list Will had made at school earlier that day during his domestic science class. After ticking them off, they stowed each item in their rucksacks. When they were finished, Will closed the flap on his and shrugged it on to his back.

'Right, let's do it,' he said with a look of sheer determination on his face as he reached for his trusty spade.

Will drew back the shelves and, once both he and Chester were inside, pulled them shut and secured them by means of a makeshift latch he had rigged up. Then Will squeezed past Chester to lead the way, moving swiftly ahead on all fours.

'Hey, wait for me,' Chester called after him, quite taken aback by his friend's impetuous enthusiasm.

At the face, they dislodged the remaining blocks of stone, which fell away into the darkness and landed with dull splashes. Chester was about to speak when Will pre-empted him.

'I know, I know, you think we're about to be swept away in a flood of raw sewage or something.' Will peered through the enlarged opening. 'I can see where the rocks fell – they're sticking up out of the water. It can only be about ankle-deep.'

With that, he turned around and started to climb backwards through the hole. He paused on the brink to grin at Chester, and then ducked out of sight, leaving his friend dumbfounded for an instant until he heard Will's feet land in the water with a loud splash.

There was a drop of about two metres. 'Hey, pretty cool,'

Will said, as Chester scrambled through after him. Will's voice echoed eerily about the cavern, which was around seven metres in height and at least thirty metres long, and, as far as they could make out, crescent-shaped, with much of the floor submerged. They had entered near one end, and so were only able to see as far as the curve of the wall allowed.

Stepping out of the water, they shone their lights around for a few seconds, but when the beams came to rest on the side of the cavern nearest to them they were both immediately transfixed. Will held his torch steady on the intricate rows of stalactites and stalagmites, all of varying sizes from the width of pencils to much larger ones, as thick as the trunks of young trees. The stalactites speared down as their counterparts reached up, some meeting to form columns, and the ground was covered with overlapping swells of the encrusted calcite.

'It's a grotto,' Will said quietly, reaching out to feel the surface of an almost translucent milky-white column. 'Isn't it just beautiful? Looks just like icing on a cake, or something.'

'I think it looks more like frozen snot,' Chester said in a whisper, also touching a small column as if he didn't believe what he was seeing. He drew back his hand and rubbed his fingers together with an expression of distaste.

Will laughed, ramming the heel of his hand against a stalactite with a soft thud. 'Hard to believe it's actually rock, isn't it?'

'And the whole place is made of it,' Chester said, turning to look further along the wall. He shivered slightly from the chill air, and screwed up his nose. The whole chamber smelled dank and stale – not very pleasant at all. But to Will it was the sweet smell of success. He'd always dreamed of finding something important, but this grotto surpassed his wildest expectations. So strong was his exhilaration, Will almost felt intoxicated.

'Yes!' he said, triumphantly punching the air. At that instant, standing there in the grotto, he was the great adventurer he'd always dreamed of being, like Howard Carter in Tutankhamun's burial chamber. He whipped his head this way and that, trying to take in everything at once.

'You know, it probably took thousands of years for all this to grow . . .' Will was babbling as he took a step backwards, stopping short as his foot snagged on something. He bent down to see what it was: a small object protruded from the flowstone. Dark and flaking, its colour had seeped into the pale whiteness around it. He tried to work it free, but his fingers slipped off. It was stuck solid.

'Shine your light on this, Chester. It feels like a rusty bolt or something. But it can't be.'

'Er, Will . . . you might want to look at this . . .' Chester replied, his voice a little shaky.

At the centre of the grotto, in the deepest part of the clouded pool that lay there, stood the remains of a massive machine of some description. The boys' lights revealed ranks of large red-brown cogwheels that were still held together within what remained of a shattered cast-iron frame, so tall that in places the stalactites growing from the rock ceiling above touched it. It was as if a locomotive had been mercilessly disembowelled and then left to die.

'What the hell is it?' Chester asked, as Will stood silently beside him, examining the scene.

'Search me,' Will answered. 'And there are bits of metal all over the place. Look!'

He was shining his light around the margins of the water,

following them as far as he could into the furthest reaches of the cavern. Will's first thought had been that the banks were streaked with minerals or something similar, but on closer inspection he discovered that they were littered with more bolts like the one he'd just found, all with chunky hexagonal heads. In addition to these, there were spindles and countless pieces of jagged cast-iron shrapnel. The red oxide from these intermingled with darker, inky streaks which, from their appearance, Will took to be oil spills.

As they stood there in amazed silence and surveyed this worthless treasure trove, they became aware of a faint scratching sound.

'Did you hear that?' Chester whispered as they trained their lights in the direction of the sound. Will moved a little further into the cavern, treading carefully on the uneven floor, now invisible beneath the water.

'What was it?' gasped Chester.

'Shh!' Will stopped, and they both listened, peering around.

A sudden movement and a small splash made them jump. Then a sleek white object leaped from the rippling water and streaked along one of the metal members, stopping still on the top of a huge gearwheel. It was a large rat with a glistening, perfectly white coat and large, bright-pink ears. It wiped its snout with its paws and flicked its head, spraying droplets into the air. Then it reared up on its hind legs, its whiskers twitching and vibrating in their torchlight as it sniffed the air.

'Look! It doesn't have any eyes,' Will hissed excitedly.

Chester shuddered in response. Sure enough, where there should have been eyes, there was not even the tiniest break in the sleek, snowy fur.

'Yuck, that's disgusting,' Chester exclaimed as he took a step back.

'Adaptive evolution,' Will replied.

'I don't care what it is!'

The animal twitched and arched its head in the direction of Chester's voice. Then, the next instant, it was gone, diving into the water and swimming to the opposite bank where it scurried away.

'Great! He's probably gone to get his mates,' Chester said. 'This place will be swarming with them in a minute.'

Will laughed. 'It's only a bloody rat!'

'That was no normal rat – who's ever heard of *eyeless* rats?'

'Come on, will you, you big girl. Don't you remember the Three Blind Mice?' Will said with a wry grin as they began to move around the crescent bank, playing their torches into the nooks and crannies in the walls and up to the ceiling above them. Chester was stepping apprehensively between the rocks and iron debris, constantly peering behind him for an imagined army of sightless rats. 'Oh, God, I hate this,' he grumbled.

As they approached the shadows at the far end of the grotto, Will increased his pace. Chester did likewise, determined not to be left behind.

'Whoa!' Will stopped in his tracks, Chester bumping into him. 'Just look at that!'

Set into the rock was a door.

Will's torch flicked over its dull, scarred surface – it looked ancient but substantial, with rivet heads like halves of golf balls spaced around its frame, and three massive handles down one side. He reached forward to touch it.

'Hey! No!' Chester fretted.

But Will paid him no heed and tapped lightly on it with his knuckles. 'It's metal,' he said, running his palm over the surface – it was shiny, black and uneven, like burned treacle.

'So what? You're *not* thinking of going in there, are you?'

Will turned to him, his hand still resting on the door. 'This is the only way my dad could've gone. Of course I damned well am!'

With that he reached up, grasped the topmost handle and tried to pull down on it. It refused to budge. He thrust his torch at Chester and then, using both hands, tried again, heaving down with all his weight. Nothing happened.

'Try the other way,' suggested Chester resignedly.

Will tried again, this time pushing upwards. It creaked a little at first and then, to his surprise, swivelled smoothly until it clunked decisively into what he assumed was the open position. He did the same with the other two handles, then stood back. Retrieving his torch from Chester, he placed one hand against the centre of the door, ready to push it open.

'Well, here goes,' he said to Chester, who for once did not raise any objection.

PART TWO

THE COLONY

CHAPTER TWENTY

The door swung open with a subdued metallic groan. Will and Chester paused for a moment, adrenaline coursing through their veins as they directed their lights into the dark space beyond. They were both ready to turn and flee in an instant but, hearing and seeing nothing, they stepped carefully over the metal lip at the base of the door frame, holding their breath while their hearts pounded in their ears.

Their torch beams licked unsteadily about the interior. They were standing in an almost cylindrical chamber, no more than five metres long, with pronounced corrugations along its length. In front was another door, identical to the one they had just come through, except for a small panel of misty glass held within a riveted frame, like a small porthole.

'Looks like some sort of airlock,' Will observed as he moved further into the chamber, his boots thudding on the grooved iron flooring. 'Get a move on,' he said unnecessarily to Chester, who had followed him in and, without being asked, was closing the door behind them, turning the handles so all three were engaged again.

'Better leave everything as we find it,' Chester said. 'Just in case.'

Having tried to see through the opaque porthole with no success, Will cranked open the three handles on the second door and pushed it outwards. There was a small hiss, as if air was leaking from a tyre valve. Chester threw Will a questioning look, which he ignored as he ventured into what appeared to be a corridor. It had walls like the keel of an old boat, a patchwork quilt of rusting metal plates held together with crude welds.

'There's a number on here,' Chester observed as he locked down the handles on the second door. Peeling and yellowing with age, there was a large figure 5 painted on the door beneath the murky porthole.

As they moved cautiously forwards, their lights picked out the first details of something in front of them. It was a trellis of interwoven metal bars, running from floor to ceiling and completely blocking the way. Will's light projected jerky shadows against the surfaces beyond as he pushed on the trellis with his hand. It was solid and unyielding. He tucked his torch away and, gripping the damp metal, pulled himself as close as he could.

'I can see the walls, and I think I can see the roof, but . . .' he said, twisting his head around, 'but the floor is—'

'A long way down,' Chester interjected, the brim of his hard hat scraping against the trellis as he tried to get a better view.

'I can tell you there's nothing remotely like this on the town plans. Do you think I'd have missed something like this?' Will said, as if to dispel any self-doubt that he might have indeed overlooked something so remarkable on the maps.

'No, hang on, Will! Look at the cables!' Chester said loudly as he spied the chunky matt lines through the trellis. 'It's a lift shaft,' he added enthusiastically, his spirits suddenly buoyed by the thought that far from being something inexplicable and menacing, what they had encountered was recognizable and familiar. *It was a lift shaft*. For the first time since they had left the relative normality of the Burrows' cellar he felt safe, imagining that the shaft must descend to something as ordinary as a railway tunnel. He even dared to let himself think that this could mean the end of their half-cocked expedition.

He looked down to his right, located a handle and, yanking on it, slid the panel across. It grated horribly on its runners. Will took a step back in surprise: in his haste, he'd failed to notice that the barrier was in fact a sliding gate, and now watched as it opened before them. Once Chester had pushed it all the way back they had an unobstructed view of the dark shaft. Their helmet lamps played on the heavy greased cables running down the middle of the shaft into the darkness below, into the abyss.

'It's one hell of a drop,' Chester shivered, gripping the edge of the old lift gate tightly as his gaze was swallowed up by the vertiginous depths. Will turned his attention from the shaft and began to look around the iron-clad corridor behind them. Sure enough, attached to the wall at his side he found a small box made of dark wood with a tarnished brass button protruding from its centre.

'Yes!' he cried triumphantly, and without a word to Chester, pressed the button, which felt greasy beneath his fingertip.

Nothing happened.

He tried again.

And once more, *nothing*.

'Chester, close the gate, close it!' he shouted, unable to contain his excitement.

Chester rammed it across and Will jabbed at the button again. There was a distant vibration, and a clank reverberated from deep inside the shaft. And then the cables jerked into life and began to move, the shaft filling with a loud, whining groan from the winching equipment, which must have been housed not far above them. They listened to the clanging echoes of the approaching lift.

'Bet it's the way down to an Underground station.' Chester turned to Will, a look of anticipation on his face.

Will frowned with annoyance. 'No way. I *told* you there's nothing here. This is something else altogether.'

Chester's optimism evaporated, his face falling as they both approached the lift gate again, pushing their heads against it so their helmet lamps dipped into the black shaft.

'Well, if we don't know what this is . . .' Chester said, 'there's still time to go back.'

'Come on, we can't give up. Not now.'

They both stood listening to the approaching lift for a couple of minutes until Chester spoke. 'What if there's someone in it?' he said, drawing back from the gate and starting to panic again.

But Will couldn't tear himself away. 'Hang on, I can't quite . . . it's still too dark . . . wait! I can see it, I can see it! It's like a miners' cage-lift!' Staring hard at the lift as it inched ponderously towards them, Will found he was able to see through the grille that formed its roof. He turned to Chester. 'Relax, will you? There's nobody in it.'

'I didn't really think there was,' Chester retorted defensively.

'Yeah, right, you big wuss.'

Satisfying himself that it was empty, Chester shook his head and sighed with relief as the lift arrived at their level. It shuddered to a clangorous halt, and Will lost no time in pulling back the gate and taking a few steps in. Then he turned to Chester who was hovering on the brink, looking decidedly uncomfortable.

'I don't know, Will, it looks well shonky,' he said, his gaze shifting around the lift's interior. It had cage walls and a scratched steel-plate floor, and the whole thing was covered with what looked like years of oily grime and dust.

'Come on, Chester, this is the *big time*!' Not for a second did Will stop to consider there was any way to go but down. If he'd been filled with exhilaration at the discovery of the grotto, then this surpassed even his wildest expectations. 'We're going to be famous!' he laughed.

'Oh sure, I can see it now . . . *Two dead in lift disaster!*' Chester rejoined morosely, stretching his hands in front of him to indicate the newspaper headline. 'It just doesn't look safe . . . probably hasn't been serviced in ages.'

Without a moment's hesitation Will jumped up and down a couple of times, his boots clanging on the metal flooring. Chester looked on, terrified, as the lift cage rattled.

'Safe as houses.' Will grinned impishly and, resting his hand on the brass lever inside the lift, he looked Chester in the eye. 'So are you coming . . . or are you going back to fight the rat?'

That was enough for Chester, who immediately moved into the lift. Will slid the gate shut behind him, and, pushing and holding the lever down, the lift once again shuddered into motion and began to descend. Through the caging, interrupted every so often by the dark mouths of other levels, they saw the rock face slowly sweeping by in muted shades of browns and blacks and greys, ochres and yellows.

A damp breeze blew about them, and at one point Chester shone his light through the grille above them, up into the shaft and on to the cables, which looked like a pair of dirty laser beams fading into deep space.

'How far down do you think it goes?' Chester asked.

'How should I know?' Will replied gruffly.

In fact, it was almost five minutes before the lift finally came to a stop with an abrupt and bone-shaking bump that made them fall against the sides of the cage.

'Maybe I should have let go of the lever a bit earlier,' Will said sheepishly.

Chester threw his friend a blank look, as if nothing really mattered any more, and then they both stood there, their lights throwing giant diamond silhouettes from the lift cage on to the walls beyond.

'Here we go again,' Chester sighed as he slid back the gate and Will pushed impatiently past him into another metal-plate corridor, rushing through it to get to the door at the far end.

'This is just like the one above,' Will noted as he busied himself with the three handles on the side of the door. This one had a large 0 painted on it.

They took a few tentative steps into the cylindrical room, their boots ringing out against the undulating sheet-metal flooring and their torch beams illuminating yet another door in front of them.

'Seems we only have one way to go,' Will said, striding towards it.

'These things look like something out of a submarine,' Chester muttered under his breath. 'Like airlocks.'

Standing on tiptoe, Will looked through the small glass porthole, but couldn't make out anything on the other side. And when he tried to shine his torch through it, the grease and the scratches on the ancient glass only refracted the beam, so that it became more opaque than ever.

'Useless,' he said to himself.

Passing his torch to Chester, he rotated the three handles and then pushed against the door. 'It's stuck!' he grunted. He tried again, without success. 'Give me a hand, will you?'

Chester joined in, and with their shoulders braced against the door they pushed and shoved with all their might. Suddenly, it burst open with a loud hiss and a massive rush of air, and they stumbled through into the unknown.

Their boots now ground on cobblestones as they regained their footing and straightened up. Before them was a scene that they both knew, for as long as they lived, they would never forget.

It was a street.

They found themselves in a huge space almost as wide as a motorway, which curved off into the distance to their left and right. And looking across to the opposite side, they saw that it was lit by a row of tall street lamps.

But what stood beyond these lights, on the far side of the cavern, was what really took their breath away. Stretching as far as they could see, in both directions, were *houses*.

As if in a trance, Will and Chester moved towards this apparition. As they did so, the door slammed shut behind them with such force that they both wheeled around.

'A breeze?' Chester asked his friend, with a baffled expression.

Will shrugged in response – he could definitely feel a faint draught on his face. He put his head back and sniffed, catching the stale mustiness in the air. Chester was shining his beam at the door and then began to play it over the wall above, illuminating the huge blocks of stone that formed it. He raised the circle of light, higher and higher, and their eyes were compelled to follow the wall up into the shadows above, where it met the opposing wall in a gentle arch, like the vaulted roof of a huge cathedral.

'What is all this, Will? What is this place?' Chester asked, grabbing him by the arm.

'I don't know – I've never heard about anything like this before,' Will replied, staring wide-eyed around the huge street. 'It's truly awesome.'

'What do we do now?'

'I think we . . . we should have a look around, don't you? This is just incredible,' Will marvelled. He struggled to order his thoughts, infused with the first heady flush of discovery, and consumed with the irresistible urge to explore and to learn more. 'Must record it,' he muttered as he hoisted his camera out and began to take photographs.

'Will, don't! The flash!'

'Oops, sorry.' He slung the camera around his neck. 'Got a little carried away there.' Without another word to Chester, he suddenly strode across the cobblestones towards the houses. Chester followed behind his fellow explorer, half crouched and grumbling under his breath as he scanned up and down the road for any sign of life.

The buildings appeared to be carved out of the very walls

themselves, like half-excavated architectural fossils. Their roofs were fused with the gently arching walls behind, and where one might have expected chimneys there was an intricate net-work of brick ducts sprouting from the tops of the roofs, which ran up the walls and disappeared above, like petrified smoke plumes. As the boys reached the pavement, the only sound apart from their footfalls was a low humming, which seemed to be coming from the very ground itself. They paused briefly to inspect one of the street lights.

'It's like the—'

'Yes,' Will interrupted, unconsciously touching his pocket where his father's luminescent orb was carefully wrapped in a handkerchief. The glass sphere of the street light was a much larger version of this, almost the size of a football, and held in place by a four-pronged claw atop a cast-iron post. A pair of snow-white moths circled erratically about it like epileptic moons, their dry wings fluttering against the surface of the glass.

Will stiffened abruptly and, lifting his head back, sniffed – looking not unlike the eyeless rat on the cogwheel.

'What's up?' Chester asked with trepidation. 'Not more trouble?'

'No, just thought . . . I smelled something. It was kind of like . . . ammonia . . . something sharp. Didn't you notice it?'

'No.' Chester sniffed several times. 'I hope it's not poisonous.'

'Well, it's gone now, whatever it was. And we're fine, aren't we?'

'Suppose so. But do you think anyone really lives here?' Chester replied, as he looked up at the windows of the build-ings. They turned their attention to the nearest house, silent and ominous, as if daring them to approach.

'I don't know.'

'Well, what's it all doing here, then?'

'Only one way to find out,' Will said as they crept gingerly towards the house. It was simple and elegant, constructed of sandstone masonry, almost Georgian in style. They could just make out heavily embroidered curtains behind the twelve-paned windows either side of the front door, which was painted with treacle-thick green gloss and had on it a door knocker and bell push of deeply burnished brass.

'167,' Will said in wonder as he spotted the digits above the knocker.

'What *is* this place?' Chester was whispering as Will caught a faint flicker of light in a chink between the curtains. It shimmered, as if it came from a fire.

'Shhh!' he said, as he crept over and crouched down below the window, then slowly rose above the sill and peered with one eye through the small gap. His mouth gaped open in silent awe. He could see a fire burning in a hearth. Above this was a dark mantelpiece on which there were various glass ornaments. And as the light from the fire danced around the room, he could just make out some chairs and a sofa, and the walls, which were covered in framed pictures of varying sizes.

'Come on, what's there?' Chester said nervously, continually looking back at the empty street, as Will squashed his face against the dirty pane of glass.

'You won't believe this!' Will replied, moving aside to let his friend see for himself. Chester eagerly pressed his nose against the window.

'Wow! It's a proper room!' he said turning to look at Will, only to find he was already on the move, working his way along the front of the house. He stopped as he reached the corner of the building.

'Hey! Wait for me,' Chester hissed, terrified that he was going to be left behind.

Between this building and the next one in the row, a short alley ran straight back to the tunnel wall. Will poked his head around the corner and, once he was satisfied that it was clear, beckoned to Chester that they should move on to the next house.

'This one's number 166,' Will said as he examined its front door, which was almost identical to the one on the first house. He tiptoed to the window, but was unable to see anything at all through the dark panes.

'What's there?' Chester asked.

Will held a finger to his lips, then retraced his steps back to the front door. Examining it closely, a thought occurred to him and his eyes narrowed. Recognizing the look, Chester reached out to try to stop him, spluttering: 'Will, no!'

But it was too late. Will had barely touched the door when it swung inward. They exchanged glances and then both inched slowly inside, twinges of excitement and fear simultaneously surging through them.

The hallway was spacious and warm, and they both became aware of a potpourri of smells – cooking, fire smoke – and of human habitation. It was laid out just like any normal house; wide stairs started halfway down the corridor, with brass carpet rails at the base of each riser. Waxed wood panelling ran up to a handrail, above which was wallpaper of light- and dark-green stripes. Portraits in ornate, dull-gold-coloured frames hung on the walls, depicting sturdy-looking people with huge shoulders and pale faces. Chester was peering at one of these when a terrible thought struck him.

'They're just like the men that chased us,' he said. 'Oh, great, we're in a house that belongs to one of those nutters, aren't we? This is bloody nutty town!' he added as the awful realization hit him.

'Listen!' Will hissed. Chester stood riveted to the spot as Will cocked an ear in the direction of the stairs, but there was nothing, only an oppressive silence.

'I thought I heard . . . no . . .' he said, and moved towards the open doorway to their left, then looked cautiously around the corner. 'This is awesome!' He couldn't help himself – he had to go in. And by this time, Chester was also being swept along by the need to know more.

A cheery fire crackled in the hearth. Around the walls were small pictures and silhouettes in brass and gilt frames. One in particular caught Will's eye: *The Martineau House*, he read on the inscription below. It was a small oil painting of what appeared to be a stately home surrounded by rolling grasslands.

By the fireplace were chairs upholstered in a dark-red material with a dull sheen. There was a dining table in one corner, and in another a musical instrument that Will recognized as a harpsichord. In addition to the light from the fire, the room was lit by two tennis-ball-sized spheres suspended from the ceiling in ornate pinchbeck cages. The whole thing brought to Will's mind a museum his father had taken him to with a display called *How We Used To Live*. As he looked around, he reflected that this room wouldn't have been out of place there.

Chester sidled up to the dining table, where two plain white bone china cups sat in their saucers.

'There's something in these,' he said with an expression of sheer surprise. 'Looks like tea!'

He hesitantly touched the side of one of the cups and looked up at Will, even more startled.

'It's still warm. What's going on here? Where are all the people?'

'Don't know,' Will replied. 'It's like . . . like . . .'

They looked at each other with dumbfounded expressions.

'I honestly don't know what it's like,' Will admitted.

'Let's just get out of here,' Chester said, and they both bolted for the door. As they reached the pavement again, Chester collided with Will as he stopped dead.

'What are we running for?' Will asked.

'Er . . . the . . . well . . .' Chester blathered in confusion as he struggled to put his concerns into words. For a moment they lingered indecisively under the sublime radiance of a street light. Then Chester noticed with dismay that Will was staring intently at the road as it curved into the distance. 'Come on, Will. Let's just go home.' Chester shivered as he glanced back at the house and up at the windows, certain that there was someone there. 'This place gives me the creeps.'

'No,' Will replied, not even looking at his friend. 'Let's follow the road along for a bit. See where it goes. Then we can leave. I promise – all right?' he said, already striding off.

Chester stood his ground for a moment, looking longingly across the road at the metal doorway through which they had first come. Then, with a groan of resignation, he followed Will along the line of houses. Many had lights in their windows, but as far as they could tell there were no signs of any occupants.

As they came to the last house in the row, where the road curved off to the left, Will paused for a moment, deliberating whether to go on or call it a day. His voice squeaking with desperation, Chester started pleading that enough was enough and that they should turn back, when they became aware of a sound behind them. It began like the rustling of leaves, but quickly grew in intensity to a dry, rippling cacophony.

'What the—?' Will exclaimed.

Shooting down from the roof, a flock of birds the size of sparrows dived down towards them, like living tracer bullets. Will and Chester instinctively ducked, raising their arms to shield their faces as the pure white birds whirled around them.

Will began to laugh. 'Birds! It's only birds!' he said, swatting at the mischievous flock, but never making contact. Chester lowered his arms and began to laugh too, a little nervously, as the birds darted between them. Then, as quickly as they'd appeared, the birds swept upwards and vanished round the bend in the tunnel. Will straightened up and staggered a few steps after them, but then froze.

'Shops!' he announced with a startled voice.

'Huh?' Chester said.

Sure enough, down one side of the street stretched a parade of bow-fronted shops. Without speaking, they both began to walk towards them.

'This is unreal,' Chester muttered as they reached the first shop with windows of hand-blown glass that distorted the wares inside like badly-made lenses.

'Jacobson Cloths,' Chester read from the shop sign, then peered at the rolls of material laid out in the eerie, green-lit interior.

'A grocer's,' Will said as they moved on.

'And this one's some sort of hardware shop,' Chester observed.

Will gazed up at the arching roof of the cavern above them. 'You know, by now we must nearly be under the High Street.'

Peering into the windows and soaking up the strangeness of the ancient shops, they kept walking, driven by their careless curiosity, until they came to a place where the tunnel split into three. The centre fork appeared to descend into the earth at a marked angle.

'Right, that's it,' Chester said resolutely. 'We're leaving now. I'm *not* going to get lost down here.' All his instincts were screaming that they should turn back.

'All right,' Will agreed, 'but—'

He was just stepping off the pavement on to the cobbled road when there was an ear-splitting crash of iron on stone. In a blinding flash, four white horses bore down on him, sparks spraying from their hooves, breathing hard and pulling behind them a sinister black coach. Will didn't have time to react, as that very instant they were both yanked off their feet and hoisted into the air by the scruffs of their necks.

A single man held them both, dangling helplessly, in his huge gnarled hands. 'Interlopers!' the man shouted, his voice fierce and gravelly as he lifted the pair up to his face and inspected them with a look of repugnance. Will tried to bring his spade up to beat him off, but it was wrested from his grip.

The man was wearing a ridiculously small helmet and a dark-blue uniform of coarse material that rasped as he moved. Beside a row of dull buttons Will caught sight of a five-pointed star of orange-gold material stitched into the coat. Their massive, menacing captor was clearly some sort of policeman.

'Help,' Chester mouthed silently at his friend, his voice deserting him as they were buffeted about in the man's vice-like grip.

'We've been expecting you,' the man rumbled.

'What?' Will stared at him blankly.

'Your father said you'd be joining us before long.'

'My father? Where's my father? What have you done with him? Put me down!' Will tried to swivel around, kicking out at the man.

'No use wriggling.' The man hoisted the struggling boy even higher in the air and sniffed at him. 'Topsoilers. Disgusting!'

Will sniffed back.

'Don't smell too good yourself.'

The man gave Will a look of withering scorn, then he held Chester up and sniffed at him too. In sheer desperation, Chester tried to head-butt the man. He jerked his face away, but not before Chester, with a wild swing of his arm, had swiped his helmet. It spun from his head, exposing his pale scalp, which was covered with short tufts of wispy white hair.

The man shook Chester violently by the collar and then, with a horrible growl, knocked the boys' heads together. Although their hard hats protected them from any injury as they crashed noisily against each other, they were so shocked by his ferocity that they immediately abandoned any further thoughts of resistance.

'Enough!' the man shouted, and the stunned boys heard a chorus of bitter laughter from behind him, becoming aware for the first time of the other men who were peering at them with pale, unsmiling eyes.

'Think you can come down here and break into our houses?' the man growled as he swept them down towards the centre fork, where the road descended.

'It's the clink for you two,' snarled someone behind them.

They were frogmarched unceremoniously through the streets, which were now filling with people emerging from various doorways and alleys to gawp at this unfortunate pair of strangers. Half dragged and half stumbling, each time they lost their footing the boys would be yanked savagely to their feet by the enormous officer. It was as if he was playing up to the audience and making a big show of having complete control of the situation.

In all their confusion and panic, Will and Chester looked frantically around in the vain hope that they might find an opportunity for escape, or that someone would come to their rescue. But their faces drained of blood as this hope receded, and they realized the gravity of their situation. They were being dragged deeper into the bowels of the earth, and there was absolutely nothing they could do about it.

Before they knew it, they were heaved around a bend in the tunnel and the space around them opened up. They were struck dumb by a dizzying confusion of bridges, aqueducts and raised walkways criss-crossed above a lattice of cobbled streets and lanes, all bordered with buildings.

Dragged on at an impossible rate by the policeman, they were watched by huddled groups of people, their wide faces curious and yet impassive. But not all the faces were like those of their captor or the men who had pursued them up in Highfield, with their wan skin and washed-out eyes. If it hadn't been for their old-fashioned dress, some would have appeared quite normal and could easily have passed unnoticed in any English street.

'Help, help!' Chester cried hopelessly as he half-heartedly resumed his efforts to extricate himself from the policeman's grip. But Will hardly noticed any of this. His attention had been seized by a tall, thin individual standing beside a lamp-post, whose hard face was set atop a stark white collar and a long, dark coat that reflected the light as if it was made from polished leather. He stood out strikingly from the squat people about him, his shoulders slightly bent over like a highly strung bow. His whole being emanated evil and his dark eyes never left Will's, who felt a wave of dread wash over him.

'I think we're in real trouble here, Chester,' he said, unable to tear his gaze from the sinister man, whose thin lips were twisted into a sardonic smile.

CHAPTER TWENTY-ONE

Will and Chester stumbled and tripped as they were hauled up a small flight of steps into a single-storey building nestling between what Will took to be drab offices or factories. Once inside, the policeman pulled them to an abrupt halt and, spinning them around, roughly yanked their rucksacks off their backs. Then he literally hurled the two boys at a slippery oak bench, its surface dipping here and there with polished indentations, as if years of wrongdoers had rubbed along its length. Will and Chester gasped as their backs slammed against the wall and the breath was knocked out of them.

'Don't you move!' the policeman roared, positioning himself between them and the entrance. By craning his neck forward Will could just see past the man and through the half-windowed doors into the street outside, where a mob had gathered. Many were jostling for a view, and a few started to shout angrily and wave their fists as they caught sight of Will. He quickly sat back and tried to catch Chester's eye, but his friend, frightened out of his wits, was staring fixedly at the floor in front of him.

Will saw a noticeboard next to the door, on which a large number of black-edged papers were pinned. Most of the writing was too small to decipher from where he sat, but he could just make out handwritten headings such as *Order* or *Edict*, followed by strings of numbers.

The walls of the station were painted black from the floor up to a handrail, above which they were an off-white colour, peeling in places and streaked with dirt. The ceiling itself was an unpleasant nicotine yellow with deep cracks running in every direction, like a road map of some unidentified country. On the wall directly above Will was a picture of a forbidding-looking building, with slits for windows and huge bars across its main entrance. He could just make out the words 'Newgate Prison' written under it.

Across from the boys ran a long counter, on which the policeman had placed their rucksacks and Will's spade, and beyond that was an office of some sort, where three desks were surrounded by a forest of narrow filing cabinets. A number of smaller rooms led off this main room, and from one came the rapid tapping of what could have been a typewriter.

Just as Will was looking into the far corner of the room, where a profusion of burnished brass pipes ran up the walls like the stems of an ancient vine, there was a screeching hiss that ended with a solid clunk. The noise was so sudden that Chester sat up and blinked like a nervous rabbit, stirred from his anxious torpor.

Another policeman emerged from a side room and hurried over to the brass pipes. There he glanced at a panel of antiquated dials from which a cascade of twisted wires spiralled down to a wooden box. Then he opened a hatch in one of the pipes, prising out a bullet-shaped cylinder the size of a small rolling pin. Unscrewing a cap from one end of it, he extracted a scroll of paper that crackled as he straightened it out to read it.

'Styx on their way,' he said gruffly, striding over to the counter and opening up a large ledger, not once looking in the boys' direction. He also had an orange-gold star stitched on to his jacket, and although his appearance was much like that of the other officer, he was younger and his head was covered with a neatly cut stubble of white hair.

'Chester,' Will whispered. As his friend didn't react, he stretched over to nudge him. In a flash, a truncheon lashed out, smacking smartly across his knuckles.

'Desist!' the policeman next to them barked.

'Ouch!' Will jumped up from the bench, his fists clenched. 'You stupid . . .' he shouted, his body trembling, trying to control himself. Chester reached out and grabbed hold of his arm.

'Be quiet, Will!'

Will angrily shook Chester's hand off and stared into the policeman's cold eyes. 'I want to know why we're being held,' he demanded.

For a horrible moment they thought the policeman's face was going to explode, it turned such a livid red. But then his huge shoulders begin to heave, and a low grating laugh rumbled up, which grew louder and louder. Will threw a sidelong glance at Chester, who was eyeing the policeman with alarm.

'ENOUGH!' The voice of the man behind the counter cracked like a whip as he looked up from the ledger, his gaze falling on the laughing policeman, who immediately fell silent. 'YOU!' the man glowered at Will. 'SIT DOWN!' His voice held such authority that Will didn't hesitate for a second, quickly taking his place next to Chester again. 'I . . .' the man continued, puffing out his barrel chest self-importantly, 'am the First Officer. You are already acquainted with the Second Officer.' He nodded in the direction of the policeman standing by them.

The First Officer looked down at the roll of paper from the message tube. 'You are hereby charged with unlawful entry and trespass into the Quarter under Statute Twelve, Sub-section Two,' he read in a monotone.

'But . . .' Will began meekly.

The First Officer ignored him and read on. 'Furthermore you did uninvited enter a property with the intent to pilfer, contrary to Statute Six, Sub-section Six,' he continued matter-of-factly. 'Do you understand these charges?' he asked.

Will and Chester exchanged confused looks, and Will was about to reply when the First Officer cut him off.

'Now what have we here?' he said, opening their rucksacks and emptying the contents on to the counter. He picked up the foil-wrapped sandwiches Will had prepared and, not bothering to open them, merely sniffed at them. 'Ah, swine,' he said with a flicker of a smile. And from the way he briefly licked his lips and slid it to one side, Will knew he'd seen the last of his packed lunch.

Then the First Officer turned his attention to the other items, working his way through them methodically. He lingered on the compass, but was more taken by the Swiss army knife, levering out each of its blades in turn and squeezing the little scissors with his thick fingers before he finally put it down. Casually rolling one of the balls of string on the countertop with one hand, he used the other to flick open the dog-eared geological map that had been in Will's rucksack, giving it a cursory inspection. Finally, he leaned over and smelled the map, wrinkling his face with a look of distaste, before moving on to the camera.

'Hmmm,' he muttered thoughtfully, turning it in his banana-like fingers to consider it from several angles.

'That's mine,' Will said.

The First Officer completely ignored him and, putting the camera down, picked up a pen and dipped it in an inkwell set into the counter. With the pen poised over a page of the open ledger, he cleared his throat.

'NAME!' he bellowed, throwing a glance in Chester's direction.

'It's, er, Chester . . . Chester Rawls,' the boy stammered.

The First Officer wrote in the ledger. The scratching of the nib on the page was the only sound in the room, and Will suddenly felt utterly helpless, as if the entry in the ledger was setting in motion an irreversible process, the workings of which were quite beyond his understanding.

'AND YOU?' he snapped at Will.

'He told me my father was here,' Will said, bravely stabbing his finger in the direction of the Second Officer. 'Where is he? I want to see him now!'

The First Officer looked across at his colleague and then back to Will. 'You won't be seeing anyone unless you do as you are told.' He shot another glance at the Second Officer and frowned with barely disguised disapproval. The Second Officer averted his gaze and shifted uneasily from foot to foot.

'NAME!'

'Will Burrows,' Will answered slowly.

The First Officer picked up the scroll and consulted it again. 'That is not the name I have here,' he said, shaking his head and then fixing Will with his steely eyes.

'I don't care what it says. I know my own name.'

There was a deafening silence as the First Officer continued to stare at Will. Then he abruptly slammed the ledger shut with a loud slap, causing a cloud of dust to billow up from the counter's surface.

'GET THEM TO THE HOLD!' he barked apoplectically.

They were dragged to their feet and, just as they were being pushed roughly through a large oak door at the end of the reception area, they heard another long hiss followed by a dull clunk as a further message arrived in the pipe system.

The connecting corridor of the Hold was about twenty metres long and dimly lit by a single globe at the far end, beneath which stood a small wooden desk and chair. A blank wall ran along the right-hand side, and on the wall opposite were four dull iron doors set deep into solid brick surrounds. The boys were pushed along to the farthest door, on which the number four was marked in Roman numerals.

The Second Officer opened it with his keys and it swung back silently on its well-greased hinges. He stepped aside. Looking at the boys, he inclined his head towards the cell and as they hovered uncertainly on the threshold, he lost patience and shoved them in with his large hands, slamming the door behind them.

Inside the cell, the clang of the door reverberated sickeningly about the walls, and their stomachs turned as the key twisted in the lock. They tried to make out the detail of the dark and dank cell by feeling their way around, Chester managing to send a bucket clattering over as he went. They discovered there was a metre wide, lead-covered ledge along the length of the wall that directly faced the door, and, without a word to each other, both sat down on it. They felt its rough surface, cold and clammy, under their palms as their eyes gradually adjusted to the only source of light in the cell, the meagre illumination that filtered through an observation hatch in the door. Finally, Chester broke the silence with a loud sniff.

'Oh, man, what *is* that smell?'

'I'm not sure,' said Will as he too sniffed. 'Sick? Sweat?' Then he sniffed again and pronounced, with the air of a connoisseur, 'Carbolic acid and . . .' Sniffing once more, he added: 'Is that sulphur?'

'Huh?' his friend muttered.

'No, cabbage! Boiled cabbage!'

'I don't care what it is, it stinks,' Chester said, screwing his face up. 'This place is just gross.' He turned to look at his friend in the gloom. 'How are we going to get out of here, Will?'

Will drew his knees up under his chin and rested his feet on the edge of the ledge. He scratched his calf but said nothing. He was quietly furious with himself, and didn't want his friend to pick up any sense of what he was feeling. Maybe Chester, with his cautious approach and his frequent warnings, had been right all along. He clenched his teeth and balled his fists in the darkness. Stupid, stupid, stupid! They had blundered in like a couple of amateurs. He'd allowed himself to get totally carried away. And how was he ever going to find his father now?

'I've got the most awful feeling about all this,' Chester continued, now looking desolately at the floor. 'We're never going to see home again, are we? '

'Look, don't you worry. We found a way in here, and we're sure as hell going to find a way out again,' Will said confidently, in an effort to reassure his friend, though he himself couldn't have felt more uncomfortable about their current predicament.

Neither of them felt much like talking after that, and the room was filled with the sound of the ever-present thrumming, and the erratic scuttling of unseen insects.

Will woke with a start, catching his breath as if coming up for air. He was surprised to find he had actually dozed off in a half-sitting position on the lead sill. How long had he slept? He looked blearily about the shadowy gloom. Chester was standing with his back pressed against the wall, staring wide-eyed at the cell door. Will could almost feel fear emanating from him. He automatically followed Chester's gaze to the observation hatch: framed in the opening was the leering face of the Second Officer, but owing to the size of his head only his eyes and nose were visible.

Hearing the keys jangle in the lock Will watched as the man's eyes narrowed, and then the door swung open to reveal the officer silhouetted in the doorway, like a monstrous cartoon illustration.

'YOU!' he said to Will. 'OUT NOW!'

'Why? What for?'

'MOVE IT!' the officer barked.

'Will?' Chester said anxiously.

'Don't worry, Chester, it'll be all right,' Will said weakly as he stood up, his legs cramped and stiff from the damp. He stretched them as he walked awkwardly out of the cell and into the aisle. Then, unrequested, he began to make his way to the main door of the Hold.

'Stand still!' snapped the Second Officer as he locked the

door again. Then, grabbing Will's arm in a painful grip, he steered him out of the Hold and down a succession of bleak corridors, their footfalls echoing emptily about the flaking whitewashed walls and bare stone floors. Eventually, they turned a corner into a narrow stairwell that led into a short, dead-ended passage. It smelled damp and earthy, like an old cellar.

A bright light issued from an open door about halfway down. A sense of dread was growing in the pit of Will's stomach as they approached the doorway, and sure enough, he was pushed into the well-lit room by his escort and brought to an abrupt halt. Dazzled by the brightness, Will squinted as he peered around him.

The room was bare except for a bizarre chair and a metal table, behind which two tall figures were standing, their thin bodies bent over so that their heads were almost touching as they talked quietly in urgent, conspiratorial whispers. Will strained to catch what they were saying, but it didn't seem to be in any language he recognized, punctuated as it was by an alarming series of the most peculiar high-pitched, scratchy noises. Try as he might, he couldn't make out a single word; it was completely unintelligible to him.

So, with his arm still held tight in the officer's crushing grip, Will stood and waited, his stomach knotting with nervous tension as his eyes became accustomed to the brightness. From time to time the strange men glanced fleetingly at him, but Will didn't dare utter a word in the presence of this new and sinister authority.

They were dressed identically, with pristine, stark white collars at their necks. These were so large that they draped over the shoulders of their stiff, full-length leather coats, which creaked as the men gesticulated to each other. The skin of their gaunt faces, the colour of new putty, only served to emphasize their jet-black eyes. Their hair, shaved high at the temples, was oiled back against their scalps so that they looked as though they were wearing shiny skullcaps.

Quite unexpectedly, they stopped what they were doing and turned to face Will.

'These gentlemen are the Styx,' said the Second Officer behind him, 'and you will answer their questions.'

'Chair,' the Styx on the right said, his black eyes staring unwaveringly at Will.

He pointed with a long-fingered hand at the strange chair that stood between the table and Will. Overcome by a sense of foreboding, Will didn't protest as the officer sat him down. An adjustable metal bar rose from the back of the chair, with two padded clamps at the top to hold the occupant's head firmly in place. The officer adjusted the height of the bar, then tightened the clamps, pressing them hard against Will's temples. He tried to turn his head to look at the officer, but the restraints held him fast. While the officer continued to secure him, Will realized he had absolutely no choice but to face the Styx, who were poised behind the table like avaricious priests.

The officer stooped. Out of the corner of his eye Will saw him pull something from underneath the chair, then heard the old leather straps creak and the large buckles rattle as each of his wrists was strapped to the corresponding thigh.

'What's this for?' Will dared to ask.

'Your own protection,' the officer said as, crouching down, he proceeded to loop further straps around Will's legs, just below the knees, fastening them to the legs of the chair. Both of Will's ankles were then secured in a similar fashion, the officer pulling the bindings so taut that they bit mercilessly and made Will writhe with discomfort. He noticed with some dismay that this appeared to amuse the Styx. Finally, a strap some ten centimetres thick was drawn tightly across his chest and arms, and fastened behind the back of the chair. The officer then stood to attention until one of the Styx nodded mutely to him and he left the room, closing the door behind him.

Alone with them, Will watched in terrified silence as one of the Styx produced an odd-looking lamp and placed it in the centre of the table facing Will. It had a solid base and a short curved arm topped with a shallow conical shade. This held what appeared to be a dark-purple bulb; it reminded Will of an old sunlamp he'd seen in his father's museum. A small black box with dials and switches was placed next to it, and the lamp was plugged into this by means of a twisted brown cable. The Styx's pale finger jabbed at a switch and the box began to hum gently to itself.

One Styx stepped back from the table as the other continued to lean over the lamp, manipulating the controls behind the shade. With a loud click, the bulb flared a dim orange for an instant, and then appeared to go out again.

'Going to take my picture?' Will asked in a weak attempt at humour, as he tried to steady the tremor in his voice. Ignoring him, the Styx turned a dial on the black box, as if he was tuning a radio.

Alarmingly, an uncomfortable pressure began to build up behind Will's eyes. He opened his mouth in a silent yawn, trying to relieve this strange tension in his temples, when the room began to darken, as if the device was literally sucking all the light from it. Thinking he was going blind, Will blinked several times and opened his eyes as wide as he could. With the greatest difficulty, he could just make out the two Styx silhouetted by the dim light reflecting off the wall behind them.

He became aware of an incessant pulsing drone, but for the life of him he couldn't pinpoint where it was coming from. As it grew more intense, his head began to feel decidedly strange, as if every bone and sinew were vibrating. It was like a plane flying too low overhead. The resonance seemed to form into a spiked ball of energy in the very centre of his head. Now he *really* began to panic, but not being able to move a muscle he could do nothing to resist.

As the Styx manipulated the dials, the ball appeared to shift, slowly sinking through his body into his chest and then circling his heart, causing him to catch his breath and cough involuntarily. Then it was moving in and out of his body, sometimes coming to a rest, and hovering a little distance behind him. It was as if a living thing was homing in and searching for something. It shifted again, and now floated half in and half out of his body, at the nape of his neck.

'What's going on?' Will asked, trying to summon up some bravado, but there was no response from the ever-darkening figures. 'You're not scaring me with all this, you know.'

They remained silent.

Will closed his eyes for a second, but when he reopened them, he found he couldn't even distinguish the outlines of the Styx in the total darkness that now confronted him. He began struggling against his bonds.

'Does the absence of light unsettle you?' asked the Styx on the left.

'No, why should it?'

'What is your name?' The words cut into Will's head like a knife out of the darkness.

'I've told you, it's Will. Will Burrows.'

'Your real name!' Again the voice caused Will to wince with pain – it was as if each word was setting off electric shocks in his temples.

'I don't know what you mean,' he answered through gritted teeth.

The ball of energy began to edge into the centre of his skull, the humming growing more intense now, the throbbing pulse enveloping him in a thick blanket of pressure.

'Are you with the man called Burrows?'

Will's head was swimming, waves of pain rippling through him. His feet and hands were tingling unpleasantly with intense pins and needles. This horrible sensation was slowly enveloping his whole body.

'He's my dad!' he shouted.

'What is your purpose here?' The precise, clipped voice was closer now.

'What have you done to him?' Will said in a choked voice, swallowing back the rush of saliva flooding into his mouth. He felt he was going to be sick at any moment.

'Where is your mother?' The measured but insistent voice now seemed to be emanating from the ball inside his head. It was as though both Styx had entered his cranium and were searching feverishly through his mind, like burglars ransacking drawers and cupboards for valuable items.

'What is your purpose?' they repeated again.

Will tried again to struggle against his bonds, but realized he could no longer feel his body. In fact it felt as if he had been reduced to nothing but a floating head, cast adrift into a fog of darkness, and he couldn't fathom which way was up or down any more.

'NAME? PURPOSE?' The questions came thick and fast as Will felt all his remaining energy seep out of him. Then the incessant voice became fainter, as if Will was moving away from it. From a great distance, words were being shouted after him, and each word, when it finally arrived, set off small pin-pricks of light at the edge of his vision, which swam and jittered until the darkness before him was filled with a boiling sea of white dots, so bright and so intense that his eyes ached. All the time, the scratchy whispers swept around him and the room spun and pitched. Another deep wave of nausea over-whelmed him, and a burning sensation filled his head to bursting point. White, white, blinding white, cramming into his head until it felt as if it was going to explode.

'I'm going to be sick . . . please . . . I'm going to be . . . I feel faint . . . please,' and the light of the white space seared into him and he felt himself growing smaller and smaller, until he was a tiny fleck in the huge white emptiness. Then the light began to recede and the burning sensation grew less and less, until everything was black and silent, as if the uni-verse itself had gone out.

He came round as the Second Officer, supporting him under one arm, turned the key in the cell door. He was shaky and weak. Vomit was streaked down the front of his clothes, and his mouth was dry with an acrid metallic taste that made him gag. His head was pounding with pain, and as he tried to look up it was as though part of his vision was missing. He couldn't stop himself from groaning as the door was pulled open.

'Not so cocky now, eh?' the officer said, letting go of Will's arm. He tried to walk, but his legs were like jelly. 'Not after your first taste of the Dark Light,' the officer sneered.

After a couple of steps Will's legs gave way and he fell heavily on to his knees. Chester dashed over to him, panic-stricken at his friend's condition.

'Will, Will, what have they done to you?' Chester was frantic as he helped him over to the ledge. 'You've been gone for hours.'

'Just tired . . .' Will managed to mumble as he slumped down on the ledge and rolled up in a ball, grateful for the coolness of the lead lining against his aching head. He shut his eyes . . . he just wanted to sleep . . . but his head was still spinning and waves of nausea were breaking over him.

'YOU!' the officer bellowed. Chester jumped up from beside Will and turned to the officer, who beckoned to him with a thick forefinger.

'Your turn.'

Chester looked down at Will, who now lay unconscious.

'Oh no.'

'NOW!' the officer ordered. 'Don't make me ask you again.'

Chester reluctantly came out into the aisle. After locking the door the officer took him by the arm and marched him off.

'What's a Dark Light?' Chester said, his eyes glazed with fear.

'Just questions,' the officer smiled. 'Nothing to worry about.'

'But I don't know anything . . .'

*

Will was woken by the sound of a hatch being pulled back at the base of the door.

'Food,' a voice announced coldly.

He was starving. He lifted himself up on to one arm, his body aching dully as if he had the flu. Every bone and muscle complained when he tried to move.

'Oh, God!' he groaned, and then suddenly thought of Chester. The open food hatch shed a little more illumination than usual into the cell and, as he looked about him, there on the floor at the base of the lead-covered ledge, was his friend, lying in a foetal position. Chester's breathing was shallow, and his face pale and feverish.

Will staggered up on to his legs and, with difficulty, fetched the two trays back to the ledge. He inspected the contents briefly. There were two bowls with something in them and some liquid in battered tin cups. It all looked terribly unappetizing, but at least it was hot, and didn't smell too bad.

'Chester?' he said, crouching down by his friend. Will felt awful – he, and he alone, was responsible for everything that was happening to both of them. He began to shake Chester gently by the shoulder. 'Hey, are you all right?'

'Urgh . . . wha . . .?' his friend moaned and tried to lift his head. Will could see his nose had been bleeding; the blood was caked and smudged across his cheek.

'Food, Chester. Come on, you'll feel better once you've eaten something.'

Will pulled Chester into a sitting position, propping his back against the wall. He moistened his sleeve with the liquid from one of the cups and began to dab at the blood on Chester's face with it.

'Leave me alone!' Chester objected weakly, trying to push him away.

'That's an improvement. Here, eat something,' Will said, handing a bowl to Chester, who immediately pushed it away.

'I'm not hungry. I feel terrible.'

'At least drink some of this. I think it's some sort of herb tea.' Will handed the drink to Chester, who cupped his hands around the warm mug. 'What did they ask you?' Will mumbled through a mouthful of the grey mush.

'Everything. Name . . . address . . . your name . . . all that stuff. I can't remember most of it. I think I fainted . . . I really thought I was going to die,' Chester said in a flat voice, staring into the middle distance.

Will began to chuckle quietly. Strange as it may seem, his own suffering seemed to be relieved somewhat by hearing his friend's complaints.

'What's so funny?' Chester asked, outrage in his voice. 'It's not funny at all.'

'No,' Will laughed. 'I know. Sorry. Here, try some of this. It's actually quite good.'

Chester shuddered with disgust at the grey slurry in the bowl. Nevertheless, he picked up the spoon and poked at it, somewhat suspiciously at first. Then he sniffed at it.

'Doesn't smell too bad,' he said, trying to convince himself.

'Just bloody eat it, will you?' Will said, filling his mouth again. He felt his strength begin to return with each mouthful. 'I keep thinking I said something about Mum and Rebecca to them, but I'm not sure if I didn't dream it.' He swallowed, then was silent for several seconds, biting the inside of his mouth as something began to trouble him. 'I just hope I haven't got them in trouble too.' He took another mouthful and, still chewing, continued speaking as the recollections came back to him. 'And Dad's journal – I keep seeing it in my mind, clear as anything – as if I'm there, watching, as their long white fingers open it and turn the pages, one by one. But that can't have happened, can it? It's all mixed up. What about you?'

Chester shifted a little. 'I don't know. I might have mentioned the cellar in your house . . . and your family . . . your mum . . . and Rebecca . . . yes . . . I could have told them something about her . . . but . . . oh God, I don't know . . . it's so jumbled up. It's like I can't remember if it's what I *said*, or what I *thought*.' He put his mug down and cradled his head in his hands while Will leant back, peering up at the dark ceiling.

'Wonder what time it is,' he sighed, 'up there.'

Over what must have been the next week, there followed more interrogations with the Styx, the Dark Light leaving both of them with the same awful side effects as before: exhaustion, a befuddled uncertainty about just what it was that they had told their tormentors, and the appalling bouts of sickness that ensued.

Then came a day when the boys were left alone. Although they couldn't be certain, they both felt that surely the Styx must have got all they wanted for now, and hoped against hope that the sessions were finally over.

And so the hours passed and the two boys slept fitfully, mealtimes came and went, and they divided their time between pacing the floor, when they felt strong enough, and resting on the ledge, even occasionally shouting at the door, but to no avail. And in the constant, unchanging light, they lost all sense of time, and of day or night.

Beyond the walls of their cell, serpentine processes were in play: investigations, meetings and chatterings, all in the scratchy secret language of the Styx, were deciding their fate.

Ignorant of this, the boys worked hard to keep their spirits up. In hushed tones, they talked at length about how they might escape, and whether Rebecca would eventually piece it all together and lead the authorities to the tunnel in the cellar. How they kicked themselves for not leaving a note! Or maybe Will's father was the answer to their problems – would he somehow get them out of there? And what day of the week was it? And more importantly, not having washed for some time now, their clothes must have taken on a decidedly funky aroma, and that being the case, why did they not smell any worse to each other?

It was during one particularly lively debate, about who these people were and where they had come from, that the inspection hatch shot back and the Second Officer leered in. They both immediately fell silent as the door was unlocked and the grim, familiar figure all but blotted out the light from the aisle. *Which of them was it to be this time?*

'Visitors.'

They looked at each other in disbelief.

'Visitors? For us?' Chester asked incredulously.

The officer shook his massive head, then looked at Will. 'You.'

'What about Ches—?'

'You, come on. NOW!' the officer shouted.

'Don't worry, Chester, I won't go anywhere without you,' Will said confidently to his friend, who sat back with a pained smile and nodded in silent affirmation.

Will stood up and shuffled out of the cell. Chester watched as the door clanged shut. Finding himself once more alone, he looked down at his hands, rough and ingrained with dirt, and longed for home and comfort. He felt the increasingly frequent sting of frustration and helplessness, and his eyes filled with hot tears. No, he wouldn't cry, he would not give them the satisfaction. He knew Will would work something out, and that he'd be ready when he did.

'Come on, stupid,' he said quietly to himself, wiping his eyes with his sleeve. 'Drop and give me twenty,' he mimicked his football coach's voice as he got down on the floor and began to do press-ups, counting as he did so.

Will was shown into a whitewashed room with a polished floor and some chairs arranged around a large oak table. Sitting behind this were two figures, still a little bleary to him as his sight hadn't yet adjusted from the darkness of the Hold. He rubbed his eyes and then glanced down at his front. His shirt was filthy and, worse still, specked with dried traces of his vomit. He brushed at it feebly before his attention was drawn to an odd-looking hatch or window on the wall to his left. The surface of the glass, if it *was* glass, had a peculiar blue-black depth to it. And this matt and mottled surface didn't seem to be reflecting any of the light from the orbs in the room.

For some reason, Will couldn't take his eyes off the surface. He felt a sudden twinge of recognition. A new, yet familiar feeling swept over him: *they* were behind there. *They* were watching all this. And the longer he stared, the more the darkness filled him, just as it had with the Dark Light. He felt a sudden spasm in his head. He pitched forward as though he was about to faint and his left hand groped wildly and found the back-rest of the chair in front of him. The officer, seeing this, caught him by his other arm and helped him to sit down, facing the pair of strangers.

Will took some deep breaths and the light-headedness passed. He looked up as someone coughed. Opposite him sat a large man and, at his side but a little behind him, a young boy. The man was much like all the others Will had seen – it could easily have been the Second Officer in civilian clothing. He was staring fixedly at Will with barely concealed contempt. Will felt too drained to care, and numbly returned the stranger's gaze.

Then, as chair legs grated loudly on the floor and the boy moved closer to the table, Will focused his attention on him. The boy was looking at Will with an expression of wonder. He had an open and friendly face, the first friendly countenance that Will had seen down there since he had been arrested. Will estimated that the boy was probably a couple of years younger than himself. His hair was almost white and closely cropped, and his soft blue eyes shimmered with mischievousness. As the corners of the boy's mouth curled into a smile, Will thought that he seemed vaguely familiar. He tried desperately to remember where he'd seen him before, but his mind was still too cloudy and unclear. He narrowed his eyes at the boy and tried again to work out where he knew him from, but it was no use. It was as if he was casting around in a murky pool, trying to find something precious with only his sense of touch to guide him. His head began to spin, and he clenched his eyes shut and kept them that way.

He heard the man clear his throat. 'I am Mr Jerome,' he said in a flat and perfunctory tone. It was clear from his voice that he was uncomfortable with the situation, and very resentful at being there. 'This is my son . . .'

'Cal,' Will heard the boy say.

'Caleb,' the man quickly corrected.

There was a long and awkward pause, but Will still didn't open his eyes. He felt insulated and safe with them shut. It was oddly comforting.

Mr Jerome looked testily at the Second Officer. 'This is useless,' he grunted. 'It's a waste of bloody time.'

The officer leaned forward and brusquely prodded Will's shoulder. 'Sit up and be civil to your family. Show some respect.'

Startled, Will's eyes snapped open. He swivelled in his chair to look at the officer in amazement.

'What?'

'I said be civil,' he nodded to Mr Jerome, 'to your *family*, like.'

Will swivelled back to face the man and boy.

'What are you on about?'

Mr Jerome shrugged and looked down, and the boy frowned, his gaze switching between Will, the officer and his father, as if he didn't quite understand what was happening.

'Chester's right, you're all bloody mad down here,' Will exclaimed, and flinched as the Second Officer took a step towards him with his hand raised. But the situation was defused by the boy as he spoke out.

'You must remember this?' he said, delving into an old canvas bag on his lap. All eyes were on him as he finally produced a small object and placed it on the table in front of Will. It was a carved wooden toy, a rat or a mouse. Its white painted face was chipped and faded and its little formal coat was threadbare, yet its eyes glowed eerily. Cal looked expectantly at Will.

'Grandma said it was your favourite,' he continued, as Will failed to react. 'It was given to me after you went.'

'What are you . . .?' Will asked, perplexed. 'After I went where?'

'Don't you remember anything?' Cal asked. He looked deferentially at his father, who was now sitting back in his chair with his arms crossed.

Will reached out and picked up the little toy to examine it more closely. As he tipped it back, he noticed that the eyes closed, a tiny shutter counterbalancing in the head to extinguish the light. He realized that there must be a minute light orb within its head, which gave out light through the glass beads that were the animal's eyes.

'It sleeps,' Cal said, then added, 'You had that very toy . . . in your cot.'

Will dropped it on the table as abruptly as if it had bitten him. 'What are you talking about?' he snapped at the boy.

There was a moment of uncertainty on everyone's part, and once again an unnerving silence descended over the room, broken only by the Second Officer who began to hum quietly to himself. Cal opened his mouth as if about to speak, but seemed to be struggling to find the words. Will sat looking at the toy animal, until Cal took it off the table and put it away again. Then, looking up at Will, he frowned.

'Your name is Seth,' he said, almost resentfully. 'You're my brother.'

'Hah!' Will laughed dryly in Cal's face and then, as all the bitterness from his treatment at the hands of the Styx welled up inside him, he shook his head and spoke to him harshly. 'Yeah. Right. Anything you say.' Will had just about had enough of this charade. He knew who his family was, and it wasn't this pair of jokers before him.

'It's true. Your mother was my mother. She tried to run away with both of us. She took you Topsoil, but left me with Grandma and Father.'

Will rolled his eyes and twisted around to face the Second Officer. 'Very clever. It's a good trick, but I'm not buying it.'

The officer pursed his lips but said nothing.

'You were taken in by a family of Topsoilers . . .' Cal said, raising his voice.

'Sure, and I'm not about to be *taken in* by a family of stark raving loonies down here!' Will replied angrily, really starting to lose it.

'Don't waste your breath on him, Caleb,' said Mr Jerome, putting a hand on his shoulder. But Cal shook it off and continued, his voice beginning to crack with despair.

'They're not your *real* family. We are. We're your flesh and blood.'

Will stared at Mr Jerome, whose reddened face exuded nothing but loathing. Then he looked again at Cal, who had now sat back despondently, his head bowed. But Will was unimpressed. It was all some sick joke. *Do they really think I'm so stupid that I'd be taken in by this?* he said to himself.

Buttoning his coat, Mr Jerome rose hastily to his feet. 'This is going nowhere,' he said.

And Cal, rising with him, spoke quietly. 'Grandma always said you'd come back.'

'I don't have any grandparents. They're all dead!' Will shouted, jumping up from his chair, his eyes now burning with anger and brimming with tears. He tore over to the glass window in the wall and pressed his face against the surface.

'Very clever!' he yelled at it. 'Nearly had me going there!' He shielded his eyes from the light of the room in an effort to see beyond the glass, but there was nothing, only an unrelenting darkness. The Second Officer grabbed his arm and pulled him away. Will did not resist – the fight had gone out of him for now.

CHAPTER TWENTY-TWO

Rebecca lay on top of her bed, staring up at the ceiling. She'd just had a hot bath and was dressed in her acid-green dressing gown, with her hair up in a towel turban. She was humming softly along to the classical music station on her bedside radio as she mulled over the events of the last three days.

It had all kicked off when she was woken very late one evening by a frantic knocking and ringing at the front door. She'd had to get up and answer it as Mrs Burrows, on the strong sleeping pills she'd recently been prescribed, was dead to the world. A drunken brass band couldn't have roused her if they'd tried.

As Rebecca had opened the front door she'd almost been knocked off her feet by Chester's father, who had burst into the hallway and immediately begun to bombard her with questions.

'Is Chester still here? He hasn't come home yet. We tried to phone, but no one answered.' His face was ashen and he was wearing a crumpled beige mac with the collar skew-whiff, as if he'd put it on in a great hurry. 'We thought he must've decided to stay over. He *is* here, isn't he?'

'I'm not . . .' she started to say, as she happened to look into the kitchen, and realized that the plate of food she'd left out on the side for Will hadn't been touched.

'He said he was helping Will with a project, but . . . is he here? Where's your brother . . . can you get him, please?' Mr Rawls' words tripped over each other as he glanced anxiously down the hall and up the stairs.

Leaving the man fretting to himself, Rebecca ran up to Will's room. She didn't bother to knock; she already knew what she would find. She opened the door and turned on the light. Sure enough, Will wasn't there, and his bed hadn't been slept in. She turned out the light and closed the door behind her, returning downstairs to Mr Rawls.

'No, no sign of him,' she said. 'I think Chester *was* here, though, last night; but I don't know where they might've gone. Maybe—'

On hearing this, Mr Rawls became almost incoherent, gabbling something about checking their usual haunts and getting the police involved as he tore out of the front door, leaving it open behind him.

Rebecca remained in the hallway, chewing her lip. She was furious with herself that she hadn't been more vigilant. With all his secretive behaviour and the skulking about with his new bosom buddy, Will had been up to something for weeks – there was no question about that. *But what?*

She knocked on the sitting-room door and, getting no answer, entered. The room was dark and stuffy, and she could hear regular snoring.

'Mum,' she said with gentle insistence.

'Urphh?'

'Mum,' she said more loudly, shaking Mrs Burrows' shoulder.

'Wha? Nnno . . . smmumph?'

'Come on, Mum, wake up, it's important.'

'Nah,' said an obdurate, sleepy voice.

'Wake up. Will's missing!' Rebecca said urgently.

'Leave . . . me . . . alone,' grumbled Mrs Burrows through an indolent yawn, swinging an arm to warn Rebecca off.

'Do you know where he's gone? And Chester . . .'

'Oh, go awayyyy!' her mother screeched, turning on her side in the chair and pulling the old travelling rug right over her head. The shallow snoring resumed as she returned to her state of hibernation. Rebecca sighed with sheer frustration as she stood next to the shapeless form.

She went into the kitchen and sat down. With the DCI's number in her hand and the cordless phone lying on the table in front of her, she deliberated for a long time over what to do next. It wasn't until the small hours that she actually made the call and, getting only the answering service, left a message. She returned upstairs to her bedroom and tried to read a book while she waited for a response.

The police turned up at precisely 7.06 a.m. After that, events took on a life of their own. The house was filled with uniformed officers searching every room, poking around every closet and chest of drawers. Wearing rubber gloves, they began in Will's room and worked through the rest of the house, ending in the cellar, but apparently found nothing much of interest. She was almost amused when she saw they were retrieving articles of Will's clothing from the laundry basket on the landing and meticulously sealing each item in its own polythene bag before carrying it outside. She wondered what his dirty Y-fronts could possibly tell them.

At first, Rebecca busied herself by straightening up the mess the searchers had left behind, using the activity as an excuse to move around the house and see if she could glean anything from the various conversations that were taking place. Then, as no one seemed to be taking the blindest bit of notice of her, she dropped the pretence of tidying and just strolled around wherever she wanted, spending most of her time in the hallway outside the sitting room where the DCI and a female detective were interviewing Mrs Burrows. From what Rebecca could catch, she seemed to be detached and disturbed in turn, and wasn't able to shed any light at all on Will's current whereabouts.

The searchers eventually decamped to the front of the house, where they stood around smoking and laughing amongst themselves. Shortly afterwards the DCI and the female detective emerged from the sitting room, and Rebecca followed them to the front door. As the DCI walked down the path to the row of parked squad cars, she couldn't help but overhear his words.

'That one's a few volts short of a full charge,' he said to his colleague.

'Very sad,' the female detective said.

'You know . . .' the DCI said, pausing to glance back at the house, 'to lose one family member is unfortunate . . .' His colleague had nodded.

'. . . but to lose two is downright iffy,' the DCI continued. '*Very* bloody iffy, in my book.'

The female detective nodded again, a grim smile on her face.

'We'd better have a sweep of the common, just to be sure,' Rebecca heard him say before he was finally out of earshot.

The next day the police had sent a car for them, and Mrs Burrows was interviewed for several hours, while Rebecca was asked to wait in another room with a lady from the Social Services.

Now, three days later, Rebecca's mind was running over the chain of events again. Closing her eyes, she recalled the deadpan faces down at the police station and the exchanges she'd heard.

'This won't do,' she said, glancing at her watch and seeing the time. She got up from her bed, unwound the towel from her head and dressed quickly.

Downstairs, Mrs Burrows was ensconced in her armchair, curled up fully clothed under the travelling rug that was tucked around her like a drab tartan cocoon. The only light in the room came from a muted Open University programme, the cool blue light pulsing intermittently and causing the shadows to jump and jerk, lending a sort of animation to the furniture and objects in the room. She was sleeping deeply when a noise in the room brought her awake. A deep murmur, like a strong wind combing through the branches of the trees in the garden outside. She opened her eyes a fraction. In the far corner of the room, by the half-opened curtains of the French windows, she could make out a large, shadowy form. For a moment she wondered if she was dreaming, as the shadow shifted and changed under the light cast by the television. She strained to make out just what was there. She wondered if it could be an intruder. *What should she do? Pretend to be asleep? Or lie quite still so the intruder wouldn't bother her?*

She held her breath, trying to control her rising panic. The seconds felt like hours as the shape remained stationary. She began to think that maybe it was just an innocent shadow after all. A trick of the light and an overactive imagination. She let the air out of her lungs, opening her eyes fully.

All of a sudden there was a snuffling sound and, to her horror, the shadow split into two distinct ghost-like blurs and closed in on her with blinding speed. As her senses reeled in shock and terror, a calm and collected voice in her head told her with absolute conviction, 'THEY ARE NOT GHOSTS.'

In a flash the figures were upon her. She tried to scream, but no sound came. Rough material brushed against her face as she smelled a peculiar mustiness, something like mildewed clothes. Then a powerful hand struck her and she curled up in pain, winded and struggling for air, until, like a newborn baby, she caught her breath and let out an unholy shriek.

She was powerless to resist as she was scooped out of her chair and borne aloft into the hallway. Now, howling like a banshee and bucking and straining, she glimpsed another figure looming from the doorway of the cellar, and a huge damp hand was clapped over her mouth, stifling her screams.

Who were they? What were they after? Then a terrible thought sprung to mind. Her precious TV and video recorders! That was it! That was what they'd come for! The sheer injustice of it all. It was just too much to take, on top of everything else she'd had to put up with. Mrs Burrows saw red.

Finding energy from nowhere, she summoned the super-human strength of the desperate. She wrestled one of her legs free and instantly kicked out. This caused a flurry of activity as her assailants tried to seize it, but she kicked out again and again as she twisted around. The face of one of her attackers appeared within reach; she saw her chance and lunged forwards, biting down as hard as she could. She found that she had it by its nose, and she shook her head like a terrier with a rat.

There was a bloodcurdling wail, and its hold on her relaxed for a moment. That was enough for Mrs Burrows. As the figures lost their grip on her and fell backwards against each other she found the ground with her feet and swung her arms behind her like a downhill skier. With a yell, she hurtled away from them and into the kitchen, leaving them grasping only the travelling rug that had been around her, like the discarded tail of a fleeing lizard.

In the blink of an eye, Mrs Burrows was back. She swooped into the midst of the three hulking forms. All hell broke loose.

Rebecca, from her vantage point at the top of the stairs, was perfectly placed to watch as it all unfolded. In the half-light of the hallway below, something metallic flashed back and forth and from side to side, and she saw a wild face. Mrs Burrows' face. Rebecca realized that she was wielding a frying pan, swinging it left and right like a cutlass. It was the new one with the extra-wide base and the special non-stick surface.

Time and time again the shadowy forms renewed their attack on her but Mrs Burrows stood her ground, repelling them with multiple blows, the pan resounding satisfyingly as it connected with a skull here or an elbow there. In all the confusion Rebecca could see the streaks of movement as the salvo of blows continued at an incredible rate, boinging away to a chorus of grunts and groans.

'DEATH!' screamed Mrs Burrows. 'DIE, DIE!'

One of the shadowy figures reached out in an attempt to grab Mrs Burrows' pan arm as it wheeled around in figures of eight, only to be walloped by a tremendous bone-shattering swipe. He let out a deep howl like a wounded dog, and staggered back, the others falling back with him. Then, as one, they turned on their heels, and the three of them scuttled out through the open front door. They moved with startling speed, like cockroaches caught in the light, and were gone.

In the stillness that ensued, Rebecca crept down the stairs and flicked on the hall light. Mrs Burrows, her bedraggled hair hanging in dark wisps across her white face like limp horns, immediately shifted her maniacal gaze on to Rebecca.

'Mum,' Rebecca said softly.

Mrs Burrows raised the pan above her head and lurched towards her. The feral look of wild-eyed fury on her face made Rebecca take a step back, thinking she was about to turn on her.

'Mum! Mum, it's me, it's all right, they've gone . . . they've all gone now!'

A look of odd self-satisfaction spread across Mrs Burrows' face as she checked herself and nodded slowly, appearing to recognize her daughter.

'It's all right, Mum, really.' Rebecca tried to pacify her. She ventured closer to the rapidly panting woman and gently eased the frying pan from her grip. Mrs Burrows didn't put up any resistance.

Rebecca sighed with relief and, looking around, noticed some dark splatters on the hall carpet. It could have been mud or – she looked closer and frowned – blood.

'If they bleed,' Mrs Burrows intoned, following Rebecca's gaze, 'I can kill them.' She drew her lips back revealing her teeth as she let out a low growl, then started to laugh horribly, an unnatural, grating cackle.

'How about a nice cup of tea?' Rebecca asked, forcing a smile as Mrs Burrows quietened down again. Putting an arm around her waist, she steered her in the direction of the sitting room.

CHAPTER TWENTY-THREE

W ill was rudely woken by the cell door crashing back and the First Officer hauling him to his feet. Still thick with sleep, he was bundled out of the Hold, through the reception area of the station, out of the main entrance and on to the top of the stone stairs.

The officer let go of him and he tottered down a couple of steps until he found his footing. There he stood, groggy and more than a little disoriented. He heard a thump next to him as his rucksack landed by his feet, and without a word the officer turned his back and went into the station.

It was a strange feeling, standing there bathed in the glow of the street lights after being confined in that gloomy cell for so long. There was a slight breeze on his face – it was damp and musty but, all the same, it was a relief after the airlessness of the Hold.

What happens now? he thought to himself, scratching his neck under the collar of the coarse shirt he'd been given by one of the officers. His mind still befuddled, he started to yawn, but stifled it as he heard a noise: a restless horse brayed and stamped a hoof against the damp cobbles. Will immediately looked up and saw a dark carriage a little way down on the other side of the road, to which two pure-white horses were hitched. At the front, a coachman sat holding the reins. The carriage door swung open, and Cal jumped out and crossed the street towards him.

'What's this?' Will asked suspiciously, backing up a step as Cal approached.

'We're taking you home,' Cal replied.

'Home? What do you mean, home? With you? I'm not going anywhere without Chester!' he said resolutely.

'Shhhh, don't. Listen!' Cal now stood close to him and spoke with urgency. 'They're watching us.' He inclined his head down the street, his eyes never leaving Will's.

On the corner was a sole figure, dark as a disembodied shadow, standing stock-still. Will could just make out the white collar.

'I'm not leaving without Chester,' Will hissed.

'What do you think will happen to him if you *don't* come with us? Think about it.'

'But—'

'They can be easy on him, or they can not. It's up to you.' Cal looked pleadingly into Will's eyes.

Will glanced back at the station one last time, then sighed and shook his head. 'All right.'

Cal smiled and, picking up Will's rucksack for him, led the way over to the waiting carriage. He held the door open for Will who followed grudgingly, his hands in his pockets and his head down. He didn't like this at all.

As the carriage pulled away, Will studied the austere interior. It certainly wasn't built for comfort. The seats, like the side panels, were made of a hard, black-lacquered wood, and the whole thing smelled of varnish with a faint hint of bleach, rather reminiscent of a school gym on the first day of term. Still, anything was better than the cell in which he'd been locked up for so many days with Chester. Will felt a sudden pang as he thought of his friend, still incarcerated and now alone in the Hold. He wondered if Chester had even been told that he'd been whisked away, and swore to himself that he'd find a way of getting his friend out of there if it was the last thing he did.

He slumped back dejectedly in his seat and put his feet up on the opposite bench, then pulled back the leathery curtain and stared through the open window of the carriage. As the coach rattled through the cavernous, deserted streets, bleak houses and unlit shop fronts passed with monotonous regularity. Copying Will, Cal also settled back and rested his feet on the seat in front of him, occasionally giving Will sidelong glances and smiling contentedly to himself.

Both boys remained silent, lost in their own thoughts, but it wasn't long before Will's natural inquisitiveness began to revive slightly. He made a concerted effort to take in the murky sights passing him by but, after a short while, his eyelids grew heavier and heavier as his extreme weariness and the seemingly endless underworld got the better of him. Finally, lulled by the rhythmic beat of the horses' hooves, he nodded off, occasionally waking with a start when the carriage's buffeting roused him. With a somewhat startled expression, he would look about self-consciously, much to Cal's amusement, and then his head would droop and he'd succumb to his fatigue again.

He didn't know if he'd been asleep for minutes or even hours when the driver cracked his whip, waking him again.

The carriage surged forwards, and the lampposts flicked past the window at less regular intervals. Will assumed they must be reaching the outskirts of the town. Wider areas opened up between the buildings, carpeted by dark green, almost black beds of lichens or something similar. Then came strips of land at either side of the road, which were divided into plots by rickety-looking fences, and contained beds of what appeared to be some sort of large fungi.

At one point, their speed dropped as they crossed a small bridge spanning an inky-looking canal. Will stared down into the slow and torpid water, flowing like crude oil, and for some reason it filled him with an inexplicable dread.

He had just settled back into his seat and was beginning to doze off again, when the road suddenly dipped down a steep incline and the carriage veered left. Then, as the road levelled out once more, the driver shouted 'Whoa!' and the horses slowed to a trot.

Will was wide awake now, and stuck his head out of the window to see what was going on. There was a huge metal gate blocking the way, and to the side of this a group of men huddled around a brazier as they warmed their hands. Standing apart from them in the middle of the road, a hooded figure held a lamp high and was waving it from side to side as a signal for the coachman to stop. As the carriage ground to a halt, to Will's horror he spotted the instantly recognizable figure of a Styx emerging from the shadows. Will quickly yanked the curtain shut and ducked back into the carriage. He looked questioningly at Cal.

'It's the Skull Gate. It's the main portal to the Colony,' Cal explained in a reassuring tone.

'I thought we were already in the Colony.'

'No,' Cal replied incredulously, 'that was only the Quarter. It's sort of . . . like an outpost . . . our frontier town.'

'So there's more beyond this?'

'More? God, there's *miles* of it!'

Will was speechless. He looked fearfully at the door as the clipped sound of boot heels on cobblestones drew nearer. Cal grabbed his arm. 'Don't worry, they check everyone who goes through. Just say nothing. If there's a problem, I'll do all the talking.'

At that very moment, the door on Will's side was pulled open and the Styx shone a brass lamp into the interior. He played the beam across their faces, then took a step back and shone it up at the coachman, who handed him a piece of paper. He read it with a cursory glance. Apparently satisfied, he returned to the boys once more, directed the dazzling light straight into Will's eyes and, with a contemptuous sneer, slammed the door shut. He handed the note back to the driver, signalled to the gateman, turned on his heels and walked away.

Hearing a loud clanking, Will warily lifted the hem of the curtain and peered out again. As the guard waved them on, the light from his lantern revealed that the gate was in fact a portcullis. Will watched as it rose jerkily into a structure that made him blink with astonishment. Carved from a lighter stone and jutting from the wall above the portcullis, it was an immense toothless skull.

'That's pretty creepy,' Will muttered under his breath.

'It's meant to be. It's a warning,' Cal replied indifferently as the coachman lashed his whip and the carriage lurched through the mouth of the fearsome apparition and into the cavern beyond.

Leaning out of the window, Will watched the portcullis juddering down behind them again until the curve of the tunnel hid it from sight. As the horses picked up speed, the carriage turned a corner and raced down a steep incline into a giant tunnel hewn out of the dark-red sandstone. It was completely devoid of buildings and houses. As the tunnel continued to descend, the air began to change – it began to smell of smoke – and for a moment the ever-present background hum grew in intensity until it rattled the very fabric of the carriage itself.

They made a final sharp turn, and the humming lessened and the air grew cleaner again. Cal joined Will at the window as a massive space yawned before them. Either side of the road stood rows of buildings, a complex forest of brick ducts running over the cavern walls above them, like bloated varicose veins. In the distance, dark stacks vented cold blue flames and streamed vertical plumes of smoke which, largely undisturbed by air currents, rose to the roof of the cavern. Here the smoke accumulated, rippling slowly and resembling a gentle swell on the surface of an inverted brown ocean.

'This is the Colony, Will,' said Cal, his face next to Will's at the narrow window. 'This is . . .'

Will just stared in wonder, hardly daring to breathe.

'. . . home.'

CHAPTER TWENTY-FOUR

Around the same time that Will and Cal were arriving at the Jerome house, Rebecca was standing patiently beside a lady from Family Welfare on the thirteenth floor of Mandela Heights, a dreary, run-down tower block on the seamier side of Wandsworth. The social worker was ringing the bell of Number 65 for the third time without getting a reply, whilst Rebecca looked about her at the dirty floor. With a low, remorseful moan, the wind was blowing through the broken windows of the stairwell and flapping the partially filled bin bags heaped in one corner.

Rebecca shivered. It wasn't just because of the chill wind, but because she was about to be delivered to what she considered to be one of the worst places on Earth.

By now, the social worker had given up pressing the grimy doorbell and had started knocking loudly. There was still no reply, but the sound of the television could clearly be heard from within. She knocked again, more insistently this time, and stopped as she finally heard the sound of coughing and a woman's strident voice from the other side of the door.

'All right, all right, for Gawd's sake, giv'us a chance!'

The social worker turned to Rebecca and tried to smile reassuringly. She only managed something approaching a pitying grimace.

'Looks like she's in.'

'Oh, good,' Rebecca said sarcastically, picking up her two small suitcases.

They waited in an awkward silence as, with much fumbling, the door was unlocked and the chain removed, accompanied by mutterings and curses, and punctuated by intermittent coughing. The door finally swung open and a rather dishevelled middle-aged woman, a cigarette hanging from her bottom lip, looked the social worker up and down suspiciously.

'What's all this about?' she asked, one eye squinting from the smoke streaming from her cigarette, which twitched with all the vigour of a conductor's baton as she spoke.

'I've brought your niece, Mrs Boswell,' the social worker announced, indicating Rebecca standing beside her.

'You what?' the woman said sharply, shedding ash on the social worker's immaculate shoes. Rebecca cringed.

'Don't you remember . . . we spoke on the phone yesterday?'

Her watery gaze settled on Rebecca, who smiled and leaned forward a little to come within her limited field of vision. 'Hello, Auntie Jean,' she said, doing her best to smile.

'Rebecca, love, of course, yes, look at you, 'aven't you grown? Quite the young lady.' Auntie Jean coughed and opened the door fully. 'Yes, come in, come in, I've got something on the boil.' She turned and shuffled back into the small hallway, leaving Rebecca and the social worker to survey the haphazard piles of curling newspapers stacked along the walls, and the huge number of unopened letters and pamphlets littering the filthy carpet. Everything was covered with a fine film of dust, and the corners of the hallway were festooned with cobwebs. The whole place stank of Auntie Jean's cigarettes. The social worker and Rebecca stood in silence until the social worker, as if pulling herself out of a trance, abruptly bade Rebecca goodbye and good luck. She seemed in a mad haste to leave and Rebecca watched her as she made for the stairs, pausing on the way to glance at the lift doors as if she was hoping that by some miracle it was back in service and that she wasn't facing the long trek down.

Rebecca gingerly entered the flat, and followed her aunt into the kitchen.

'I could do with some 'elp in 'ere,' Auntie Jean said, picking out a packet of cigarettes from amongst the debris on the table.

Rebecca surveyed the squalid vision that lay before her. Shafts of sunlight cut through the ever-present fog of cigarette smoke that hung about her aunt like a personal storm cloud. She wrinkled her nose as she caught the acrid taint of yesterday's burned food lacing the air.

'If you're going to be staying in my gaff,' her aunt said through a fit of coughing, 'you're going to 'ave to pull your weight.'

Rebecca didn't move; she feared any motion, however slight, would result in her being covered in the grime that covered every surface.

'C'mon, Becs, put your bags down, roll up your sleeves. You can start by putting the kettle on.' Auntie Jean smiled as she sat down at the kitchen table. She lit a fresh cigarette from the old one before stubbing out its glowing stump directly on the Formica tabletop, completely missing the overflowing ashtray.

The interior of the Jerome household was rich and comforting, with subtly patterned carpets, burnished wood surfaces and walls of deep greens and burgundies. Cal took Will's rucksack from him and set it down by a small table, on which an oil lamp with a vaseline glass shade stood on a creamy linen doily.

'In here,' Cal said, indicating Will should follow him through the first door leading off the hallway. 'This is the drawing room,' he announced proudly.

The atmosphere in the room was warm and muggy, with tiny gusts of fresh air coming from a dirt-encrusted grille above where they now stood. The ceiling was low with ornate plaster mouldings, turned an off-white by the smoke and soot from the fire that even now roared in the wide hearth. In front of this, sprawled on a worn Persian rug, was a large, mangy-looking animal asleep on its back with its legs in the air, shamelessly displaying a pair of pendulous testicles.

'A dog!' Will was a little surprised to see a domestic pet down here. The animal was the colour of rubbed slate; it was almost completely bald, with just the odd patch of dark stubble or tuft of hair erupting here and there from its loose skin, which sagged like an ill-fitting suit.

'Dog? That's Bartleby, he's a cat, a Rex variant. An excellent hunter.'

Astonished, Will looked again. *A cat?* It was the size of a well-fed, badly-shaved Dobermann. There was nothing the slightest bit feline about the animal, whose large ribcage slowly rose and fell with its regular breathing. As Will bent over to examine it more closely, it snorted loudly in its sleep, and its huge paws twitched.

'Careful, he'll take your face off.'

Will swung around to see an old woman in one of the two large leather winged chairs positioned either side of the fire-place. She had been sitting well back when he had come in and he hadn't seen her.

'I wasn't going to touch him,' he answered defensively, straightening up.

The old woman's pale-grey eyes twinkled and never left Will's face.

'He doesn't have to be touched,' she said, and added, 'He's very instinctive, is our Bartleby.' Her face glowed with affection as she glanced at the luxuriating and oversized animal.

'Grandma, this is Will,' Cal said.

Once again the old lady's knowing gaze returned to Will and she nodded. 'Of that I am well aware. He's a Macaulay from head to toe, and has his mother's eyes, and no mistake. Hello, Will.'

Will was struck dumb, transfixed by her gentle manner and the vibrant light dancing in her old eyes. It was as though some part of him, a vague memory, had been lit, just as a dying ember is rekindled by a faint breeze. He felt immediately at ease in her presence. *But why?* He was naturally wary when meeting adults for the first time, and down here in this strangest of places he couldn't afford to let his guard drop. He'd decided to go along with these people, to play their game, but he wasn't about to trust any of them. However with this old woman, it was different. It was as if he *knew* her . . .

'Come and sit yourself down, talk to me. I'm sure there's lots of fascinating tales you can tell me from your life up there.' She lifted her face momentarily towards the ceiling. 'Caleb, put the kettle on and let's have some fancies. Will's going to tell me all about himself,' she said, motioning towards the other leather chair with a delicate yet strong hand. It was the hand of a woman who'd had to work hard all her life.

Will perched on the edge of the seat, the lively fire warming and relaxing him. Although he couldn't explain it to himself, he felt as if he'd reached a place of safety at last, a sanctuary.

The old lady looked intently at him and he unselfconsciously looked straight back at her, the warmth of her attention every bit as comforting as the fire in the hearth. All the horror and the trials of his time in prison were forgotten for the moment, and he sighed and sat back, regarding her with mounting curiosity.

Her hair was fine and a snowy white, and she wore it in an elaborate bun at the top of her head, held in place by a tortoiseshell slide. She was dressed in a plain blue long-sleeved dress, with a white ruffled collar high up on the neck.

'Why do I feel as though I know you?' he asked suddenly. He had the oddest feeling that he could say whatever was on his mind to this complete stranger.

'Because you do,' she smiled. 'I held you as a baby, I sang you lullabies.'

He opened his mouth, about to protest that what she'd said couldn't be true, but he stopped himself. He frowned. Once again, from deep within him came a glimmer of recognition. It was as if every fibre of his body was telling him that she was speaking the truth. There was just something so familiar about the old lady. His throat tightened and he swallowed several times, trying to control his feelings. The old woman saw the emotion welling up in his eyes.

'She would've been so proud of you, you know,' Grandma Macaulay said. 'You were her first-born.' She inclined her head towards the mantelpiece. 'Would you hand me that picture – there, in the middle?'

Will stood up to examine the many photographs in frames of different shapes and sizes. He didn't immediately recognize any of the subjects; some were grinning preposterously, and some had the most solemn faces. They all had the same ethereal quality as the daguerreotypes, the old photographs showing the ghost-like images of people from the distant past, which he'd seen in his father's museum in Highfield. As the old lady had asked, he reached for the largest photograph of them all, which held pride of place in the very centre of the mantelpiece. Seeing that it was of Mr Jerome and a younger version of Cal, he hesitated.

'Yes, that's the one,' the old lady confirmed.

Will handed it to her, watching as she turned it over on her lap, unclipped the catches and lifted off the back. There was another picture concealed within it, which she levered out with her fingernails and passed to him without comment.

Turning it to catch the light, he studied the print closely. It showed a young woman in a white blouse and a long black skirt. In her arms, the woman held a small bundle. Her hair was the whitest of whites, identical to Will's, and her face was beautiful, a strong face with kind eyes and a fine bone structure, a full mouth and a square jaw . . . *his* jaw, which he now touched involuntarily.

'Yes,' the old lady said softly, 'that's Sarah, your mother.

You're just like her. That was taken just weeks after you were born.'

'Huh?' Will gasped, nearly dropping the picture.

'Your real name is Seth . . . that's what you were christened. That's you she's holding.'

He felt as though his heart had stopped. He peered at the bundle. He could see it was a baby but couldn't make out its face clearly because of the swaddling. His mind raced and his hands trembled, as his feelings and thoughts bled into one another. But through all this, something definite emerged and *connected*, as if he'd been wrestling with a hitherto insoluble problem and suddenly discovered the answer. As if buried deep in his subconscious there had been a tiny question hidden away, an unadmitted suspicion that his family, Dr and Mrs Burrows and Rebecca, all he'd known for his life, were somehow different from him.

He was having problems focusing on the picture, and forced himself to look at it again, scouring it for detail.

'Yes,' Grandma Macaulay said in a gentle voice, and he found himself nodding. However irrational it may seem, he knew, knew with absolute certainty that what she was saying was true. That this woman in the photograph, with the monochrome and slightly blurry face, was his *real* mother, and that all these people he'd so recently met were his *true* family. He couldn't explain it even to himself, he just knew.

His suspicions that they were trying to deceive him, and that this was all some elaborate trick, evaporated and a tear ran down his cheek, drawing a pale, delicate line on his unwashed face. He hurriedly brushed it away with his hand. As he passed the photograph back to Grandma Macaulay, he was aware that his face was flushing.

'Tell me what it's like up there – Topsoil,' she said, to spare him his embarrassment. He was grateful, still standing awkwardly by her chair as she put the frame together again, then held it out for him to replace on the mantelpiece.

'Well . . .' he began falteringly.

'You know, I've never seen daylight or felt the sun on my face. How does that feel? They say it burns.'

Will, now back in his chair, looked across at her. He was staggered. 'You've never seen the sun?'

'Very few here have,' Cal said, coming back into the room and squatting down on the hearth rug at his grandmother's feet. He began gently kneading the loose and rather scabby flap of skin under the cat's chin; almost at once a loud, throbbing purr filled the room.

'Tell us, Will, tell us what it's like,' Grandma Macaulay said, her hand resting on Cal's head as he leaned against the arm of her chair.

So Will started to tell them, a little hesitantly at first, but then, as if a torrent had been unleashed, he found he was almost babbling as he spoke about his life above. It astounded him how easy it was, and how very natural it felt, to talk to these people whom he'd only known for such a brief time. He told them about his family and his school, regaling them with stories about the excavations with his father – or rather, the person he'd believed was his father until this moment – and about his mother and his sister.

'You love your Topsoiler family very much, don't you?' Grandma Macaulay said, and Will could only bring himself to nod in response. He knew that none of this, none of these revelations that he might have a *real* family down here in the Colony, would change the way he felt about his father. And no matter how difficult Rebecca had made his life, he had to admit to himself that he missed her terribly. He felt a tremendous surge of guilt, knowing that by now she'd be racked with worry about what had happened to him. Her small and well-ordered world would be unwinding around her. He swallowed hard. *I'm sorry, Rebecca, I should have told you, I should have left a note!* He wondered if she'd called the police after it was discovered that he was missing, the same rather ineffective procedure they'd put into motion when their father had gone. But all this was pushed aside in an instant when the image of Chester, alone and still incarcerated in that awful cell, flashed before him.

'What will happen to my friend?' he blurted out.

Grandma Macaulay didn't answer, staring absently into the fire, but Cal was quick to respond.

'They'll never let him go back . . . or you.'

'But why?' Will asked. 'We'll promise not to say anything . . . about all this.'

There were a few seconds of silence and then Grandma Macaulay coughed gently.

'It wouldn't wash with the Styx,' she said. 'They couldn't have anyone telling the Topsoilers about us. It might bring about the Discovery.'

'The Discovery?'

'It's what we're taught in the Book of Catastrophes. It is the end of all things, when the people are ferreted out and perish at the hands of those above,' Cal said flatly, as if reciting verse.

'God forbid,' the old lady murmured, averting her eyes and staring into the flames again.

'So what will they do with Chester?' Will asked, dreading

the answer.

'Either he'll be put to work, or he might be Banished . . . sent on a train down to the Deeps, and left to fend for himself,' Cal replied.

Will was about to ask what the Deeps were, when out in the hall the front door was flung open with a bang. The fire flared and threw up a shower of sparks, which glowed briefly as they were drawn up the chimney. Grandma Macaulay peered around the side of her armchair, smiling as Cal and Bartleby both leaped to their feet. A powerful man's voice bellowed, 'HELLO IN THERE!'

Still sleep-ridden, the cat blundered sideways against the underside of an occasional table, which crashed to the ground at the same instant as the drawing-room door burst open. A massive, thickset man entered the room like dirty thunder, his pale yet ruddy-cheeked face beaming with undisguised excitement.

'WHERE IS HE? WHERE IS HE?' he shouted, and locked his fierce gaze on Will, who rose apprehensively from his chair, uncertain what to make of this human explosion. In two strides, the man had crossed the room and clasped Will in a bear hug, hoisting him off his feet as if he weighed no more than a bag of feathers. Letting out a deafening roar of a laugh, he held Will at arm's length with his feet dangling helplessly in midair.

'Let me look at you. Yes . . . yes, you're your mother's boy, no mistake; it's the eyes, isn't it, Ma? He's got her eyes, and her chin . . . the shape of her handsome face, by God, ha, ha, ha!' he bellowed.

'Do put him down, Tam,' Grandma Macaulay said.

The man lowered Will back down to the floor, still staring

intently into the startled boy's eyes, and grinning and shaking his head.

'It's a great day, a great day indeed.' He stuck out a huge ham of a hand towards Will. 'I'm your Uncle Tam.'

Will automatically held out his hand and Tam took it into his giant palm, shook it in an iron grip and pulled Will in towards him, ruffling his hair with his other hand and sniffing at the top of his head loudly in an exaggerated manner.

'He's awash with Macaulay blood, this one,' he boomed. 'Wouldn't you say so, Ma?'

'Without a doubt,' she said softly. 'But don't you be frightening him with your horseplay, Tam.'

Bartleby was rubbing his massive head against Uncle Tam's oily black trouser legs and insinuating his long body between his and Will's, all the while purring and making an unearthly low whining sound. Tam glanced briefly down at the creature and then up at Cal, who was still standing next to his grandmother's chair, enjoying the spectacle.

'Cal, the magician's apprentice, how are you, lad? What do you think of all this, eh?' He looked from one boy to the other. 'By God, it's good to see you two under the same roof again.' He shook his head in disbelief. 'Brothers, hah, brothers, my nephews. This calls for a drink. A *real* drink.'

'We were just about to have some tea,' Grandma Macaulay intervened quickly. 'Would you care for a cup, Tam?'

He swung around to his mother and smiled broadly with a devilish glint in his eye. 'Why not? Let's have a cup of tea, and catch up.'

With that the old woman disappeared into the hall and Uncle Tam sat down in her vacated chair, which groaned under his weight. Stretching out his legs, he took out a short pipe from the inside of his huge overcoat and filled it from a tobacco pouch. Then he used a taper from the fireside to light the pipe, sat back and blew a cloud of bluish smoke up at the ornate ceiling, all the while looking at the two boys.

For a time, all that could be heard was the crackling of the burning coal, the intrusive purring of Bartleby and the distant sounds of the old woman busy in the kitchen. No one felt the need to talk as the flickering light played on their faces and threw trembling shadows over the walls behind. Eventually, Uncle Tam spoke.

'You know your Topsoiler father passed through here?'

'You saw him?' Will leaned towards Uncle Tam.

'No, but I talked to them that did.'

'Where is he? The policeman said he was safe.'

'Safe?' Uncle Tam sat forward, yanking the pipe from his mouth, his face becoming deadly serious. 'Listen, don't you believe a word those spineless scum say to you; they're all snakes and half-inchers. They're the poisonous toadies of the Styx.'

'That's quite enough, Tam,' Grandma Macaulay said as she entered the room rattling a tray of tea in her unsteady hands, and a plate laden with some 'fancies', as she called them, shapeless lumps topped with white icing. Cal got up and helped her, handing cups to Will and Uncle Tam. Then Will let Grandma Macaulay have his chair and sat next to Cal on the hearth rug.

'So, about my dad?' Will asked a little sharply, unable to contain himself any longer.

Tam nodded and relit his pipe, unleashing voluminous shrouds of smoke that enveloped his head in a haze. 'You only missed him by a week or so. He's gone to the Deeps.'

'Banished?' Will sat bolt upright, his face filled with concern as he remembered the term that Cal had used.

'No, no,' Tam exclaimed, gesticulating with his pipe. 'He wanted to go! Curious thing, by all accounts he went willingly . . . no announcements . . . no spectacle . . . none of the usual Styx theatricals.' Uncle Tam drew a mouthful of smoke and blew it out slowly, his brow furrowed. 'I suppose it wouldn't have been much of a show for the people, no ranting and wailing from the condemned.' He stared into the fire, his frown remaining as if he was profoundly baffled by the whole affair. 'In the weeks before he left, he'd been seen wandering around, scribbling in his book . . . bothering folk with his foolish questions. I reckon the Styx thought he was a little . . .' Uncle Tam tapped the side of his head.

Grandma Macaulay cleared her throat and looked at him sternly.

'. . . harmless,' he said, checking himself. 'Reckon that's why they let him roam around like that, but you can bet they watched his every move.'

Will shifted uneasily where he sat on the Persian rug; it felt wrong to be demanding answers from this good-natured and friendly man, this man who was purportedly his uncle, but he couldn't help himself.

'What exactly *are* the Deeps?' he asked.

'The inner circles, the Interior,' Uncle Tam pointed with the stem of his pipe at the floor. 'Down below us. The Deeps.'

'It's a bad place, isn't it?' Cal put in.

'Never been there myself. It's not somewhere you'd choose to go,' Uncle Tam said with a measured look at Will.

'But what's there?' Will asked, dying to learn more about where his father had gone.

'Well, five or so miles down, there are other . . . I suppose you could call them settlements. That's where the Miners' Train stops, where the Coprolites live.' He sucked loudly on his pipe. 'The air's sour down there. It's the end of the line, but the tunnels go further, miles and miles, they say. Legends even tell of an inner world down deep, at the centre, older towns and older cities, larger than the Colony.' Uncle Tam chortled dismissively. 'Reckon it's a load of codswallop, myself.'

'But has anyone ever been down these tunnels?' Will asked, hoping in his heart of hearts that someone had.

'Well, there've been stories. In the year 220 or thereabouts they say a Colonist made it back after years of Banishment. What was his name . . . Abraham something?'

'Abraham de Jaybo,' Grandma Macaulay said quietly.

Uncle Tam glanced at the door and lowered his voice. 'When they found him at the Miners' Station, he was in a ter-rible state, covered in cuts and bruises, his tongue missing – cut out, they say. He was almost starved to death, like a walk-ing corpse. He didn't last long; died a week later from some unknown disease that made his blood boil up through his ears and mouth. He couldn't speak, of course, but some say he made drawings, loads of them, as he lay on his deathbed, too afraid to sleep.'

'What were the drawings of?' Will was wide-eyed.

'All sorts, apparently, infernal machines, strange animals and impossible landscapes, and things no one could under-stand. The Styx said it was all the product of a diseased mind, but others say the things he drew really exist. To this very day the drawings are kept under lock and key in the Governors' vaults . . . though no one I know's ever seen them.'

'God, I'd give anything to look at those,' Will said, enthralled by what he'd just heard.

Uncle Tam gave a deep chuckle.

'What?' Will asked.

'Well, apparently, that Burrows fellow said the selfsame thing when he was told the tale . . . the *selfsame* words, he used.'

CHAPTER TWENTY-FIVE

After all the talk, the tea, the cake and the revelations, Uncle Tam finally rose with a cavernous yawn and stretched his powerful frame with several bone-chilling clicks. He turned to Grandma Macaulay.

'Well, come on, Ma, high time I got you home.'

And with that, they bade their farewells and were gone. Without Tam's booming voice and infectious guffaws to fill it, the house suddenly seemed a very different place.

'I'll show you where you'll be sleeping,' Cal said to Will, who only mumbled in response. It was as though he was under some kind of spell, his mind teeming with new thoughts and feelings that, try as he might, he couldn't keep from rising to the surface like a shoal of hungry fish.

They wandered out into the hallway, where Will perked up slightly. He began to study the succession of portraits hanging there, working his way gradually along.

'I thought your granny lived in this house,' he asked Cal in a distant voice.

'She's allowed to visit me here.' Cal immediately looked away from Will, who wasn't slow in noticing there was more to this than Cal was letting on.

'What do you mean, *allowed to?*'

'Oh, she's got her own place, where Mother and Uncle Tam were born,' Cal said evasively, with a shake of his head. 'C'mon, let's go!' He was halfway up the stairs with the rucksack hooked over his arm when, to his exasperation, he found Will wasn't following him. Peering over the banisters, he saw that he was still hovering by the portraits, his curiosity piqued by something at the end of the hallway.

Will's hunger for discovery and adventure took hold of him again, sweeping aside his sheer fatigue and his preoccupation with all he'd so recently learned. 'What's through here?' he asked, pointing at a black door with a brass handle.

'Oh, it's nothing. Just the kitchen,' Cal replied impatiently.

'Can I have a quick look?' Will said, already heading for the door.

Cal sighed. 'Oh, all right, but there's really nothing to see,' he said in a resigned tone and descended the stairs, stowing the rucksack at the bottom. 'It's *just* a kitchen!'

Pushing through the door, Will found himself in a low-ceilinged room resembling something from a Victorian hospital. And it not only looked but smelled like one too, a strong undercurrent of carbolic blending with indistinct cooking smells. The walls were a dull mushroom colour, and the floor and work surfaces were covered with large white tiles, crazed with a myriad of scratches and fissures. In places, they had been worn into dappled hollows by years of scrubbing.

His attention was drawn to the corner, where a lid was gently clattering on one of a number of saucepans being heated on an antiquated stove of some kind, its heavy frame swollen and glassy with burned-on grease. He leaned over the nearest saucepan but its simmering contents were obscured by wisps of steam as it gave off a vaguely savoury aroma. To his right, beyond a solid-looking butcher's block with a large-bladed cleaver dangling from a hook above, Will spotted another door leading off the kitchen.

'Where does that go?'

'Look, wouldn't you rather . . . ?' Cal's voice tailed off as he realized it was futile to argue with his brother, who was already nosing into the small adjoining room.

Will's eyes lit up when he saw what was in there; it was like an alchemist's storeroom, with shelf upon shelf of squat jars containing unrecognizable pickled items, all horribly distorted by the curvature of the thick glass and discoloured by the oily fluid in which they were immersed. They resembled anatomical specimens preserved in formaldehyde.

On the bottom shelf, laid out on dull metal trays, Will noticed a huddle of objects the size of small footballs, which had a grey-brown dusty bloom to them.

'What are these?'

'They're pennybuns – we grow them all over, but mostly in the lower chambers.'

'What do you use them for?' Will was crouching down, examining their velvety, mottled surfaces.

'They're mushrooms. You eat them. You probably had some in the Hold.'

'Oh, right,' Will said, pulling a face as he stood upright. 'And that?' he said, pointing at some strips of what appeared to be beef jerky hanging from racks above.

Cal smiled broadly. 'You should be able to tell what it is.'

Will hesitated for a moment and then leaned a little closer to one of the strips; it was definitely meat of some description.

It looked like elongated sinews and was the colour of new scabs. He sniffed tentatively, then shook his head.

'No idea.'

'Come on. The smell?'

Will closed his eyes and sniffed again. 'No, it doesn't smell like anything I—' His eyes snapped open and he looked at Cal. 'It's rat, isn't it?' he said, both pleased that he was able to identify it and, at the same time, rather appalled by the finding. 'You eat rat?'

'It's delicious . . . there's nothing wrong with that. Now, tell me what *kind* is it?' Cal asked, revelling in Will's evident disgust. 'Pack, sewer or sightless?'

'I don't *like* rats, let alone eat them. I haven't got the faintest.'

Cal shook his head slowly, with an expression of mock disappointment.

'It's easy, this is sightless,' he said, lifting the end of one of the lengths with his finger and sniffing it himself. 'More gamey than the others – it's a bit special. We usually have it on Sundays.'

They were interrupted by a loud, machine-gun-like humming behind them, and both spun around at the same time. There, purring with all his might, sat Bartleby, his huge amber eyes fixed on the meat strips, and drops of anticipatory saliva dripping off his bald chin.

'Out!' Cal shouted at him, pointing at the kitchen door. The cat didn't move an inch, but sat resolutely on the tiled floor, completely mesmerized by the sight of the meat.

'Bart, I said get out!' Cal shouted again, making to close the door as he and Will entered the kitchen again. The cat snarled threateningly and bared his teeth, a pearly stockade of viciously sharp pegs, as his skin erupted with a wave of goose pimples.

'You insolent mutt!' Cal snapped. 'You know you don't mean that!'

Cal aimed a playful kick at the disobedient animal, which dodged sideways, easily avoiding the blow. Turning slowly, Bartleby gave them both a slightly scornful look over his shoulder, then padded lethargically away, his naked, spindly tail flicking in a gesture of defiance behind him.

'He'd sell his soul for rat, that one,' Cal said, shaking his head and smiling.

After the brief tour of the kitchen, Cal showed Will up the creaking wooden staircase to the top floor.

'This is Father's room,' he said, opening a dark door halfway down the landing. 'We're not supposed to go in here. There'll be hell to pay if he catches us.'

Will quickly glanced back down the stairs to assure himself the coast was clear before following. A huge four-poster bed dominated Mr Jerome's room, so tall it almost touched the ceiling that sagged ominously down towards it. The space around it was bare and featureless, and a single light burned in one corner.

'What was here?' Will asked, noticing a row of lighter patches on the grey wall.

Cal looked at the ghostly squares and frowned. 'Pictures – there used to be lots of them before Father stripped the room out.'

'Why'd he do that?'

'Because of Mother – she'd furnished it, it was her room really,' Cal replied. 'After she left, Father . . .' He fell silent, and as he didn't seem inclined to volunteer any more on the subject Will felt he shouldn't probe further, for the moment anyway. He certainly hadn't forgotten how the photograph Grandma Macaulay had shown him of his mother had been inexplicably hidden away. None of these people – Uncle Tam, Grandma Macaulay or Cal – were divulging the whole story. Whether or not they were indeed his true family – and at moments Will couldn't quite bring himself to accept the fantastical notion that they were – there was evidently more to all this than he was being told. And he was determined to find out what it was.

Back out on the landing, Will paused to admire an impressive light orb supported by a ghostly bronze hand protruding from the wall.

'These lights, where do they come from?' he asked, touching the cool surface of the sphere.

'I don't know. I think they're made in the West Cavern.'

'But how do they work? Dad had one looked at by some experts, but they didn't have a clue.'

Cal regarded the light with a noncommittal air. 'I don't really know. I do know that it was Sir Gabriel Martineau's scientists who discovered the formula—'

'Martineau?' Will interrupted, recalling the name from the entry in his father's journal.

Cal carried on regardless: 'No, I couldn't really tell you what makes them work – I think they use Antwerp glass, though. It has something to do with how the elements mix under pressure.'

'There must be thousands of these down here.'

'Without them we couldn't survive,' Cal replied. 'Their light is like sunlight to us.'

'How do you turn them off?'

'Turn them off?' Cal looked at Will quizzically, the illumination bathing his pale face. 'Why in earth would you want to do that?'

He started down the landing, but Will stayed put. 'So are you going to tell me about this Martineau?' he demanded.

'Sir Gabriel Martineau,' Cal said carefully, as if Will was showing a distinct lack of respect. 'He's the Founding Father – our saviour – he built the Colony.'

'But I read he died in a fire in . . . er . . . well, several centuries ago.'

'That's what they'd have you Topsoilers believe. There was a fire, but he didn't die in it,' Cal replied with a scornful curl of his lip.

'So what happened then?' Will shot back.

'He came down here with the Founding Fathers to live, of course.'

'The Founding Fathers?'

'God!' Cal said in exasperation. 'I'm not going into all that now. You can read about it in the Book of Catastrophes, if you're so interested.'

'The Book . . . ?'

'Oh, do come on,' Cal snapped. He stared at Will and ground his teeth with such irritation that Will refrained from asking any further questions. They continued down the landing and went through a door.

'This is my room. Father arranged another bed when he was told you had to stay with us.'

'Told? Who by?' Will asked in a flash.

Cal raised his eyebrows as if he ought to know better, so Will just looked around the simple bedroom, not much larger than his own back home. Two narrow beds and a wardrobe almost filled it, with very little space in between. He perched on the end of one of the beds and, noticing a set of clothes left on the pillow, glanced up at Cal.

'Yes, they're yours,' Cal confirmed.

'I suppose I could do with a change,' Will muttered, looking down at the filthy jeans he was wearing. He opened the bundle of new clothes and felt the fabric of the waxy trousers. The material was rough, almost scaly to the touch – he guessed it was a coating to keep out the damp.

While Cal lay back on his bed, Will began to get changed. The clothes felt strange and cold next to his skin. The trousers were stiff and scratchy, and fastened with metal buttons and a belt-tie. He wrestled into the shirt without bothering to undo it, and then slowly wriggled his shoulders and arms as if trying to get a new skin to fit. Last of all, he shrugged on the long jacket with the familiar shoulder mantle that they all wore. Although pleased to be out of his filthy clothes, the replacements felt stiff and restrictive.

'Don't worry, they loosen up once they're warm,' Cal said, noticing his discomfort. Then Cal got up and clambered across Will's bed to get to the wardrobe, where he knelt down and slid out an old Peek Freans biscuit tin from beneath it.

'Have a look at these.' He put the tin on Will's bed and prised off the lid.

'This is my collection,' he announced proudly. He fished about in the tin, taking out a battered mobile phone which he handed to Will, who immediately tried to turn it on. It was dead. *Neither use nor ornament*: Will remembered the oft-used phrase his father would trot out on such occasions, which was ironic considering most of Dr Burrows' prize possessions didn't fit into either category.

'And this,' Cal produced a small blue radio and, holding it up to show Will, he clicked on the switch. It crackled with tinny static as he swivelled one of the dials.

'You won't pick anything up down here,' Will said, but Cal was already taking something else out of the tin.

'Look at these, they're fantastic.'

He straightened out some curling car brochures, mottled with chalky spots of mildew, and passed them to Will as if they were priceless parchments. Will frowned as he surveyed them.

'These are very old models, you know,' Will said as he browsed through the pages of sports cars and family saloons. 'The new Capri,' he read aloud and smiled to himself.

He glanced at Cal and noticed the look of total absorption on the boy's face as he lovingly arranged a selection of chocolate bars and a bag of cellophane-wrapped sweets in the bottom of the tin. It was as if he was trying to find the perfect composition.

'What's all the chocolate for?' Will asked, rather hoping that Cal might offer him some.

'I'm saving it for a very special occasion,' Cal said as he lovingly handled a bar of Fruit and Nut. 'I just love the way it smells.' He drew the bar under his nose and sniffed extravagantly. 'That's enough for me . . . I don't need to open it.' He rolled his eyes in ecstasy.

'So where did you get all this?' Will asked, putting down the car brochures, which curled slowly back into a dishevelled tube. Cal glanced warily at the bedroom door and moved a little closer to Will.

'Uncle Tam,' he said in a low voice. 'He often goes beyond the Colony – but you mustn't tell anyone. It would mean Banishment.' He hesitated and glanced at the door again. 'He even goes Topsoil.'

'Does he now?' Will said, scrutinizing Cal's face intently. 'And when does he do that?'

'Every so often.' Cal was speaking so softly that Will had difficulty hearing him. 'He trades things that . . .' he faltered, realizing that he was overstepping the mark, '. . . that he finds.'

'Where?' Will asked.

'On his trips,' Cal said obliquely as he packed the items back into the tin, replaced the lid and pushed it once again under the wardrobe. Still kneeling, he turned to Will.

'You're going to get out, aren't you?' he asked with a sly grin.

'Huh?' Will said, taken aback by the abruptness of the question.

'Come on, you can tell me. You're going to escape, aren't you? I just know it!' Cal was literally vibrating with excitement as he waited for Will's response.

'You mean back to Highfield?'

Cal nodded energetically.

'Maybe, maybe not. I don't know yet,' Will said guardedly. Despite his emotions and everything he felt for his new-found family, he was going to play it safe for now; a small voice in his head was still warning him that this could be part of an elaborate plan to ensnare him and keep him here for ever, and that even this boy who claimed to be his brother could be working for the Styx. He wasn't quite ready to trust him yet, not completely.

Cal looked directly at Will.

'Well, when you do, I'm coming with you.' He was smiling, but his eyes were deadly serious. Will was taken completely unawares by this suggestion, and didn't know how he was going to answer, but at that point was saved by a gong sounding insistently from somewhere in the house.

'That's dinner, Father must be home. Come on.' Cal leaped up and ran out of the door and down the stairs to the dining room, Will following closely behind. Mr Jerome was already seated at the head of a deep-grained wooden table. As they entered, he didn't look up, his eyes remaining fixed on the table in front of him.

The room couldn't have been more different from the sumptuous drawing room Will had seen earlier. It was spartan and the furniture basic, appearing to be constructed from wood that had endured centuries of wear. On closer inspection, he could see that the table and chairs had been fabricated from a mishmash of different woods of conflicting shades and with grains at odds to each other; some parts were waxed or varnished, while others were rough with splintery surfaces. The high-backed dining chairs looked particularly rickety and archaic, with spindly legs that creaked and complained when the boys took their places either side of the sullen-faced Mr Jerome, who barely gave Will a glance. Will shifted in his seat, trying to get comfortable and wondering idly how the chairs could accommodate someone of Mr Jerome's impressive bulk without giving up the ghost.

Mr Jerome cleared his throat loudly and without any warning he and Cal leaned forward, their eyes closed and their hands folded on the table in front of them. A little self-consciously Will did likewise.

'The sun shall no longer set, nor shall the moon withdraw itself, for the Lord will be your everlasting light and the dark days of your mourning will be ended,' Mr Jerome droned.

Will couldn't stop himself from peeping at the man through his half-closed eyes. He found all this a little odd – no one would have *ever* thought of saying grace in his house. Indeed, the closest they ever got to anything resembling a prayer was when his mother yelled, 'For God's sake, shut up!'

'As it is above, so it is below,' Mr Jerome finished.

'Amen,' he and Cal said in unison, too quickly for Will to join in. They sat up, and Mr Jerome tapped a knife on the tumbler in front of him.

There was a moment of uncomfortable silence during which no one at the table was looking at anyone else. Then a man with long, greasy hair shambled into the room. His face was deeply lined and his cheeks were gaunt. He was wearing a leather apron, and his tired and listless eyes, like dying candle flames in cavernous hollows, lingered briefly on Will and then quickly turned away.

As Will watched the man making repeated trips in and out of the room and shuffling to each of them in turn to serve the food, he came to the conclusion that he must have endured great suffering, possibly a severe illness.

The first course was a thin broth. From its steamy vapours, Will could detect a spiciness, as if copious amounts of curry powder had been ladled into it. This came with a side dish of small white objects, similar in appearance to peeled gherkins. Cal and Mr Jerome wasted no time in starting on their soup and, between loud exhalations, they both made the most out-rageous noises as they sucked the liquid from their spoons, splashing large amounts of it over their clothes, which they simply ignored. The symphony of slurps and loud gulps reached such a ridiculous crescendo that Will couldn't stop himself from staring at both of them in utter disbelief.

Finally he picked up his own spoon and was just on the point of taking his first tentative mouthful when, out of the corner of his eye, he saw one of the white objects on his side plate twitch. Thinking he'd imagined it, he emptied the contents of his spoon back into his bowl and used it to roll the object over.

With a shock he found it had a row of tiny dark-brown pointed legs neatly folded beneath it. It was a grub of some kind! He sat bolt upright and watched with horror as it curved its back, its minuscule spiky legs rippling open in a Mexican wave, as if to greet him.

His first thought was that it had got there by mistake, so he glanced at Mr Jerome's and Cal's side plates, wondering if he should say something. At that very moment Cal picked up one of the white objects from his own plate and bit into it, chewing it with gusto. Between his thumb and forefinger, the remaining half of the grub twitched and writhed, oozing a clear fluid over his fingertips.

Will felt his stomach heave, and dropped his spoon in his soup dish with such a crash that the serving man came in and, finding that he was not wanted, promptly exited again. As Will tried to quell his nausea, he saw that Mr Jerome was looking straight at him. It was such a hateful stare that Will immediately averted his eyes. As for Cal, he was intent on finishing the still-writhing half-grub, sucking it into his mouth as if he was devouring a very fat strand of spaghetti.

Will shuddered; there was absolutely no way he could bring himself to drink his soup now, so he sat there feeling distinctly unnerved and out of place until the serving man cleared the bowls away. Then the main course appeared, a gravy-soaked mush just as indeterminate as the broth. Will prodded suspiciously at everything on his plate just to make sure that nothing was still alive. It seemed harmless enough, so he began to pick at it without enthusiasm, quailing involuntarily with each mouthful, all the while accompanied by his fellow diners' gastronomic cacophony.

Although Mr Jerome hadn't said a single word to Will during the whole meal, the unbridled resentment radiating from him was overwhelming. Will had no idea why this was, but he was vaguely beginning to wonder if it had something to do with his real mother, the person no one seemed to be prepared to talk about. Or perhaps the man simply despised Topsoilers like him? Whatever it was, he wished the man would say something, anything at all, just to break the agonizing silence. From Mr Jerome's demeanour, Will knew full well that it wouldn't be pleasant when it came; he was prepared for that. He just wanted to get it over with. He began to sweat and tried to loosen the starched collar of his new shirt by running his finger inside it. It felt to Will as if the room was filling with a chilled and poisonous aspic; he felt suffocated by it.

His reprieve finally came when, finishing his plate of mush, Mr Jerome downed a glass of murky water and then abruptly got up. He folded his napkin twice and tossed it carelessly on to the table. He reached the door just as the wretch of a serving man was entering with a copper bowl in his hands. To Will's horror, Mr Jerome elbowed him brutally aside. Will thought the man was going to fall as he lurched against the wall. He fought to regain his balance as the contents of the bowl tipped out, and apples and oranges rolled about the floor and under the table.

As if Mr Jerome's behaviour was nothing out of the ordinary, the serving man didn't so much as murmur. Will could see a cut on his lip and blood trickling down his chin as the unfortunate man crawled around the base of his chair, retrieving the fruit.

Will was flabbergasted, but Cal seemed to be ignoring the incident altogether. Will watched the pathetic man until he left the room and then, deciding there was nothing he could do, turned his attention to the bowl of fresh fruit – there were bananas, pears and a couple of figs in addition to the apples and oranges. He helped himself, grateful for something familiar and recognizable after the first two courses.

At that moment the front door slammed with such a crash that the casement windows shook. Will and Cal listened as Mr Jerome's footsteps retreated down the front path. It was Will who broke the silence.

'Doesn't like me much, does he?'

Cal shook his head as he peeled an orange.

'Why—?' Will stopped short as the servant returned and stood submissively behind Cal's chair.

'You can go,' Cal ordered rudely, not even bothering to look at the man, who slipped quietly out of the room.

'Who was that?' Will enquired.

'Oh, that was just Watkins.'

Will didn't speak for a moment, then asked, '*What* did you say his name was?'

'Watkins . . . Terry Watkins.'

Will repeated the name to himself several times. 'I'm sure I know that from somewhere.' Although he couldn't quite put his finger on it, the name triggered a sense of foreboding in him.

Cal continued eating, enjoying Will's confusion, and then Will remembered with a start. 'They went missing, the whole family!'

'Yes, they certainly did.'

Taken aback, Will quickly looked across at Cal. 'They were snatched!'

'They had to be, they were a problem. Watkins stumbled on to an air channel and we couldn't have him telling anybody.'

'But that's never Mr Watkins – he was a big man. I've seen him . . . his sons were at my school,' Will said. 'No, that can't be the same person.'

'He and his family were put to work,' Cal said coldly.

'But . . .' Will stuttered as he juggled the mental image of Mr Watkins as he used to appear with how he looked now, '. . . he looks a hundred years old. What happened to him?' Will couldn't help but think of his own predicament, and of Chester's. So was that to be their lot? Pressed into slavery for these people?

'Just as I said, they were all put to work,' Cal repeated, lifting a pear to smell its skin. Noticing there was a smear of Mr Watkins' blood on it, he polished it on his shirt before taking a bite.

Will was regarding his brother now with renewed scrutiny, trying to work him out. The warmth he'd been beginning to feel towards him had all but evaporated. There was a vindictiveness, a hostility even, evident within the younger boy which Will didn't understand or very much care for. One moment he was saying he wanted to escape from the Colony, and the next he was acting as if he was completely at home here.

Will's train of thought was broken as Cal glanced over at his father's empty chair and sighed. 'This is very hard on

Father, but you have to give him time. I suppose you bring back too many memories.'

'About *what*, exactly?' Will shot back, not feeling an ounce of sympathy for the surly old man. That was where the notion of his new-found family fell apart – if he never saw Mr Jerome again, it would be too soon.

'About Mother, of course. Uncle Tam says she always was a bit of a rebel.' Cal sighed, then fell silent.

'But . . . did something bad happen?'

'We had a brother. He was only a baby. He died from a fever. After that, she ran away.' A wistful look came into Cal's eyes.

'A brother,' Will echoed.

Cal stared at him, any hint of his usual grin absent from his face. 'She was trying to get both of us out when the Styx caught up.'

'So she escaped?'

'Yes, but only just, and that's why I'm still here.' Cal took another mouthful of pear and was still chewing when he spoke again. 'Uncle Tam says she's the only one he knows of who got out and stayed out.'

'She's still alive?'

Cal nodded. 'As far as we know. But she broke the laws, and if you break the law the Styx never let go, even if you make it Topsoil. It doesn't end there. One day they *will* catch up with you, and then they *will* punish you.'

'Punish? How?'

'In Mother's case, execution,' he said succinctly. 'That's why you have to tread so very carefully.' Somewhere in the distance a bell began to toll. Cal got to his feet and glanced through the window. 'Seven bells. We should go.'

*

Once they were outside Cal forged ahead and Will found it difficult to keep up, his new trousers chafing against his thighs with every stride. It was as though they'd stepped into a river of people. The streets heaved with them, all dashing frantically in different directions as if they were late for something. It looked and sounded like a confused flock of leathery birds taking flight. Will followed Cal's lead and after several turns they joined the end of a queue outside a plain-looking building that resembled a warehouse. In front of each of the studded wooden doors at the entrance a pair of Styx stood in their characteristic poses, arched over like vindictive headmasters about to strike. Will bowed his head, trying to blend in with the crowd and avoid the jet-black pupils of the Styx, which he knew would be upon him.

Inside, the hall was deceptively big – around half the size of a football pitch. Large flagstones, shiny with dark patches of damp, formed the floor. The walls were roughly plastered and whitewashed. Looking around, he could see elevated platforms in the four corners of the hall, crude wooden pulpits, each with a Styx in place, hawkishly scrutinizing the gathering.

Halfway down the left and right walls were two huge oil paintings. Because of the sheer mass of people in the way, Will didn't have a clear view of the painting on the right, so turned to examine the one nearer to him. In the foreground was a man dressed in a black coat and a dark-green waistcoat, and sporting a top hat above his somewhat lugubrious and mutton-chopped face. He was studying a large sheet of paper, which might have been a plan, spread open in his hands. And he appeared to be standing in the midst of some kind of earthworks. Huddled at his sides were many other men with pickaxes and shovels, all of them looking at him with rapt admiration. For no particular reason, it brought to Will's mind pictures he'd seen of Jesus and his disciples.

'Who's that?' Will asked Cal, motioning towards the painting as people bustled past them.

'Sir Gabriel Martineau, of course. It's called the "Breaking of the Ground".'

With the ever-increasing crowds of people milling about in the hall Will had to jig his head from side to side to make out more of the painting. Other than the main figure, who Will now knew was Martineau himself, the ghostly faces of the workmen fascinated him. Silvery rays of what could have been moonlight radiated from above and fell on their faces, which glowed with a soft, saintly luminosity. And, adding to this effect, many of them appeared to have an even brighter light directly above their heads, as if they had halos.

'No,' Will murmured to himself, realizing with a start that they weren't halos at all, but that it was their white hair.

'Those others?' he said to Cal. 'Who are they?'

Cal was about to reply when a portly Colonist barged rudely into him, almost spinning him completely around. The man continued determinedly on his way without so much as an apology, but Cal didn't seem to be the slightest bit put out by the man's conduct. Will was still waiting for an answer as Cal wheeled back to face him again. He spoke as if he was addressing someone who was irretrievably stupid.

'They're our ancestors, Will,' he sighed.

'Oh.'

Despite the fact that Will was burning with curiosity about the picture, it was hopeless – his view was now almost completely blocked by the massing crowd. Instead, he turned to the front of the hall, where there were ten or so carved wooden pews, packed with closely seated Colonists. Going up on tiptoes to try to see what was beyond them, he caught sight of a massive iron crucifix fixed to the wall – it seemed to be made from two sections of railway track, bolted together with huge round-headed rivets.

Cal tugged him by the sleeve and they pushed their way through the gathering to a position closer to the pews. The doors thudded shut and Will realized that the hall had been crammed to capacity in scarcely any time at all. He found it stifling, squashed against Cal on one side and bulky Colonists on the others. The room was warming up quickly, and wraith-like wisps of steam were beginning to rise from the damp clothes of the crowd and encircle the hanging lights.

The hubbub of conversation died down as a Styx mounted the pulpit by the side of the metal cross. He wore a full-length black gown, and his shining eyes lanced through the fuggy air. For a brief moment, he closed them and inclined his head forward. Then he slowly looked up, his black gown opening, making him look like a bat about to take flight as he extended his arms towards the congregation, and started to speak in a sibilant monastic drone. At first, Will couldn't quite catch what he was saying, even though from the four corners of the room the voices of the other Styx were reiterating the words of the preacher in scratchy whispers, a sound not unlike the massed tearing of dry parchments. Will listened more intently as the preacher raised his voice.

'Know this, brethren, know this,' he said, his gaze scything through the congregation as he drew breath melodramatically.

'The surface of the Earth is beset by creatures in a constant state of war with one another. Millions perish on either side, and there is no limit to the brutality of their malice. Their nations fall and rise, only to fall again. The vast forests have been laid low by them, and the pastures defiled with their poison.' All around him Will heard mumbled words of agreement. The preacher Styx leaned forward, grasping the edge of the pulpit with his pale fingers.

'Their gluttony is matched only by their appetites for death, affliction, terror and ruination of every living thing. And, despite their iniquities, they aspire to rise to the firmament . . . but, *mark this*, the excessive weight of their very sins will weigh them down.' There was a pause as his black eyes scanned the flock and, raising his left arm above his head, a long, bony index finger pointing upwards, he continued.

'Nothing remains on the soil or in the great oceans that shall not be hunted, disturbed or despoiled. To the living things slain in droves, these defilers are both the sepulchre and the means of transition.

'And when the judgement comes,' he lowered his arm now and pointed forebodingly at members of the congregation through the hazy atmosphere, 'and mark these words, it will . . . then they will be hurled into the abyss and for ever lost to the Lord . . . and on that day, the truthful, the righteous, we of the true way, will once again return to reclaim the surface, to begin again, to build the new dominion . . . the new Jerusalem. For this is the teaching and the knowledge of our forefathers, passed down to us through the ages by the Book of Catastrophes.'

A hush filled the hall, absolute and unbroken by a single cough or shuffle. Then the preacher spoke again, in a calmer, almost conversational tone.

'So let it be known, so let it be understood.' He bowed his head.

Will thought he glimpsed Mr Jerome seated in the pews, but couldn't be sure because he was so completely hemmed in.

Then, without warning, the whole congregation joined in with the Styx's monotone: 'The Earth is the Lord's, and the followers thereof, the Earth and all that dwell therein. We give our eternal gratitude to our Saviour, Sir Gabriel, and the Founding Fathers for their shepherdship and for the flowing together into one another, as all that happens in God's Earth is also on the highest level, the Kingdom of God.'

There was a moment's pause and the Styx spoke again. 'As above, so below.'

The voices of the congregation boomed Amens as the Styx took a step back and Will lost sight of him. He swung around to Cal to ask him a question, but there was no time as the congregation immediately started to file towards the doorway, leaving the hall as swiftly as it had collected. The boys were swept along in the tide of people until they found themselves back on the street, where they stood watching them depart in all directions.

'I don't get this "As below, so above" stuff,' Will asked Cal in a low voice. 'I thought everybody hated Topsoilers.'

'*Above* isn't *Topsoil*,' Cal replied, so loudly and in such a petulant tone that several burly men in earshot turned to regard Will with snarls of disgust. He winced – he was beginning to wonder if having a younger brother was all it was cut out to be.

'But how often do you have to do that – go to church?'

Will ventured, when he had recovered sufficiently from Cal's last response.

'Once a day,' Cal said. 'You go to church Topsoil too, don't you?'

'Our family didn't.'

'How strange,' Cal said, looking shiftily around to check that no one could overhear him. 'Load of drivel, anyway,' he sneered under his breath. 'C'mon, we're going to see Tam. He'll be at the tavern in Low Holborn.'

As they reached the end of the street and turned off it, a flock of white starlings spiralled above them and swung into a barrel roll towards the area of the cavern where the boys were now heading. Appearing from nowhere, Bartleby joined them, flicking his tail and wobbling his bottom jaw at the sight of the birds, and giving a rather sweet and plaintive mew that was totally at odds with his appearance.

'Come on, you daft beast, you'll never catch them,' Cal said as the animal sauntered past, his head held high as he hankered after the birds.

As the boys walked, they passed hovels and small work-shops: a smithy where the blacksmith, an old man, backlit by the blaze from his furnace, hammered relentlessly on an anvil, and places with names like Geo. Blueskin Cartwrights and Erasmus Chemicals. Of particular fascination to Will was a dark, oily-looking yard full of carriages and broken machinery.

'Shouldn't we really be getting back?' Will asked, stopping to peer through the wrought-iron railings at the strange contraptions.

'No, Father won't be home for a while yet,' Cal said. 'Hurry up, we should get a move on.'

As they progressed towards what Will assumed was the

centre of the cavern, he couldn't stop himself from looking all around at the amazing sights and the packed houses, huddled together in seemingly endless rows. Until now he hadn't fully appreciated just how huge this place was. And looking up he saw a shimmering haze, a shifting, living thing that hung like a cloud above the chaos of rooftops, fed by the collective glow of all the light of the orbs below.

For a moment, it reminded Will of Highfield during the summer doldrums, except that where there should have been sky and sunlight, there were only glimpses of an immense stone canopy. Cal quickened his pace as they passed Colonists who, from their lingering glances, evidently knew who Will was. A number crossed the road to avoid him, muttering under their breath, and others stopped where they stood, glowering at him. A few even spat in his direction.

Will was more than a little distressed by this.

'Why are they doing that?' he asked quietly, falling back behind his brother.

'Ignore them,' Cal replied confidently.

'It's like they hate me or something.'

'It's always the same with outsiders.'

'But . . .' Will began.

'Look, really, don't worry about it. It'll pass, you'll see. It's because you're new and, don't forget, they all know who your mother is,' Cal said. 'They won't do anything to you.' All of a sudden, he drew to a halt and turned to Will. 'But through here keep your head down, and keep moving. Understand? Don't stop for *anything*.'

Will didn't know what Cal was talking about until he saw the entrance by the other boy's side: it was a passage barely more than shoulder-width. Cal slipped in, with Will reluctantly following behind. It was dark and claustrophobic, and the sulphurous stench of old sewage hung in the air. Their feet splashed through unseen puddles of unidentifiable liquids. He was careful not to touch the walls, which were running with a dark, greasy slime.

Will was grateful when they finally emerged into the dim light, but then he gasped as he beheld a scene that was straight out of Victorian London. Buildings loomed either side of the narrow alleyway, slanting inwards at such precarious angles that their upper storeys almost met. They were timber-framed and in a terrible state of disrepair. Most of their windows were either broken or boarded up.

Although he couldn't tell where they originated, Will heard the sound of voices, and cries and laughter, coming from all around. There were odd snatches of music, as if scales were being played on a strangled zither. Somewhere a baby was wailing persistently and dogs were barking. As they strode quickly past the badly deteriorated façades Will caught whiffs of charcoal and tobacco smoke and, through open doorways, glimpsed people huddled at tables. Men in shirtsleeves hung out of windows, staring at the ground listlessly as they smoked their pipes. There was an open channel in the middle of the alley, down which a sluggish trickle of raw sewage ran through vegetable waste and other filth and detritus. Will nearly blundered into it, and stepped smartly to the edge of the alleyway to avoid it.

'No! Watch yourself!' Cal warned quickly. 'Keep away from the sides!'

As they hurried along Will hardly let himself blink as he feasted his eyes on everything he saw around him. He was muttering 'Just fantastic,' over and over again to himself, wondering if his father had come across this place, a piece of living history, when his attention was caught by something else. There were people in the narrow passageways that branched off on either side. Mysterious shadowy outlines were stirring within them, and he heard hushed voices, snatches of hysterical muttering, and even, at one point, the far-off sound of someone screaming in agony.

From one of these passageways a dark figure lurched. It was a man with a black shawl over his head, which he hoisted up to reveal his gnarled face. It was covered with a sickly layer of sweat, and his skin was the colour of old bone. He grabbed at Will's arm with his hand, his rheumy yellow eyes looking deep into the startled boy's.

'Ah, what is it you're after, my sweet thing?' he wheezed asthmatically, his lopsided smile revealing a row of jagged brown stumps for teeth. Bartleby snarled as Cal hurriedly pushed himself between Will and the man, yanking Will from the man's grasp and not letting go of him through several twists and turns of the alley until at last they were out, and back on to a well-lit street again. Will breathed a sigh of relief.

'What *was* that place?'

'The Rookeries. It's where the paupers live. And you only saw the outskirts – you really wouldn't want to find yourself in the middle of it,' Cal said, dashing ahead so quickly that Will had a job to keep up. He was still feeling the after-effects of the ordeal in the Hold; his chest ached and his legs were leaden. But he wasn't about to let Cal see any weakness, and forced himself on.

As the cat bounded ahead into the distance Will doggedly followed Cal's lead as he leaped over the larger pools of water and skirted around the occasional gushing downpour. Falling from the shadows of the cavern roof above, these torrents seemed to spring from nowhere, like upturned geysers.

They wound their way through a series of broad streets jam-packed with narrow terraced houses until, in the distance, Will spotted the lights of a tavern at the apex of a sharp corner where two roads met. People thronged outside it in various states of intoxication, laughing raucously and shouting, and from somewhere a woman's voice was singing shrilly. As he got closer Will could make out the painted sign, 'The Buttock & File', with a picture of the weirdest-looking locomotive he had ever seen, which had, it appeared, an archetypal devil as its driver, scarlet-skinned and replete with horns, trident and an arrow-tipped tail.

The frontage and even the windows of the tavern were painted black and covered in a film of grey soot. People were so tightly packed in that they were overflowing on to the pavements outside. To a man, they were drinking from dented pewter tankards, while a number smoked either long clay pipes or turnip-shaped objects, which Will didn't recognize, but which reeked of chronically soiled nappies.

As he stuck close behind Cal they passed a top-hatted man standing at a small folding table. He was calling 'Find the painted lady! Find the painted lady!' to a couple of interested onlookers as he deftly cut a pack of cards using only a single hand. 'My good sir,' the man proclaimed as one of the onlookers stepped up and slapped a coin down on the green baize of the table. The cards were dealt and Will was sorry not to see the outcome of the game, but there was absolutely no way he was going to become separated from his brother as they pushed deeper into the midst of the throng. Surrounded by all these people he felt very vulnerable, and was just debating whether he could persuade Cal to take him home when a friendly voice boomed out.

'Cal! Bring Will over here!'

There was an immediate lull in the chatter around them and in the silence all heads turned on Will. Uncle Tam emerged from a group of people and waved the two boys over extravagantly. The faces in the crowd outside the tavern were varied: curious, grinning, blank – but for the most part sneering with unbridled hostility. Tam seemed not the slightest bit bothered by this. He threw his thick arms around the boys' shoulders and turned his head to face the crowd, staring back at them in mute defiance.

The cacophony continued inside the tavern, only serving to make the yawning silence outside, and the rising tension that accompanied it, even more intense. This horrible hush filled Will's ears, crashing and swelling and drowning everything out.

Then an ear-splitting belch, the longest and loudest Will had ever heard, ripped from someone in the crowd. As the last echoes rang back from the neighbouring buildings, the spell was broken and the whole crowd exploded into peals of harsh laughter, intermingled with cheers and the odd wolf whistle.

It wasn't long before all this merriment subsided and people settled down again, the chatter resuming as a small man was widely congratulated, and patted on the back so forcibly that he had to cover his drink with his hand to prevent it from slopping on to the pavement.

Still acutely self-conscious, Will kept his head bowed. He couldn't help noticing when Bartleby, stretched out under the bench where the men sat, jerked suddenly, as if some parasite or other had bitten him. Doubling up, the cat began to lick his nether regions with a hind leg pointing heavenwards, looking remarkably like a badly plucked turkey.

'Now you've met the great unwashed,' Uncle Tam said, his eyes briefly flicking back over the crowd, 'let me introduce you to royalty, the crème de la crème. This is Joe Waites,' he said, manoeuvring Will face to face with a wizened old man. His head was topped with a tightly fitting skullcap that seemed to compress the upper half of his face, making his eyes bulge out and hoisting his cheeks up into an involuntary grin. A solitary tooth protruded from his top jaw like an ivory tusk. He proffered his hand to Will who shook it reluctantly, somewhat surprised to find it warm and dry.

'And this,' Tam inclined his head to a dapper man sporting a tawdry chequered three-piece suit and black-rimmed glasses, 'is Jesse Shingles.' The man bowed gracefully and then chuckled, raising his thick eyebrows.

'And, not least, the one and only Imago Freebone.' A man with long, dank hair plaited into a biker's ponytail shot out a mittened hand, his voluminous leather coat flapping open to reveal his immense deep-chested barrel of a body. Will was so intimidated by the sheer mass of the man he almost took a step back.

'Deeply pleased to meet such a hallowed legend, we being such 'umble personages,' Imago said, bending his bulk forward and tugging a non-existent forelock with his other hand.

'Er . . . hello,' Will said, uncertain what to make of him.

'Knock it off,' grimaced Tam.

Imago straightened up, offering his hand again and in a normal voice said, 'Will, very good to meet you.' Will shook it again. 'I shouldn't tease,' Imago added earnestly. 'We all know what you've been through, only too well.' His eyes were warm and sympathetic as he continued to clasp Will's hand between both of his, finally releasing it with a comforting squeeze. 'I've had the pleasure of the Dark Light myself several times, courtesy of our dear friends,' he said.

'Yeah, gives you the most God-awful heartburn,' Jesse Shingles said with a smirk.

Will was more than a little daunted by Uncle Tam's associates and their strange appearances, but, looking around, it struck him that they weren't that different from most of the revellers outside the tavern.

'I got you both a quart of New London.' Tam handed the two tankards to the boys. 'Go easy on it, Will, you won't have tasted anything like that before.'

'Why? What's in it?' Will asked, eyeing with suspicion the greyish liquid with a thin froth on top of it.

'You don't wanta know, my boy, really you don't,' Tam said, and his friends laughed; Joe Waites made peculiar bird-like noises, while Imago threw his head back and gave an extravagant but completely silent laugh, his great shoulders heaving violently. Under the bench, Bartleby grunted and licked his lips noisily.

'So you've been to your first service,' Uncle Tam asked. 'What did you make of it?'

'It was, er . . . interesting,' Will said noncommittally.

'Not after years of it, it ain't,' Tam said. 'Still, it keeps the White Necks at bay.' He took a deep swig from his tankard, then straightened his back and let out a contented sigh. 'Yep, if I had a florin for every "As above, so bloody below" I've said, I'd be a rich man today.'

'As yesterday, so tomorrow,' Joe Waites said in a weary, nasal voice, mimicking a Styx preacher. '"So sayeth The Book of Catastrophes.'" He gave a huge exaggerated yawn, which afforded Will a rather unsettling view of his pink gums and the sad, lone tooth.

'And if you've heard one catastrophe, you've heard them all.' Imago nudged Will in the ribs.

'Amen,' chorused Jesse Shingles and Joe Waites, knocking their tankards together and laughing. 'Amen to that!'

'Now, now, it brings comfort to them as don't have minds of their own,' Tam said.

Will looked out of the corner of his eye at Cal and saw that he was joining in and laughing with the rest of them. This puzzled Will; at times his brother appeared to be filled with a religious zeal, but at others he didn't stint at showing a total lack of respect, even a contempt, for it.

'So, Will, what do you miss most about life up top?' Jesse Shingles suddenly asked, jerking his thumb towards the rock roof above their heads. Will looked uncertain and was about to say something when the little man went on. 'I'd miss the fish and chips; not that I've ever tasted them.' He winked conspiratorially at Imago.

'That's enough of that.' Tam's brow creased with concern as he cast his eyes over the people milling around them. 'Not the time or the place.'

Cal had been happily supping his drink, but noticed Will was being a little reticent with his. He wiped his mouth with the back of his hand and turned to his brother, gesticulating towards his so far untouched tankard. 'Go on, try it!'

Will tentatively took a mouthful of the chalky fluid and held it in his mouth for a moment before gulping it down.

'Well?' Cal enquired.

Will ran his tongue around his lips. 'Not bad,' he said.

Then it bit. His eyes widened and watered as his throat began to burn. He spluttered, trying vainly to stifle the coughing fit that followed. Uncle Tam and Cal grinned. 'I'm not old enough to drink alcohol,' Will croaked, putting the tankard on the edge of the table.

'Who's to stop you? Whole different set of rules here. As long as you stay within the law, pull your weight and attend their services, nobody minds if you let off a little steam. It's nobody's business, anyway,' Tam said, slapping him gently on the back.

As if to show their agreement, the assembled group held up their tankards and clanked them together with salutations of 'Up yer cludgy!'

And so it went, drink after drink, until about the fourth or fifth round – Will had lost count. Tam had just finished telling a convoluted and unfathomable joke about a flatulent policeman and a blind orb-juggler's daughter that Will could make neither head nor tail of, although all the others found it hilarious.

Picking up his tankard and still chuckling, Tam suddenly peered into his drink and, with his thumb and forefinger, pulled something out of the froth. 'I got the bloody slug again,' he said, as the others burst once more into fits of uncontrolled laughter.

'You'll be married in the month if you don't eat it,' Imago roared.

'In that case . . . !' Tam laughed and, to Will's amazement, placed the limp grey object on his tongue. He moved it around inside his mouth before chewing and then swallowing it, to shouts of applause from his friends.

In the lull that followed, Will felt sufficiently emboldened with Dutch courage to speak up.

'Tam – Uncle Tam – I need your help.'

'Anything, lad,' Tam said, resting his hand on Will's shoulder. 'You only have to ask.'

But where did he start? Where did he begin? He had so many concerns swirling through his drink-befuddled mind . . . finding his father . . . and what about his sister . . . and his mother . . . but *which* mother? Through this haze, one pressing thought crystallized – one thing, above all else, that he had to do.

'I have to get Chester out,' Will blurted.

'Shhh!' Tam hissed. He glanced nervously around. They all drew together to encircle him in a secretive huddle.

'Have you any idea what you're asking?' Tam said under his breath.

Will looked at him blankly, not sure how to respond.

'And where would you go? Back to Highfield? Think you'd ever be safe there again, with the Styx hunting you? You wouldn't last a week. Who'd protect you?'

'I could go to the police,' Will suggested. 'They'd—'

'You're not listening. They have people everywhere,' Tam reiterated forcefully.

'And not just in Highfield,' Imago interjected in a low voice. 'You can't trust anyone Topsoil, not the police . . . not *anyone*.'

Tam nodded in agreement. 'You'd need to lose yourself somewhere they'll never think of looking for you. Do you know where you might go?'

Will didn't know whether it was fatigue or the effect of the alcohol, but he was finding it hard to fight back the tears. 'But I can't just do *nothing*. When I needed help to find my dad,' he said hoarsely, his throat tightening with emotion, 'the one person I could rely on was Chester, and now he's stuck in the Hold . . . because of me. I owe it to him.'

'Have you any idea what it's like to be a fugitive?' Tam asked. 'To spend the rest of your years running from every shadow, without a single friend to help you because you're a danger to anyone you're around?'

Will swallowed noisily as Tam's words sank in, aware that all eyes in their little group were on him.

'If I were you, I'd *forget* about Chester,' Tam said harshly.

'I . . . just . . . can't,' Will said in a strained voice, looking into his drink. 'No . . .'

'It's the way things are down here, Will . . . you'll get used to it,' Tam said, shaking his head emphatically.

The high spirits of only a few minutes earlier had completely evaporated, and now Cal's face and those of Tam's men, gathered closely around Will, were stern and unsympathetic. He didn't know if he'd put his foot in it, and said totally the wrong thing, but he couldn't just leave it at that – his feelings were too strong. He lifted his head and looked Tam straight in the eye.

'But why do you all stay down here?' he asked 'Why doesn't everyone just get out . . . escape?'

'Because,' Tam began slowly, 'all said and done, this is *home*. It might not be much, but it's all most people know.'

'Our families are here,' Joe Waites put in forcefully. 'Do you think we could we just clear off and leave them? Have you any idea what would happen if we did?'

'Reprisals,' Imago said in a voice that was barely audible. 'The Styx would slaughter the lot of them.'

'Rivers of blood,' Tam whispered.

Joe Waites pressed even closer to Will. 'Do you really think we'd be happy living in a strange place where everything is so completely foreign to us? Where would we go? What would we do?' he gushed, trembling with agitation as he spoke. It was obvious he was extremely upset by Will's questions, only beginning to regain his composure when Tam laid a comforting hand on his shoulder.

'We'd be out of place . . . out of time,' Jesse Shingles said.

Will could only nod, cowed by the sheer intensity of emotion he'd aroused in the group. He sighed shakily.

'Well, whatever, I have to get Chester out. Even if I have to do it myself,' he said.

Tam regarded him for a moment and then shook his head. 'Stubborn as a mule. Talk about like mother, like son,' he said, a grin returning to his face. 'D'you know, it's uncanny how much you sound like her. Once Sarah set her mind on something there was no budging her.' He ruffled Will's hair with his large hand. 'Stubborn as a bloody mule.'

Imago tapped Tam's arm. 'It's him again.'

Relieved that he was no longer the centre of attention, Will was a little slow to catch on, but when he did he observed that across the street a Styx was talking to a hefty man who had wiry white hair and long sideburns, and wore a shiny brown coat with a grimy red neckerchief coiled around his stubby neck. As he watched, the Styx nodded, turned and walked away.

'That Styx has been dogging Tam for a long time now,' Cal whispered to Will.

'Who is he?' Will asked.

'Nobody knows their names, but we call him the Crawfly, on account he can't so easily be shaken off. He's on a personal vendetta to bring Uncle Tam down.'

Will watched as the figure of the Crawfly dissolved into the shadows.

'He's had it in for your family ever since your ma gave the White Necks the slip and went Topsoil,' Imago said to Will and Cal.

'And till my dying day I'll swear he did for my pa,' Tam said, his voice flat and oddly lacking in any emotion. 'He killed him all right . . . that was no accident.'

Imago shook his head slowly. 'That was a horrible thing,' he agreed. 'A *horrible* thing.'

'So what's he cooking up with that scum over there?' Tam said, frowning as he turned to Imago.

'Who was he was talking to?' Will asked, peering across at the other man who was now crossing the road towards the crowd outside the tavern.

'Don't look at him . . . that's Heraldo Walsh. A cut-throat . . . nasty piece of work,' Cal warned.

'A burglar, lowest of the low,' Tam growled.

'But what's he doing talking to a Styx, then?' Will said, totally confused.

'Wheels within wheels,' Tam muttered. 'The Styx are a devious bunch. A belt becomes a snake with them.' He turned to Will. 'Look, I may be able to help you with Chester, but you've got to promise me one thing,' he whispered.

'What's that?'

'If you get caught, you'll never implicate Cal, me or any of us. Our lives and our families are here and, like it or not, we have to stay in this place with the White Necks . . . the Styx. That's our lot. And I'll say it again: they'll never let it rest if you cross them . . . they will do *everything* they can to catch up with you—' Suddenly Tam broke off.

Will saw the alarm in Cal's eyes. He spun around. Heraldo Walsh was standing not two metres away. And behind him a throng of drunkards had parted fearfully to allow a phalanx of brutish-looking Colonists through. They were clearly Walsh's gang – Will saw the fiery hatred in their faces. His blood ran cold. Tam immediately stepped to Will's side.

'What do you want, Walsh?' Tam said, his eyes narrowed and his fists clenched.

'Ah, my old friend, Tamfoolery,' Heraldo Walsh said with a vile, gappy grin. 'I just wanted to see this Topsoiler for myself.'

Will wished the ground would open up and swallow him.

'So you're the type of scum that chokes our air channels and pollutes our houses with your foul sewage. My daughter died because of your kind.' He took a step closer to Will, raising his hand threateningly, as if he was going to grab at the petrified boy. 'Come 'ere, you stinking filth!'

Will cowered. His first impulse was to run, but he knew his uncle wasn't about to let anything happen to him.

'That's far enough, Walsh.' Tam took a step towards the man, to block his approach.

'You're fraternizing with the godless, Macaulay,' Walsh yelled, his eyes never leaving Will's face.

'And what do *you* know of God?' Tam retorted, stepping fully in front of Will to shield him. 'Now, you leave it! He's family!'

But Heraldo was like a dog with a bone – he wasn't about to let go. Behind him, his supporters were egging him on and cursing.

'You call *that* family?' He thrust a dirt-stained finger at

Will. 'Sarah Jerome's mongrel?'

At this, several of his men let out wild howls and whoops.

'He's the bastard offspring of a traitorous bitch who ran for the sun,' Heraldo snapped.

'That's it,' Tam hissed through his clenched teeth. He slung the dregs of his beer at the man, hitting him square in the face, dousing his hair and sideburns in the watery grey fluid.

'Nobody insults my family, Walsh. Step up to the scratch,' Tam scowled.

Heraldo Walsh's coterie began to chant, 'Milling, milling, milling!' and very soon cheers filled the air as everyone outside on the pavement joined in. Others came rushing out of the tavern door to see what all the commotion was about.

'What's going on?' Will asked Cal, terrified out of his wits as the huge crowd hemmed them in. Right in the centre of the closely packed, overexcited rabble, Tam stood resolutely in front of the dripping Heraldo Walsh, locked in an angry staring match.

'A fist fight,' Cal said.

The landlord, a stocky man in a blue apron, with a sweaty red face, pushed through the tavern doors and threaded his way through the mob until he reached the two men. He barged in between Tam and Heraldo Walsh and knelt down to fix shackles to their ankles. As they both took a step back, Will saw that the shackles were connected by a length of rusty chain, so that the two fighters were bound together.

Then the landlord reached into his apron pocket and brought out a piece of chalk. He drew a line on the pavement halfway between them.

'You know the rules,' his voice boomed melodramatically,

as much for the benefit of the crowd as for the two men. 'Above the belt, no weapons, biting or gouging. It stops on a KO or death.'

'*Death?*' Will whispered shakily to Cal, who nodded grimly.

Then the landlord ushered everyone back until a human boxing ring had been squared off. This wasn't an easy task, as people were jostling against each other as they vied for a view of the two men.

'Step up to the mark,' the man said loudly. Tam and Heraldo Walsh positioned themselves either side of the chalk line. The landlord held their arms to steady them. Then he released them with the shouted order 'Commence!' and quickly retreated.

In an attempt to knock his opponent off balance, Walsh immediately swung his foot back and the length of chain – two metres or so long – snapped taut, yanking Tam's leg forward.

But Tam was ready for the manoeuvre and used the forward momentum to his advantage. He leaped towards Walsh, a huge right fist flying at the shorter man's face. The blow glanced off Walsh's chin, drawing a gasp from the crowd. Tam continued with a fast combination of blows, but his opponent avoided them with apparent ease, ducking and diving like a demented rabbit, as the chain between them rattled noisily on the pavement amidst the shouts and cries.

'By Jove, he's quick, that one,' Joe Waites observed.

'But he don't have Tam's reach, do he?' Jesse Shingles countered.

Then Heraldo Walsh, crouching low, shot up under Tam's guard and landed a blow on his jaw, a sharp uppercut that jarred Tam's head. Blood burst from his mouth, but he didn't hesitate in his retaliation, bringing his fist down squarely on the top of Walsh's skull.

'The pile-driver!' Joe said excitedly, and then shouted, 'Go on, Tam! Go on, you beauty!'

Heraldo Walsh's knees buckled and he reeled backwards, spitting with anger, and came back immediately with a frenzied salvo of punches, clipping Tam around the mouth. Tam moved back as far as the limits of the chain would allow, colliding with the crowd behind him. As people stepped on those behind to give the two fighters more room, Walsh pursued him. Tam used the time to collect himself and reorganize his guard. As Walsh closed in, his fists swiping the air in front of him, Tam ducked down and exploded back into his opponent with a combination of crushing blows to his ribcage and stomach. The noise of the thudding wallops, like bales of hay being thrown on the ground, could be heard over the shouts and jeers of the spectators.

'He's softening him up,' Cal said gleefully.

Sporadic skirmishes were breaking out among the mob as arguments raged between the supporters of the two fighters. From his vantage point Will saw heads bobbing up and down, fists flailing and tankards flying, beer going everywhere. He also noticed that money was changing hands, as bets were feverishly taken – people were holding up one, two or three fingers and swapping coins. The atmosphere was carnivalesque.

Suddenly the crowd let out a deep 'Oooh!' as, without warning, Heraldo Walsh landed a mighty right hook on Tam's nose. There was a dramatic lull in the shouting, as the crowd watched Tam drop to one knee, the chain snapping tightly between them.

'That's not good,' Imago said worriedly.

'Come on, Tam!' Cal shouted for all he was worth. 'Macaulay, Macaulay, Macaulay . . .' he yelled, and Will joined in.

Tam stayed down. Cal and Will could see blood running from his face and dripping on to the cobblestones of the street. Then Tam looked across at them and winked slyly.

'The old dog!' Imago said under his breath. 'Here it comes.'

Sure enough, as Heraldo Walsh stood over him, Tam rose up with all the grace and speed of a leaping jaguar, throwing a fearsome uppercut that smashed into Walsh's jaw, forcing his teeth together in a bloodcurdling crunch. Heraldo Walsh staggered back, and Tam was on him, pounding him with deadly precision, striking the face of the smaller man so rapidly and with such force that he had no time to mount any form of defence.

Something covered with spittle and blood shot from Heraldo Walsh's mouth and landed on the cobblestones. With a shock Will saw it was a large part of a shattered tooth. Hands reached into the ring in an attempt to snatch it away. A man in a moth-eaten trilby was the fastest off the mark, whisking it away and then vanishing into the throng behind him.

'Souvenir hunters,' Cal said. 'Ghouls!'

Will looked up just as Tam closed on his opponent, who was now being held up by some of his followers, exhausted and gasping for breath. Spitting out blood, his left eye swollen shut, Heraldo Walsh was pushed forward just in time to see Tam's fist as he landed a final, crushing blow.

The man's head snapped back as he fell against the crowd, which this time parted and watched him as he danced a slow, drunken, bent-leg jig for a few agonizing moments. Then he simply folded to the ground like a sodden paper doll, and the crowd fell silent.

Tam was bent forwards, his raw knuckles resting on his knees as he tried to catch his breath. The landlord came forward and nudged Heraldo Walsh's head with his boot. He didn't move.

'Tam Macaulay!' the landlord yelled out to the silent mob, which suddenly erupted with a roar that filled the cavern and must have rattled the windows on the other side of the Rookeries.

Tam's shackle was removed, and his friends ran over to him and helped him to the bench, where he sat down heavily, feeling his jaw as the two boys took their places either side of him.

'Little bastard was faster than I thought,' he said, looking down at his bloodied knuckles as he flexed them painfully. He was handed a full tankard by someone who slapped him on the back and then disappeared into the tavern.

'The Crawfly's disappointed,' Jesse said, as they all turned to see the Styx at the end of the street, his back to them as he strolled away, drumming a pair of peculiar eyeglasses on his thigh as he went.

'But he got what he wanted,' Tam said despondently. 'The word will go around that I've been in another brawl.'

'Don't matter,' Jesse Shingles said. 'You were justified. Everyone knows it was Walsh started it.'

Tam looked at the sorry limp figure of Heraldo Walsh, left where he'd dropped. Not one of his cronies had come forward to move him off the street.

'One thing's for sure – he'll feel like a Coprolite's dinner when he wakes up,' Imago chortled as a barman threw a bucket of water over the poleaxed figure and then returned inside the tavern, laughing as he went.

Tam nodded thoughtfully and took a huge mouthful of his drink, wiping his bruised lips with his forearm.

'That's if he wakes up at all,' he said quietly.

CHAPTER TWENTY-SIX

Rebecca's room was filled with the heavy rumble of Monday morning traffic, car horns hooting impatiently from the streets thirteen floors below. A slight breeze ruffled the curtains. She wrinkled her nose disdainfully as she smelled the stale stench of cigarettes from Auntie Jean's non-stop smoking the night before. Although the door to her bedroom was firmly shut the smoke nosed its way into every nook and cranny, like an insidious yellow fog searching out new corners to taint.

She got up, slipped on her dressing gown and made her bed as she trilled the first couple of lines of 'You Are My Sunshine'. Lapsing into vague la-las for the rest of the song, she carefully arranged a black dress and a white shirt on the top of the duvet.

She went over to the door and, placing her hand on the handle, stopped completely still, as if she had been struck by a thought. She turned slowly and retraced her steps to her bed. Her eyes alighted on the pair of little silver-framed photographs on the table beside it.

Taking them in her hands she sat on her bed, looking

between the two. In one, there was a slightly out-of-focus photograph showing Will leaning on a spade. In the other, a youthful Dr and Mrs Burrows sat on stripy deckchairs on an unidentified beach. In the picture, Mrs Burrows was staring at an enormous ice cream, while Dr Burrows appeared to be trying to swat a fly with a blurred hand.

They had all gone their separate ways – the family had fallen apart. Did they seriously think she was going to stick around to nursemaid Auntie Jean, someone even more slothful and demanding than Mrs Burrows?

'No,' Rebecca said aloud. 'I'm done here.' A thin smile flickered momentarily across her face. She glanced at the photographs one last time and then drew in a long breath.

'Props,' she said and threw them with such vehemence that they struck the discoloured skirting board with a tinkle of breaking glass.

Twenty minutes later she was dressed and ready to leave. She put her little suitcases next to the front door and went into the kitchen. In a drawer next to the sink was Auntie Jean's 'fag stash'. Rebecca tore open the ten or so packets of cigarettes and shook their contents into the sink. Then she started on Auntie Jean's bottles of cheap vodka. Rebecca twisted off the screw caps and poured them, all five bottles, into the sink, dousing the cigarettes.

Finally she picked up the 'wipe-clean' box of kitchen matches from beside the gas cooker and slid it open. Taking out a single match, she struck it and set light to a crumpled-up sheet of kitchen roll.

She stood well back, and chucked the flaming ball into the sink. The cigarettes and alcohol went up with a satisfying whoosh, flames leaping out of the sink over the chrome-effect plastic taps and the chipped floral tiles behind them. Rebecca didn't stay to savour it. The front door slammed, and she and her little suitcases were gone. With the sound of the smoke alarm receding behind her, she made her way across the landing and into the stairwell.

Since his friend had been spirited away, Chester, in the permanent night of the Hold, had passed beyond the point of despair.

'One. Two. Thre . . .' He tried to straighten his arms to complete the press-up, part of the daily training routine he'd started in the Hold.

'Thre . . .' He breathed deeply and tensed his arms without any real enthusiasm.

'Thre . . .' He exhaled hollowly and sank down defeated, his face coming to rest against the unseen filth on the stone floor. He slowly rolled over and sat up, glancing at the observation hatch in the door to make sure he wasn't being watched as he brought his hands together. *Dear God . . .*

To Chester, praying was something from the self-conscious cough-filled silences at school assembly . . . something that followed the badly sung hymns, which, to the glee of their giggling confederates, some boys salted with dirty lyrics.

No, only nerds prayed in earnest.

. . . please send someone . . .

He pressed his hands together even harder, no longer feeling any embarrassment. What else could he do? He remembered the great-uncle who had one day appeared in the spare room at home. Chester's mum had taken Chester to one side and told him the funny little twig-like man was having cancer therapy at a London hospital and, although Chester had never set eyes on him before, she said he was 'family', and that that was important.

Chester pictured the man, with his *Racing Post* and his harsh 'I don't eat any of that foreign filth,' when he was presented with a perfectly good plate of spag bol. He remembered the rasping cough punctuating the numerous 'rollies' he still insisted on smoking, much to the exasperation of Chester's mother.

In the second week of car trips to the hospital the little man had got weaker and more withdrawn, like a leaf withering on a branch, until he didn't talk of 'life up north', or even try to drink his tea. Chester had heard how, but never understood why, the little man had cried out to God in their spare room in horrible wheezing breaths, in those days before he died. But he understood now.

. . . help me, please . . . please . . .

Chester felt lonely and abandoned and . . . and why, oh why, had he gone with Will on this ridiculous jaunt? Why hadn't he just stayed at home? He could be there now, tucked up warm and safe, but he *wasn't*, and he *had* gone with Will . . . and now there was nothing he could do but mark the passage of days by the two depressingly identical bowls of mush that arrived at regular intervals, and the intermittent periods of unfulfilling sleep. He had now grown used to the continual thrumming noise that invaded his cell – the Second Officer had told him it was due to machinery in the 'Fan Stations'. He had actually begun to find it rather comforting.

Of late, the Second Officer had mellowed slightly in his treatment of Chester and occasionally deigned to respond to his questions. It was almost as though it didn't matter any more whether or not the man maintained his officious bearing, which left Chester with the dreadful feeling that he might be there for ever, or, on the other hand, that something was just around the corner; that things were coming to a head – and not for the better, he suspected.

This suspicion had been further heightened when the Second Officer slung the door open and ordered Chester to clean himself up, providing him with a bucket of dark water and a sponge. Despite his misgivings, Chester was grateful for the opportunity to wash, although it hurt like hell as he did it because his eczema had flared up like never before. In the past it had been limited to his arms, only very occasionally spreading to his face, but now it had broken out all over, until it seemed that every inch of his body was raw and flaking. The Second Officer had also chucked in some clothes for him to change into, including a pair of huge trousers that felt as if they were made of sackcloth and made him itch even more, if that was possible.

Other than this, time tottered wearily by. Chester had lost track of how long he'd been alone in the Hold; it may have been as much as a month, but he couldn't be sure.

At one point he got very excited when he discovered that by gently probing with his fingertips he could make out letters scratched into the stone of one of the cell walls. There were initials and names, some with numbers that could have been dates. And at the very bottom of the wall someone had gouged in large capitals: I DIED HERE, SLOWLY. After finding this, Chester didn't feel like reading any more of them.

He'd also found out that by standing on his toes on the lead-covered ledge, he could just reach the bars on a narrow slit window high up on the wall. Gripping these bars, he was able to pull himself up so he could see the gaol's neglected

kitchen garden. Beyond that, there was a stretch of road leading into a tunnel, lit by a few ever-burning orb lampposts.
Chester would stare relentlessly at the road where it disappeared into the tunnel, in the forlorn hope that maybe, just
maybe, he might catch a glimpse of his friend, of Will returning to save him, like some knight errant galloping to his
rescue. But Will never came, and Chester would hang there,
hoping and praying fervently, as his knuckles turned white
with the strain, and until his arms gave out and he would fall
back into the cell, into the shadows, and back into despair.

CHAPTER TWENTY-SEVEN

'Wakey, wakey!'
Will was rudely woken from a deep and dreamless sleep by Cal shouting and shaking his shoulder mercilessly.

Will's head throbbed dully as he sat up in his narrow bed. He felt more than a little fragile.

'Get up, Will, we have duties.'

He had no idea what time it was, but he was certain it was very early indeed. He burped and, as the taste of the ale from the night before soured his mouth, he groaned and lay back down on his narrow bed.

'I said get up!'

'Do I have to?' Will protested.

'Mr Tonypandy's waiting, and he's not a patient man.'

How did I end up here? His eyes firmly shut, Will lay still, longing to go back to sleep. It felt to him exactly like the first day of school all over again, such was the sensation of dread that flooded through him. He had absolutely no idea what they had in store for him, and he wasn't in the mood to find out.

'Will!' Cal shouted.

'All right, all right.' With sickening resignation he got up and dressed and followed Cal downstairs, where a short, heavy-set man with a severe expression stood on the doorstep. He regarded Will with a look of overt disgust before turning his back on him.

'Here, put these on quickly.' Cal handed Will a heavy black bundle. Will unfolded it and struggled into what could only be described as ill-fitting oilskins, uncomfortably tight under the arms and around the crutch. He looked down at himself and then at Cal, who was dressed in the same clothing.

'We look ridiculous!' he said.

'You'll need them where you're going,' Cal replied tersely.

Will presented himself to Mr Tonypandy, who didn't utter a word. He stared blankly at Will for a moment, and then flicked his head to indicate that he should follow.

On the street, Cal headed off in a different direction altogether. Although he was also on a work detail, it was in another quadrant of the South Cavern, and Will was seized with trepidation that he wouldn't be accompanying him. As irksome as Will sometimes found his brother, Cal was his touchstone, his keeper in this incomprehensible place with its primitive practices. He felt terribly vulnerable without him by his side.

Following unenthusiastically behind, Will stole occasional glances at Mr Tonypandy as he walked slowly along with a pronounced limp, his left leg heaving waywardly in its own orbit, and his foot beating the cobbles with a soft thwack at each step. Practically as broad as he was tall, he wore a peculiar black ribbed hat that was pulled down almost to his eyebrows. It looked as though it was made of wool but, on closer inspection, appeared to be woven from a fibrous material, something rather like coconut hair. His short neck was as wide as his head and it suddenly occurred to Will that, from behind, the whole thing resembled a big thumb sticking out of an overcoat.

As they progressed along the street, other Colonists fell in behind them until the troop was a dozen or so in number. They were mostly young, between the ages of ten and fifteen, Will reckoned. He saw that many of them were carrying spades, while a few had bizarre long-handled tools that looked vaguely like pickaxes, with a spike on one side but a long, curved scoop on the other. From the wear on the leather-bound shafts and the state of the ironwork, Will could tell the tools had seen a great deal of use.

Curiosity overcame him, and he leant over to one of the boys walking beside him and asked in a low voice: 'Excuse me, what's that thing you've got there?'

The boy glared charily at him and muttered: 'It's a pitch cleaver, of course.'

'A pitch cleaver,' Will repeated. 'Er, thanks,' he added as the boy deliberately slowed his pace, dropping back from him. At that point, Will felt more alone than he could ever remember feeling, and was suddenly overwhelmed by the strongest yearning to turn around and go back to the Jerome house. But he knew he had no alternative but to do what he was told down here in this place. He had to toe the line.

Eventually, they entered a tunnel, the tramping of their boots echoing about them. The tunnel walls had diagonal veins of a shiny black rock running through them, like strata of obsidian or even, as he looked more closely, polished coal. *Was that what they were on their way to do?* Will's head immediately filled with images of miners stripped to the waist, crawling into narrow seams and hacking away at the dusty black coalface. His mind swam with apprehension.

After a few minutes they crossed through into a cavern, smaller than the one they had just left. The first thing Will noticed was that the air was different in here; the humidity had increased to the point that he could feel the moisture collect on his face and mingle with his sweat. Then he noticed that the cavern walls were shored up with huge slabs of limestone. Cal had told him that the Colony was made up of an interlinking series of chambers, some naturally formed and others like this one, man-made with partially reinforced walls.

'God, I hope Dad's seen this!' Will said under his breath, longing to stop and savour his surroundings, perhaps even to do a sketch or two to record it. But he had to be content with taking in as much as he could as they tramped quickly along.

There were fewer buildings in this cavern, giving it an almost rural feel, and a little further on, they marched by some oak-beamed barns and single-storey houses like little bungalows, some freestanding but mostly built into the walls. As for the residents of the cavern, he saw only a handful of people carrying bulky canvas bags on their backs or pushing loaded barrows.

The troop followed Mr Tonypandy as he veered off the road and down into a deep trench, the bottom of which was full of sodden clay. Slippery and treacherous, it clung to their boots, hampering their progress as they weaved their way through a meandering course. Soon the trench opened into a sizeable crater at the base of the cavern wall itself, and the work party drew up beside two crude stone-built buildings with flat roofs. The boys seemed to know that they should just wait, leaning against their spades and pitch cleavers as Mr

Tonypandy began a lively discussion with two older men who had emerged from one of the buildings. The boys in the troop joked and chatted noisily together, sometimes giving Will sidelong glances as he stood apart from them. Then Mr Tony-pandy left, limping off in the direction of the road, and one of the older men shouted over at Will.

'You're with me, Jerome. Go to the huts.'

The man had a livid red scar in the shape of a crescent across his face. It began just above his mouth and ran up across his left eye and forehead, parting the man's snow-white hair and ending somewhere at the back of his head. But for Will, the man's eye, permanently weeping and shot through with a mottled cloudiness, was the most distressing aspect. The eyelid over it was so torn and ragged that each time the man blinked, it was like a defective windscreen wiper strug-gling to function.

'In there! In there!' he barked, as Will failed to acknowl-edge the order.

'Sorry,' Will answered quickly. Then he and two other youngsters followed the scar man into the nearest building.

The interior was dank and, except for some equipment in the corner, appeared to be empty. They stood idly about as the scar man kicked at the dirt floor as if looking for something he'd lost. He began to swear wildly under his breath until his boot finally struck something solid. It was a metal ring. He pulled at it with both hands and there was a loud creaking as a steel plate lifted to reveal a metre-square opening.

'Right, down we go.'

One by one they filed down a wet, rusty stepladder, and once they had all reached the bottom, the scar man took the lantern from his belt and played it around the brick-lined tunnel. It wasn't quite high enough to stand up in and, judging by the state of the masonry, was clearly eroded and badly in need of repointing where the chalky mortar had crumbled away. Will guessed that it must have been in use for decades, if not centuries.

Ten centimetres or so of brackish water stood in the bottom of the tunnel and it wasn't long before it plunged over the tops of Will's boots as he tagged behind the others. They had sloshed along for about ten minutes when the scar man stopped and turned to them again.

'Under here . . .' the man spoke condescendingly to Will, as if he was explaining something to a young child, '. . . are boreholes. We remove the sediment . . . we unblock them. Yes?'

The scar man swung the lantern to illuminate the tunnel floor, which was heavily silted with little island aggregations of flint and limestone shards rising out of the water. He slipped several coils of rope off his shoulder and Will watched as each boy in turn took an end from him and knotted it securely around his waist. The scar man tied the other end of each rope around himself, so that they were connected like a group of mountaineers.

'Topsoiler,' the scar man snarled, 'we tie the rope around ourselves . . . we tie it well.' Will didn't dare to question why as he took the rope and looped it around his waist, knotting it as best he could. As he tugged at it to test it, the man held out a battered pitch cleaver for him.

'Now we dig.'

The two boys began to hack away at the floor of the tunnel, and Will knew he was meant to do likewise. Probing with the unfamiliar tool, he edged his way along the brick lining under the swilling waters until he came to a softer patch of compacted sediment and stones. He hesitated, glancing at the other boys to reassure himself he was doing the right thing.

'We keep digging, we don't stop,' the scar man shouted as he shone the lantern on Will, who immediately began to dig. It was hard going, both because of the cramped conditions and because the tool he was using, the pitch cleaver, was unfamiliar. And the job wasn't made any easier by the water, which, however fast he worked, would keep washing back into the deepening hole after every stroke.

It wasn't long before Will had got to grips with this new tool and mastered his technique. Now well into his stride, it felt good just to be digging again and all of his worries seemed to be forgotten, even if only for a short while, as he threw load after load of stone and sopping earth out of the hole. With the water rushing in after every scoopful, he was soon thigh-deep in the borehole, and the other boys were having to work furiously just to keep up with him. Then, with a bone-shaking judder, his pitch cleaver jarred against something immovable.

'We dig around it!' the scar man snapped.

With sweat running down his dirty face and stinging his eyes, Will glanced at the scar man and then back at the water lapping against his oilskins, trying to work out the reason for their task. He knew he'd get short shrift from the scar man if he asked, but his curiosity was getting the better of him. He was just looking up to ask a question when there was an urgent cry, cut off almost as soon as it started.

'BRACE!' the scar man screamed.

Will turned just in time to see one of the other boys completely vanish with a loud gurgling, as the water gushed down into what now looked like a huge drain the size of a manhole.

The rope yanked tight, cutting into Will's waist and jerking with the fallen boy's desperate movements. The scar man leaned back and dug his boots into the grit and debris of the tunnel floor. Will found he was pinned to the edge of his borehole.

'Pull yourself up!' the scar man shouted in the direction of the swirling hole. Will watched with alarm, until he saw grimy fingers snaking up the rope as the boy heaved himself out against the flow. As he got to his feet again Will saw the terrified look on his mud-streaked face.

'One hole down. Now the rest of you get a bloody move on,' the scar man said, lounging back against the wall behind him as he took out a pipe and began to clean its bowl with a pocket knife.

Will stabbed away blindly at the tightly compacted sediment around the object wedged in the hole, until most of it had been removed. He couldn't tell what it was, but when he jabbed at the obstruction itself, it felt a little spongy, as if it was water-logged timber. As he drove his heel down in an attempt to loosen it, there was a sudden whoosh as it dislodged and the surface beneath his feet literally gave way. There was nothing he could do, he was in free fall, water sluicing down around him with a cascade of gravel and slurry. His body banged against the sides of the borehole, his hair and face drenched and covered in grit.

He twitched like a marionette as the rope broke his fall. In less than a second, he'd gathered his wits; he guessed he'd dropped at least six metres, but he had no idea what lay below him in the blackness.

Now's my chance, it suddenly occurred to him in a flash.

He desperately groped under his oilskins, in his trouser

pockets, his hand closing on the penknife.

. . . to escape . . .

He peered below him into the absolute darkness of the unknown, calculating the odds, the rope tensing as the others began to pull.

. . . and Dad's down here . . . somewhere . . . The idea blinked through his mind as keenly as a neon sign.

. . . down here, down here, down here . . . it repeated, flashing on and off with the irksome buzz of an electrical discharge.

. . . water, I can hear water . . .

'CLIMB THE ROPE, BOY!' he heard the scar man bellowing from somewhere above. 'CLIMB THE ROPE!'

Will's mind raced as he tried to catch the sounds below him; faint splashes and the gurgle of moving water were just audible over the pendulum creaks of the thick rope that bit into his waist, his lifeline back to the Colony above.

. . . but how deep is it?

There was water below, that much was certain, but he didn't know if it was sufficient to cushion his fall. He flicked the blade open and pressed it against the rope, poised to cut it.

Yes . . . no?

If the water wasn't deep enough he'd be jumping to his death in this godforsaken, lonely place. He pictured jagged shards of rock, razor-sharp and deadly, like a line drawing from a comic book . . . the next frame was his lifeless body, impaled and broken as his blood pumped out of him, mingling with the darkness.

But he felt rash and daring. He drew the blade against the rope and the first braid of fibres separated beneath it.

A daring escape! flashed in his mind, even brighter than

before, like a by-line from some Hollywood adventure. The words were proud and brave, but then the image of Chester's face, laughing and happy, reared up shattering it into a million fragments. Will shivered from the cold, his body drenched and plastered with mud.

The muted hollering of the scar man once again drifted from above, as vague and confused as a yodeller down a drainpipe, wrenching Will from his thoughts. He knew he should start pulling himself back up the rope, but he couldn't bring himself to do it. Then he sighed, and all the courage and bravado were gone. In their place was the cold certainty that if not now, then there'd be another opportunity to escape, and he *would* take it next time.

He tucked away the penknife, twisted himself upright, and began the laborious climb back to the others.

Seven long hours later he'd lost count of how many boreholes they'd cleared as they progressed further and further into the tunnel. Finally, glancing at his pocket watch under the light of the lantern, the scar man told them they were finished for the day. They trudged back towards the stepladder and Will set off alone for the journey home, his hands and back aching horribly.

As he climbed out of the trench and made his way slowly along the road, he spotted a circle of Colonists outside a building with a pair of large, garage-type doors. They were surrounded by banks of stacked crates.

As one of the men stepped back from the gathering Will heard a high-pitched laugh. Then he saw something that made him blink and rub his eyes. A man in a puce-pink blazer and straw boater pranced in the middle of the group.

'Can't be! No! It is! It's Mr Clarke Junior!' he said aloud, without meaning to.

'What?' came a voice from behind. It was one of the boys who had been working with Will in the tunnel. 'You know him?'

'Yes! But . . . but . . . what on earth is he doing here?' Will was dumbfounded, as he thought of the Clarkes' shop in the High Street and struggled with the displaced apparition of Mr Clarke Junior down here, still cavorting within the circle of stocky Colonists. As he watched, Will saw that he was picking things from the boxes with little theatrical flourishes and displaying them to his audience, sweeping them along his sleeve like a dodgy watch salesman before he placed them delicately on a trestle table. Then the penny dropped.

'Don't tell me he's selling fruit!' Will said.

'And vegetables.' The boy looked curiously at Will. 'The Clarkes have been trading with us for as long as—'

'My God, what's *that*?' Will interrupted him, pointing at an outlandish figure that had stepped into view from the shadow of a towering stack of fruit boxes. Apparently ignored, it stood outside the huddle of Colonists and inspected a pineapple as if it were a rare artefact, while the exchange continued with the gesticulating Mr Clarke Junior.

The boy followed Will's finger to the stationary figure, which appeared to be human, with arms and legs, but was swathed in some kind of bloated diver's suit, which was a dull bone colour. It was bulbous, like a caricature of a fat man, and the head and face were completely obscured by a hood-like extension. Its large goggles glinted as they caught the light of a street lamp. It looked like a man-shaped slug or, rather, a slug-shaped man.

'Bloody hell, don't you know anything?' The boy laughed with undisguised scorn at Will's ignorance. 'It's only a *Coprolite*.'

Will frowned. 'Oh right, a Coprolite.'

'From down there,' the boy said, flicking his eyes towards the ground as he walked away. Will lingered behind for a moment to watch the strange being – it moved so slowly it reminded Will of the leeches that inhabited the sludge at the bottom of the school fish tank. It was an improbable scene, the pink-jacketed Mr Clarke Junior peddling his wares to the crowd, while the Coprolite examined a pineapple, deep in the bowels of the Earth.

He was deliberating whether to go over to talk to Mr Clarke Junior when he spotted two policemen at the edge of the crowd. He left quickly and went on his way, nagged by a question which elbowed all other thoughts aside. *If the Clarkes knew about the Colony, then how many others in Highfield were leading double lives?*

As the weeks passed Will was assigned to further work details in other parts of the Colony. It gave him an insight into the workings of this subterranean culture, and he was determined to document as much of it as he could in his journal. The Styx were at the very top of the pecking order and a law unto themselves, and next came a small governing elite of Colonists, to which Mr Jerome was privileged to belong. Will had no idea what he or these Governors actually did and, on detailed questioning, it appeared that Cal didn't either. Then there were the ordinary Colonists and finally an underbelly of unfortunates, who either could not work or refused to do so, and they were left to rot in ghettos, the largest of which was the Rookeries.

Every afternoon, after Will had swabbed dirt and sweat off himself using the basic facilities in the so-called bathroom of the Jerome house, Cal would watch as he sat on his bed and jotted down meticulous notes, adding the occasional sketch where he felt it was warranted. Perhaps it would be of children working at one of the rubbish tips. It was quite a scene: these tiny Colonists, little more than toddlers, so adept at scavenging the huge mounds of litter and taking so much care to sort everything into hoppers for processing.

'Nothing goes to waste,' Cal had told him. 'I should know, I used to do it!'

Or it might be a picture of the stark fortress in the farthermost corner of the South Cavern where the Styx lived, which had a huge iron stockade enclosing it. This drawing had been by far the greatest challenge for Will as he hadn't had an opportunity to get very close. With sentries patrolling the neighbouring streets, it wasn't done to be caught showing too much interest in it.

Cal was at a loss to understand why Will took such great pains to write up his journal. He persistently badgered Will, asking him what the point of it all was. Will had replied that it was something his father had taught him to do whenever they found anything during their excavations.

And there it was again, his father. Dr Burrows was still his father as far as he was concerned, and Mr Jerome, even if he was his *real* father – though he still wasn't wholly convinced of that – came a poor second in Will's estimation. And his deranged Topsoil mother, and sister, Rebecca, still felt like family. Yet he felt such affection for Cal, Uncle Tam and Grandma Macaulay that sometimes his loyalties churned in his head with the ferocity of a stoppered tornado.

As he put the finishing touches to a sketch of a Colony house his mind wandered and he began to daydream again about his father's journey into the Deeps. Will was eager to discover what lay down there, and knew that one day soon he would follow. However, every time he tried to imagine what the future might hold for him, he was brought back to bitter reality with a bump, to the plight of his friend Chester, still confined in that abysmal Hold.

Will stopped drawing and rubbed the peeling calluses on the palms of his hands together.

'Sore?' Cal asked.

'Not as bad as they were,' Will replied. His mind flashed back to the work detail earlier that day, clearing stone channels in advance of draining a huge communal cesspit. He shuddered. It had been the worst task he'd been designated so far. With aching arms he resumed his notes, but then his concentration was broken by the urgent wailing of a siren, the hollow and eerie sound filling the entire house. Will stood up, trying to pinpoint where it was coming from.

'Black Wind!' Cal jumped off the bed and rushed over to close the window. Will joined him and saw people in the street below running hell for leather in all directions, until it was completely deserted. Cal pointed excitedly, then drew back his hand, looking at the hairs rising on his forearm from the rapid build-up of static in the air.

'Here it comes!' He tugged at his brother's sleeve. 'I love this.'

But nothing seemed to be happening. The siren's haunting wail continued as Will, not knowing what to look for, scanned the empty street for anything out of the ordinary.

'There! There!' Cal shouted, peering further down into the cavern. Will followed his gaze, trying to make out just what it was, but it seemed as though something was wrong with his vision. It was as if his eyes weren't focusing properly.

Then he saw why.

A solid cloud billowed up the street like ink diffusing through water, rolling and churning and obscuring everything in its wake. As Will looked down from the window he could see the street lights bravely trying to burn even more brightly as the sooty fog almost blotted them out. It was as if nocturnal waves were closing over the submerged lights of a doomed ocean liner.

'What is it?' Will asked, enthralled. He pressed his nose against the windowpane to get a better view of the dark fog spreading quickly along the rest of the street.

'It's a sort of backwash from the Interior,' Cal told him. 'It's called a Levant Wind. It rises from the lower Deeps – a bit like a burp,' he giggled.

'Is it dangerous?'

'No, just dust and stuff, but people think it's bad luck to breathe it. They say that it carries germules,' he laughed and then adopted a mock Styx monotone. '*Pernicious to those that it encounters, it sears the flesh.*' He giggled again. 'It's great though, innit?'

Will stared, transfixed. As the street below was obliterated from view, the window turned black and he felt an uncomfortable pressure in his ears. His flesh seemed to be buzzing, and all his hairs standing on end. For several minutes, the dark cloud billowed by, filling their bedroom with the smell of burnt ozone and a deadening silence. Eventually it began to thin out, the street lamps flickering through the swirling dust like the sun breaking through clouds, and then it was gone, leaving just a few diffuse grey smudges hanging in the air, as if the scene had been swept by a watercolourist's brush.

'Now watch this!'

'Sparklers?' Will asked, not believing what he was seeing.

'It's a static storm. They always follow a Levant,' Cal said, quivering with sheer excitement. 'They give you one hell of a belt if you get in the way.'

Will watched in astounded silence as a host of fireballs spun out of the dispersing clouds all along the street. Some were the size of tennis balls, while others were as large as beach balls, all fizzing fiercely as bright sparks sprayed from their edges, as if a gang of delinquent Catherine wheels had gone on the rampage.

The two boys stood mesmerized as right in front of them a fireball as large as a melon, its vibrant light illuminating their young faces and reflecting in their wide eyes, abruptly went into a downward spiral, around and around, casting off sparks as it plummeted towards the ground, shrinking to the size of an egg. As it hovered just above the cobblestones, the dying fireball seemed to flicker just a little more intensely before, in the blink of an eye, it had sputtered out.

Will and Cal were unable to tear themselves away from where it had been, the traces of its last seconds still imprinted on their retinas in little ecstatic trails, like optical pins and needles.

CHAPTER TWENTY-EIGHT

Far below the streets and houses of the Colony a lone figure stirred.

The wind had been a gentle breeze at first but rapidly built to a terrifying gale that spat grit in his face with all the ferocity of a sandstorm. He'd wound his spare shirt around his face and mouth as it grew even more intense, threatening to knock him off his feet. And the dust had been so dense and impenetrable that he hadn't been able to see his hands in front of him.

There was nothing else for it but to wait until it passed. He'd dropped to the ground and curled up into a ball, his eyes clogged and burning with the fine black dust. There he had remained, the wailing howl blasting out his thoughts until, frail from hunger, he fell into a half-sleeping, half-waking torpor.

Sometime later, he shuddered awake and, not knowing how long he'd been curled up on the floor of the tunnel, lifted his head for a tentative look around. The strange darkness of the wind had gone, save for a few lingering clouds. Coughing and spitting, he sat up and shook the dust from his clothes.

With a stained handkerchief he wiped his watering eyes and cleaned his spectacles.

Then, on all fours, Dr Burrows crawled about, scrabbling in the dry grit, using the light of a luminescent orb to find the little pile of organic matter that he'd gathered for kindling before the dust storm had hit. Eventually locating it, he picked out something that resembled a curling fern leaf. He squinted at it curiously – he had no idea what it was. Like everything in the last five miles of tunnel, it was as dry and crisp as old parchment.

He was becoming increasingly worried about his supply of water. As he'd boarded the Miners' Train the Colonists had thoughtfully provided him with a full canteen, a satchel of dried vegetables of some type, some meat strips and a packet of salt. He could ration the food, but the problem was definitely the water; he hadn't been able to find a fresh source from which to replenish his canteen for two whole days now, and he was running perilously low.

Having rearranged the kindling he began to knock two chunks of flint together until a spark leaped into it and a tiny flickering flame took hold. With his head resting on the grit floor, he gently blew on the flame and fanned it with his hand, nurturing it until the fire caught, bathing him in its glow. Then he squatted down next to his open journal, sweeping the layer of dust from the pages, and resumed his drawing.

What a find! A circle of regular stones, each the size of a door, with strange lettering cut into their faces. He didn't recognize the language from all his years of study. It was unlike anything he'd ever seen before. His mind raced as he dreamed of the people who had written these words, who had lived far below the surface of the Earth, quite possibly for thousands of years, yet had the sophistication to build this subterranean monument.

Thinking he heard a noise, he suddenly stopped drawing and sat bolt upright. Controlling his breathing, he held completely still, his heart pounding in his chest, as he peered into the darkness beyond the fire's illumination. But there was nothing, just the all-pervading silence that had been his companion since the start of his journey.

'Getting jumpy, old man,' he said, relaxing again. He was reassured by the sound of his own voice in the confines of the rock passage. 'It's just your stomach again, you silly old baggage,' he said, and laughed out loud.

He unwound the shirt from around his mouth and nose. His face was cut and bruised, his hair was matted and a straggly beard hung from his chin. His clothes were filthy and torn in places. He looked like a mad hermit. As the fire crackled he picked up his journal and concentrated on the circle of stones once again.

'This is truly exceptional – a miniature Stonehenge. What an incredible find!' he exclaimed, completely forgetting for the moment how hungry and thirsty he was. His face animated and happy, he continued with his sketching.

Then he laid down his journal and pencil, and sat unmoving for a few seconds as a faraway look crept into his eyes. He got to his feet and, taking the light orb in his hand, backed away from the fire until he was outside the stone circle. He began to stroll slowly around it. As he did so, he held the orb to the side of his face like a microphone. He pursed his lips and dropped his voice a tone or two in an attempt to mimic a television interviewer.

'And tell me, Dr Burrows, newly appointed Dean of Subterranean Studies, what does the Nobel Prize mean to you?'

Now walking more quickly around the circle, a jaunty spring in his step, his voice reverted to its normal tone and he moved the light orb to the other side of his face. He adopted a slightly surprised manner with pantomime hesitancy.

'Oh, I . . . I . . . I must say . . . it was truly a great honour and, at first, I felt that I was not worthy to follow in the footsteps of those great men and women—' At that very moment his toe caught against a piece of rock and he swore blindly as he stumbled for a few paces. Regaining his poise he began to walk again, simultaneously continuing with his response. 'The footsteps of those great men and women, that exalted list of winners who preceded me.'

He swung the orb back to the other side of his face. 'But, Professor, the contributions you have made to so many fields – medicine, physics, chemistry, biology, geology and, above all, archaeology – are inestimable. You are considered to be one of the greatest living scholars on the planet. Did you ever think it would come to this, the day you began the tunnel in your cellar?'

Dr Burrows gave a melodramatic 'ahem' as the orb changed sides again. 'Well, I knew that there was more for me . . . much more than my career in the museum back in . . .'

Dr Burrows' voice tailed off as he ground to a halt. His face fell and became devoid of any expression. He pocketed the orb, plunging himself into the shadows cast by the stones as he thought of his family and wondered how they were getting on without him. Shaking his bedraggled head, he slowly shuffled back into the circle and slumped down by his journal, staring blankly into the flickering flames, which grew more blurred as he watched them. Finally he removed his spectacles and rubbed the moisture from his eyes with the heels of his hands.

'I have to do this,' he said to himself as he replaced his spectacles and once again took up his pencil. '*I have to.*'

The firelight radiated out from between the stones in the circle, projecting shifting spokes of gentle light on to the floor and walls of the passage. In the centre of this wheel, totally absorbed, the cross-legged figure grumbled quietly as he rubbed out a mistake in his journal.

He hadn't a thought for anyone in the world at that moment; he was a man so obsessed that nothing else mattered, nothing at all.

CHAPTER TWENTY-NINE

As a fire spluttered in the hearth Mr Jerome reclined in one of the winged armchairs reading his newspaper. From time to time, the heavily waxed pages flopped waywardly, and he flicked his wrists reflexively to straighten them up again. Will couldn't make out a single headline from his vantage point at the table; the blocky newsprint bled into the paper to such an extent that it looked as though a swarm of ants had dipped their feet in black ink and then stampeded across the pages.

Cal played another card and waited expectantly for his brother's response, but Will was finding it impossible to keep his concentration on the game. It was the first time he'd been in the same room as Mr Jerome without being on the receiving end of hostile glances or a resentful silence. This in itself represented a landmark in their relationship.

There was a sudden crash as the front door was flung open, and all three looked up.

'Cal, Will!' Uncle Tam bellowed as he blundered in from the hallway, shattering the scene of apparent domestic bliss. He pulled himself up when he saw Mr Jerome staring daggers at him from his chair.

'Oh, sorry, I . . .'

'I though we had an understanding,' Mr Jerome growled as he rose and folded the paper under his arm. 'You said you wouldn't come here . . . when I'm at home.' He walked stiffly past Tam without so much as a glance.

Uncle Tam pulled a face and sat down next to Will. With a conspiratorial wave of his hand, he indicated to the boys to come closer. He waited until Mr Jerome's footsteps had receded into the distance before he spoke.

'The time has arrived,' Tam whispered, extracting a dented metal canister from inside his coat. He flipped off the cap from one end and they watched as he slid out a tattered map and laid it over their cards on the tabletop, smoothing out the corners so that it lay flat. Then he turned to Will.

'Chester is to be Banished tomorrow evening,' he said.

'Oh, God.' Will sat up as if he'd had an electric shock. 'That's a bit sudden, isn't it?'

'I only just found out – it's planned for six,' Tam said. 'There'll be quite a crowd. The Styx like to make a spectacle out of these things. They believe a sacrifice is good for the soul.'

He turned back to the map, humming softly as he searched the complex grid of lines, until finally his finger came to rest on a tiny dark square. Then he looked up at Will as if he'd just remembered something.

'You know, it's not a difficult thing . . . to get *you* out, alone. But Chester too, that's a very different kettle of fish. It's taken a lot more thought, but,' he paused and Will and Cal stared into his eyes, 'I've cracked it. There might be a way to escape to the Topsoil . . . through the Eternal City.'

Will heard Cal gasp, but much as he wanted to ask his uncle about this place, it didn't seem appropriate as Tam went on. He proceeded to talk Will through the escape plan, tracing the route on the map as the boys listened raptly, absorbing every detail. The tunnels had names like Watling Street, The Great North and Bishopswood. Will interrupted his uncle only once as he was talking, with a suggestion which, after some considerable thought, Tam incorporated into the plan. Although on the exterior he was composed and businesslike, Will felt excitement and fear building in the pit of his stomach.

'The problem with this,' Tam sighed, 'is the unknowns, the variables, that I can't help you with. If you hit any snags when you're out there you'll just have to play it by ear . . . do the best you can.' At this point, Will noticed that some of the sparkle had gone out of Tam's eyes – he didn't look his normal confident self.

Tam ran through the whole plan from beginning to end once again and, when he'd finished, he fished something out of his pocket and passed it over to Will. 'Here's a copy of the directions once you're outside the Colony. If they catch up with you, heaven forbid, eat the damn thing.'

Will unfolded it carefully. It was a piece of cloth, the size of a handkerchief when completely opened. The surface was covered with a mass of infinitesimally small lines in brown ink, like an unruly maze, each representing a different tunnel. Although Will's route was clearly marked in a light red ink, Tam quickly took him through it.

Tam watched as Will refolded the cloth map, and then spoke in a low voice. 'This has to go like clockwork. You'd put *all* your kin in the very worst danger if the Styx thought for one second I'd had a hand in this . . . and it wouldn't just end with me; Cal, your grandmother and father would all be in the firing line.' He grasped Will's forearm tightly across the table and squeezed it to emphasize the gravity of his warning. 'Another thing, when you're Topsoil, you and Chester are going to have to disappear. I haven't had time to arrange anything, so—'

'What about Sarah?' Will blurted as the idea occurred to him, although her name still felt a little odd on his lips. 'My *real* mother? Couldn't she help me?'

A suggestion of a smile dropped into place on Tam's face. 'I wondered when you'd think of that,' he said. The smile disappeared, and he spoke as if choosing his words carefully. 'If my sister is still alive, and nobody knows that for sure, she'll be well and truly hidden.' He glanced down at the palm of his hand as he rubbed it with the thumb of the other. 'One plus one can sometimes add up to zero.'

'What do you mean?' Will asked.

'Well, if by some miracle you did happen to find her, you might lead the Styx her way. Then *both* of you would end up feeding the worms.' He raised his head again and shook it just once as he fixed Will with a thoughtful stare. 'No, I'm sorry, but you're on your own. You're going to have to run hard and long, for all our sakes, not just yours. Mark my words, if the Styx get you in their clutches, they *will* make you spill your guts, sooner or later, and that would endanger us all,' he said ominously.

'Then we'd have to get out too, wouldn't we, Uncle Tam?' Cal volunteered, his voice full of bravado.

"You've got to be kidding!" Tam turned sharply on him. 'We wouldn't have a hope. We wouldn't even see them coming.'

'But . . .' began Cal.

'Look, this isn't some game, Caleb. If you cross them once too often, you won't be around long enough to regret it. Before you know it, you'll be dancing Old Nick's Jig.' He paused. 'You know what that is?' Tam didn't wait for an answer. 'It's a choice little number. Your arms are stitched behind your back . . .' he shifted uncomfortably in his seat, '. . . with copper thread, your eyelids are stripped off and you're dropped in the darkest chamber you can imagine, full of Red Hots.'

'Red *whats*?' Will asked.

Tam shuddered and, ignoring Will's question, went on. 'How long do you think you'd last? How many days of knocking into the walls in the pitch black, dust burning into your ruined eyes, before you collapsed from exhaustion? Feeling the first bites on your skin as they start to feed? I wouldn't wish that on my worst . . .' He didn't finish the sentence.

The two boys both swallowed hard, but then Tam's expression brightened up again. 'Enough of that,' he said. 'You've still got that light, haven't you?'

Still stunned by what he'd just heard, Will looked at him blankly. He pulled himself together and nodded.

'Good,' Tam said as he took out a small cloth bundle from his coat pocket and put it on the table in front of Will. 'And these might come in handy.'

Will touched the bundle tentatively.

'Well, go on, have a look.'

Will untied the corners. Inside, there were four knobbly brown-black stones the size of marbles.

'Node stones!' Cal said.

'Yes. They're rarer than slugs' boots,' Tam smiled. 'They're described in the old books, but nobody 'cept me and my boys has ever seen one before. Imago found this lot.'

'What do they do?' Will asked, looking at the strange stones.

'Down here, it's not like you're going to beat a Colonist or, worse still, a Styx in a straight fight. The only weapons you have are *light* and *flight*,' Tam said. 'If you get in a tight corner, just crack one of these things open. Chuck it against something hard and keep your eyes shut – it'll give a burst of the brightest light you can imagine. I hope these are still good,' he said, weighing one in his hand. He looked at Will. 'So you think you're up to this?'

Will nodded.

'Right,' the big man said.

'Thanks, Uncle Tam. I can't tell you how . . .' Will said falteringly.

'No need, my boy.' Tam ruffled his hair. He looked down at the table and didn't speak for a few seconds. It was totally unexpected; silence and Uncle Tam didn't go together. Will had never before seen him like this, this gregarious and massive man. He could only think that he was upset and trying to hide it. But when Tam raised his head, the broad smile was there and his voice rumbled as it always did.

'I saw all this coming . . . it was bound to happen sooner or later. The Macaulays are loyal and we will fight for those we love and believe in, no matter what the price. You would've tried to do something to save Chester, and gone after your father, whether I'd helped you or not.'

Will nodded, feeling his eyes fill with tears.

'Thought as much!' Tam boomed. 'Like your mother . . . like Sarah . . . a Macaulay through and through!' He grabbed

Will firmly by his shoulders. 'My head knows you have to go, but my heart says otherwise.' He squeezed Will and sighed. 'Pity is . . . we could have had some times down here, the three of us. Some high times indeed.'

Will, Cal and Tam talked well into the early hours, and when he finally got to bed Will hardly slept a wink.

Early in the morning, before there was a stir in the house, Will packed his rucksack and tucked the cloth map Uncle Tam had given him into the top of his boot. He checked that the node stones and light orb were in his pockets, then went over to Cal and shook him awake.

'I'm off,' Will said in a low voice as his brother's eyes flickered open. Cal sat up, scratching his head.

'Thanks for everything, Cal,' Will whispered, 'and say goodbye to Granny from me, won't you?'

'Course I will,' his brother replied, then frowned. 'You know I'd give anything to come too.'

'I know, I know . . . but you heard what Tam said, I have more chance by myself. Anyway, your family are here,' he said finally, and turned to the door.

Will tiptoed down the stairs. He felt exhilarated to be on the move again, but this was tempered by an unexpected pang of sadness that he was leaving. Of course, he could stay here, somewhere he actually belonged, if he chose, rather than venturing out into the unknown and risking it all. It would be so easy just to go back to bed. As he reached the hallway he could hear Bartleby snoring somewhere in the shadows. It was a comforting sound, the sound of home. He would never hear that sound again if he went now. He stood by the front door and hesitated. No! How could he ever live with himself if he chose to leave Chester to the Styx? He would rather die trying to free him. He took a deep breath and, glancing behind him into the still house, he slipped the heavy catch on the door. He opened it, stepped over the threshold and then closed it gently behind him. He was out.

He knew he had a considerable distance to cover, so he walked quickly, his rucksack thumping a rhythm on his back. It took him a little under forty minutes to reach the building at the edge of the cavern that Tam had described. There was no mistaking it, as unlike most structures in the Colony it had a tiled rather than a stone roof.

He was now on the road that led to the Skull Gate. Tam had said that he had to keep his wits about him as the Styx changed sentries at random intervals, and there was no way of knowing whether one was just about to appear around the corner.

Leaving the road, Will climbed over a gate and sprinted through the yard that lay in front of the building, a ramshackle farm property. He heard a pig-like grunting coming from one of the outlying buildings, and spotted some chickens penned up in another area. They were spindly and malnourished, but had perfectly white feathers.

He entered the building with the tiled roof and saw the old timber beams leaning against the wall just as Tam had described. As he crept in under them, something moved towards him.

'What—?'

It was Tam. He immediately silenced Will by putting a finger to his lips. Will could hardly contain his surprise. He looked at Tam questioningly but the man's face was grim and unsmiling.

There was hardly enough room for both of them under the beams, and Tam squatted awkwardly as he slid a massive paving slab along the wall. Then he leaned in towards Will.

'Good luck,' he whispered in his ear, and literally pushed him into the jagged opening. Then the slab grated shut behind Will and he was on his own.

In the pitch darkness he fumbled in his pocket for the light orb to which he'd already attached a length of thick string. He slipped this around his neck, so leaving his hands free. At first, he moved along the passage with ease, but then, after nine or ten metres, it pinched down to a crawlway. The roof of the tunnel was so low that he ended up on his hands and knees. The passage angled upwards, and as he heaved himself painfully over jagged plates of broken rock his rucksack kept snagging on the roof.

He caught a movement in front of him, and froze on the spot. With some trepidation he lifted the light orb to see what it was. He held his breath as something white flashed across the passage and then landed with a soft thump no more than two metres ahead of him. It was an eyeless rat, the size of a well-fed kitten, with snowy fur and whiskers that oscillated like butterfly wings. It stood up on its hind legs, its muzzle twitching and its large, glistening incisors in full view. It showed absolutely no sign that it was afraid of him.

Will found a stone on the tunnel floor and threw it as hard as he could. It missed, glancing off the wall next to the animal, which didn't even flinch. Will's indignation that a mere rat was holding him up welled over, and he lunged towards the animal with a growl. In a single effortless bound it leaped at him, landing smartly on his shoulder, and for a split second neither boy nor rat moved. Will felt its whiskers, as delicate as eyelashes, brush his cheek. He shook his shoulders frantically and it launched itself off, springing once on the back of Will's leg as it sped away in the opposite direction.

'Little sh . . .' Will muttered, as he tried to compose himself before setting off again.

He crawled for what seemed like hours, his hands becoming cut and tender from the razor-sharp shards strewn across the floor. Then, much to his relief, the passage increased in height and he was almost able to stand up again. Now he could move at speed he became almost euphoric and felt an irrepressible urge to sing as he negotiated the bends in the tunnel. He thought better of it when it occurred to him that the sentries at the Skull Gate probably weren't very far from his current position and might somehow be able to hear him.

Eventually he reached the end of the passage, which was cloaked with several layers of stiff sacking, dirtied up to camouflage them against the stone. He brushed them aside and drew his breath as he saw the tunnel had come out just under the roof of a cavern, and that there was at least a thirty-metre drop to the road below. He was pleased that he'd got this far, past the Skull Gate, but he felt certain that this couldn't be right. He was at such a dizzying height that he immediately assumed he must be in the wrong place. Then Tam's words came back to him: '*It'll look impossible, but take it slowly. Cal managed it with me when he was much younger, so you can do it.*'

He leaned over to scan the array of ledges and nooks in the rock wall below him. Then he cautiously clambered out over the edge of the tunnel lip and began the descent, checking and rechecking each shaking handhold and foothold before he made the next move.

He'd climbed no more than six metres when he heard a noise below. A desolate groan. He held still and listened, his heart thudding in his ears. It came again. He had one foot on a small ridge with the other dangling in midair, while his hands gripped an outcrop of rock at chest height. He slowly twisted his head and peered down over his shoulder.

Swinging a lantern, a man was strolling in the direction of the Skull Gate with two emaciated cows a couple of paces in front of him. He shouted something at them as he drove them along, completely unaware of Will's presence above him.

Will was totally exposed but there was nothing he could do. He held absolutely still, praying that the man wouldn't stop and look up. Then just the thing Will was dreading happened: the man came to an abrupt halt.

Oh, no, this is it!

With his bird's-eye view Will could clearly make out the man's shiny white scalp as he took something out of a shoulder bag. It was a clay pipe with a long stem, which he loaded with tobacco from a pouch and lit, puffing out little clouds of smoke. Will heard him say something to the cows, and then he started on his way again.

Will breathed a silent sigh of relief and, checking that the coast was clear, quickly finished the descent, criss-crossing from ledge to ledge until he was safely back on the ground. Then he dashed as fast as he could along the road, on either side of which were fields of impossibly proportioned mushrooms, their bulbous ovoid caps standing on thick stalks. He now recognized these as pennybuns and, as he went, the motion of his light bobbing in his hand threw a multitude of their shifting shadows over the cavern walls behind them.

Will slowed his pace as he developed a painful stitch in his side. He took a series of deep breaths to try to ease it, then forced himself to speed up again, aware that every second counted if he was going to reach Chester in time. Leaving cavern after cavern behind him, the fields of pennybuns eventually gave way to black carpets of lichen, and he was relieved when he spotted the first of the lampposts and the hazy outline of a building in the distance. He was getting closer. Suddenly he found himself at a huge stone archway hewn into the rock. He went through it, into the main body of the Quarter. Soon the dwellings were crowding the sides of the road and he was becoming more and more nervous. Although nobody seemed to be around, he kept the sound from his boots to a minimum by running on his toes. He was terrified that someone was going to appear from one of the houses and spot him.

Then he saw what he'd been looking for. It was the first of the side tunnels that Tam had mentioned.

'*You're going to take the backstreets.*' He remembered his uncle's words. '*It's safer there.*'

'Left, left, right.' As he went, Will repeated the sequence Tam had drummed into him.

The tunnels were just wide enough for a coach to pass through them. '*Go quickly through these,*' he'd said. '*If you bump into anyone, just brass it out, like you're supposed to be there.*'

But there was no sign of anyone as Will ran with all his might, his rucksack crashing on his back at every step. By the time he re-emerged in the main cavern he was sweating and out of breath. He recognized the squat outline of the police station between the two taller structures on either side, and slowed to a walk to give himself a chance to cool off.

'Made it this far,' he muttered to himself. The plan had seemed so easy when Tam had described it, but now he was wondering if he'd made a dreadful mistake. *'You haven't got time to think,'* Tam had said, pointing a finger at him to emphasize his words. *'If you hesitate, the momentum will be lost – the whole thing will go cockeyed.'*

Will wiped the sweat from his forehead and steeled himself for the next stage.

As he drew nearer, the sight of the police station's entrance brought back memories of the first time he and Chester had been dragged up its steps, and the gruelling interrogations that had followed. It all came flooding back, and he tried to put them from his mind as he slipped into the shadows by the side of the building and heaved his rucksack off. He dug out his camera, checking it quickly before he put it into his pocket. Then he hid his rucksack and headed for the steps. As he climbed them, he took a deep breath and pushed through the doors.

The Second Officer was reclining in a chair with his feet on the counter. His eyes swivelled to regard the newcomer, his movements dull as if he'd been dozing. It took him almost a second to recognize who was standing before him, and then a confounded expression crept over his beefy face.

'Well, well, well, Jerome. What on earth are you doing back here?'

'I've come to see my friend,' Will replied, praying that his voice didn't crack. He felt as if he were edging out on the branch of a tree, and the further he went the thinner and more precarious the branch became. If he lost his balance now, the fall could be fatal.

'So who let you come back here?' the Second Officer said

suspiciously.

'Who d'you think?' Will tried to smile calmly.

The Second Officer pondered for a moment, looking him up and down. 'Well, I suppose . . . if they let you through the Skull Gate, it must be all right,' he reasoned aloud as he lumbered slowly to his feet.

'They told me I could see him,' Will said, 'one last time.'

'So you know it is to be tonight?' the Second Officer said with the suggestion of a smile. Will nodded and saw that this had dispelled any doubts in the man's mind. At once the officer's manner was transformed.

'Didn't walk the whole way, did you?' he asked. A friendly, generous smile creased his face like a gash in a pig's belly. Will hadn't seen this side of him before, and it made it all the more difficult for him to do what he had to.

'Yes, I had an early start.'

'No wonder you look hot. Better come with me, then,' the Second Officer said as he lifted up the flap at the end of the counter and came through, rattling his keys. 'I hear you're fitting in well,' he added. 'Knew you would . . . the moment I first laid eyes on you. Deep down he's one of us, I told the First Officer. Looks the part, I said to him.'

They went through the old oak door into the gloom of the Hold. The familiar smell gave Will the creeps as the Second Officer swung back the cell door and ushered him in. It took a moment for his eyes to adjust, then he saw him: Chester was sitting in the corner on the ledge, his legs drawn up under his chin. His friend didn't react immediately, but stared emptily at Will. Then, with a flash of recognition and sheer disbelief, he was on his feet.

'Will?' he said, his jaw dropping. 'Will! I can't believe it!'

'Hi, Chester,' Will said, trying to keep the excitement from his voice. He was elated to see him again, but at the same time his whole body was shaking with adrenaline.

'Have you come to get me out, Will? Can I leave now?'

'Er . . . not quite.' Will half turned, aware that the Second Officer was just behind him and could hear every word.

The Second Officer coughed self-consciously. 'I have to lock you in, Jerome. Hope you understand – it's the regulations,' he said as he shut the door and turned the key.

'What is it, Will?' Chester asked, sensing that something was wrong. 'Is it bad news?' He took a step away from Will.

'You all right?' Will replied, too preoccupied to answer his friend as he listened to the Second Officer leave the Hold through the oak door and close it firmly. Then he took Chester into the corner of the cell and they huddled together while Will explained what they had to do.

Minutes later came the sound that Will was dreading: the Second Officer was walking back into the Hold towards them. 'Time, gentlemen,' he said. He turned the key and opened the door, and Will made his way out slowly.

'Bye, Chester,' he said.

As the Second Officer began to close the door, Will put his hand on the man's arm.

'Just a second, I think I've left something in there,' he said.

'What's that?' the man asked.

The Second Officer was looking directly at him as Will brought his hand out of his pocket. He saw that the little red light was on: the camera was ready. Thrusting it at the man, Will clicked the shutter.

The flash caught the policeman full in the face. He howled and dropped his keys, clapping his hands over his eyes as he sank to the floor. The flash had been so bright compared with the sublime glow of the light orbs that even Will and Chester, who had both shielded themselves from it, felt the aftershock of its brilliance.

'Sorry,' Will said to the groaning man.

Chester was standing motionless in the cell, a stupefied look on his face.

'Get a move on, Chester!' Will shouted as he leaned in and yanked him past the Second Officer, who was starting to fumble his way to the wall, still moaning horribly.

As they entered the reception area, Will happened to glance over the counter.

'My spade!' he exclaimed as he ducked underneath and grabbed it from against the wall. He was on his way back when he saw the Second Officer stagger out from the Hold. The man snatched blindly at Chester, and before Will knew what was happening he had got hold of him around the neck.

Chester let out a strangled yelp and tried to wrestle free.

Will didn't stop to think. He swung the spade. With a bone-crunching clang, it connected with the Second Officer's forehead and he crumpled to the floor with a whimper.

Chester wasn't so slow off the mark this time. He was right behind Will as they bolted out of the station, slowing just long enough for Will to retrieve his rucksack before they both turned down the stretch of road that Chester had spent so many hours watching from his cell. Then they veered off down a side tunnel.

'Is this the right way?' Chester said, breathing heavily and coughing.

Will didn't answer, but kept on running until they reached the end of the tunnel.

There they were, just as Tam had described them, three partially demolished houses on the perimeter of a circular cavern as large as an amphitheatre. The rich, loamy surface was springy underfoot as they tramped over it, and the air reeked of old manure. The walls of the cavern caught Will's attention. What at first he'd taken to be clusters of stalagmites were, in fact, petrified tree trunks, some broken halfway down and others twisted around each other. These fossilized remains stood like a carved stone forest in the shadows.

Will felt increasingly uneasy, as if something unwholesome and threatening was radiating from between the ancient trees. He was relieved when they reached the middle house and pushed through the front door, which opened crookedly on a single hinge.

'*Through the hall, straight ahead . . .*'

Chester shouldered the door shut behind them as Will entered the kitchen. It was roomier than the one in the Jerome house. As they crossed the tiled floor, a thick carpet of dust was stirred into life. It whipped up into a miniature storm and in the glow of the light orb every movement they made left a trace in the airborne motes.

'*Locate the wall tile with the painted cross.*'

Will found it and pushed. A small hatch clicked open under his hand. Inside was a handle. He twisted it to the right and a whole section of the tiled wall opened outwards – it was a cleverly disguised door. Behind was an antechamber with boxes stacked on either side, and a further door set into its far wall. But this was no ordinary door – it was made of heavy iron studded with rivets, and there was a handle by its side to crank it open.

'*It's airtight – keeps the germules out.*'

There was an inspection port at head height, but no light was visible through the clouded glass.

'Get going on that while I find the breathing apparatus,' Will ordered Chester, pointing at the crank. His friend leaned on the handle and there was a loud hiss as the thick rubber seal at the base of the door lifted from the ground. Will found the masks Tam had said would be left there, old canvas hoods with black rubber pipes attached to cylinders. They resembled some sort of ancient diving equipment.

Then, from the dark outside, Will heard a plaintive mew. He knew what it was even before he'd turned around.

'Bartleby!' The cat scampered in through the hallway. His paws scrabbling excitedly in the dust, he went straight to the secret door, shoving his muzzle into the gap and sniffing inquisitively.

'What is *that*?' Chester was so flabbergasted by the vision of the oversized cat that he let go of the crank handle. It spun freely as the door trundled down on its runners and slammed shut. Bartleby leaped back.

'For Christ's sake, Chester, just get that door open!' Will shouted.

Chester nodded and began again.

'Need a hand?' Cal asked, moving into view.

'No! Not you, too! What the *hell* are you doing here?' Will gasped.

'Coming with you,' Cal replied, taken aback by his brother's reaction.

Chester stopped turning the crank, and glanced rapidly from one brother to the other and back again. 'He looks just like you!'

Will had reached a point at which the whole situation had

taken on an insanity all of its own, a random and hopeless insanity. Tam's plan was falling apart before his very eyes, and he had the most awful feeling that they were all going to be caught. He had to get things back on track . . . somehow . . . and *quickly*.

'FOR GOODNESS' SAKE GET THAT DOOR OPEN, WILL YOU!' he bawled at the top of his voice, and Chester meekly resumed the cranking. The door was now half a metre off the ground and Bartleby stuck his head under for an exploratory look, dropped low and then slid through the opening, disappearing from sight altogether.

'Tam doesn't know you're here, does he?' Will grabbed his brother by his coat collar.

'Of course not. I decided it was time to go Topsoil, like you and Mother.'

'You're not coming,' Will snarled through gritted teeth. Then, as he saw the hurt in his brother's face, he let go of his coat and softened his voice. 'Really, you can't . . . Uncle Tam would kill you for being here. Go home right—' Will never finished the sentence. Both he and Cal had smelled the strong pulses of ammonia rippling through the air.

'The alarm!' Cal said with panic-stricken eyes.

They heard a commotion outside, some shouting and then the crash of breaking glass. They ran to the kitchen window and peered through the cracked panes.

'Styx!' Cal gasped.

Will estimated there were at least thirty of them drawn up in a semicircle in front of the house, and those were just the ones he could see from his limited vantage point. How many there were in total, he shuddered to think. He ducked down and shot a glance at Chester, who was frenziedly cranking the door, the opening now high enough for them to get through.

Will looked at his brother and knew there was only one thing for it. He couldn't leave him at the mercy of the Styx.

'Go on! Get under the door,' he whispered urgently.

Cal's face lit up and he started to thank Will, who shoved the breathing apparatus into his hands and propelled him towards the door.

As Cal slithered through the gap, Will turned back to the window just in time to see the Styx advancing on the house. That was enough – he launched himself at the door, frantically shouting at Chester to grab a mask and follow him. As he heard the front door to the house smash open, he knew there was just enough time for them both to get away.

Then one of those terrible things happened.

One of those events which, afterwards, you replay in your mind over and over again . . . but you know, deep down, there was nothing you could have done.

That was when they heard it.

A voice they both knew.

CHAPTER THIRTY

'Same old Will,' she said, rooting them to the spot.

Will was halfway under the door, his hand gripping Chester's forearm ready to pull him in, when he glanced at the kitchen doorway and froze.

A young girl walked into the room, two Styx flanking her.

'Rebecca?' Will gasped, and shook his head as if his eyes were deceiving him.

'Rebecca!' he said again, incredulously.

'Where are we going, then?' she said coolly. The two Styx edged forwards a fraction, but she held her hand up and they halted.

Was this some trick? She was wearing their clothes, their uniform – the black coat with the stark white shirt. And her jet-black hair was different – it was raked back tightly over her head.

'What are you . . . ?' was all Will managed to say before the words failed him.

She'd been captured. That must be it. Brainwashed, or held hostage.

'Why do we keep doing these things?' she sighed

theatrically, raising one eyebrow. She looked relaxed and in control. Something wasn't right here, something jarred.

No.

She was one of them.

'You're . . .' he gasped.

Rebecca laughed. 'Quick, isn't he?'

Behind her, more Styx were entering the kitchen. Will's mind reeled, his memories playing back at breakneck speed as he tried to reconcile Rebecca, his sister, with this Styx girl before him. Were there signs, any clues he'd missed?

'How?' he cried.

Revelling in his confusion, Rebecca spoke. 'It's really very simple. I was placed in your family when I was two. It's the way with us . . . to rub shoulders with the Heathen . . . it's the training for the elite.'

She took a step forward.

'Don't!' Will said, his mind starting to work again and his hand surreptitiously reaching inside his coat pocket. 'I can't believe it!'

'Hard to accept, isn't it? I was put there to keep an eye on you – and, if we were lucky, flush your mother into the open . . . your *real* mother.'

'It's not true.'

'It doesn't matter what you believe,' she replied curtly. 'My job had run its course, so here I am, back home again. No more play-acting.'

'No!' Will stuttered as he closed his hand around the little cloth package that Tam had given him.

'Come on, it's over,' Rebecca said impatiently. With a barely perceptible nod of her head, the Styx on either side of her lurched forward, but Will was ready. He slung the node stone across the kitchen with all his might. It soared between the two advancing Styx and struck the dirty white tiles, breaking into a tiny snowstorm of fragments.

Everything stopped.

For a split second Will thought nothing was going to happen, that it wasn't going to work. He heard Rebecca laugh, a dry, mocking laugh.

Then there was a whooshing sound, as if air was being sucked from the room. Each tiny splinter, as it sprinkled to the ground, flared with a dazzling incandescence, loosing beams that blasted the room like a million searchlights. These were so intense that everything was shot through with an unbearable, searing whiteness.

It didn't seem to bother Rebecca in the slightest. With the light ablaze about her, she stood out like some dark angel, her arms folded in her characteristic pose as she clucked with disapproval.

But the two advancing Styx stopped in their tracks, and let out screams like fingernails being dragged down a blackboard. They staggered back blindly, trying to cover their eyes.

This gave Will the opportunity he was looking for. He yanked Chester over, pulling him from the crank handle.

But already the light was dwindling, and another two Styx were pushing aside their blinded comrades. They lunged at Will, their claw-like fingers raking out towards him. As he continued to pull on one of Chester's arms, both Styx had latched on to the other. It turned into a tug-of-war between Will and the Styx, with the terrified, whimpering Chester caught in the middle. Worse still, now nobody was bracing the crank handle, it was whirring wildly around as the massive door sank slowly down on its runners. And Chester was right in its path.

'Push them off!' Will cried.

Chester tried to kick out but it was no use; they had too strong a hold on him. Will wedged himself against the door in a vain attempt to slow its progress, but it was just too heavy and nearly unbalanced him. There was no way he could do anything about it and save Chester at the same time.

As the Styx grunted and strained, and Chester tried with all his might to resist, Will knew the Styx couldn't be beaten. Chester was slipping out of his hands and screaming in pain as the Styx's fingernails bit deep into the flesh of his arm.

Then, as the door continued its relentless descent, the real-ization hit Will – Chester was going to be crushed unless he let go.

Unless he released Chester to the Styx.

The crank handle was spinning madly. The door was now little more than a metre from the ground, and Chester was being bent double – its entire weight pressing down on his back. Will had to do something, and quick.

'Chester, I'm sorry!' Will screamed.

For an instant Chester stared with horror-stricken eyes into those of his friend, and then Will let go of his arm and he flew straight back into the Styx, the momentum bowling them over in a tumbling confusion of arms and legs. Chester shouted Will's name once as the door clanged down with a terrible finality. Will could only watch numbly through the milky glass of the porthole as Chester and the Styx came to rest in a heap against the wall. One of the Styx immediately picked himself up and raced back towards the door.

'JAM THE HANDLE!' Cal's shout galvanized Will. As Cal held a light orb, Will set to work on the mechanism by the side of the door. He whipped out his penknife and, using the largest blade, attempted to wedge the gear wheels with it.

'Please, please work!' Will begged. He tried several places before the blade slipped in between two of the largest gear wheels, and stayed in place. Will took his hands away, praying it would do the trick. And it did, the little red penknife quivering as the Styx applied pressure to the handle on the other side.

Will glanced through the porthole again. Like some macabre silent film, he couldn't help but watch the desperation on Chester's face as he valiantly battled with the Styx. He'd somehow managed to get hold of Will's spade and was trying to beat them off with it. But he was overpowered by their sheer numbers as they swarmed over him with the insect intent of devouring locusts.

But then one face blocked out everything else as it loomed in the porthole.

Rebecca's face. She pursed her lips sternly and shook her head at Will, as if she was telling him off. Just like she'd done for all those years in Highfield. She was saying something, but it was inaudible through the door.

'We have to go, Will. They'll get it open,' Cal said urgently. Will tore his eyes away with difficulty. She was still mouthing something at him. And with a sudden, chilling realization, he knew just what it was. *Exactly* what it was. She was singing to him.

'Sunshine . . . !' he said bitterly. 'You are my sunshine!'

They fled down the rock passage with Bartleby bringing up the rear, and eventually came to a dome-shaped atrium with numerous passages leading off it. Everything was rounded and smoothed, as if aeons of flowing water had rubbed away any sharp edges. It was dry now, every surface coated in an abrasive silt, like powdered glass.

'We've only got one mask,' Will said suddenly to Cal, as the realization hit him. He took the canvas and rubber contraption from his brother and examined it.

'Oh, no!' Cal's face dropped. 'What do we do now? We can't go back.'

'The air in the Eternal City,' Will said, 'what's wrong with it?'

'Uncle Tam says there was some sort of plague. It killed off all the people . . .'

'But it's not still there, is it?' Will asked quickly, dreading the answer.

Cal nodded slowly. 'Tam says it is.'

'Then you're using the mask.'

'No way!'

In a flash, Will whipped the mask over Cal's head, muffling his protests. Cal struggled, trying to take it off, but Will wouldn't let him.

'I mean it! You're going to wear it,' Will insisted. 'I'm the oldest, so I get to choose.'

At this Cal stopped resisting, his eyes peeking anxiously through the glass strip as Will made sure the hood was seated correctly on his shoulders. Then he buckled up the leather strap to secure the pipes and stubby filter around his brother's chest. He tried not to think what the implications of letting Cal have the mask might be for himself, and could only hope that the plague was yet another of the Colonists' superstitions, of which there seemed to be so many.

Then Will slipped the map Tam had given him from inside his boot, counted the tunnels in front of them, and pointed to

340

the one they were to take.

'How did the Styx girl know you?' Cal's voice was indistinct through the hood.

'My sister.' Will lowered the map and looked at him. 'That was my sister . . .' he spat contemptuously, '. . . or so I used to think.'

Cal didn't show any sign of surprise, but Will could see just how frightened he was by the way he kept glancing at the stretch of tunnel behind them. 'The door won't hold them for long,' his brother warned, looking nervously at Will.

'Chester . . .' Will began hopelessly, then fell silent.

'There was nothing we could've done to help him. We were lucky to get out of there alive.'

'Maybe,' Will said as he rechecked the map. He knew he didn't have time to think about Chester, not right now, but after all the risks he'd taken to save his friend the whole exercise had failed horribly, and he was finding it hard to focus on what to do next. He took a deep breath. 'I suppose we should go, then.'

And so the two boys, with the cat trailing behind, broke into a steady trot, penetrating deeper into the complex of underground tunnels that would eventually lead them to the Eternal City – and then, Will hoped, out into the sunlight again.

PART THREE

THE ETERNAL CITY

CHAPTER THIRTY-ONE

O *ne two, one two, one, one, one two.*

As they jogged along, Will had settled into the easy rhythm he frequently used for the more strenuous bouts of digging back in Highfield. The tunnels were dry and silent; there wasn't the slightest sign that anything lived down here. And as their feet tramped over the sandy floors, not once did Will catch sight of any airborne dust or motes behind them in the beam of his light orb. It was as if their passage had gone completely unnoticed.

But it wasn't long before he began to notice the faintest scintillations before his eyes, smears of light that materialized and then, just as abruptly, vanished from his field of vision. He watched, fascinated, until it dawned on him that something was not quite right. At the same time a dull ache gripped his chest and a clammy sweat broke out on his temples.

One two, one two, one . . . one . . . one two . . .

He slowed his pace, feeling the resistance as he drew breath. It was peculiar; he couldn't quite put his finger on what was wrong. At first he thought it was simply exhaustion, but no, it was more than that. It was as if the air, having lain undisturbed in these deep tunnels, maybe ever since prehistoric times, was behaving like a sluggish fluid.

One two, one . . .

Will came to an abrupt halt, loosening his collar and massaging his shoulders under the straps of his rucksack. He had an almost irresistible urge to throw the weight off his back – it made him feel constricted and uneasy. And the walls of the passage bothered him – they were too close, they were smothering him. He backed away into the middle of the tunnel, where he leaned on his knees and took in several gulps of air. After a while, he felt a little better and forced himself to straighten up.

'What's wrong?' Cal asked, eyeing him worriedly through the glass slit of his mask.

'Nothing,' Will replied as he fumbled in his pocket for the map. He didn't want to admit to any weakness, certainly not to his brother. 'I . . . I just need to check our position.'

He'd taken it upon himself to navigate their route through the many twists and turns, aware that a single mistake would lose them in this subterranean maze of such extraordinary complexity. He remembered how Tam had referred to it as the 'Labyrynth' and likened it to pumice stone with innumerable interlocking pores worming randomly through it. At the time, Will hadn't thought much about his uncle's words, but he now knew precisely what he'd meant. The sheer scale of the area was daunting and although they had been making good time as they were moving rapidly through the passages Will reckoned they had a long way to go yet. They were helped considerably by a gentle downward gradient, but this in itself caused him some consternation; he was only too aware that

346

every metre they descended would have to be climbed again before they reached the surface.

He glanced from the map to the walls. They had a pinkish hue to them, probably due to the presence of iron deposits, which could explain why his compass was worse than useless down here. The needle dithered lazily around the dial, never settling in the same position long enough to give any sort of reading.

As Will looked around him he reflected that the passages could have been formed by gas trapped under a solidified plug of some kind, as it tried to escape through the still-molten volcanic rock. Yes, that could be the reason there weren't any vertical tunnels. Or possibly they'd been formed by water exploiting lines of weakness in the millennia after the rock cooled. 'I wonder what Dad would make of this,' he thought before he could stop himself, his face falling as he realized that he'd probably never see him again. Not now.

And try as he might, he couldn't stop remembering that last glimpse of Chester as he'd rolled helplessly across the floor, and straight back into the clutches of the Styx. Will had let him down yet again . . .

And Rebecca! There it was, incontrovertible, he'd seen it with his own eyes. She was a Styx! Despite the fact he felt so weak his blood boiled. He wanted to laugh out loud as he thought back to how worried he'd been about her.

But there was no time to reflect now – if they were going to get through this alive he had to make sure they didn't stray off course. He took one last glance at the map, and refolded it before they resumed their journey.

One two, one two, one, one, one two.

As their feet crunched in the fine red sand Will longed for

a change, a landmark, *anything* to break the monotony, to confirm that they were still on the right track. He began to despair that they were ever going to reach the end. For all he knew, they could be going round in circles.

He was thrilled when they eventually came across what looked like a small headstone, with a flat face and a rounded top, set against the passage wall. With Cal looking on, he crouched down to brush the sand from its surface.

A sweep of his hand revealed a symbol carved into the pink rock about halfway down the face. It was comprised of three diverging lines, which fanned out like rising rays or the prongs of a trident. Below were two rows of angular lettering. The symbols were unfamiliar and made no sense to him at all.

'What's this? Some kind of marker or milestone?' Will looked up at his brother, who shrugged his shoulders unhelpfully.

Several hours later, the going had become slow and laborious. They were coming to fork after fork in the tunnel, and Will was having to consult the map even more frequently. They'd already taken one wrong turn; luckily they hadn't gone too far before Will realized his mistake, and they had painstakingly retraced their steps and found their way back on to the correct path again. Once there, they had flopped on to the sandy floor, stopping just long enough to catch their breath. Although he was trying to fight it, Will felt unusually tired, as if he were running on empty. And when they resumed their journey, he felt weaker than ever.

Whatever state he was in, though, Will didn't want Cal to suspect anything was wrong. He knew they must keep going; they must keep ahead of the Styx, they had to get out. He turned to his brother beside him.

'So what does Tam do in this Eternal City?' he said, breathing heavily. 'He was very cagey when I asked him about it.'

'He searches for coins and stuff like that, gold and silver,' Cal said, then added, 'Most of it from graves.'

'Graves?'

'In the burial grounds,' Cal nodded.

'So people really lived there?'

'A long time ago. He reckons that several races occupied it, one after the other, each building on top of the last. He says there are fortunes just waiting to be found.'

'But who were the people?'

'Tam told me the Bruteans were the first, centuries ago. I think he said they were Trojans. They constructed it as a stronghold or something, while the Topsoil London was built above.'

'So the two cities were connected?'

Cal's mask nodded ponderously. 'In the beginning. Later the entrances were blocked up and the stones marking them were lost . . . the Eternal City was just *forgotten*,' he said, puffing noisily through the air filter. He looked nervously back up the tunnel, as if he'd heard something.

Will immediately followed his glance, but all he could see was the shadowy form of Bartleby as he loped impatiently from one side of the tunnel to the other. It was clear that he wanted to go faster than the two boys and from time to time he would speed past them but then stop to sniff at a crevice or the ground up ahead, often becoming visibly agitated and letting out a low whine.

'At least the Styx will never find us in this place,' Will said confidently.

'Don't count on it. They'll be following us all right,' Cal said. 'And then there's still the Division in front of us.'

'The *what*?'

'The Styx Division. They're sort of a . . . well . . . border guard,' Cal said, searching for the right words. 'They patrol the old city.'

'What for? I thought it was empty?'

'There's talk that they're rebuilding whole areas and patching up the cavern walls. It's said the whole Colony might be moved there, and there's rumours of work parties of condemned prisoners, working like slaves. It's only rumours though – no one knows for sure.'

'Tam never mentioned anything about more Styx.' Will didn't attempt to hide the alarm in his voice. 'Bloody brilliant,' he said angrily, kicking a rock in his path.

'Well, maybe he didn't think it would be a problem. We didn't exactly leave the Colony quietly, did we? Don't get too worried though; it's a huge area to cover and there'll only be a handful of patrols.'

'Oh, great! That's a real comfort!' Will replied, as he imagined what might be in store for them ahead.

They wandered on for several hours, eventually scrabbling down a steep incline, their feet slipping and sliding in the red sand until they finally reached a level area. Will knew that if he'd been reading the map correctly they should be approaching the end of the Labyrynth. But the tunnel narrowed before them, and appeared to end in a blind alley.

Fearing the worst Will raced ahead, stooping as the roof lowered. To his relief, he found that there was a small passage to one side. He waited until Cal caught up, and they looked apprehensively at each other as Bartleby sniffed the air. Will hesitated, looking repeatedly from Tam's map to the opening, and back again. Then he met Cal's eyes and smiled broadly as he edged into the narrow passageway. It was bathed in a subdued green light.

'Careful,' Cal warned.

But Will was already at the corner. He became aware of a familiar sound: the patter of falling water. He moved his head until just one eye was peering around the edge. He was struck dumb by what he glimpsed, and inched slowly into the open, into the bottle-green glow, to get a better view. From Tam's description, and the pictures his imagination had conjured up, he was expecting something out of the ordinary. But nothing could have prepared him for the sight that met his eyes.

'The Eternal City,' he whispered to himself, as he began to move down a huge escarpment. As he looked up, his wide eyes scrutinizing the roof of the immense domed space, water splashed on to his upturned face and made him flinch.

'Underground rain?' he muttered, immediately realizing how ridiculous that sounded. He blinked as it dripped into his eyes, stinging them.

'It's seepage from above,' Cal said, coming to a halt behind him.

But Will wasn't listening. He was finding it hard to come to terms with the titanic volume of the cavern, so massive that its farthest reaches were hidden by fog and the mists of distance. The drizzle continued to fall in slow, languorous swathes as they set off again down the escarpment.

It was almost too much to take in. Basaltic columns, like windowless skyscrapers, arced down from the mammoth span of the roof into the centre of the city. Others speared upwards from the outlying ground in mind-bending curves, encasing the city with gigantic drunken buttresses. It dwarfed any of the Colony's caverns with its scale, and brought to Will's mind the image of a gargantuan heart, its chambers criss-crossed by huge, heartstring-like columns.

He pocketed the light orb and instinctively sought the source of the emerald-green glow that gave the scene a dream-like quality. It was as though he was looking at a lost city in the depths of an ocean. He couldn't be sure but the light seemed to be coming from the very walls themselves – so subtly that at first he thought they were simply reflecting it.

He crossed over to the side of the escarpment and examined the cavern wall more closely. It was covered in a wild growth of tendrils, dark and glistening with moisture. It was algae of some kind, made up of many trailing shoots, and thickly layered, like ivy on an old wall. As he held up the palm of his hand he could feel the warmth radiating from it and, yes, he could see that there was indeed a very dim glow coming from the edges of the curled leaves.

'Bioluminescence,' he said aloud.

'Mmmmph?' came the vague response from under Cal's canvas hood, which was twitching absurdly from side to side as he kept watch for the Styx Division.

As he continued down the incline Will switched his attention back to the cavern, focusing on the most wondrous sight of all, the city itself. Even from this distance his eyes hungrily took in the archways, impossible terraces and curving stone stairways sweeping up into stone balconies. Columns, Doric and Corinthian, sprang up to support dizzying galleries and walkways. His intense excitement was tinged with a sadness that Chester wasn't seeing all this with him as he should rightly have been. And as for his father, it would have blown his mind! It was just too much to absorb all at once. In every direction Will looked there were the most fantastic structures: colosseums and ancient domed cathedrals in beautifully crafted stone.

Then, as he came to the bottom of the escarpment, the smell hit him. It had been deceptively gentle at first, like old pond water, but with each step they'd descended it had become more pungent. It was rancid, catching in Will's throat like a mouthful of bile. He cupped a hand over his nose and mouth, and looked at Cal in desperation.

'This is just gross!' he said, gagging on the stench. 'No wonder you need to wear one of those things!'

'I know,' Cal said flatly, his expression hidden by the breathing mask as he pointed to the gully by the foot of the escarpment. 'Come over here.'

'What for?' Will asked as he joined his brother. He was astonished to see him thrust his hands into the treacle-like slurry that lay stagnating there. Cal lifted out two handfuls of the black algae and rubbed it over his mask and his clothes. Then he grabbed Bartleby by the scruff of the neck. The cat let out a low howl and tried to get away, but Cal streaked him from head to tail. As the filth dripped over his naked skin, Bartleby arched his back and trembled, looking at his master balefully.

'God, the stink is worse than ever now. What the hell are you doing?' Will demanded, thinking his brother had taken leave of his senses.

'The Division use stalker dogs round here. Any whiff of the Colony on us, we're as good as dead. This slime will help cover our scent,' he said, scooping up fresh handfuls of the brackish vegetation. 'Your turn.' Will braced himself as Cal doused the fetid weed over his hair, chest and shoulders, and then down each of his legs.

'How can you smell anything over this?' Will asked irately, looking at the oily patches on his clothes. The reek was overpowering. 'Those dogs must have *some* sense of smell!' It was all he could do to stop himself from being sick.

'Oh, they do,' Cal said as he shook his hands to rid them of the tendrils, then wiped them on his jacket. 'We need to get out of sight.'

Crossing one by one, they passed swiftly over a stretch of boggy ground and into the city. They went under a tall stone arch with two malevolent gargoyle faces glaring down contemptuously at them, and then into an alley with high walls either side. The dimensions of the buildings, the gaping windows, arches and doorways, were huge, as if they'd been built for incredibly tall beings. At Cal's suggestion, they slipped through one of these openings, at the base of a square tower.

Now out of the green light, Will needed his light orb to study the map. As he pulled it out from under his coat, it illuminated the room, a stone chamber with a high ceiling and several inches of water on the floor. Bartleby scampered into one corner and, finding a heap of something rotten, he investigated it briefly before lifting a leg over it.

'Hey,' Cal said abruptly. 'Just look at the walls.'

They saw skulls – row upon row of carved death's heads covered the walls, all with toothy grins and hollow, shadowy eyes. As Will moved the orb, the shadows shifted and the skulls appeared to be turning to face them.

'My dad would've loved this. I bet this was a—'

'It's grisly,' Cal interrupted, shivering.

'These people were pretty spooky, weren't they?' Will said, unable to suppress a wide grin.

'The ancestors of the Styx.'

'What?' Will looked at him questioningly.

'Their forebears. People believe a group escaped from this city at the time of the Plague.'

'Where to?'

'Topsoil,' Cal replied. 'They formed some sort of secret society there. It's said that the Styx gave Sir Gabriel the idea for the Colony.'

Will didn't have the chance to question Cal any further, as suddenly Bartleby's ears pricked up and his unblinking eyes fixed on the doorway. Although neither of the boys had heard anything Cal became agitated.

'Come on, quick, check the map, Will.'

They left the chamber, cautiously picking their way through the ancient streets. It gave Will an opportunity to inspect the buildings at close hand. Everywhere about them the stone was decorated with carvings and inscriptions. And he saw the decay; the masonry was crumbling and fractured. It cried out with abandonment and neglect. Yet the buildings still sat proudly in all their magnificence – they had an aura of immense power to them. Power, and something else – an ancient and decadent menace. Will was relieved that the city's inhabitants weren't still in residence.

As they jogged down lanes of ancient stone their boots scattered the murky water on the ground and churned up the algae, leaving faintly glowing blotches in their wake like luminous stepping stones. Bartleby was agitated by the water and pranced through it with the precision of a performing pony, trying not to splash himself.

Crossing a narrow stone bridge, Will stopped briefly and looked over the eroded marble balustrade at the slow-moving river below. Slick and greasy, it snaked lazily through the city, crossed here and there with other small bridges, its waters lapping turgidly against the massive sections of masonry that formed its banks. On these, classical statues stood watch like water sentinels: old men with wavy hair and impossibly long beards, and women in flowing gowns, held out shells and orbs – or just the broken stumps of their arms – towards the water as if offering up sacrifices to gods that no longer existed.

They came to a large square surrounded by towering buildings but held back from entering it, taking refuge behind a low parapet.

'What is that?' Will whispered. In the middle of the square was a raised platform supported by an array of thick columns. On top of the platform were human forms: chalky statues in twisted postures of frozen agony, some with their features obliterated and others with limbs missing. Rusting chains wound around the contorted figures and the posts next to them. It looked like a sculpture of some long-forgotten atrocity.

'The Prisoners' Platform. That's where they were punished.'

'Gruesome statues,' Will said, unable to take his eyes off it.

'They're not statues, they're real people. Tam said the bodies have been calcified.'

'No!' Will said, staring even more intently at the figures and wishing he had time to document the scene.

'Shhhhh,' Cal warned. He grabbed Bartleby and pulled him to his chest. The cat kicked out but Cal wouldn't let go.

Will looked at him enquiringly.

'Get down,' Cal whispered. Ducking behind the parapet, he cupped his hand over the cat's eyes and clasped the animal even more tightly.

As he followed suit Will caught sight of them. At the far end of the square, as silent as ghosts, four figures appeared to float on the surface of the waterlogged ground. They wore breathing masks over their mouths, and goggles with large, circular eyepieces making them appear like nightmarish man-insects. Will could tell from their outlines that they were Styx. They wore leather skullcaps and long coats. Not the lustrous black ones Will had seen in the Colony; these were matt, and camouflaged with streaky green and grey blocks of dark and light hues.

With easy military efficiency, they were advancing in a line, as one controlled an immense dog straining on a lead. Vapour was blowing from the muzzle of the impossibly large and ferocious animal – it was unlike any dog that Will had ever seen before.

The boys cowered behind the parapet, acutely aware that they had nowhere to run if the Styx came their way. The hoarse panting and snorting of the dog was growing louder – Will and Cal looked at each other, both thinking that at any moment the Styx would appear from around the edge of the parapet. They angled their heads, straining to catch the least sound of the Styx approaching, but there was only the hushed gurgle of running water and the unbroken patter of cavern rain.

Will and Cal's eyes met. All the signs were that the Styx had gone, but what should they do? *Had the patrol moved on, or was it lying in ambush for them?* They waited and, after what seemed like an age, Will tapped his brother on the arm and pointed upward, indicating he was going to take a look.

Cal shook his head violently, his eyes flaring with alarm behind the half-fogged glass; they pleaded with Will to stay put. But Will ignored him, and raised his head a fraction over the parapet. The Styx had vanished. He gave the thumbs-up and Cal rose slowly to see for himself. Satisfied the patrol had moved on, Cal let go of Bartleby and he sprang away, shaking himself down and then glowering resentfully at both of them.

They skirted cautiously around the side of the square and chose a lane in the opposite direction to the one they assumed the Styx had taken. Will was feeling increasingly tired, and it was getting harder for him to catch his breath. His lungs were rattling like an asthmatic's, and a dull ache gripped his chest and rib cage. He summoned up all his energy and they darted from shadow to shadow until the buildings ran out and the cavern wall was in front of them. They ran alongside it for several minutes until they came to a huge stone staircase cut into the rock.

'That was too close by half,' Will panted, glancing behind them.

'You can say that again,' Cal agreed, then peered at the staircase. 'Is this the one?'

'I think so.' Will shrugged. At that point, he didn't much care; he just wanted to put as much distance between them and the Styx Division as possible.

The base of the stairs was badly damaged by a massive pillar that had crashed down and shattered it, and at first the boys were forced to clamber up several broken sections. Once they had reached the steps, it wasn't much better; they were slick with black weed, and the boys nearly lost their footing more than once.

They climbed higher and higher up the stairway and, forgetting how ill he felt for the moment, Will stopped to take in the view now they were so high up. Through the haze, he caught sight of a building topped with a huge dome.

'That's the spitting image of St Paul's,' he puffed, getting his breath back as he peered at the magnificent domed roof in the distance. 'I'd love to have a closer look,' he added.

'You've got to be joking,' Cal replied sharply.

As they continued, the stairs eventually disappeared into a jagged arch in the rock wall. Will turned for a last glance at the emerald strangeness of the Eternal City, but as he did so he slipped from the edge of the step, tottering forward on to the one below. For a heartbeat he faced the sheer drop in front of him and cried out, thinking he was about to plunge down it. He clutched frantically at the black tendrils covering the wall. Handful after handful broke off, then he finally managed to get a grip and steady himself again.

'Jesus, are you all right?' Cal said, now at his side. As Will didn't answer him, he became increasingly concerned. 'What's the matter?'

'I . . . I just feel so dizzy,' Will admitted in a wheezing voice. He was panting in small, shallow breaths – it was as if he was breathing through a clogged straw. He climbed a few steps, but came to a standstill again as he broke into a racking cough. He thought the coughing fit was never going to stop. Bent double, he hacked away and then spat. He clutched his forehead, soaked with rain and clammy with an unhealthily cold sweat, and knew there was no way he could hide it from his brother any longer.

'I need to rest,' he said hoarsely, using Cal for support as the coughing subsided.

'Not now,' Cal said urgently, 'and not here.' Grabbing Will's arm, he helped him through the archway and into the gloomy stairway beyond.

CHAPTER THIRTY-TWO

There is a point at which the body is spent, when the muscles and sinews have nothing left to give, when all that remains is a person's mettle, his sheer bloody-mindedness.

Will had reached that point. His body felt drained and worthless, but still he slogged on, driven by the responsibility he felt towards his brother and his duty to get him to safety. At the same time, gnawing away at him was the unbearable guilt that he'd let Chester down, let him fall into the Colonists' hands for a second time.

I'm useless, bloody useless. The words ran in a loop through Will's mind, over and over again. But neither he nor his brother spoke as they climbed, grinding their way up the never-ending spiral stairway. At the very limits of his endurance, Will pushed himself on, step after painful step, flight after flight, his thighs burning as much as his lungs. Slipping and sliding on water-drenched stone treads and the stringy weed that clung to them, he fought to suppress the dread realization that they still had far to go.

'I'd like to stop now,' he heard Cal pant.

'Can't . . . don't think . . . I'd ever . . . get going . . . again,'

Will grunted in time with his plodding steps.

The excruciating hours crawled by, until he had lost track of how long they'd been climbing, and nothing in the world existed or mattered to him except the gruelling notion that he had to take the next step, and the next, and so on . . . and just when Will thought he'd reached his limits and that he couldn't go any further, he felt the faintest of breezes on his face. He knew instinctively it was untainted air. He stopped and sucked at the freshness, hoping to lift the leaden weight from his chest and relieve the interminable rattle in his lungs.

'Don't need it,' he said, pointing at Cal's mask. Cal removed it from his head and tucked it in his belt, the sweat running down his face in rivulets and his eyes rimmed with red.

'Phew,' he exhaled. 'Bit hot under that thing.'

They resumed the climb, and it wasn't long before the steps ended and they entered a sequence of narrow passages. Every so often they were forced to scramble up rusted iron ladders, their hands turning orange as they tested each precarious rung.

Eventually they reached a steeply angled shaft no more than a metre wide. They hauled themselves up its pockmarked surface using the thick knotted rope they discovered hanging there (Cal was certain his Uncle Tam had rigged it up). Hand over hand they went, their feet finding purchase in the shallow cracks and fault lines as they climbed. The incline became steeper and they had a devil of a job to scrabble over the remaining stretch of slime-covered stone, but despite losing their footing a few times they eventually reached the top, hauling themselves up into a circular chamber. Here there was a small vent in the floor. Leaning into it, Will could see the remnants of an iron grating, long since rusted away.

'What's down there?' Cal panted.

'Nothing, can't see a damn thing,' Will said despondently, squatting down to rest on his haunches. He brushed the sweat from his face with a raw hand. 'I suppose we do what Tam said. We climb down.'

Cal looked behind and then to his brother, nodding. For several minutes neither of them made a move, immobilized with fatigue.

'Well, we can't stay here for ever,' Will sighed. He swung his legs into the vent and, with his back pressed against one side and feet hard against the other, began to ease himself down.

'What about the cat?' Will shouted after he had gone a short distance. 'Is it going to be able to cope with this?'

'Don't worry about him,' Cal smiled. 'Anything we can do—'

Will never heard the rest of Cal's sentence. He slipped. The sides of the vent shot by and he landed with a large splash – he was submerged in an icy coldness. He thrashed out with his arms, then his feet found the bottom and he stood up and blew out a mouthful of freezing liquid. He found he was chest-deep in water, and after he'd wiped it out of his eyes and pushed back his hair, he looked around. He couldn't be certain, but there seemed to be a dim light in the distance.

He heard Cal's frantic shouts from above. 'Will! Will! Are you all right?'

'Just had a quick dip!' Will shouted, laughing weakly. 'Stay there, I'm going to check something out.' His exhaustion and discomfort were ignored for the moment as he stared at the weak glow, trying to make out the faintest detail of what lay ahead.

Soaked to the skin he clambered out of the pool and, stooping under the low roof, crept slowly towards the light. After a couple of hundred metres, he could clearly see the circular mouth of the tunnel and, with his heart racing, he sped towards it. Dropping more than a metre off a ledge he'd failed to notice, he landed roughly, finding himself under a jetty of some kind. Through a forest of heavy wooden stanchions, draped with weed, he could see the dappled reflections of light on water.

Gravel crunched underfoot as he walked into the open. He felt the invigorating chill of the wind on his face. He breathed deeply, drawing the fresh air into his aching lungs. It was such sweetness. Slowly he took stock of the surroundings.

Night. Lights reflected off a river in front of him. It was a wide river. A two-tiered pleasure boat chugged past – bright flashes of colour pulsed from its two decks as indistinct dance music throbbed over the water. Then he saw the bridges either side of him and, in the distance, the floodlit dome of St Paul's. The St Paul's he knew. A red double-decker bus crossed the bridge closest to him. This wasn't any old river. He sat down on the bank with surprise and relief.

It was the *Thames.*

He lay back on the bank and closed his eyes, listening to the droning hubbub of traffic. He tried to remember the names of the bridges, but he didn't really care – he'd got out, he'd escaped, and nothing else mattered. He'd made it. He was home. Back in his own world.

'The sky,' Cal said with awe in his voice. 'So that's what it's like.' Will opened his eyes to see his brother craning his neck this way and that, as he stared at the stray wisps of cloud caught in the amber radiation of the street lights. Although Cal was sopping from his immersion in the pool, he was smiling broadly, but then he wrinkled his nose up. 'Phew, what's that?' he asked loudly.

'What do you mean?' Will said.

'All those smells!'

Will propped himself up on one elbow and sniffed. 'What smells?'

'Food . . . all sorts of food . . . and . . .' Cal grimaced. 'Sewage – lots of it – and chemicals . . .'

As Will sniffed the air, thinking again how fresh it was, it occurred to him that he hadn't once considered what they were going to do next. Where were they going to go? He'd been so intent on escaping, he hadn't given anything beyond it a second thought. He stood up and examined his sodden, filthy Colonists' clothes and those of his brother, and the unfeasibly large cat that was now nosing around the bank like a pig searching for truffles. A brisk winter wind was picking up and he shivered violently, his teeth starting to chatter. It struck him that neither his brother nor Bartleby had experienced the relative extremes of Topsoil weather in their sheltered, subterranean lives. He had to get them moving. And quickly. But he didn't have any money on him – not a penny.

'We're going to have to walk home.'

'Fine,' Cal replied unquestioningly, his head back as he stared at the stars, losing himself in the canopy of the sky. 'At last I've seen them,' he whispered to himself.

A helicopter drifted across the horizon.

'Why's that one moving?' he asked.

Will felt too tired to explain. 'They do that,' he said flatly.

They set off, keeping close to the bank so as not to be noticed, and almost immediately came upon a set of steps leading up to the walkway above. It was next to a bridge. Will knew then where they were – it was Blackfriars Bridge.

A gate blocked the top of the steps so they hastily clambered over the broad wall beside it to reach the walkway. Dripping water on the pavement and freezing in the night air, they looked around them. Will was seized by the dreadful thought that even here the Styx might have spies watching out for them. After seeing one of the Clarke brothers in the Colony he felt that he couldn't trust anybody, and regarded the few people in the immediate area with mounting suspicion. But nobody was close, with the exception of a young couple walking hand in hand. They strolled past, so involved with each other that they didn't seem to pay the boys or their huge cat the least attention.

With Will taking the lead they climbed the steps to the bridge itself. Arriving at the top, Will saw that the IMAX cinema was to their right. He immediately knew they didn't want to be on that side of the river. To him, London was a mosaic of places, each familiar to him from museum visits with his father or school expeditions. The rest, the interconnecting areas, were a complete mystery to him. There was only one thing for it; trust in his sense of direction and try to head north.

As they turned left and quickly traversed the bridge, Will spotted a sign to King's Cross and knew instantly they were heading the right way. Traffic passed them as they arrived at the end of the bridge, and Will paused to look at Cal and the cat under the glow of a street light. Talk about three suspicious-looking lost souls – they stuck out a mile. Although it was dark Will was painfully aware that a pair of young boys soaked to the skin and wandering the streets of London at this late hour, with or without a giant cat, were likely to attract attention, and the last thing he needed now was to be picked up by the police. He made an attempt at concocting a story, rehearsing it in his mind, just in case it happened.

'Ello, 'ello, ello, the pair of fictitious policemen said. *What 'ave we 'ere then?*

Er . . . just out walking the . . . the . . . Will's imagined response came to a faltering stop. No, that wouldn't do, he had to be better prepared than that. He started again: *Good evening, officers. We're just taking the neighbour's pet for a walk.*

The first policeman leaned in to peer curiously at Bartleby, his eyes narrowing as he grimaced in open distaste. *Looks dangerous to me, son. Shouldn't it be on a lead?*

What is it, exactly? the second imaginary policeman chimed in.

It's a . . . Will began. What could he say? Ah yes . . . *It's very rare . . . a very rare hybrid, a cross between a dog and a cat called a . . . a Dat,* Will informed them helpfully.

Or is it a Cog, perhaps? the second policeman suggested drily, the glint in his eye telling Will he wasn't buying a word of it.

Whatever it is, it's bloody ugly, his partner said.

Shhh! You'll hurt his feelings.

Suddenly Will realized that he was wasting his time with all of this. The reality was that the policemen would simply ask for their names and addresses, and radio in to double-check them. And they'd probably be rumbled even if they tried to give false ones. So that would be it. They'd be taken back to the station and held there. Will suspected he was probably wanted for abducting Chester, or something equally ridiculous, and would likely as not end up in a young offenders' institution. As for Cal, he would be a real conundrum – of course, there wouldn't be a record of him anywhere, no Topsoil identity whatsoever. No, they'd have to avoid the police, at all costs.

Perversely, as he contemplated the future, there was a part of him that almost wanted them to be stopped. It would remove the dreadful burden which at the moment lay squarely on his shoulders; he glanced at the cowed figure of his brother. Cal was a stranger, a freak in this cold and inhospitable place, and Will had no idea how he was going to protect him.

But Will knew if he turned himself in to the authorities and tried to get them to investigate the Colony – that's if they believed a runaway teenager in the first place – he could be risking countless lives, his *family's* lives. Who knew how it would end? He shuddered at the thought of the Discovery, as Grandma Macaulay had called it, and tried to imagine her being led out into the daylight after her long subterranean life. He couldn't do that to her – it didn't bear thinking about. It was too big a decision for him to take alone, and he felt so terribly alone and isolated.

He pulled his damp jacket around himself, and hustled Cal and Bartleby down into the subway at the end of the bridge.

'It's very pissy down here,' his brother commented. 'Do all Topsoilers mark their territories?' He turned to Will enquiringly.

'Er . . . not usually. But this *is* London.'

As they emerged from the subway and back on to the pavement Cal seemed confused by the traffic, looking this way and that. Coming to a main road, they stopped at the kerb. Will gripped his brother's sleeve with one hand and the cat's hairless scruff with the other. Crossing when there was a lull, they made it to the traffic island. He could see people peering curiously at them from the passing cars, and a white van slowed down almost to a halt right beside them, the driver talking excitedly into his mobile. To Will's relief it sped off again. They crossed the remaining two lanes and after a short distance, Will steered them into a dimly lit side street. His brother stood with one hand on the brick wall beside him – he looked completely disoriented, like a blind man in unfamiliar surroundings.

'Foul air!' he said vehemently.

'It's only car fumes,' Will replied as he untied the thick string from his light orb and fashioned a slipknot lead for the cat, who didn't seem to mind one bit.

'It smells wrong. It must be against the laws,' Cal said with complete conviction.

''Fraid not,' Will answered as he led them down the street. He would have to stay off the main road and keep to the backstreets as far as possible, even though it would make their journey even more difficult and circuitous.

And so the long march north began. On their way out of central London they only saw a single police car, but Will was able to usher them around a corner in the nick of time.

'Are they like Styx?' Cal asked.

'Not quite,' Will replied.

With the cat on one side and Cal twitching nervously on the other, they trudged along. From time to time his brother would stop dead, as if invisible doors were being slammed in his face.

'What is it?' Will asked on one of these occasions when his brother refused to move.

'It's like . . . anger . . . and fear,' Cal said in a strained voice as he glanced nervously up at the windows over a shop front. 'It's so strong. I don't like it.'

'I can't see anything,' Will said as he failed to make out what was troubling his brother. They were just ordinary windows, a sliver of light showing between the curtains in one of them. 'It's nothing, you're imagining it.'

'No, I'm not. I can smell it,' Cal said emphatically, 'and it's getting stronger. I want to go.'

After several miles of tortuous ducking and diving, they came to the brow of a hill, at the bottom of which was a busy main road with six lanes of speeding traffic.

'I recognize this – it's not far now. Maybe a couple of miles, that's all,' Will said with relief.

'I'm not going near it. I can't – not with that stench. It'll kill us,' Cal said, backing away from Will.

'Don't be so bloody stupid,' Will said. He was just too tired for any nonsense, and his frustration now turned to anger. 'We're so close.'

'No,' Cal said, digging his heels in. 'I'm staying right here!'

Will tried to pull the boy's arm, but he yanked it away. Will had been fighting his exhaustion for miles and was still struggling to breathe; he didn't need this. All of a sudden, it got too much for him. He thought he was actually going to break down and cry. It just wasn't fair. He pictured the house and his welcoming clean bed. All he wanted to do was lie down and sleep. Even as he was walking, his body kept going loose, as if he was dropping through a hole into a place where everything was so comforting and warm. Then he would yank himself out of it, back to wakefulness, and urge himself on again.

'Fine!' Will spat. 'Suit yourself!' He set off down the hill, tugging Bartleby by the lead.

As he reached the road Will heard his brother's voice over the din of the traffic.

'Will!' he yelled. 'Wait for me! I'm sorry!'

Cal came hurtling down the hill – Will could see that he was genuinely terrified. He kept jerking his head to look around him, as if he was about to be attacked by some imagined assassin.

They crossed the road at the lights, but Cal insisted on pressing his hand over his mouth until they were a good distance from it. 'I can't take this,' he said glumly. 'I liked the idea of cars when I was in the Colony . . . but the brochures didn't say anything about the way they smell.'

'Got a light?'

Startled by the voice, they whirled round. They'd stopped for a minute's rest and, as if he had appeared from nowhere, a man was standing very close behind them, a lopsided grin on his face. He wasn't terribly tall, but was well dressed in a tightly fitting dark-blue suit, and a shirt and tie. He had long black hair, which he kept stroking back at the temples and tucking behind his ears, as if it was bothering him. 'Left mine at home,' he continued, his voice deep and rich.

'Don't smoke, sorry,' Will replied, quickly edging away. There was something forced and sleazy in the man's smile, and alarm bells were ringing in Will's head.

'You boys all right? You look done in. I got a place you can warm up. Not far from here,' the man said ingratiatingly.

'Bring your doggy too, of course.' He held out a hand towards Cal, and Will saw that the fingers were stained with nicotine and his fingernails were black with filth.

'Can we really?' Cal said, returning the man's smile.

'No . . . very kind of you, but . . .' Will interrupted, glaring at his brother but failing to get his attention. The man took a step towards Cal and addressed him, completely ignoring Will, as if he wasn't there.

'Something hot to eat too?' he offered.

Cal was on the point of replying when Will spoke.

'Must go, our parents are waiting just round the corner. Come on, Cal,' he said, a note of urgency creeping into his voice. Cal looked perplexedly at Will, who shook his head, frowning. Realizing that something wasn't quite right, Cal fell into step beside his brother.

'Shame, maybe next time?' the man said, his eyes still locked on Cal. He made no move to follow them, but pulled a lighter from his jacket pocket and lit a cigarette. 'Be seeing you!' he called after them.

'Don't you look back,' Will hissed through his teeth as he walked rapidly away with Cal in tow. 'Don't you *dare* look back.'

An hour later they entered Highfield. Will avoided the High Street in case he was recognized, taking the back alleys and side roads until they turned into Broadlands Avenue.

There it was. The house, completely dark, with an estate agent's sign in the front garden. Will led them around the side and under the carport into the back garden. He kicked over a brick where the spare back-door key had always been hidden, and muttered a silent prayer of thanks when he saw it was still there. He unlocked the door and they took a few wary paces into the dark hallway.

'Colonists!' Cal said straight away, recoiling as he continued to sniff the air. 'They've been here . . . and not long ago.'

'For God's sake.' It merely smelled a little fusty and unoccupied to Will, but he couldn't be bothered to argue. Not wanting to alert the neighbours, he left the lights off and used his light orb to check each room, whilst Cal remained in the hall, his senses working overtime.

'There's nothing . . . no one here at all. Satisfied?' Will said as he returned downstairs. With some consternation, his brother edged further into the house with Bartleby at his heels, and Will shut and locked the door behind them. He shepherded them into the sitting room and, making sure the curtains were tightly closed, turned the television on. Then he went to the kitchen.

The fridge was completely bare except for a tub of margarine and an old tomato, which was green and shrunken. For a moment Will stared uncomprehendingly at the bare shelves. To him this was unprecedented, confirming just how far things had gone. He sighed as he shut the door and spotted a scrap of lined paper taped to it. It was in Rebecca's precise hand, one of her shopping lists.

Rebecca! The fury suddenly rose in him. The thought of that impostor masquerading as his sister for all those years made him rigid with anger. She had changed everything. Now he couldn't even think back to the comfortable and predictable life he'd been leading before his father went missing, because she had been there, watching and spying . . . her very presence tainted all his memories. Hers was the worst kind of betrayal – she was a Judas sent by the Styx.

'Bitch!' he shouted, tearing off the list, crumpling it up and slinging it to the floor.

As it came to rest on the pristine lino floor which Rebecca had mopped week in and week out with mind-numbing regularity, Will looked at the stopped clock on the wall and sighed. He shuffled over to the sink and filled glasses with water for himself and Cal, and a bowl for Bartleby, then returned to the sitting room. Cal and the cat were already curled up asleep on the sofa, Cal with his head resting drowsily on his arm. He could see that they were both shivering, so fetched a couple of duvets from the beds upstairs and draped them over their slumbering forms. The house didn't have its central heating on and it was cold, but not that cold. He'd been right in thinking that they just weren't used to these lower temperatures, and made a mental note to sort out some warm clothing for them in the morning.

Will drank the water quickly and climbed into his mother's chair, wrapping himself in her travelling rug. His eyes barely registered the death-defying snowboarding stunts on the television as he curled up, precisely as his mother had done for so many years, and fell into the deepest of sleeps.

CHAPTER THIRTY-THREE

T am stood silent and defiant. He was determined not to show any sign of his trepidation as he and Mr Jerome faced the long table, their hands clenched behind their backs as if standing to attention.

Behind the table of highly polished oak sat the Panoply. These were the most senior and powerful members of the Styx Council. At either end of the table sat a few high-ranking Colonists: representatives from the Board of the Governors, men that Mr Jerome had known all his life, men that were his friends. He quaked with shame as he felt the disgrace wash over him, and couldn't bring himself to look at them. He'd never thought it would come to this.

Tam was less intimidated; he'd been carpeted before and always managed to get off by the skin of his teeth. Although these allegations were serious, he knew his alibi had passed their scrutiny. Imago and his men had made sure of that. Tam watched as the Crawfly conferred with a fellow Styx and then leant back to speak to the Styx child who stood half hidden behind the high back of his chair. Now, that was *irregular*. Their children were usually kept well out of sight and far away from the Colony; the newborn were never seen, while the older offspring, it was said, were closeted away with their masters in the rarefied atmosphere of their private schools. He'd never heard of them accompanying their elders in public, let alone being present at meetings such as these.

Tam's thoughts were interrupted as a scratchy outburst of intense debate ran back and forth through the Panoply. Chinese whispers rippled from one end to the other as their skinny hands communicated in a series of harsh gestures. Tam glanced quickly at Mr Jerome, whose head hung low. He was quietly mumbling a prayer as sweat coursed from his temples. His face was puffy and his skin an unhealthy pink. All this was taking its toll on him.

The commotion abruptly ceased amidst nods and staccato words of agreement, and the Styx settled back in their seats, a chilling silence descending over the room. Tam readied himself. A pronouncement was about to be delivered.

'Mr Jerome,' the Styx to the left of the Crawfly intoned. 'After due consideration and full and proper investigation,' he fixed his beady pupils on the quivering man, 'we will allow you to step down.'

Another Styx promptly took over. 'It is felt that the injustices brought upon you from specific of your family members, past and present, are unjust and unfortunate. Your honesty is not in question and your reputation has not been tarnished. Unless you would like to speak for the record, you are unconditionally discharged.'

Mr Jerome bowed dolefully and backed away from the table. Tam heard his boots scuffing on the flagstones, but dared not turn to watch him leave. Instead, his gaze flicked to the ceiling of the stone hall, then to the ancient wall hangings behind the Panoply, alighting on one depicting the Founding Fathers digging a perfectly round tunnel in the side of a verdant hill.

He knew that all eyes now rested on him.

Another Styx spoke. Tam immediately recognized the Crawfly's voice, and was obliged to face his avowed enemy. He's loving every minute of this, Tam thought to himself.

'Macaulay. You are a different kettle of fish. Though not proven yet, we believe that you did aid and abet your nephews, Seth and Caleb Jerome, in their foiled attempt to liberate the Topsoiler Chester Rawls, and then to escape to the Eternal City,' said the Crawfly with evident relish.

A second Styx continued. 'The Panoply has recorded your plea of not guilty and your continuing protestations.' With a single, disapproving shake of his head he fell silent for a moment. 'We have reviewed the evidence submitted in your defence but at this time we are unable to reach a resolution. Accordingly we have decreed that the investigation will remain open, and that you are to be held on remand and your privileges revoked until further notice. Do you understand?'

Tam nodded sombrely.

'We said, do you understand?' snapped the Styx child, stepping forward.

An evil grin flicked across Rebecca's face as her icy glare drilled into Tam. There was a stir of hushed astonishment from the Colonists that the minor had dared to speak, but not the smallest indication from the Styx that anything out of the ordinary had taken place.

To say Tam was staggered would be a rank understatement. Was he really supposed to respond to this mere child? As he didn't answer right away she repeated the question, her hard little voice as sharp as a whip-crack.

'WE SAID, DO YOU UNDERSTAND?'

'I do,' Tam muttered, 'only too well.'

Of course, it wasn't a final ruling by any means, but it meant he would live in limbo until they decided either that he was cleared or . . . well . . . the alternative didn't bear thinking about.

As a surly Colonist officer escorted him away he couldn't help but notice the smarmy look of self-congratulation that passed between Rebecca and the Crawfly.

'Well, I'll be blowed!' Tam thought to himself. 'It's his daughter!'

Aroused from his sleep by the booming sound of the television, Will sat up in the armchair with a start. He automatically groped for the remote control and clicked the volume down a couple of notches; it was only when he looked around that he fully realized where he was, and remembered how he'd got there. He was home, and in a room he knew so well. Although he was surrounded by uncertainty about what he was going to do next, for the first time in a long time he felt that he had a measure of control over his destiny, and it felt good.

He flexed his stiff limbs and took several deep breaths, coughing sharply. Despite the fact that he was ravenous, he felt a little better than he had the day before; the sleep had done him some good. He scratched, then tugged vaguely at his matted hair, its usual whiteness discoloured with dirt. Clambering out of the chair, he stumbled over to the curtains and parted them a couple of inches to let the morning sun into the room. Real light. It was such a welcome sight that he pulled them wider.

'Too bright!' Cal screeched repeatedly, burying his face in a cushion. Bartleby, roused by Cal's cries, flicked his eyes open. He immediately shied away from the glare, his long legs propelling him backwards until he tumbled off the rear of the sofa. Here he remained, hiding from the light and making noises somewhere between hisses and low meows.

'Oh, God, I'm sorry,' Will stuttered, kicking himself as he hurriedly yanked the curtains shut again. 'I completely forgot.'

He helped his brother into a sitting position. He was moaning quietly behind the cushion and Will could see that it was already soaked with his tears. He wondered if Cal's and Bartleby's eyes would ever adjust to natural light. It was just one more problem Will had to contend with.

'That was *so* stupid,' he said helplessly. 'I'll . . . er . . . I'll find some sunglasses for you.'

Upstairs he began to search through a chest of drawers in his parents' room only to find that it had been emptied. As he was checking the last drawer he picked out a little bag of lavender languishing on the cheap Christmas gift wrap that his mother had used as a paper liner, and held it up to catch the familiar scent. He closed his eyes as the smell conjured up a vivid picture of her. Wherever they'd sent her to recuperate she'd be lording it over the other patients by now. He was willing to bet she'd commandeered the best chair in the television room, and had cajoled someone into bringing her regular cups of tea. He smiled. In a way, she was probably happier now than she'd been for years. And maybe a little safer too, if the Styx decided to pay a visit.

For no reason in particular, as he rummaged through a bedside cupboard, he thought of his real mother. He wondered where she was right at this very moment, if indeed she was still alive at all. The only person in the long history of the Colony ever to evade the Styx and survive. He set his jaw with a determined look as he caught his reflection in a mirror. Well, now there were going to be two more Jeromes with that distinction.

On a high shelf in his mother's wardrobe he found what he was looking for, a pair of bendy plastic sunglasses she wore on the rare occasions she ventured out in the summer. He went back to Cal, who was squinting at the television in the darkened room, and completely absorbed by the mid-morning talk show in which the perma-tanned and obsequious host, oozing sincerity, was comforting the inconsolable mother of a teenage drug addict. Cal's eyes were a little red and still wet with tears, but he said nothing, and indeed did not shift his gaze once from the screen as Will placed the glasses on his head, looping an elastic band around the arms to hold them firmly in place.

'Better?' Will asked.

'Much better, yes,' Cal said, adjusting them. 'But I'm really hungry,' he added, rubbing his stomach. 'And I'm so cold.' He rattled his teeth together dramatically.

'Showers first, I reckon. That'll warm you up,' Will said as he lifted his arm to sample the accumulated odour of many days' sweat. 'And some clean clothes.'

'Showers?' Cal peered at him blankly through the lenses of the sunglasses.

Will managed to get the boiler fired up and went first, the hot water stinging his flesh with painful relief as the clouds of steam enveloped him in an ecstasy of forgetfulness. Then it was Cal's turn. Will showed his fascinated brother how the power shower worked and left him to it. From the wardrobe in his bedroom he dug out clean sets of clothes for himself and Cal, although his brother's needed a little adjustment to make them fit.

'I'm a real Topsoiler now,' Cal announced, admiring the baggy jeans with rolled-up bottoms and the voluminous shirt with two sweaters over the top of it.

'Yeah, very trendsetting,' Will laughed.

Bartleby was more problematic. It took much coaxing by Cal to even get the shivering animal as far as the bathroom door, and then they had to push him from the rear, like a recalcitrant donkey, to get him in. As if he knew what was in store in the steamy room he leaped away and tried to hide under the sink.

'Come on, Bart, you stinker, into the bath!' Cal ordered, finally running out of patience, and the cat grudgingly crept into the bath and looked at them with the most hangdog of expressions. He let out a warbled, low whine when the water first trickled over his sagging skin, and, deciding he'd had enough, his paws scrabbled on the plastic of the bath as he tried to get out. But with Will holding him down they managed to finish the task, although all three of them were completely drenched by the end of the exercise.

Once out of the bath Bartleby ricocheted around the bedrooms like a whirling dervish while Will took great pleasure in ransacking Rebecca's room. As he chucked all her incredibly neatly folded clothes on to the floor he wondered how on earth he was going to find anything that was remotely suitable to dress a cat. But in the end some brown legwarmers were cut down to size for the animal's hind legs and an old purple

Benetton jumper took care of his top half. Will found a pair of Bugs Bunny sunglasses in Rebecca's holiday holdall, and these stayed in place on the cat's head once a yellow-and-black striped Tibetan hat was pulled firmly down.

Bartleby looked quite bizarre in his new outfit. Out on the landing, the two brothers stood back to admire their handiwork, promptly falling about in hysterics.

'Who's a pretty boy then?' Cal chuckled between outbursts of breathless laughter.

'Better looking than most around here!' Will said.

'Don't you worry, Bart,' Cal said soothingly, patting the peeved animal on the back. 'Very . . . er . . . striking,' he managed to say before they both lapsed once again into uncontrolled laughter. Behind the pink-tinted lenses, the indignant Bartleby watched them sideways out of his large eyes.

Fortunately Rebecca, much as Will cursed her, had left the freezer in the utility room well stocked. He read the microwave instructions and heated up three beef dinners complete with dumplings and French beans. They wolfed these down in the kitchen, Bartleby standing with both paws on the table, his tongue rasping against the tinfoil dish as he hungrily devoured every last scrap of the meat. Cal thought it was just about the best thing he'd ever tasted, but claimed he was still hungry so Will retrieved another three meals from the freezer. This time, they had pork dinners with roast potatoes. They washed this down with a bottle of Coke, which sent Cal into fits of rapture.

'So what happens next?' he said finally, tracing the rising bubbles on the side of his glass with a finger.

'What's the mad rush? We'll be all right for a while,' Will replied. He hoped that they would be able to hole up there, even if for just a few days, to give him time to work out their next move.

'The Styx know about this place – someone's already been here, and they'll be back. Don't forget what Uncle Tam said. There's absolutely no way we can stay put.'

'I suppose so,' Will agreed reluctantly, 'and we could get spotted by the estate agents if they show people round.' He gazed in an unfocused way at the net curtains over the sink and spoke decisively. 'But I still have to get Chester out.'

His brother looked aghast. 'You don't mean go back? I can't go back, not now, Will. The Styx would do something terrible to me.'

Cal was not alone in his fear at returning underground. Will could barely contain his terror at the prospect of facing the Styx again. He felt as though he had pushed his luck as far as it would go, and to imagine he could carry out some audacious rescue attempt was sheer lunacy.

On the other hand, what would they do if they remained Topsoil? Go on the run? When he really thought about it, it just wasn't realistic. Sooner or later they'd be apprehended by the police, and he and Cal would probably be separated and placed in care. Worse than that, he'd live the rest of his life under the shadow of Chester's death, and with the knowledge that he could have joined his father in one of the greatest adventures of the century.

'I don't want to die,' Cal said in a faint voice. 'Not like that.' He pushed his glass away and looked pleadingly into Will's eyes.

This wasn't getting any easier. Will couldn't cope with much more pressure. He shook his head. 'What am I supposed to do? I can't just leave him there. I can't. I won't.'

*

Later, while Cal and Bartleby lounged in front of the television watching children's programmes and eating crisps, Will couldn't resist going into the cellar. Just as he expected, when he swung the shelves out, there wasn't a trace of the tunnel – they had even gone to the trouble of painting the newly laid brickwork to blend in with the rest of the wall. He knew that behind it would be the usual backfill of stone and earth. They'd done the job properly. No point in wasting any further time there.

Back in the kitchen he balanced on a stool while he hunted through the jars on top of the cupboards. He found his mother's video money in a porcelain honey pot – there was about £20 in loose change.

He was in the hallway on his way to the sitting room when he began to see tiny dots of light dancing before his eyes, and all over his body pinpricks of heat broke out. Then, without any warning, his legs went from under him. He dropped the jar, which glanced off the edge of the hall table and shattered, scattering the change over the floor. It was as if he was in slow motion as he collapsed, a fierce pain burning through his head until everything turned black and he lost consciousness.

Cal and Bartleby came rushing out of the sitting room at the noise. 'Will! What's the matter?' Cal cried, kneeling next to him.

Will slowly came round, his temples throbbing painfully. 'I don't know,' he said feebly. 'Just felt awful, all of a sudden.' He started to cough, and had to hold his breath in order to stop.

'You're burning up,' Cal said, feeling his forehead.

'Freezing . . .' Will could barely talk as his teeth rattled together. He made an effort to get up, but didn't have the strength.

'Oh, God,' Cal's face was creased with concern, 'it could be something from the Eternal City. Plague!'

Will was silent as his brother pulled him over to the bottom step of the staircase and propped his head on it. He fetched the travelling rug and put it around him. After a while Will directed Cal to the bathroom to fetch some aspirin. He swallowed them down with a sip of Coke and, after a brief rest, managed to get shakily to his feet with assistance from Cal.

Will's eyes were feverish and unfocused, and his voice trembled. 'I really think we should get help,' he said, mopping the sweat from his brow.

'Is there anywhere we can go?' Cal asked.

Will sniffed, swallowed and nodded, his head feeling as though it was about to burst. 'There's only one place I can think of.'

'Get yerself out here!' the Second Officer bawled into the cell, his head pushed so far forward that the tendons in his bull-like neck stood proud, like knotted lengths of rope.

From the shadows came several sniffs as Chester did his best to control his terrified sobbing. Ever since he had been recaptured and brought back to the Hold the Second Officer had been treating him brutally. The man had taken it upon himself to make Chester's life a living hell, withholding his meals and waking him up if he happened to nod off on the ledge by emptying a bucket of ice-cold water over his head or by screaming threats through the inspection hatch. All this probably had something to do with the thick bandage around the Second Officer's head – Will's blow with the spade had knocked him out cold – and, what was worse, when he came to the Styx had spent the best part of a day interrogating him over the accusation that he had been negligent in his duties. So to say that the Second Officer was now very bitter and vindictive would be putting it mildly.

Chester, half starved and exhausted to the point of collapse, wasn't sure how much more of this treatment he could take. If life had been hard for him before the botched escape attempt, it was that much worse now.

'Don't make me come in there and get you!' the Second Officer was yelling. Before he'd finished, Chester shuffled barefoot into the wan light of the aisle. Shielding his eyes with one hand, he lifted his head. It was streaked grey with ingrained dirt and his shirt was torn.

'Yes, sir,' he mumbled subserviently.

'The Styx want to see you. They've got something to tell you,' the Second Officer said, his voice distorted with malice, and then he began to chortle. 'Something that'll fix you good and proper.' He was still laughing as, unbidden, Chester started down the aisle towards the main door to the Hold, the soles of his feet rasping sluggishly across the gritty flags.

'Shift it!' the Second Officer snapped, thrusting his bunch of keys into the small of Chester's back.

'Ow,' Chester complained in a pitiful voice.

As they went through the main door Chester had to cover his eyes altogether, he was now so unused to the light. He continued to shuffle along, heading on a course that would have taken him through to the front desk of the police station if the Second Officer hadn't stopped him.

'And where do you think you're off to? You don't think

you're going home, do you?' The man started to guffaw and then became deadly serious again. 'No, you go *right*, into the corridor, you do.'

Chester, lowering his hands and trying to see through his screwed-up eyes, made a slow quarter turn and then froze, rooted to the spot.

'The Dark Light?' he asked fearfully, not daring to turn his face towards the Second Officer.

'No, we're past all that now. This is where you get your comeuppance, you worthless little squit.'

They passed through a series of corridors, the Second Officer chivvying Chester along with further jabs and shoves, chuckling to himself all the way. He quietened down as they rounded a corner and came in sight of an open doorway. From this an intense light streamed out, illuminating the whitewashed wall opposite.

Although Chester's movements were languid and his expression blank, inwardly his fears were raging. Frantically he debated with himself whether he should make a run for it and bolt down the corridor ahead. He hadn't got the slightest idea where it led, or how far he'd get, but it would, at the very least, put off facing whatever was waiting for him in that room. For a while anyway.

He slowed even further, his eyes hurting as he forced himself to look directly at the blaze of light flooding from the doorway. He was getting closer. He didn't know what was waiting inside - another of their exquisitely horrible tortures? Or maybe . . . maybe *an executioner*.

His whole body stiffened, every muscle wanting to do anything but carry him into that dazzling light.

'Nearly there,' the officer said over Chester's shoulder, and

Chester knew that he had no alternative but to cooperate. There were going to be no miraculous reprieves, no timely escapes.

He was dragging his heels so much that he was barely moving at all when the Second Officer gave him such a hefty shove that he was knocked clean off his feet and sent flying through the doorway into the light. Skidding over the stone floor on his front he came to a rest and lay there, a little stunned.

The light was all around him, and he was blinking rapidly in its harsh glare. He heard the door slam and, from a rustle of papers, he knew at once there was someone else in the room. He immediately imagined who it, or they, would be – two tall Styx, most likely looming behind a table, just as there'd been during the Dark Light sessions.

'Stand up,' ordered a reedy, nasal voice.

Chester did so, and slowly raised his eyes to the source. He couldn't have been more astonished by the sight that greeted him.

It was a single Styx and he was wizened and small, his thinning grey hair pulled back at the temples and his face criss-crossed with so many lines and wrinkles that he looked like a bleached raisin. Hunched sharply over a tall desk with a slanted top, he resembled an ancient schoolmaster.

Chester was completely disarmed by this apparition with the sheer light all around it. This was not what he'd been expecting at all. He was beginning to feel relieved, telling himself that perhaps things were going to turn out better than he'd thought after all, when his eyes met those of the old Styx.

They were the coldest, darkest eyes Chester had ever seen. They were like two bottomless wells that drew him towards them and by some unnatural and unwholesome power pulled him down into their voids. Chester felt a chill descend over him as if the temperature had plummeted in the room, and he shivered violently.

The old Styx dropped his eyes to the desk and Chester swayed unsteadily on his feet, as if he'd been abruptly released from something that had had him in its relentless grip. He let out his breath in a rush, unconscious until now that he'd been holding it in. Then the Styx began to read in a measured tone.

'You have been found guilty,' he said, 'under Order 42, Edicts 18, 24, 42 . . .'

The numbers went on, but it meant nothing to Chester until the Styx paused, and, very matter-of-factly, said the word 'Sentence'. Chester really began to listen at this point.

'The prisoner will be taken from this place and conveyed by train to the Interior, and there be Banished, relinquished to the forces of nature. So be it,' the old Styx finished, clapping his hands and holding them pressed hard together, as if he was wringing something out. Then he slowly raised his head from his papers and said, 'May the Lord have mercy on your soul.'

'What . . . what do you mean?' Chester asked, reeling under the Styx's icy gaze and the implications of what he'd just heard.

Without needing to consult the papers before him the Styx simply reiterated the punishment and then fell silent again. Chester grappled with the questions that were racing through his head, moving his lips but emitting no sound at all.

'Yes?' the old Styx asked, in such a way that suggested he'd been in this situation many times before, and found it thoroughly tiresome to have to converse with the lowly prisoner before him.

'What . . . what does that mean?' Chester eventually managed.

The Styx stared at Chester for several seconds and, with total impassivity, said, 'Banished. You will be escorted as far as the Miner's Station, many fathoms down, and then left to do as you will.'

'Taken deeper into the Earth?'

The Styx nodded. 'We have no need for your sort in the Colony. You attempted to escape, and the Panoply takes a dim view of that. You are not worthy of service here.' He clapped his hands together again. 'Banished.'

Chester suddenly felt the immense weight of all the millions of tons of earth and rock above, as if they were pressing directly down on him, squeezing out his lifeblood. He staggered backwards.

'But I've done *nothing*. I'm not *guilty* of anything!' he cried, holding his hands out and pleading with the emotionless little man. He felt as if he was being buried alive, and that he would never again see home, or the blue sky, or his family . . . everything he loved and yearned for. The hope he had clung on to ever since he'd been captured and locked up in that dark room gushed out of him, as air from a burst balloon.

He was doomed.

This hateful little man didn't give a stuff about him . . . Chester saw that in the Styx's impassive face and in his frightful eyes – reptilian, inhuman eyes. And Chester knew that there was absolutely no point in trying to persuade him, or to beg for his life. These people were savage and merciless, and they had arbitrarily condemned him to the most awful fate. *An even deeper grave.*

'But why?' Chester asked, tears wetting his face as he wept openly.

'Because it is the law,' the old Styx answered. 'Because I am sitting here, and you are standing there.' He smiled without the remotest trace of any warmth.

'But—' Chester objected with a howl.

'Officer, take him back to the Hold,' the old Styx said, gathering up his papers with his arthritic fingers, and Chester heard the door creak open behind him.

CHAPTER THIRTY-FOUR

Will was thrown forward as a fist landed squarely in the middle of his back. Staggering drunkenly for a few steps, he rebounded off the handrail and turned slowly round to face his assailant.

'Speed?' he said, recognizing the school bully's scowling face.

'Where've you sprung from, snowdrop? Thought you'd snuffed it. People said you were dead or something.'

Will didn't reply. He was deep in the insulated cocoon of the unwell; he felt as though he was looking at the world from behind a frosted sheet of glass. It was all Will could do to stand there, his body quivering as Speed pushed his snarling face just centimetres in front of his. Out of the corner of his eye, Will glimpsed Bloggsy closing in on Cal a little further down the sloping path.

They had been on their way to the Tube station and right now a fight was the last thing Will wanted.

'So where's Fat Boy?' Speed crooned, the moisture on his breath clouding in the cold air. 'Bit different without your minder, innit, dipstick?'

'Oi, Speed, check this out, it's Mini Me!' Bloggsy said, looking from Cal to Will and back again. 'What's in your bag, loser?'

At Will's insistence, Cal had been carrying their dirty Colonists' clothes in one of Dr Burrows' old expedition holdalls.

'Payback time,' Speed shouted, and simultaneously jabbed a fist in Will's stomach. Winded, Will slumped to his knees and then toppled over, curling up with his arms wrapped protectively around his head as he hit the ground.

'This is too easy,' Speed crowed and kicked Will in the back several times.

Bloggsy was making ludicrous whooping noises and crouching in a mock kung fu fighting stance as he prodded two fingers at Cal's sunglasses. 'Prepare to meet your maker,' he said, drawing his arm back ready to throw a punch.

Everything happened too quickly for Will after that. There was a streak of purple-and-brown lightning as Bartleby landed smack in the middle of Bloggsy's shoulders. The impact knocked the boy away from Cal and sent him tumbling untidily down the slope, the cat still latched on to his back. As Bloggsy came to rest face down on the ground he was writhing and trying to use his elbows to beat off the flurry of pearl-white canines and barbaric-looking claws, all the while letting out the most awful high-pitched cries and screaming for someone to help.

'No,' Will shouted weakly. 'Enough!'

'Leave it, Bart!' Cal yelled.

The cat, still on top of Bloggsy, spun his head about to look at Cal, who shouted another command.

'See him off!' Cal pointed at Speed, who had remained

standing over Will through all this, not believing what he was seeing. Speed's jaw dropped, and a look of sheer horror crept over his face. Bartleby fixed his eyes on the new quarry through the bizarre pink sunglasses, the Tibetan hat now slightly askew on his head. With a loud hiss, he bounded up the slope towards the startled bully.

'Jesus! Call it off!' Speed shrieked, as he started to run up the path as if his life depended on it. It did. In the blink of an eye, the cat had caught up with him. Sometimes at his side, sometimes blocking his way, Bartleby circled around him like a playful whirlwind, attacking his calves and slashing at his legs through his school trousers, lacerating his skin. The terrified boy stumbled and tottered in a spasmodic, comic dance as he frantically tried to escape, his feet sliding hopelessly on the tarmac.

'I'm sorry, Will, I'm sorry! Just get it off me! Please!' Speed was gibbering, his trousers reduced to tatters.

With a look from Will, Cal stuck two fingers in his mouth and whistled. The cat stopped instantly, and allowed Speed to run away. Not once did the boy turn to look back.

Will glanced past Cal to the bottom of the slope, where Bloggsy had picked himself up and was half-running, half falling in his haste to make an escape.

'I think we've seen the last of them,' Cal laughed.

'Yes,' Will agreed faintly as he slowly got to his feet. Wave upon wave of the fever ebbed through him, and he felt as if he was going to pass out again. He could quite happily have lain back down, opened his coat to the cold and gone to sleep right there and then on the frosty path. The only way Will could get down the remaining stretch of the slope was with Cal supporting him, but they eventually made it to the bottom and into the Tube station.

'So even Topsoilers like to go underground,' he said, looking at the dirty old station, long overdue a refurbishment. His manner was instantly transformed; he seemed genuinely at ease for the first time since they had emerged on to the banks of the Thames - relieved that there was a tunnel around him rather than open sky.

'Not really,' Will said listlessly as he started to feed change into the ticket machine, while Bartleby slavered over a lichen-like patch of freshly deposited chewing gum on the tiled floor. Will's shaking fingers fumbled with the coins, then he stopped and leaned against the machine. 'It's no good,' he gasped. Cal took the change from him and, as Will told him what to do, he finished paying for the tickets.

Down on the platform, it wasn't long before a train arrived. Once aboard the southbound train, neither boy spoke as they pulled out of the station. As it gained speed Cal watched the cables rippling along the tunnel sides and played with his ticket. Licking his paws, Bartleby was propped on his haunches in the seat next to Cal. There weren't many people in the carriage, but Cal was conscious that they were attracting some pretty curious glances.

Opposite Cal and Bartleby, Will was sitting slumped against the side of the carriage, soothed by the chill glass on his temple as his head lolled against the window. Between stops, he drifted in and out of a fitful sleep, and during a period of wakefulness saw that a pair of old ladies had taken the seats across the aisle from them. Snatches of their conversation drifted into his consciousness and mixed with the platform announcements like voices in a confused dream.

'Just look at him . . . disgraceful . . . feet all over the seats . . .

MIND THE GAP . . . funny-looking child . . . LONDON UNDERGROUND APOLOGIZES . . .'

Will forced his eyes open and looked at the two women. He realized immediately it was Bartleby who was the cause of their apparent distress. The one who was doing all the talking had purple-rinsed hair and wore translucent white-framed bifocals that rested crookedly on her poppy-red nose.

'Shhh! They'll hear you,' her companion whispered, eyeing Cal. She was wearing a wig that had seen better days. They both held identical shopping bags on their laps, as if they were some form of defence against the miscreants sitting opposite.

'Nonsense! Bet they don't speak a word of English. Probably got here on the back of a lorry. I mean, look at the state of their clothes. And that one – he don't look too bright to me. He's probably on drugs or something.' Will felt their rheumy eyes linger on him.

'Send them all back, I say.'

'Yes, yes,' the old ladies said in unison, and with a mutual nod of agreement fell to discussing, in morbid detail, the ill health of a friend. Cal glowered furiously at them while they gabbled away, now apparently too preoccupied to pay further attention to anyone else. The train came to a stop and as the old ladies were getting up from their seats Cal lifted the ear flap of Bartleby's Tibetan hat and whispered something into his ear. Bartleby suddenly reared up and hissed in their faces so forcefully that Will was shocked from his feverish stupor.

'Well, I never!' the red-nosed lady cried out, dropping her shopping bag. While she retrieved it, her companion bustled and pushed her from behind, trying to hurry her up.

In a flap, both women struggled off the train, shrieking.

'Bloody gyppos!' the red-nosed lady huffed from the platform. 'You bloody animals!' she screamed through the doors as they slid shut.

The train moved off and Bartleby kept his eyes fixed demonically on them as they stood on the platform, still huffing with indignation.

His curiosity getting the better of him, Will leant over to his brother.

'Tell me . . . what did you say to Bartleby?' he asked.

'Oh, nothing much,' Cal replied innocently, smiling at his cat proudly before he turned to look out of the window again.

Will was dreading the last half-kilometre to the block of flats. He staggered along like a sleepwalker, resting when it became too much for him.

When they finally reached the tower block the lift wasn't working. Will peered into the graffiti-strafed greyness with quiet desperation. That was the last straw. He sighed and, steeling himself for the climb, stumbled towards the squalid stairwell. After a stop on each landing to allow him to catch his breath, they eventually reached the right floor and made their way through the obstacle course of discarded rubbish bags.

There was no response when Cal rang the bell, so he had resorted to hammering on the door with his fist when Auntie Jean opened it suddenly. She clearly hadn't been up for long – she looked as tired and crumpled as the moth-eaten overcoat that she'd evidently been asleep in.

'What is it?' she said indistinctly, rubbing the nape of her neck and yawning. 'I didn't order nothing and I don't buy nothing from salesmen.'

'Auntie Jean, it's me . . . Will,' he said, as the blood drained from his head and the image of his aunt blanched, as if all the colours had been washed out of it.

'Will,' she said vaguely, and cut another yawn short as it sank in. 'Will!' She lifted her head and eyed him disbelievingly. 'Thought you'd gone missing.' She peered at Cal and Bartleby, and added, 'Who's this?'

'Er . . . cousin . . .' Will gasped as the floor began to tip and sway, and he was forced to take a step forward to steady himself against the door jamb. He was aware of the cold sweat trickling from his scalp. '. . . south . . . from down south.'

'Cousin? Didn't know you—'

'Dad's,' Will said huskily.

She surveyed Cal and Bartleby with suspicion and not a little distaste. 'Your bloody sister was 'ere, you know.' She glanced past Will. 'Is she wiv you?'

'She . . .' Will began to say in a shaky voice.

''Cos the little tramp owes me money. Should've seen what she did to my—'

'She's *not* my sister, she's a vile . . . scheming . . . little . . . she's a . . .' With that, Will keeled over in a dead faint before a very surprised Auntie Jean.

Cal stood at the window of the darkened room. He peered down at the streets below, with their dotted lines of amber lights and sweeping cones of car headlamps. Then, with foreboding, he slowly raised his head and looked up at the moon, its shining silver spread out against the icy sky. Not for the first time he struggled to grasp, to comprehend, the vast space which yawned before him, the likes of which he'd never before seen in his life. He gripped the windowsill, barely able to control the mounting sense of dread. The soles of his feet clenched involuntarily and almost ached with vertigo.

On hearing his brother moan he tore his eyes from the window and went to sit by the shivering form that was stretched out on the bed with just a sheet over it.

'How's 'e doing then?' Cal heard Auntie Jean's anxious voice as she appeared in the doorway.

'He's a little better today. I think he's cooling down a bit,' he said as he doused a flannel in a bowl of water clunking with ice cubes and dabbed it to Will's forehead.

'Do you want to get someone in to see 'im?' Auntie Jean asked. ''E's been like this for a long time.'

'No,' Cal said firmly. 'He said he didn't want that.'

'Don't blame 'im, don't blame 'im at all. I've never 'ad no time for quacks – or them shrinks, neither, for that matter. Once you're in their clutches, there's no telling what—' She stopped short as Bartleby, who had been curled up asleep in the corner, woke with a small sneeze then ambled over and started to lap at the water in the bowl.

'Get off, you stupid cat!' Cal said, pushing him away.

''E's just thirsty,' Auntie Jean said, then assumed the most preposterous baby voice. 'Poor puss, are you a liccle firsty?' She took hold of the astounded animal by the scruff of his neck and began to lead him towards the door. 'You come with mummy, for a treat.'

A lava flow moves portentously in the distance, its heat so fierce on Will's exposed skin that he can hardly bear it. Silhouetted by the vertical wall of streaming crimson behind him, Dr Burrows frantically indicates something sprouting out of a massive slab of granite. He shouts excitedly, as he always does when he makes a discovery, but Will isn't able to catch the words due to the deafening white noise intercut with the cacophonous babble of many voices, as if someone is randomly scanning the airwaves on a damaged radio.

The scene shifts into close-up. Dr Burrows is using a magnifying glass to examine a thin stalk with a bulbous tip, which rises half a metre or so out of the solid rock. Will sees his father's lips moving but can only understand brief snatches of what he is saying.

'. . . a plant . . . literally digests rock . . . silicon-based . . . reacts to stim— . . . observe . . .'

The image cuts to extreme close-up. Between two fingers Dr Burrows plucks the grey stalk from the rock. Will feels uneasy as he sees it writhe in his father's hand and shoot out two needle-like leaves that entwine around his fingers.

'. . . gripping me like iron . . . feisty little . . .' Dr Burrows says, frowning.

There are no more words, they are replaced by laughter, but his father seems to be screaming as he tries to shake the thing off, its leaves piercing his hand and threading straight through the flesh of his palm and wrist and carrying on up his forearm, the skin bruising, bruising and bursting open and becoming smeared with blood as they twist, interweaving in a snake-like waltz. They cut tighter and tighter into his forearm, like two possessed cheese wires. Will tries to reach out to his father, to help him as he battles hopelessly against this horrific attack, as he is fighting his own arm.

'No, no . . . Dad . . . Dad!'

'It's all right, Will, it's all right,' came his brother's voice from a long way away.

The lava glow was gone. In its place was a shaded light,

and he could feel the soothing coolness of the flannel Cal was pressing against his forehead. He sat up with a start.

'It's Dad! What happened to Dad?' he cried and looked around wildly, unsure where he was.

'You're all right,' Cal said. 'You were dreaming.'

Will slumped back against the pillows, realizing he was lying in bed in a narrow room.

'I saw him. It was all so clear and real,' Will said, his voice breaking. He couldn't stem the flood of tears that suddenly filled his eyes. 'It was Dad. He was in trouble.'

'It was just a nightmare.' Cal spoke softly, averting his eyes from his brother, who was now sobbing silently.

'We're at Auntie Jean's, aren't we?' Will said, pulling himself together as he saw the floral wallpaper.

'Yes, we've been here for nearly three days.'

'Huh?' Will tried to sit up again, but it was too much for him and he rested his head against the pillow again. 'I feel so weak.'

'Don't worry, everything's fine. Your aunt's been great. Rather taken a shine to Bart too.'

Over the ensuing days, Cal nursed Will back to health with bowls of soup or baked beans on toast, and seemingly endless cups of over-sugared tea. Auntie Jean's sole contribution to his convalescence was to perch at the foot of his bed and burble on incessantly about the 'old days', though Will was so exhausted he fell asleep before she could bore him senseless.

When Will finally felt strong enough to stand he tested his legs by trying to walk up and down the small bedroom. As he hobbled around with some difficulty he noticed something lying discarded behind a box of old magazines.

He stooped down and picked up two objects. Shards of broken glass dropped to the floor. He recognized the pair of buckled silver frames straight away. They were the ones Rebecca had kept on her bedside table. Looking at the photograph of his parents, and then the one of himself, he slumped back on to the bed, breathing heavily. He was distraught. He felt as though someone had stuck a knife into him and was very slowly twisting it. *But what did he expect from her?* Rebecca wasn't his sister, and never had been. He remained on the bed for some time, staring blankly at the wall.

A little later he got to his feet again and staggered down the hall and into the kitchen. Dirty plates lay in the sink and the bin was overflowing with empty tins and torn microwave-ready food boxes. It was a scene of such carnage that he barely registered the plastic tops of the taps, melted and brown, and the flame-blackened tiles behind them. He grimaced and turned back into the hall, where he heard Auntie Jean's gruff voice. Its tones were vaguely comforting, reminding him of the Christmases when she would come to stay, chatting to his mother for hours on end.

He stood outside the door and listened as Auntie Jean's knitting needles rattled away furiously while she spoke.

'Dr bleedin' Burrows . . . soon as I laid eyes on 'im, I warned my sister . . . I did, you know . . . you don't want to be getting 'itched to some overeducated layabout . . . I mean, I ask you, what good's a man who grubs around in 'oles in the ground when there's bills to pay?'

Will peered around the corner as Auntie Jean's needles stopped their metronomic clicking and she took a sip from a tumbler. The cat was looking adoringly at Auntie Jean, who looked back at him with an affectionate, almost loving smile.

Will had never seen this side of her before – he knew he should say something to announce his presence, but somehow he couldn't bring himself to break the moment.

'I tell you it's nice to 'ave you 'ere. I mean, after my little Sophie passed on . . . she was a dog and I know you don't much like them . . . but at least she was there for me . . . that's more than you can say for any man I ever met.'

She held up her knitting in front of her, a garishly coloured pair of trousers, which Bartleby sniffed curiously. 'Nearly done. In just a mo' you can try 'em on for size, my lovely.' She leaned over and tickled Bartleby under the chin. He lifted his head and, closing his eyes, began to purr with the amplitude of a small engine.

Will turned to make his way back to the bedroom, and was resting against the wall in the hallway when there was a crash behind him. Cal was standing just inside the front door, two bags of dropped shopping spilling open in front of him. He had a scarf wrapped around his mouth and was wearing Mrs Burrows' sunglasses. He looked like the Invisible Man.

'I can't take much more of this,' he said, squatting down to retrieve the groceries. Bartleby padded out from the sitting room, followed by Auntie Jean, a cigarette perched on her lip. The cat was wearing his newly knitted trousers and mohair cardigan, both a strident mix of blues and reds, topped off with a multicoloured balaclava from which his scabby ears stuck comically. Bartleby looked like the survivor of an explosion in an Oxfam shop.

Cal glanced at the outlandish figure before him, taking in the shocking display of colours, but didn't comment. He appeared to be in the depths of despondency. 'This place is full of hate – you can smell it everywhere.' He shook his head slowly.

'Oh, it is that, love,' Auntie Jean said quietly. 'Always 'as been.'

'Topsoil isn't what I expected,' Cal said. He thought for a moment. 'And I can't go home . . . can I?'

Will stared back as he searched for something to say to console his brother, some form of words to quell the boy's anxiety, but he was unable to utter a word.

Auntie Jean cleared her throat, bringing the moment to an end.

'Suppose this means you're all going?'

As she stood there in her scruffy old coat Will saw for the first time how very vulnerable and frail she seemed.

'I think we are,' he admitted.

'Righto,' she said hollowly. She put her hand on Bartleby's neck, tenderly caressing the loose flaps of his skin with her thumb. 'You know you're all welcome 'ere – any time you want.' Her voice became choked and she turned quickly away from them. 'And do bring kitty back wiv you.' She shuffled into the kitchen, where they could hear her trying to stifle her sobs as she rattled a bottle against a glass.

Over the next few days, they planned and planned. Will felt himself growing stronger as he recovered from the illness, his lungs clearing and his breathing returning to normal. They went on shopping expeditions: an army surplus shop yielded gas masks, climbing rope and a water bottle for each of them; they bought some old camera flash units in a pawn shop and, as it was the week after Guy Fawkes' night, several large boxes of remaindered fireworks from a newsagent's. Will wanted to make sure they were ready for any eventuality, and anything that gave off a bright light might come in useful. They stocked up on food, choosing lightweight but high-energy provisions so as not to weigh themselves down. After the kindness she had shown them, Will felt bad that he was dipping into his aunt's grocery money to pay for it all, but he didn't have any alternative.

They waited until lunchtime to leave Highfield. They donned their now clean Colonists' clothes and said their goodbyes to Auntie Jean, who gave Bartleby a tearful cuddle, then they took the bus into central London and walked the rest of the way to the river entrance.

CHAPTER THIRTY-FIVE

Cal was still pressing a handkerchief to his face and muttering about the 'foul gases' as they left Blackfriars Bridge and took the steps down to the Embankment. Everything looked so different in the daylight that for a moment Will had doubts that they were even in the right place. With people bustling all about them on the walkway it seemed so fanciful to suppose that somewhere below them was an abandoned and primitive London, and that the three of them were going to go back down there.

But they were in the right place, and it was only a short walk to the entrance of that strange *other* world. They stood by the gate and peered down, watching the brown water lapping lazily below.

'Looks deep,' Cal remarked. 'Why's it like that?'

'Duh!' Will groaned, thumping his palm against his forehead. 'The tide! I didn't think of the tide. We'll just have to wait for it to go out.'

'How long will that be?'

Will shrugged, checking his watch. 'I don't know. Could be hours.'

There was no alternative but to kill time by pacing the backstreets around the Tate Modern and return to the bank every so often to check the water, trying not to attract too much attention in the process. By lunchtime they could see the gravel breaking through.

Will decided they couldn't hang around any longer. 'Right, all systems go!' he announced.

They were in full view of many passers-by on their lunch breaks, but hardly anyone took any notice of the motley-looking trio, eccentrically dressed and laden with rucksacks, as they clambered over the wall and on to the stone steps. Then an old man in a woolly hat and matching scarf spotted them and began to shout 'Ruddy kids!', wagging his fist furiously at them. One or two people gathered around to see what the fuss was all about, but they quickly lost interest and moved on. This seemed to dampen the old man's outrage, and he too shuffled off, muttering loudly to himself.

At the bottom of the steps, the water splashed up around the boys' legs as they galloped with all their might along the partially submerged foreshore, only letting up when they were out of sight under the jetty. Without any hesitation Cal and Bartleby clambered into the mouth of the drainage tunnel.

Will paused for a moment before following. He took a last lingering look at the pale-grey sky through the gaps in the planking and inhaled deeply, savouring his last breaths of fresh air.

Now he'd recovered his strength he felt like a completely different person – he was prepared for whatever lay ahead. As if the fever had purged him of any doubts or weaknesses, he was feeling the resigned assurance of the seasoned adventurer. But as he lowered his eyes to the slow-moving river, he experienced the deepest pang of loss and melancholy, aware he might never see this place again. Of course, he didn't have to go through with it, he could stay here if he chose, but he knew it would never be the same as before. Too much had changed, things that could never be undone.

'Come on,' he said, shaking himself from his thoughts and entering the tunnel where Cal was waiting for him, impatient to get going. With a single glance Will could read conflicting emotions in his brother's face: although the anxiety was plain to see, there was also a hint of something else, a deep sense of relief brought about by the promise of an imminent return to the underworld. It was his home, after all.

Although circumstances had forced his hand Will reflected on what a terrible mistake it had been to bring Cal with him to the surface. Cal would need time to adjust to Topsoil life – and that was one luxury they didn't have. Like it or not, Will's destiny lay in rescuing Chester and finding his father. And Cal's destiny was inextricably bound to his.

It irked Will that he'd lost so many days to the fever – he had no idea if he was too late to save Chester. Had he already been exiled to the Deeps, or come to some unimaginable end at the hands of the Styx? Whatever the truth might be, he had to find out. He had to go on believing Chester was still alive; he had to go back. He could never live with that hanging over him.

They found the vertical shaft and Will reluctantly lowered himself into the pool of freezing water below it. Cal climbed on to Will's shoulders so he could reach the shaft, then shimmied up it, trailing a rope behind him. When his brother was safely at the top, Will knotted the other end of the rope around Bartleby's chest and Cal began to hoist him up. This proved to be completely unnecessary as, once in the vent, the animal used his sinewy legs to scrabble up with startling agility. Then the rope was dropped for Will, who hauled himself into the shadows above. Once he was there he jumped up and down to shake the water off and warm himself.

Then they slid down the convex ramp on the seats of their pants, landing with a thump on the ledge that marked the beginning of the rough stairs. Before proceeding, they carefully removed Bartleby's knitted clothes and left them on a high ledge - they couldn't afford to carry any dead weight now. Will didn't really have any idea what he was going to do once they were back in the Colony, but he knew he had to be completely practical . . . he had to be like Tam.

The boys put on their army surplus gas masks, looked at each other for a moment, nodded an acknowledgement, and with Cal leading the way they began the long descent.

The going was arduous at first, the stairs hazardous from the constantly seeping water and, further down, the carpet of black algae. Will found he had very little recollection of their previous passage through, realizing that this must have been because the mysterious illness had already got a hold on him by then.

In what seemed like no time at all they had arrived at the opening to the Eternal City.

'What the hell is *this*?' Cal exclaimed the moment they walked out on to the top of the huge flight of steps, their eyes quickly sweeping down its dark course. Something was very wrong. Approximately thirty metres down, the steps vanished from view.

'That's what I believe they called a real pea-souper,' Will said quietly, his glass eyepieces glinting with the pale-green glow.

From their vantage point high above the city they looked out on what appeared to be the undulating surface of a huge opaline lake. The thickest of fogs covered the entire scene, suffused by an eerie light, as if it were one immense radioactive cloud. It was very daunting to think that the vast extent of the huge city lay obscured beneath this opaque blanket. Will automatically scrabbled in his pockets for the compass.

'This is going to make life a little difficult,' he remarked, frowning behind his mask.

'Why?' Cal retorted. His eyes crinkled behind his eyepieces as a broad smile spread across his face. 'They won't be able to see us in all that, will they?'

But Will's demeanour remained grim. 'True, but we won't see them either.'

Cal held Bartleby still while Will tied a rope lead around his neck. They couldn't risk him wandering off under these conditions.

'You'd better keep hold of my rucksack so you don't get lost. And whatever you do don't let go of that cat,' Will urged his brother as they took their first steps in the fog, descending slowly into it, like deep-sea divers sinking beneath the waves. Their visibility was immediately reduced to no more than half a metre – they couldn't even see their boots, making it necessary to feel for the edge of each step before venturing to the next.

Thankfully, they reached the bottom of the stairway without incident and at the start of the mud flats they repeated the black weed ritual, wiping the stinking goo all over each other, this time to mask the Topsoil smells of London.

Traversing the edge of the marshland, they eventually bumped into the city wall and followed it round. If anything, the visibility was getting even worse, and it took them an age to find a way in.

'An archway,' Will whispered, stopping so abruptly that his brother nearly fell over him. The ancient structure briefly solidified before them, and then the fog closed up, obscuring it again.

'Oh, good,' Cal replied, without an ounce of enthusiasm.

Once inside the city walls, they had to grope their way through the streets, practically walking on top of each other so that they wouldn't become separated in these impossible conditions. The fog was almost tangible, sucking and rolling like sheets in the wind, sometimes parting to allow them the briefest glimpse of a section of wall, a stretch of water-sodden ground or the glistening cobbles underfoot. The squelch of their boots on the black algae and their laboured breathing through their masks sounded unnervingly loud to them. The way the fog was twisting and playing with their senses made everything feel so intimate and yet, at the same time, so removed.

Cal grabbed Will's arm, and they stopped still. They were beginning to notice other noises all around them that weren't of their making. At first vague and indistinct, these sounds were growing louder. As they listened, Will could have sworn he caught a scratchy whispering, so close that he flinched. He pulled Cal back a couple of steps, convinced they had already done the very thing he was dreading, that they had stumbled headlong into the Styx Division. However, Cal swore he hadn't heard anything at all, and after a while they nervously resumed their journey.

Then, from the distance, came the bloodcurdling baying of a dog – there was no question about it this time. Cal tightened his grip on Bartleby's lead as the cat raised his head high, his ears pricking up. Although neither boy said anything to each other they were both thinking the same thing: the need for them to get through the city as rapidly as they could had become all the more pressing.

As they crept along, their hearts were pounding as Will referred to Tam's map and repeatedly checked his compass with his shaking hands in an attempt to fix their position. In truth, the visibility was so poor he had only the roughest idea where they were. For all he knew, they might be wandering in circles. They seemed to be making no headway at all, and Will was at his wits' end. What a great leader he was turning out to be!

He finally brought them to a halt and they huddled down in the lee of a crumbling wall. In low whispers they debated what to do next.

'If we start running it won't matter if we come across a patrol. We can easily shake them off in this,' Cal suggested quietly, his eyes darting left and right under the moisture-spotted lenses of his gas mask. 'We just keep running.'

'Yeah, right,' Will replied. 'So you *really* think you could outrun one of those dogs? I'd like to see that.'

Cal humphed angrily in response.

Will went on. 'Look, we don't have a clue where we are, and if we have to leg it, we'll probably hit a dead end or something . . .'

'But once we're in the Labyrynth, they'll never catch us,' Cal insisted.

'Fine, but we've got to get there first, and for all we know it's still a bloody long way off.' Will couldn't believe his brother's absurd suggestion. It dawned on him that a couple of months ago *he* might have been the one advocating the crazy dash through the streets and lanes of the city. Somehow, imperceptibly, he'd changed. Now he was the sober one and Cal was the impulsive, headstrong youngster, chock-full of madcap confidence and willing to risk all.

The furious whispered exchange continued, growing more and more heated until Cal finally relented. It was to be the 'softly, softly' approach; they would inch their way to the far edge of the city, keeping the sounds of their footsteps to a minimum and melting into the fog if anyone, or anything, came close.

As they stepped over hunks of rubble Bartleby's head was jerking in all directions, scenting the air and the ground, when all of a sudden he stopped. Despite Cal's best efforts to pull on the lead, the cat refused to move – he'd lowered his body as if he were hunting something, his wide head close to the ground and his skeletal tail sticking straight out behind him. His ears were pointing and twitching like radar dishes.

'Where are they?' Cal whispered frantically. Will didn't answer, but instead reached into the side pockets of Cal's rucksack and yanked out two large fireworks. He also took out Auntie Jean's little plastic disposable lighter from an inner pocket in his jacket and held it ready in his hand.

'Come on, Bart,' Cal was whispering into the cat's ear as he knelt beside him, 'it's all right.'

What little hair Bartleby had was bristling now. Cal

managed to draw the cat around and they tiptoed in the opposite direction as if walking on eggshells, Will at the rear with the fireworks poised in his hands.

They followed a wall as it curved gently around, Cal feeling the coarse masonry with his free hand as if it were some incomprehensible form of Braille. Will was walking backwards, checking behind them. Seeing nothing but the forbidding clouds, and coming to the conclusion that it was futile to try to place any reliance on sight in these conditions, he spun round only to blunder into a granite plinth. He recoiled as the leering face of a huge marble head reared out of the parting mist. Laughing at himself, he warily stepped around it and found his brother waiting only a metre ahead.

They had gone about twenty paces when the fog mysteriously folded back to reveal a length of cobbled street before them. Will hastily wiped the moisture from his eye-pieces and let his gaze ride with the retreating margins of the fog. Bit by bit the edges of the street and the façades of some of the nearest buildings came into view. Both boys felt an immense flood of relief as their immediate surroundings were tantalizingly revealed for the first time since they had entered the city.

Then their blood turned cold.

There, not ten metres away, only too real and horribly clear, they saw them. A patrol of eight Styx were fanned out across the street. They stood motionless as predators, their round goggles watching the boys as they dumbly looked back.

They were like spectres from some future nightmare in their grey-green striped long coats, strange skullcaps and sinister breathing masks. One held a ferocious-looking stalker on a thick leather strap – it was straining against its collar, its tongue lolling obscenely out of the side of its monstrous maw. It sniffed sharply, and immediately whipped its head in the boys' direction. The black pebbles of its beady eyes had sized them up in an instant. With a deep, rumbling snarl it curled back its lips to reveal huge yellowing teeth dripping with excited saliva. Its lead slackened as it crouched down, preparing to pounce.

But nobody made a move. As if time itself had stopped, the two groups merely stood and stared at each other in horrible, mute anticipation.

Something snapped in Will's head. He screamed and spun Cal around, knocking him from his shocked inertia. Then they were running, flying back into the fog, their legs pumping frantically. They ran and ran, unable to tell how much ground they were covering through the shrouds of mist. Behind them came the savage barking of the stalker and the crackling shouts of the Styx.

Neither boy had a clue where they were heading, just as long as they cleared the area. They didn't have time to think, their minds frozen with blind panic.

Then Will came to his senses. He yelled at Cal to keep going as he slowed to light the blue touchpaper on a huge Roman candle. Not really certain if he'd lit it or not, he quickly propped it against a chunk of masonry, angling it in the direction of their pursuers.

He ran on a few metres and stopped again. He flicked the lighter, but this time the flame refused to come. Swearing, he struck it desperately again and again. Nothing, just sparks. He shook it just like he'd seen the Greys do so often at school when lighting their illicit cigarettes. He took a deep breath and once again spun the tiny wheel. Yes! The flame was small, but enough to ignite the fuse of the firework, an air-bomb battery. But now the snarling and barking and voices were closing around him. He lost his nerve and simply slung the firework to the ground.

'Will, Will!' he heard up ahead. As he homed in on the shouts he was furious that Cal was making so much noise, though he knew he would never have found him otherwise. Will was running at full pelt when he caught up with his brother and almost bowled him over. They were sprinting furiously as the first firework went off. It screamed out in all directions, its bright primary colours bleeding through the texture of the fog before it ended with two deafening thunderclaps.

'Get going,' Will hissed at Cal, who had crashed head first into a wall and was acting a little stunned. 'Come on. This way!' he said pulling his brother by the arm, not allowing him any time to dwell on his injury.

The fireworks continued, exploding fireballs of light high into the cavern or in low arcs that ended in the city itself, momentarily silhouetting the buildings like the scenery in a shadow play. Each iridescent streak culminated in a dazzling flash and a cannon-shot explosion, echoing and rumbling back and forth through the city like a raging storm.

Every so often Will stopped to light another firework, picking out Roman candles, air bombs or rockets which he positioned on pieces of masonry or threw to the ground in the hope of confusing the patrol as to their position. The Styx, if they were still following, would be bearing the brunt of this onslaught and Will hoped that at the very least the smell of the smoke might put the stalker off their scent.

As the last of the fireworks went off in a cavalcade of light and sound, Will was praying he'd bought them enough time to reach the Labyrynth. They slowed to a jog to allow themselves to catch their breath, then stopped altogether to listen out for any sign of their pursuers, but there was nothing now. They appeared to have shaken them off. Will sat down on a wide step of a building that looked like it could have been a temple and took out his map and compass while Cal kept watch.

'I've no idea where we are,' he admitted, tucking the map away. 'It's hopeless!'

'We could be anywhere,' Cal agreed.

Will stood up, looking left and right. 'I say we carry on in the same direction.'

Cal nodded. 'But what if we end up right back where we started?'

'Doesn't matter. We've just got to keep moving,' Will said as he set off.

Once again the silence crowded in on them, and the mysterious shapes and shadows appeared and softened, as if the buildings were pulling in and out of focus in this invisible city. They'd made tortuously slow progress through a succession of streets when Cal pulled them up.

'I think it's clearing a little, you know,' he whispered.

'Well, that's something,' Will replied.

Once again Bartleby stiffened and crouched down low, hissing as the margins of the fog rolled back before them. The boys froze, their eyes feverishly raking the milky air.

As if veils were being lifted to reveal it, there, not ten metres away, a dark, shadowy form was hunched menacingly. They both heard a low, guttural growl.

'Oh, Jesus, a *stalker*!' Cal gulped.

Their hearts stopped with awful realization. They could only watch as it rose up, its muscular forelegs tensing into life as it pawed the earth, then began to move, accelerating forward at a bewildering speed. There was absolutely nothing they could do. There was no point in running; it was too close. Like an infernal steam engine, the black hound was pounding towards them, condensation spewing from its flaring nostrils.

Will didn't have time to think. As he saw it spring he dropped his rucksack, and shoved Cal out of the way.

The stalker soared through the air and slammed heavily against Will's chest. Its club-like paws knocked him flat on his back, his head thwacking the algae-covered ground with a hard slap. Half stunned, Will reached up and grasped the monster's throat with both hands. His fingers found its thick collar and hung on to it, as he tried to hold the brute away from his face.

But the animal was just too powerful. Its jaws snapped at his mask, then caught on to it and bit down. Will heard the squeal of its fangs tightening on the rubber as the mask was crushed against his face, and then a pop as one of the eyepieces shattered. He smelled the putrid breath of the stalker, like warm sour meat, as the animal continued to wrench and twist the mask, the straps behind his head stretched almost to breaking point.

Praying the mask would stay in place, he tried with all his might to turn his head away. The stalker's jaws slid off the wet rubber, but Will's success was short-lived. The dog pulled back slightly, but immediately lunged again. Screaming, and still hanging on to its thick collar with all his might, Will was just managing to keep it away from his face, his arms at the very limit of their strength. The collar was cutting into his fingers – he just couldn't believe how heavy the beast was. Time after time, Will whipped his head away, only just evading the snapping teeth, like the jaws of a powerful mantrap clapping shut.

Then the animal contorted and twisted its body.

One of Will's hands lost its grip, and with nothing to hinder it the animal quickly sought out a more rewarding target. It caught hold of Will's forearm and bit down hard. Will cried out from the pain, his other hand involuntarily opening and letting go of the collar.

There was nothing to stop it now.

The animal instantly scrabbled over him and sank its incisors into his shoulder. Amidst the growling and biting he heard the cloth of his jacket rip as the huge teeth, like twin rows of daggers, penetrated and tore into his flesh. Will wailed again as the animal shook its head, snarling loudly. He was helpless, a rag doll being shaken this way and that. With his free arm, he punched weakly at the animal's flanks and head, but it was no use.

Then suddenly the dog detached itself from his shoulder and reared up over him, its huge weight still pinning him down. As its frenzied eyes fixed on his, he could see its slathering jaws just centimetres from his face, strings of its drool dripping into his eyepieces. Will was aware that Cal was doing all he could to help; he was quickly lunging in to pummel and kick at the beast, then just as quickly pulling back. Each time he did this, the dog merely half turned to snarl at him, as if it knew he posed no threat. Its small savage brain was fixed on only one thing, the *kill* that was completely and utterly at its mercy.

Will tried desperately to roll over but the creature had him pinned to the floor. He knew he was no match for this hellish, unstoppable beast that seemed to be made from huge slabs of muscle, as hard and unyielding as rock.

'Go!' he yelled at Cal. 'Get away!'

Then, from out of nowhere, a fleshy bolt of grey catapulted at the stalker's head.

For one instant, it was as though Bartleby was suspended in midair, his back arched over and his claws extended like cut-throat razors just above the stalker's head. The next, he'd dropped, and there was a shocking frenzy of movement. They heard the wet slicing of flesh as Bartleby's teeth found their first mark. A dark fountain of blood was jetting over Will from a livid gash where the dog's ear had been. The beast let out a low-pitched yelp, and immediately bucked and leaped off Will, Bartleby still clamped to its head and neck, blitzing it with bites and savage flesh-tearing slashes from his raking hind feet.

'Get up! Get up!' Cal was shouting, as he helped Will to his feet with one hand and retrieved his rucksack with the other.

The boys retreated to a safe distance, then stopped, compelled to stay and watch. They were rooted to the spot, transfixed by this deadly battle between cat and dog as both writhed in mortal combat, their shapes melting together until they became an indistinguishable whirlwind of grey and red, punctuated by flashing teeth and claws.

'We can't stay here,' Will shouted. He could hear the shouts of the approaching patrol, which was quickly homing in on the fight.

'Bart, leave it! Come!'

'The Styx.' Will shook his brother. 'We have to go!'

Cal reluctantly moved off, peering back to see if his cat was following through the mist. But there was no sign of Bartleby, only the distant hisses and yelps and screeches.

Shouts and footfalls were now echoing all around. The boys ran blindly, Cal grunting with the effort of carrying both rucksacks, and Will trembling with shock, his whole arm throbbing dully with pain. He could feel the blood streaming down his side, and was alarmed to find that it was running over the back of his hand in small rivulets and dripping from the ends of his fingertips.

Out of breath, the boys hastily agreed on a direction, hoping against hope it would take them out of the city and not straight back into the arms of the Styx. Once on the marshy perimeter, they would make their way round the edge of the City until they found the mouth of the Labyrynth. And if the worst came to the worst and they missed it completely, Will knew they would eventually come to the stone staircase again and could quickly return Topsoil.

From the sounds they were hearing the patrol seemed to be zeroing in on them. The boys were dashing at full speed, but then they blundered headlong into a wall. Had they inadvertently strayed down a blind alley? The terrible thought struck both of them at the same time. They frantically felt along the wall until they found an archway, its sides crumbled away and the keystone missing at its apex.

'Thank God,' Will whispered, glancing at Cal with relief. 'That was close.'

Cal merely nodded, panting heavily. They peered briefly

behind them, before passing through the ruined archway.

With lightning speed, strong hands grabbed them roughly from either side of the opening, yanking them off their feet.

CHAPTER THIRTY-SIX

Using his good arm, Will lashed out with all the strength he could summon, but his knuckles just grazed ineffectually off a canvas hood. The man cursed sharply as Will followed with another blow, but this time his fist was caught and trapped in the iron grip of a huge hand, forcing him back effortlessly until he was pinioned against the wall.

'That's enough!' the man hissed. 'Shhh!'

Cal suddenly recognized the voice and began pushing in between Will and his hooded assailant. Will was completely baffled. What was his brother doing? Rather feebly he tried to lash out again, but the man held him fast.

'Uncle Tam!' Cal shouted joyously.

'Keep it down,' Tam rebuked.

'Tam?' Will repeated, feeling all at once very stupid and very relieved.

'But . . . how . . . how did you know we'd be . . . ?' Cal stuttered.

'We've been keeping an eye out since the escape went off the rails,' their uncle cut in.

'Yes, but how did you know it was *us*?' Cal asked again.

'We just followed the light and the noise. Who else but you lot would use those bloody fool pyrotechnics? They probably heard it Topsoil, let alone in the Colony.'

'It was Will's idea,' Cal replied. 'It sort of worked.'

'Sort of,' Tam said, looking with concern at Will, who was steadying himself against the wall, the rubber of his mask scored with deep gouges and one of his eyepieces shattered and useless. 'You all right, Will?'

'I think so,' he mumbled, holding his blood-soaked shoulder. He felt a little woozy and detached, but couldn't tell if this was because of his wounds or because of the overwhelming sense of relief that Tam had found them.

'I knew you'd not be able to rest with Chester still here.'

'What's happened to him? Is he all right?' Will asked, perking up at the mention of his friend's name.

'He's alive, at least for the time being – I'll tell you all about it later, but now, Imago, we'd better make ourselves scarce.'

Imago's massive form slipped into sight with unexpected fleetness, his baggy mask twisting furtively this way and that, like a partially deflated balloon caught in the wind as he scrutinized the murky shadows. He swung Will's rucksack over one shoulder as if it weighed nothing, and then he was off. It was all the boys could do to keep up with him. Their flight now turned into a nerve-racking game of Follow My Leader, with Imago's shadow piloting them through the miasma and unseen obstacles, while Tam brought up the rear. But the boys were so very grateful to be back under Tam's wing that they almost forgot their predicament. They felt safe again.

Imago cupped a light orb in his hand, allowing just enough light to spill from it so they could negotiate the difficult terrain. They jogged through a series of flooded courtyards, and then left the fog behind as they entered a circular building, racing at a staggering pace along corridors lined with statues and flaking murals. They slid in the mud, on the cracked marble floors of abandoned rooms and halls strewn with broken masonry, until they found themselves hurtling up stairs of black granite. Climbing higher and higher, they were suddenly out in the open again. Traversing fractured stone walkways that had long sections of their balustrades missing, Will was able to look down from giddying heights and catch views of the city below between the meshing clouds. Some of these walkways were so narrow, Will feared that if he hesitated for a second he might plunge to his death in the foggy soup that masked the sheer drops on either side. He kept going, putting his trust in Imago, who didn't waver for an instant, his unwieldy form driving relentlessly ahead, leaving little eddies of fog in its wake.

Eventually, after haring down several staircases, they entered a large room echoing with the sound of gurgling water. Imago came to a halt. He appeared to be listening for something.

'Where's Bartleby?' Tam whispered to Cal as they waited.

'He saved us from a stalker,' Cal said wretchedly, and hung his head. 'He never came after us. I think he may be dead.'

Tam put his arm around Cal and hugged him. 'He was a prince amongst animals,' he said. He patted Cal on the back consolingly before moving forward to confer with Imago in hushed tones.

'Think we should lie low for a while?'

'No, better to make a break for it,' Imago's voice was calm and unhurried. 'The Division know the boys are still here somewhere, and the whole place'll be riddled with patrols in no time at all.'

'We keep going then,' Tam concurred.

The four of them filed out of the room and travelled along a colonnade until Imago vaulted over a low wall and slid down a slimy bank into a deep gulley. As the boys followed him the stagnant water came up to their thighs, and thick fronds of glutinous black weed hampered their movements. They waded laboriously through, lethargic bubbles rising up and clumping together on the surface. Even though they were wearing masks, the putrid stench of long-dead vegetation caught in their throats. The gulley became an underground channel, and they were plunged into darkness, their splashes echoing about them until, after what felt like an eternity, they emerged into the open again. Imago motioned for them to stop, then scuttled up the side of the channel, squelching off into the fog.

'This is a risky bit,' Tam warned them in a whisper. 'It's open ground. Keep your wits about you and stay close.'

Before long Imago returned and beckoned to them. They clambered out of the water and, with sodden boots and trousers, crossed the boggy ground, the city finally behind them. They went up a slope and then seemed to reach a plateau of sorts. Will's spirits soared as he spotted the openings in the cavern wall ahead, and knew they had reached a way back into the Labyrynth. *They'd made it.*

'Macaulay!' a harsh, thin voice called out.

They all stopped dead in their tracks and wheeled around. The fog was patchier here on the higher ground, and through the thinning wisps they saw a lone figure. It was a single Styx. He stood there, tall and arrogant, with his arms folded across his narrow chest.

'Well, well, well. Funny how rats always use the same runs . . .' he shouted.

'Crawfly,' Tam replied coolly as he pushed Cal and Will towards Imago.

'. . . leaving their grease and stinking spoor on the sides. I knew I'd get you one day; it was just a matter of time.' The Crawfly uncrossed his arms and then snapped them like whips. Will's heart missed a beat as he saw two shining blades appear in the Styx's hands. Curved and about fifteen centimetres long, they looked like small scythes.

'You've been a thorn in my side for too long,' the Crawfly yelled.

Will glanced at Tam and was surprised to see he was already armed, with a brutal-looking machete he seemed to have conjured from nowhere.

'It's time I righted a few wrongs.' Tam said in a low, urgent voice to Imago and the boys. They could see the look of grim determination in his eyes. He turned in the direction of the Crawfly. 'Get going, you lot, I'll catch you up,' he called back to them as he began to advance.

But the saturnine figure, with swathes of fog curling about it, didn't give an inch. Brandishing the scythes with an expert flourish and crouching a little, the Styx had the appearance of something horribly unnatural.

'This isn't right. He's too bloody confident,' Imago muttered. 'We should make ourselves scarce.' He drew the boys back protectively to one of the tunnel mouths of the Labyrynth as Tam closed on the Crawfly.

'Oh, no . . . no . . .' Imago gulped.

Will and Cal turned, searching for the source of his alarm.

A mass of Styx had appeared through the mists, and were spreading out in a wide arc. But the Crawfly held up one glinting scythe and they came to an abrupt halt a little distance behind him, swaying and fidgeting impatiently.

Tam stopped, pausing for a moment as if weighing the odds. He shook his head just once, then he drew himself up defiantly. He tore off his hood and took a large breath, filling his lungs with the foul air.

In reply, the Crawfly yanked off his goggles and breathing apparatus, dropping them at his feet and kicking them aside. Tam and the Crawfly both stepped closer, then stopped. As they faced each other like two opposing champions, Will shuddered at the cold, sardonic smile on the thin face of the Styx.

The boys hardly dared breathe. It had grown so deathly quiet in that place, as if all the sound had been sucked from the world.

The Crawfly made the first move, his arms whipping over each other as he lunged forwards. Tam jerked back to avoid the barrage of steel and, stepping to the side, brought up his machete in a defensive move. The two men's blades met and scraped off each other with a shrill metallic scream.

With incredible dexterity, the Crawfly spun about as if performing some ritual dance, darting towards Tam and back again, slashing and slashing with his twin blades. Tam retaliated with thrusts and parries, and the two opponents attacked and defended and attacked in turn. Each sally was so blisteringly fast Cal and Will hardly dared blink. Even as they watched, there came another salvo of silver and grey, and the two men were suddenly so close they could have embraced, the razor-sharp edges of their weapons grinding coldly against each other. Almost as quickly, they fell back, breathing heavily. There was a lull while each man's eyes remained fixed on the other's, but Tam seemed to be listing slightly and clutching his side.

'This is bad,' Imago said under his breath.

Will saw it too. Between Tam's fingers and down his jacket seeped dark ribbons of liquid, which looked more like harmless black ink under the green light of the city. He was wounded and bleeding badly. He drew himself slowly up and, apparently recovering, in a flash had swung his machete at the Crawfly, who sidestepped effortlessly and swiped him across the face.

Tam flinched and staggered back. Imago and the boys saw the patch of blackness now spreading down his left cheek.

'Oh, my God,' Imago said quietly, holding on to the boys' collars so tightly that Will could feel his arms tensing as the fight resumed.

Tam attacked yet again, the Crawfly whirling backwards and forwards, this way and that, in his fluid and stylized dance. Tam's swipes and thrusts were decisive and skilful, but the Crawfly was too fast, the machete blade time and time again meeting with nothing but misty air. As Tam was twisting around to face his elusive opponent, he lost his footing. Trying to straighten up, his boots were slipping hopelessly. He was off balance, in a vulnerable position. The Crawfly couldn't miss this opportunity. He lunged at Tam's exposed flank.

But Tam was ready. He'd been waiting for this moment. He ducked forwards and rose inside his opponent's guard, bringing the machete up in a flash, so smartly that Will missed the devastating slash to the Crawfly's throat.

The air between the two combatants filled with dark spume as the Crawfly reeled back. The Styx let both of his scythes tumble to the ground and gave out a bloody, hissing gurgle as he clutched his severed windpipe.

Like a matador delivering the killing blow Tam stepped forward, using both his hands for the final thrust. The blade sank up to the hilt in the Crawfly's chest. He let out a bubbling hiss and grabbed Tam's shoulders to steady himself. He looked down with sheer disbelief at the rough wooden handle protruding from his sternum, then raised his head. For a moment they stood there absolutely motionless, like two statues in a tragic tableau, staring at each other in silent recognition.

Then Tam braced one foot against the Crawfly and wrenched out his machete. The Styx teetered on the spot, like a puppet suspended by unseen wires, his mouth shaping empty, breathless curses.

Imago and the boys watched as the mortally wounded man spluttered a last choking snarl at Tam and, tottering backwards, collapsed to the ground in a lifeless heap. Excited whispers passed down the lines of Styx, who seemed paralysed, unsure what they should do next.

Tam wasted no time in such hesitation. Holding his injured side and grimacing with the pain, he sprinted back to join Imago and the boys. This in turn mobilized the Styx, who scuttled forward to form a ring around the body of their fallen comrade.

Tam was already leading Imago and the boys down a Labyrinth passage. But they had hardly gone any distance when he lurched to one side and sought out the wall for support. He was breathing hard and sweat was pouring off him. It streamed down his face, mingling with the blood from his lacerations and dripping from his bristly chin.

'I'll hold them off,' he panted, looking back at the tunnel opening. 'It'll buy you some time.'

'No, I'll do it,' Imago said. 'You're wounded.'

'I'm finished anyway,' Tam said quietly.

Imago looked down at the blood welling out of the gaping flap on Tam's chest, and their eyes met for a fraction of a second. As Imago handed him his machete, it was clear the decision had been made.

'Don't, Uncle Tam! Please come with us,' Cal begged in a choked voice, knowing full well what this meant.

'Then we'd all lose, Cal,' Tam said, smiling wanly and hugging him with one arm. He reached into his shirt, yanked something from around his neck and pressed it into Will's hand. It was a smooth pendant with a symbol carved into it.

'Take this,' Tam said quickly. 'It might come in useful where you're going.' He let go of Cal and took a step away, but then grabbed hold of Will, his eyes never leaving the younger boy. 'And watch out for Cal, won't you, Will?' Tam tightened his grip on him. 'Promise me that.'

Will felt so numb that before he could find any words, Tam had turned away from him.

Cal began to shout frantically.

'Uncle Tam . . . come . . . come with us . . .'

'Get them away, Imago,' Tam called as he strode back towards the mouth of the tunnel, and as he did so the full horror of the approaching Styx army hove into view.

Cal was still calling Tam's name and showing not the slightest intention of going anywhere when Imago grasped hold of his collar and bundled him forcefully before him into the tunnel. The distraught boy had absolutely no choice but to do what Imago wanted, and his shouts immediately gave way to great howls of anguish and uncontrollable sobbing. Will received similarly rough treatment as Imago repeatedly slapped him on the back to drive him on. Imago only let up for the briefest moment as they rounded a sharp bend, and he seemed to hesitate. The three of them, Will, Cal and Imago, turned to catch a last glimpse of the big man, his outline dark against the green of the city as he held the two machetes in readiness at his sides.

Then Imago pushed them on again and Tam was for ever lost from view. But burned on to their retinas was that final scene, that final picture of Tam standing proud and defiant in the face of the approaching tide. A single figure before a bristling field of drawn scythes.

Even as they fled they could hear his urgent, shouted curses and the clash of blades, which grew fainter with every twist and turn of the tunnel.

CHAPTER THIRTY-SEVEN

They ran, and Will held his arm tightly to his side, his shoulder throbbing painfully with each stride. He had no idea how many miles they'd travelled when, at the end of a long gallery, Imago finally slowed the pace to allow them to catch their breath. The width of the tunnels meant they could have walked side by side, but instead they chose to remain in single file – it gave them some solitude, some privacy. Even though they hadn't exchanged a single word since they'd left Tam behind in the city, each knew only too well what the others were thinking in the wretched silence that hung like a pall over them. As they plodded mechanically along in their mournful little column, Will thought how much like a funeral procession it felt.

He just couldn't believe that Tam was really dead – the one person in the Colony who was so much larger than life, who had accepted him back into the family without a moment's hesitation. Will tried to get his thoughts into some sort of order and deal with the sense of loss and the hollowness that overwhelmed him, but wasn't helped by Cal's frequent bouts of muffled weeping.

They took innumerable turns down lefts and rights, every new stretch of tunnel as identical and unremarkable as the last. Imago didn't once refer to a map, but seemed to know precisely where they were going, muttering to himself under his mask every so often, as if endlessly reciting a poem, or even a prayer. Several times Will noticed that he would shake a dull metal sphere the size of an orange as they turned yet another corner, but he had no idea why Imago was doing this.

He was surprised when Imago drew them to a halt by what appeared to be a small fissure in the ground and looked warily up and down the tunnel either side of them. Then he started to agitate the metal sphere with vigour around the mouth of the fissure.

'What's that for?' Will asked him.

'It masks our scent,' Imago answered brusquely, and tucking the sphere away he unslung Will's rucksack and dropped it into the gap. Then he lowered himself to his knees and squeezed head first into the opening. It was a tight fit, to say the least.

For about six metres the fissure descended almost vertically, then it began to level off, narrowing even further into a tight crawl hole. Progress was slow as Will and Cal followed behind, the sounds of Imago's grunting and wriggling reaching them from up ahead as he desperately struggled through, pushing Will's rucksack before him. Will was just wondering what they would do if Imago got stuck, when they reached the end and were able to stand again.

At first Will couldn't make out much through his ruined mask, with one of its eyepieces shattered and the other fogged with condensation. It was only when Imago pulled off his mask and told the boys to remove theirs that Will saw where they were.

It was a chamber, little more than nine metres across and almost perfectly bell-shaped, with rough walls the texture of carborundum. A number of small greyish stalactites hung down in the middle of the chamber, directly over a circle of dusty metal, which was set into the centre of the floor. As they shuffled around the edges of the chamber, their boots scattered clusters of smooth spheres, which were dirty yellow in colour and varied from the size of peas to large marbles.

'Cave pearls,' Will muttered, recalling the pictures he'd seen of them in one of his father's textbooks. Despite the way he felt, he immediately cast his eye around for any sign of running water, which would have been necessary for their formation. But the floor and walls appeared to be as dry and arid as the rest of the Labyrynth. And the only way in or out that Will could see was the crawl hole they'd just come through.

Imago had been watching him, and answered his unuttered question.

'Don't worry . . . we'll be safe here, Will, for a while,' he said, his broad face smiling reassuringly. 'We call this place the Cauldron.'

As Cal stumbled wearily to the far side of the chamber and slid down against the wall with his head slumped forward on to his chest, Imago spoke to Will again.

'I should take a look at that arm.'

'It's nothing really,' Will replied. Not only did he want to be left alone, but he was also too terrified to discover just how severe his injuries might be.

'Come on,' Imago said firmly, waving him over. 'It could get infected. I need to dress it.'

Gritting his teeth Will took a deep breath and, rather stiffly and awkwardly, removed his jacket and let it slide to the ground. The material of his shirt was firmly stuck to the wounds and Imago had to work it free little by little, starting at the collar and gently peeling it back. Will watched queasily, wincing as several of the damp scabs were pulled off and he saw fresh blood well out and run down his already stained arm.

'You got off lightly,' Imago said. Will glanced at Imago's unsmiling face, wondering if he really meant what he was saying, as he nodded and went on. 'You should count yourself lucky. Stalkers usually go for more vulnerable body parts.'

Will's forearm had some livid welts, and two semicircles of puncture wounds on both sides, but there was little or no bleeding from these now. He inspected the redness on his chest and abdomen, then felt his ribs, which only hurt if he inhaled deeply. No real damage there either. But his shoulder was a different matter altogether. The animal's teeth had sunk deeper there, and the flesh had been badly mauled by the shaking of the stalker's head. In places it was so raw and torn it looked like it could have been inflicted by a shotgun blast.

'Eyshh!' Will exhaled loudly, turning his head away quickly as rivulets of blood seeped down his arm. 'It looks awful.' Now he'd actually seen it he tensed up and couldn't stop himself from trembling, realizing just how much his injuries were hurting him. For a moment all his strength deserted him, and he felt so very weak and vulnerable.

'Don't worry, it looks worse than it is,' Imago said reassuringly as he poured a clear liquid from a silver flask over a piece of lint. 'But this is going to sting,' he warned Will, and set about cleaning the wounds. When he'd finished, he pushed the flap of his coat open and reached inside to unbutton one of the many pouches on his belt. He pulled out a bag of what looked like pipe tobacco and proceeded to sprinkle it liberally over Will's wounds, concentrating on the lacerations to his shoulder. The small dry fibres stuck to the lesions, absorbing the blood. 'This might hurt a little, but I'm nearly done,' he said as he packed more of the material on top, patting it down so that it formed a thick mat.

'What's that?' Will asked, daring to look at his shoulder again.

'Shredded rhizomes.'

'Shredded *what*?' Will said with alarm. 'I hope you know what you're doing.'

'I'm the son of an apothecary. I was taught to dress a wound when I was not much older than you are.'

Will relaxed again.

'You don't need to worry, Will . . . it's been a while since I lost a patient,' Imago said, looking askance at him.

'Huh?' A little slow on the uptake, Will looked at him with alarm.

'Only joking,' Imago said, ruffling Will's hair and chuckling. But despite his attempt to lighten the mood Will could read the immense sadness in Imago's eyes as he continued to tend to his shoulder. 'There's an antiseptic in this poultice. It'll stop the bleeding and deaden the nerves,' he said, as he reached into another pouch and pulled out a grey roll of material which he began to unwind. He bound this expertly around Will's shoulder and arm and, tying the ends securely in a bow, stood back to admire his handiwork.

'How's that feel?'

'Better,' Will lied. 'Thanks.'

'You'll need to change the dressing every once in a while –

you should take some of this with you.'

'What do you mean, with me? Where are we going?' Will asked, but Imago shook his head.

'All in good time. You've lost a lot of blood and need to get some fluids in you. And we should all try to eat something.' Imago glanced across at the slumped form of Cal. 'Come on. Get yourself over here, boy.'

Cal obediently heaved himself to his feet and wandered over as Imago sat his bulk down, his legs stretched out in front of him, and began to produce numerous dull metal canisters from his leather satchel. He unscrewed the lid of the first one and proffered it at Will, who regarded the sloppy grey slabs of fungi with unconcealed revulsion. 'I hope you don't mind,' Will said, 'but we brought our own.'

Imago didn't seem to mind at all. He simply resealed his canister and waited expectantly as Will unpacked the food from his rucksack. Imago fell upon it with evident relish, sucking noisily on slices of honey-roast ham, which he held delicately in his dirty fingers. As if trying to make the experience last for ever he rolled the meat noisily around in his mouth with his tongue before chewing it. And when he did finally swallow, his eyes half closed and he let out huge blissful sighs.

In contrast Cal hardly touched a thing, picking unenthusiastically before withdrawing again to the other side of the chamber. Will didn't have much of an appetite either, particularly after witnessing Imago's performance. He pulled out a can of Coke and had just started sipping it when he suddenly thought about the jade-green pendant that Tam had given him. He found it in his jacket and took it out to examine its dull surface. It was still smeared with Tam's blood, which had congealed within the three indentations carved into one of its faces. He stared at it and ran his thumb across it lightly. He was certain he'd seen the same three-pronged symbol somewhere before. Then he remembered. It had been on the milestone in the Labyrynth.

While Imago was working his way through a bar of plain chocolate, savouring each mouthful, Cal spoke from the other side of the chamber, his voice flat and listless.

'I want to go home. I don't care any more.'

Imago choked, spitting out a hail of half-chewed chocolate globs. He spun his head around to face Cal, his horsetail plait whipping into the air. 'And what about the Styx?'

'I'll talk to them, I'll make them listen to me,' Cal replied feebly.

'They'll listen all right, while they're cutting your liver out or hacking you limb from limb!' he rebuked him. 'You little idiot, d'you think Tam gave his life just so you could chuck yours away?'

'I . . . no . . .' Cal was blinking with fright as Imago continued to shout.

Still holding the pendant tightly Will pressed it to his forehead, covering his face with his hand. He just wanted everyone to shut up; he didn't need any of this. He wanted it all to stop, if only for a moment.

'You selfish, stupid . . . what are you going to do, get your father or Granny Macaulay to hide you . . . and risk their lives too? This is going to be bad enough as it is,' Imago was yelling.

'I just thought—'

'No, you didn't!' Imago cut him off. 'You can never go

back, d'you understand? Get that into your thick head!' Casting the rest of the chocolate bar aside, he strode to the opposite side of the chamber.

'But I . . .' Cal started to say.

'Get some sleep!' Imago growled, his face rigid with anger. He wrapped his coat tightly about him and, using his satchel as a pillow, he lay down on his side with his face to the wall.

There they remained for the best part of the next day, alternately eating and sleeping with hardly a word passing between them. After all the horror and excitement of the past twenty-four hours Will welcomed the opportunity to recuperate, and spent much of the time in a heavy, dreamless sleep. He was eventually woken by Imago's voice, and lethargically opened one eye to see what was going on.

'Come over and give me a hand, will you, Cal?'

Cal quickly jumped up and joined Imago, who was kneeling by the centre of the chamber.

'It weighs a ton,' Imago grinned.

As they slid aside the metal circle in the ground it was patently obvious Imago could have managed by himself, and that this was his way of patching things up with Cal. Will opened his other eye and flexed his arm. His shoulder was stiff, but his injuries didn't hurt nearly as much as they had.

Cal and Imago were now lying full-length on the ground, peering down into the circular opening as Imago played his light into it. Will crawled over to see what they were looking at. There was a well a good metre across, and then a murky darkness below it.

'I can see something shining,' Cal said.

'Yes, railway tracks,' Imago replied.

'The Miners' Train,' Will realized, as he saw the two parallel lines of polished iron glinting in the pitch blackness.

They pulled back from the hole and sat around it, waiting eagerly for Imago to speak.

'I'm going to be blunt, because we don't have much time,' he said. 'You have two choices. Either we lie low up here for a while and then I get you Topsoil again, or—'

'No, not there,' said Cal straight away.

'I'm not saying it's going to be easy to get you there,' Imago admitted. 'Not with three of us.'

'No way! I couldn't bear it!' Cal raised his voice until he was almost shouting.

'Don't be so hasty,' Imago warned. 'If we did make it Topsoil, at least you could try to lose yourselves somewhere the Styx can't find you. Maybe.'

'No,' repeated Cal with absolute conviction.

Imago was now looking directly at Will. 'You should be aware . . .' He clammed up, as if what he was about to say was so terrible that he didn't quite know how to put it. 'Tam thinks . . .' he quickly corrected himself with a grimace, '. . . *thought*, that the Styx girl who passed herself off as your Topsoiler sister . . .' he coughed uneasily and wiped his mouth, '. . . is the Crawfly's daughter. So Tam just killed her father back there in the city.'

'Rebecca's father?' Will asked in a nonplussed voice.

'Oh, Jesus,' Cal croaked.

'Why's that important? What does—?' Will managed, before Imago cut him short.

'The Styx don't leave be. They will pursue you, anywhere you go. Anyone who gives you shelter, Topsoil, in the Colony or even in the Deeps, is in danger too. You know they have people all over the surface.' Imago scratched his belly and frowned. 'But if Tam was right, it means that as bad as your situation was before, it's worse now. You're in the very greatest danger. You are *marked* now.'

Will tried to absorb what he'd just been told, shaking his head with the unfairness, the injustice of it all.

'So you're saying that if I go Topsoil, I'm on the run. And if I went to Auntie Jean's, then . . .'

'She's dead.' Imago shifted uneasily where he sat on the dusty rock floor. 'That's the way it is.'

'But what are *you* going to do, Imago?' Will asked, finding it impossible to grasp the situation he was in.

'I can't go back to the Colony, that's for sure. But don't you worry 'bout me, it's you two that need sorting out.'

'But what should I do?' Will asked, glancing over at Cal, who was staring at the opening in the floor, and then back to Imago, who just shrugged unhelpfully, leaving Will feeling even worse. He was at a total loss. It was as though he was playing a game where you were only told the rules after you made a mistake. 'Well, I suppose there's nothing Topsoil for me anyway. Not now,' he mumbled, bowing his head. 'And my dad's down here . . . somewhere.'

Imago pulled over his satchel and rummaged inside it, fishing out something wrapped in an old piece of hessian, which he passed to Will.

'What's this?' Will muttered, folding back the hessian. With so many thoughts racing through his head, he was in a state of confusion and it took him several seconds to appreciate quite what he'd been given.

It was a flattened and solid glob of paper which easily fitted into his fist. With torn and irregular edges, it had evidently been immersed in water and then left to dry, the pieces clumped together in a crude papier mâché. He glanced enquiringly at Imago, who offered no comment, so he began to pick away at the outer layers, much as one might peel the desiccated leaves from an ancient onion. As he scratched at their furred edges with a fingernail, it didn't take him long to separate the pieces of paper. Then he laid them out to inspect them more closely under his light.

'No! I don't believe it! This is my dad's writing!' he said with surprise and delight as he recognized Dr Burrows' characteristic scrawl on a number of the fragments. They were mud-stained and the blue ink had run, making very little of it legible, but he was still able to decipher some of what was written.

'*I will resume,*' Will recited from one fragment, quickly moving on to the others, and scrutinizing each of them in turn. 'No, this bit is too smudged,' he mumbled. 'Nothing here either,' he continued, and, 'I don't know . . . some odd words . . . doesn't make any sense . . . but . . . ah, this says *Day 15*!' He continued to scour several more fragments until he stopped with a jerk. 'This bit,' he exclaimed excitedly, holding the particular scrap up to the light, 'mentions me!' He glanced across at Imago, a slight waver in his voice. '*If my son, Will, had,* it says!' With a puzzled expression, he flicked it over to check the reverse side, but found it was blank. 'But what did Dad mean? What didn't I do? What was I *meant* to do?' Will again looked to Imago for help.

'Search me,' the man said.

Will's face lit up. 'Whatever he was saying, he's still thinking about me. He hasn't forgotten me. Maybe he always hoped that somehow or other I'd try to follow after him, to find him.' He was nodding vigorously as the notion built to a crescendo in his head. 'Yes, that's it . . . that must be it!'

Something else occurred to him at that moment, deflecting his thoughts. 'Imago, this has to be from my dad's journal. Where did you get it?' Will was immediately imagining the worst. 'Is he all right?'

Imago rubbed his chin contemplatively. 'Don't know. Like Tam told you, he took a one-way on the Miners' Train.' Sticking a thumb in the direction of the hole in the floor, he went on, 'Your father's down there somewhere, in the Deeps. Probably.'

'Yes, but where did you get this?' Will demanded impatiently, closing his hand over the scraps of paper and holding them up in his palm.

''Bout a week after he arrived in the Colony he was wandering around in the outskirts of the Rookeries and got set upon.' Imago's voice became slightly incredulous at this point. 'If the story's to be believed, he was stopping people and asking them things. Round those parts they don't take kindly to anyone, least of all Topsoilers, nosing about, and he got a good kicking. By all accounts, he just lay there, didn't even try to put up a fight. Probably saved his life.'

'Dad,' Will said, with tears welling in his eyes as he pictured the scene. 'Poor old Dad.'

'Well, it can't have been too bad. He walked away from it.' Imago rubbed his hands together and his tone changed, becoming more businesslike. 'But that's neither here nor there. You need to tell me what you want to do. We can't stick around here for ever.' He looked pointedly at each boy in turn. 'Will? Cal?'

They were both silent for a while, until Will spoke up.

'Chester!' He couldn't believe that with everything else that had been going on, he'd completely forgotten about his friend. 'Whatever you say, I've got to go back for him,' he said resolutely. 'I owe it to him.'

'Chester will be all right,' Imago said.

'How can you know that?' Will immediately shot back at him.

Imago simply smiled.

'So where is he?' Will asked. 'Is he really all right?'

'Trust me,' Imago said cryptically.

Will looked into his eyes and saw the man was in earnest. He felt a huge sense of relief, as if a crushing weight had been lifted from his shoulders. He told himself that if anyone could save his friend then it would be Imago. He drew a long breath and lifted his head. 'Well, in that case, the Deeps it is.'

'And I'm going with you,' Cal put in quickly.

'You're both absolutely sure about this?' Imago asked, looking hard at Will. 'It's like hell down there. You'd be better off Topsoil, at least you'd know the lie of the land.'

Will shook his head. 'My dad is all I have left.'

'Well, if that's what you want.' Imago's voice was low and sombre.

'There's nothing for us Topsoil, not now,' Will replied, with a glance at his brother.

'Okey dokey, it's decided then,' Imago said, checking his watch. 'Now try to get some shut-eye. You're going to need all your strength.'

But none of them could sleep, and Imago and Cal ended up talking about Tam. Imago was regaling the younger boy with stories of his uncle's exploits, even chuckling at times, and Cal couldn't help but join in with him. Imago was clearly drawing comfort from reminiscing about the stunts he, Tam and his sister had pulled in their youth, when they had run rings around the Styx.

'Tam and Sarah were as bad as each other, I can tell you. Pair of wild cats,' Imago smiled sadly.

'Tell Will about the Cane Toads,' Cal said, egging him on.

'Oh, dear God, yes . . .' Imago laughed, recalling the incident. 'It was your mother's idea, you know. We caught a barrel load of the things over in the Rookeries – the sickos there chew on them to get a hit. It's a dangerous habit to have; too much of the toxin can fry your brains.' Imago raised his eyebrows. 'Sarah and Tam took the toads to a church and let them out just before the service got under way. You should have seen it . . . a hundred of the slimy little beggars hopping all over the place . . . people jumping and shrieking, and you could hardly hear the preacher for all the croaking . . . *burup, burup, burup.*' The rotund man rocked with silent laughter, then his brow furrowed and he was unable to continue.

With all the talk about his real mother Will had been trying his hardest to listen, but he was far too tired and preoccupied. The seriousness of his situation was still foremost in his mind, and his thoughts were heavy with apprehension about what he'd just committed himself to. A journey into the unknown. Was he really up to it? Was he doing the right thing, for himself and his brother?

He broke from his introspection as he heard Cal suddenly interrupt Imago, who had just started on another tale. 'Do you think Tam might have made it?' Cal asked. 'You know . . . escaped?'

Imago looked away from him quickly and began drawing absently in the dust with his finger, clearly at a loss for words.

And in the silence that ensued, the intense sorrow flooded Cal's face again.

'I can't believe he's gone. He was everything to me.'

'He fought them all his life,' Imago said, his voice distant and strained. 'He was no saint, that's for sure, but he gave us something – hope – and that made it bearable for us.' He paused, his eyes fixed on some distant point beyond Cal's head. 'With the Crawfly dead there'll be purges . . . and a crackdown the likes of which haven't been seen for years.' He picked up a cave pearl and examined it. 'But I wouldn't go back to the Colony even if I could. I suppose we're all homeless now,' he said as he flicked the pearl into the air with his thumb, and with absolute precision it fell into the dead centre of the well.

CHAPTER THIRTY-EIGHT

'Please!' Chester whimpered inside the clammy hood, which stuck to his face and neck with his cold sweat. After they had dragged him from his cell and down the aisle to the front of the police station, they had shoved rough sacking over his head, and bound his wrists. Then they'd left him standing there, enveloped in stifling darkness, with muffled sounds coming from all around.

'Please!' Chester shouted in sheer desperation.

'Shut up, will you!' snapped a gruff voice just centimetres behind his ear.

'What's happening?' Chester begged.

'You're going on a little journey, my son, a little journey,' said the same voice.

'But I haven't done anything! Please!'

He heard boots grinding on a stone floor as he was pushed from behind. He stumbled and fell to his knees, unable to rise up again with his hands tied behind his back.

'Get up!'

He was hauled to his feet and stood swaying, his legs like jelly. He'd known that this moment was looming, that his days were numbered, but he'd had no way of finding out what it would be like when it did come. Nobody would speak to him in the Hold, not that he made much of an effort to ask them, so petrified was he of provoking any further retribution from the Second Officer and his fellow warders.

So Chester had lived as a condemned man who could only guess at the form of his eventual demise. He'd clung on to every precious second he had left, trying not to let them go, and dying a little inside as, one after another, they slipped away. Now the only thing he could find solace from was the knowledge he had a train journey before him – so at least he had *some* time left. But then what? What were the Deeps like? What would happen to him there?

'Move it!'

He shambled forward a few paces, unsure of his footing and unable to see a thing. He bumped into something hard, and the sound around him seemed to change. Echoes. Shouts, but from a distance, from a larger space.

Suddenly there came the clamour of many voices.

Oh, no!

He knew without a shred of doubt exactly where he was – he was outside the police station. And what he was hearing was the baying of a large crowd. If he'd been frightened before, it was worse now. *A crowd.* The jeering and catcalls grew louder, and he felt himself being lifted under each arm and hoisted along. He was in the main street; he could feel the irregular surface of the cobbles when his feet were allowed to touch the ground.

'I haven't done anything! I want to go home!'

He was panting hard, struggling to breathe through the coarse material of the hood. Sopping with his own saliva and tears, it was sucked into his mouth with every inhalation.

'Help me! Someone!' His voice was so anguished and distorted that it was almost unrecognizable to him.

Still the crazed shouts came from all around.

'TOPSOIL FILTH!'

'STRING 'IM UP!'

One repeated shout with many voices took form. It went over and over again.

'FILTH! FILTH! FILTH!'

They were shouting at him – so many people were shouting at him! His stomach churned with the stark realization. He couldn't see them and that made it worse. He was so terrified he thought he was going to be sick.

'FILTH! FILTH! FILTH!'

'Please . . . please stop . . . help me! Please . . . please help me . . . please.' He was hyperventilating and crying at the same time – he couldn't help it.

'FILTH! FILTH! FILTH!'

I'm going to die! I'm going to die! I'm going to die!

The single thought pulsed through his head, a counterpoint to the repeated chant of the crowd. They were so close to him now – close enough that he could smell their collective stench, and the foul reek of their collective hatred.

'FILTH! FILTH! FILTH!'

He felt as if he was in the bottom of a well, with a vortex of noises and shouts and vicious laughter swirling about him. He couldn't take it any more. He had to do something. He had to escape!

In blind terror he tried to break free, struggling and twisting his body, convulsing against his captors. But the huge hands only gripped him even more savagely, and the rabble's cries and laughter reached fever pitch at this new spectacle. Exhausted and realizing it was futile, he moaned, 'No . . . no . . . no . . . no . . .'

A sickly, intimate voice came from so close that he felt the speaker's lips brush his ear. 'C'mon now, Chester, pull yourself together! You don't want to disappoint all these good ladies and gentlemen, do you?' Chester realized it was the Second Officer. He must have been relishing every second of this.

'Let them have a look at you!' said someone else. 'Let them see you for what you are!'

Chester felt numb . . . bereft. *I can't believe this. I can't believe this.*

For a moment it was as if all the jeering and chanting and catcalls had stopped. As if he was in the eye of the storm, as if time itself had stopped. Then hands took hold of his ankles and legs, guiding them on to a step of some kind.

What now? He was heaved on to a bench and shoved hard against its back, in a sitting position.

'Take him away!' someone barked. The crowd cheered, and there were rapturous yelps and wolf whistles.

Whatever he had been put on lurched forward. He thought he heard the plunging of horses' hooves. *A carriage? Yes, a carriage!*

'Don't make me go! This isn't right!' he implored them.

He began to gibber, his words making no sense.

'You're going to get exactly what you deserve, my boy!' said a voice to his right, in an almost confidential tone. It was the Second Officer again.

'And it's too good for you,' came another he didn't recognize, from his left.

Chester was now shaking uncontrollably.

This is it, then! Oh, God! Oh, God! This is it!

He thought of his home, and the memories of watching television on so many Saturday mornings popped into his head. Happy and cherished moments of normality with his mother in the kitchen cooking breakfast, the smell of the food in the air, and his father calling from upstairs to see if it was ready yet. It was like another life he was remembering, some-one else's life, from another time, another century.

I will never never see them again. They've gone . . . it's all gone . . . finished . . . for ever!

His head sank to his chest. He went limp, as the stone-cold realization that it was all over spread through his whole body.

I am FINISHED.

From the soles of his feet to the top of his head he was filled with a crushing hopelessness. As if he'd been paralysed, his breath slowly left his lips, pulling with it an involuntary animal sound, a half-whine, half-moan. An awful, dread-filled sound of resignation, of abandonment.

For what seemed like an eternity he didn't breathe at all, his mouth gaping, closing, opening, like that of a stranded fish. His empty lungs burned from the lack of air until finally his whole body jerked. He sucked in a painful breath through the clogged weave of the hood. Forcing his head up, he let go a final cry of utter and final despair.

'WWWWWWIIIIIILLLLLLLLLLLLLLLLLLL!'

Will was surprised to find he'd dozed off again. He awoke, disoriented and with no idea how long he'd actually been asleep, as a dull, far-off vibration roused him. He couldn't pin-point what it was, and in any case the cold, hard reality of the choice to go into the Deeps came flooding back to him. It was as if he'd awoken into a nightmare.

He saw Imago crouching by the well, inclining his head towards the sound, listening. Then they all heard it plainly; the distant rumbling grew louder with every second until it began to reverberate around the chamber. At Imago's direction, Will and Cal shimmied over to the opening in the floor and readied themselves. As they both sat with their legs dangling from the edge, beside them Imago was leaning his head and shoulders into the well, hanging down as far as he could.

'Slows round the corner,' they heard him shout, and the noise grew more and more intense, until the whole chamber was vibrating around them. 'Here she comes. Bang on time!' He pulled himself out, still watching the tracks below as he knelt between the boys.

'You're sure this is what you want?' he asked them.

The boys looked at each other and nodded.

'We're sure,' Will said. 'But Chester . . . ?'

'I told you, don't worry 'bout him,' Imago said with a dismissive smile.

The chamber was shaking now with the sound of the approaching train, as if a thousand drums were beating in their heads.

'Do exactly as I say – this has to be timed to perfection, so when I say jump, you jump!' Imago told them.

The chamber filled with the acrid taint of sulphur. Then, as the roar of the engine reached a crescendo, a jet of soot shot up through the opening like a black geyser. It caught Imago square in the face, spraying him with smut and making him squint. They all coughed as the thick, pungent smoke flooded the Cauldron, engulfing them.

'READY . . . READY . . .' Imago screamed, pitching the

rucksacks into the darkness below them. 'CAL, JUMP!'

For a split second Cal hesitated, and Imago suddenly pushed him. He dropped into the well, howling with surprise.

'GO, WILL!' Imago screamed again, and Will tipped himself off the edge.

The sides flashed past and then he was out and tumbling into a vortex of noise, smoke and darkness, his arms and legs flailing. His breath was knocked from him as he landed with a jarring crunch, and a pure white light burst around him, one he couldn't even begin to understand. Points of illumination seemed to be leaping over him like errant stars and, for the briefest of moments, he really wondered if he'd died.

He lay still, listening to the percussive beat of the engine somewhere up ahead, and the juddering rhythm of the wheels as the train picked up speed. He felt the wind on his face and watched the long wisps of smoke pass above him. *No, this wasn't some industrial heaven, he was alive!*

He resolved not to move for a moment while he mentally checked himself over, making sure he didn't have any broken bones to add to his already burgeoning list of injuries. Incredibly, other than a few additional grazes, everything seemed to be intact and in working order.

He lay there. If this wasn't death, he couldn't understand the bright fluxing light he still saw all around him, like a miniature aurora. He pulled himself up on to one elbow.

Countless light orbs, the size of large marbles, were rolling around the gritty floor of the truck, colliding and rebounding off each other in random paths. Some became trapped in the runnels in the floor and would dim slightly as they touched, until they became unseated and scampered off on their ways again, flaring into brilliance once more.

Then he looked behind him and found the remains of the crate and the straw packing. It all became clear. His fall had been broken by a box of light orbs, which had smashed open when he landed on it. Thanking his luck, he felt like cheering, but instead helped himself to several handfuls of the lights, stuffing them into his pockets.

He got to his feet, bracing himself against the motion of the train. Although the foul-smelling smoke streamed thickly around him, the loose orbs lit up the truck to such effect that he was able to see it in detail. It was massive. It must have been nearly thirty metres long, and half that in width, much larger and more substantial than any train he'd ever seen Topsoil. It was constructed from slab-like plates of iron, crudely welded together. The side panels were battered and covered in rust, and their tops worn and buckled, as if the truck had seen aeons of hard use.

He dropped down again and, his knees grinding in the grit on the floor and the movement of the truck buffeting him around, he went in search of Cal. He came across several other crates made from the same thin wood as the one he'd landed on, and then, near the front of the truck, he spotted Cal's boot propped up on another line of boxes.

'Cal, Cal!' he shouted, crawling frantically towards him. In the midst of a mass of splintered wood, his brother was lying still, too still. His jacket was splattered with a wet darkness, and Will could see there was something wrong with his face.

Fearing the worst, Will shouted even louder. Not wanting to knock against Cal in case he was badly hurt, he clambered rapidly across the top of the crates alongside him. Dreading what he was about to see, he slowly held a light orb up to

Cal's head. It didn't look good. His face and hair were slick with a red pulp.

Will reached out gingerly, and was touching the watery redness on his brother's face when he noticed the broken green forms scattered around him. And there were pips stuck to Cal's forehead. Will drew back his hand and tasted his fingers. *It was watermelon!* At Cal's side was another damaged crate. As Will shoved it away to make more room, tangerines, pears and apples spilled out. His brother had evidently had a soft landing, smashing into crates of fruit.

'Thank God,' Will repeated as he shook Cal gently by the shoulders, trying to stir his limp form. But his head flopped lifelessly from side to side. Not knowing what else to do, Will took his brother's wrist to check his pulse.

'Get off me, will you!' Cal yanked his arm away from Will as he sluggishly opened his eyes and moaned self-pityingly. 'My head hurts,' he complained, rubbing his forehead tenderly. He brought his other arm up, and glanced bemusedly at the banana in his hand. Then he caught the fragrant smell of the lush fruit all around him, and looked uncomprehendingly at Will.

'What happened?' he shouted over the din of the train.

'Jammy sod, you fell in the restaurant car!' Will chuckled.

'Huh?'

'Doesn't matter. Try to sit up,' Will suggested.

'In a minute.' Cal was groggy, but otherwise appeared to be unharmed, except for a few cuts and bruises and a liberal dousing of melon juice, so Will crawled back over the crates and began to investigate. He knew he should be retrieving their rucksacks from the trucks in front of them, but there was no hurry. Imago had said it would be a long trip and, anyway, his curiosity was getting the better of him.

'I'm going to . . .' he shouted over at Cal.

'What?' Cal cupped a hand to his ear.

'Explore,' Will motioned.

'Right!' Cal yelled back.

Will scrambled through the mad sea of light orbs at the rear of the truck, and pulled himself up on the end panel. He peered down at the coupling in between the trucks, and the polished sheen of the well-used rails shooting hypnotically underneath. Then he looked across to the next truck, only a metre away, and, without stopping to think, hoisted himself over the edge. With the motion of the train it was awkward, but he managed to reach across and straddle both end panels, then had no option but to jump.

He dropped into the next truck, and rolled uncontrollably over the floor until he came to rest against a pile of canvas sacks. There was nothing much of note here except for some more crates halfway down, so he crawled to the back of the section and got to his feet again. He tried to see to the very end of the train, but the combination of smoke and darkness made this impossible.

'How many are there?' Will shouted to himself as he made to clamber over the end wall. As he repeated the process over successive trucks he finally got the hang of it, and found he could hop over and steady himself before he went tumbling. He was consumed with a burning curiosity to find the end of the train, but at the same time wary about what he might come across there. He'd been warned by Imago that it was more than likely there'd be a Colonist in the guard's carriage, so he had to play it carefully.

He'd dropped over the edge of the fourth truck and was

just crawling across a loose tarpaulin when something stirred beside him.

'What the—?' Terrified he'd been caught, Will drove his heel into the shadows as hard as he could. Off balance, the kick wasn't as effective as he'd hoped, but he definitely struck something under the tarpaulin. He readied himself to strike again.

'Leave me alone!' a voice complained weakly, and the tarpaulin flew back to reveal a hunched form in the corner. Will immediately held up his light orb.

'Hey!' the voice squeaked, trying to shield its face from the illumination.

He blinked at Will, tear stains etched through the film of grime and coal smut on his cheeks. There was a pause and a gasp of recognition, and his face split into the broadest grin imaginable. It was a tired face, and had lost much of its healthy chubbiness, but it was unmistakable.

'Hi, Chester,' Will said, slumping down next to his old friend.

'Will?' Chester cried, not quite believing what he was seeing. Then, at the top his lungs, he cried out again. 'Will!'

'Didn't think I'd let you go by yourself, did you?' Will shouted back. Will realised now what Imago had had in mind. He knew Chester was to be Banished, sent to the Deeps on this very train. The sly old rogue had known all along.

It was impossible to talk with all the noise from the speeding engine up ahead, but Will was content just to be reunited with Chester. Will grinned the widest of grins, luxuriating in a wave of relief that his friend was safe. He leaned back against the end panel of the truck and shut his eyes, filled with the most intense feeling of elation that, finally, from the throes of the nightmarish situation he'd found himself in, something good had emerged, something had turned out right. *Chester was safe!* That meant the world to him.

And, to top it all, he was being borne towards his father, on the greatest adventure of his life, on a journey into undiscovered lands. In his mind, Dr Burrows was the only part of his past life that he could cling on to. Will was determined that he would find him, wherever he was. And then everything would be all right again. They'd all be all right: he, Chester and Cal, all together, with his father. This notion shone in his mind like the brightest of beacons.

All of a sudden the future didn't seem so daunting.

Will opened his eyes and leaned towards Chester's ear. 'No school tomorrow then,' he shouted.

They both burst into helpless laughter, which was drowned out by the train as it continued to gather speed, spewing dark smoke behind it, carrying them away from the Colony, away from Highfield, and away from everything they knew, accelerating into the very heart of the Earth.

EPILOGUE

The gentle heat of the sun filtered down on a beautiful day early in the New Year, so balmy it could have been spring. Unobstructed by tall buildings, the perfect blue canvas of the sky was marred only by the specks of gulls falling and rising on thermals in the distance. If it hadn't been for the occasional intrusion of traffic swerving past on the canal-side road, one might have imagined it was somewhere on the coast, perhaps a sleepy fishing village.

But this was London, and the wooden tables outside the pub were beginning to fill up as the lure of the fine weather became too tempting. Three dark-suited men with the anaemic faces of office workers swaggered out through the doors and sat down with their drinks. Leaning over the table, each tried to outdo the other as they talked too loudly and laughed raucously, like squabbling crows. Next to them was a very different group, students in jeans and faded T-shirts who hardly made any noise at all. They were almost whispering to each other as they supped their beers and rolled the occasional cigarette.

Alone on a wooden bench in the shade of the building, Reggie sipped his pint, his fourth that lunchtime. He felt slightly woozy, but as he had nothing planned for the afternoon, he'd decided to indulge himself. He took a handful of whitebait from the bowl beside him, and munched on the little fish thoughtfully.

'Hiya, Reggie,' one of the barmaids said, her arms full of precariously stacked glasses as she collected the empties.

'Hi there,' he replied hesitantly, never very good at remembering any of the bar staff's names.

She smiled pleasantly at him, then pushed the door open with her hip as she headed back inside. Reggie had been turning up on and off for years, but had recently become a firm regular, dropping in nearly every day for his favourites, a bowl of whitebait or cod and chips.

He was a quiet man who kept to himself. Other than the fact that he was over-generous with his tips, what made him stand out from the run-of-the-mill punters was his appearance. He had the most striking white hair. Sometimes he wore it like an ageing biker, plaited into a bleached snake down his back, but on other occasions it ran wild, fluffed up like a newly shampooed poodle. He was never without his heavily tinted sunglasses, whatever the weather, and his clothes were arcane and old-fashioned, as if he had borrowed them from a theatrical costumier. Given his eccentric appearance, the bar staff came to the conclusion that he must be an out-of-work musician, a 'resting' actor or even an undiscovered artist, of which there were many in the area.

He leaned back against the wall, sighing contentedly as a slim young girl with a pleasant face and a flowery cotton scarf over her head appeared. Carrying a rattan basket she went from table to table, trying to sell little sprigs of heather with foil wrapped around their stems. It was a scene that could have been lifted from Victorian times. He grinned, thinking how quaint it was that street gypsies still peddled such innocent wares, when all around the big companies were promoting their brands so relentlessly on the billboards.

'Imago.'

The name drifted towards him as a breeze picked up and a battered car swerved recklessly around the corner, its wheels squealing. He shivered, and looked suspiciously at an old man as he struggled along the pavement on his walking stick. The man's cheeks were covered with spiky grey stubble, as if he'd forgotten to shave that morning.

As the girl selling the heather brushed past with her basket Imago looked away from the old man and studied the people at the tables again. No, he was just a little jumpy. It was nothing. He must have imagined it.

He put the bowl of whitebait on his lap and helped himself to another handful, washing it down with some beer. This was the life! He smiled to himself and stretched out his legs.

Nobody saw as he was thrown back against the wall by a sudden spasm, and then pitched forward from the bench, his face locked into a grotesque contortion. As he hit the ground his eyes swivelled up into their sockets, and his mouth opened, just once, then closed for the last time.

It was all over long before the ambulance arrived. Because he might have rolled off the stretcher, the two ambulance men decided instead to carry the rigid corpse, one on each side. The crowd of onlookers gasped at the spectacle, muttering amongst themselves as Imago's body, frozen like a statue in a sitting position, was manhandled into the back of the ambulance. And there was absolutely nothing the ambulance men could do about the bowl still grasped in the corpse's hand, so

462

tightly they couldn't lever it out.

Poor old Reggie. A pretty insensitive lot when it came to the welfare of their clientele, the bar staff were genuinely disturbed by his death. Particularly so when the kitchen was closed and several of them lost their jobs. They were later told there'd been an obscure lead-based compound in his food; it was a freak occurrence, a poisoned fish in a million. His body had simply shut down, his blood clotting like quick-setting cement due to overwhelming toxic shock.

At the inquest the coroner wasn't too forthcoming about the nature of the poison. Indeed, he was rather baffled by the traces of complex chemicals, which had never been recorded before.

Only one person, the girl watching the ambulance from across the road, knew the truth. She took off her scarf and threw it into the gutter, shaking out her jet-black hair with a self-satisfied smile as she put on her sunglasses and inclined her head towards the bright sky. As she walked away, she began singing softly: 'Sunshine . . . you are my sunshine . . .'

She wasn't done yet . . .

We dedicate this book to our long-suffering families and friends who have put up with us through our prolonged obsession, and to Barry Cunningham and Imogen Cooper at Chicken House for their endless encouragement and for keeping us on the straight and narrow, and to Peter Straus at Rogers, Coleridge and White for helping a couple of guys who happened to wander in out of the rain, and to Kate Egan and Stuart Webb, and to our friend Mike Parsons who has shown bravery beyond belief.